DELHI: A SOLILOQUY

M. Mukundan was born and brought up in Mahe. He rose to critical acclaim and popularity with *Mayyazhippuzhayude Theerangalil* (1974). His stories and novels have been widely translated into various Indian languages, English and French. He has been awarded Ezhuthachan Puraskaram, the highest literary honour given by the Government of Kerala, the Crossword Book Award twice, first in 1999 for *On the Banks of the Mayyazhi* and again in 2006 for *Kesavan's Lamentations*, and the Sahitya Akademi award and N.V. Puraskaram for *Daivathinte Vikrithikal (God's Mischief)*. His other major works include *Kesavante Vilapangal* (2009) and *Prasavam* (2008). He was presented with the insignia of Chevalier in the Order of Arts and Letters by the French government in 1998. He also served as the president of the Kerala Sahitya Akademi from 2006 to 2010. Four of his books have been adapted into award-winning films. *Delhi Gathakal (2011)*, translated as *Delhi: A Soliloquy*, is based on his experiences of living and working in Delhi for forty years as a Cultural Attaché at the French embassy. In 2004, he retired from that position and returned to Mahe, his hometown.

Fathima E.V. is an award-winning writer and translator. Her translation of Subhash Chandran's *Manushyanu Oru Amukham*, translated as *A Preface to Man*, was awarded the Crossword Book Award (2017) and the V. Abdulla Translation Award (2017). She was the translator-editor of the *Indian Ink Mag*, and her poems and short fiction have appeared in international anthologies and journals. She holds an MA and a PhD from the University of Calicut, and completed the TESOL course from the University of Surrey. Currently, she heads the department of English at Krishna Menon Memorial Government Women's College, Kannur.

Nandakumar K. started his career as a sub-editor at *Financial Express*, after completing a master's degree in Economics, followed by stints in international marketing and general management in India and abroad. Having travelled in over fifty countries, he claims he can speak enough German and French to save his life. Strangely, his tryst with translation started with a paper in French on the blood diseases of fishes for his sister-in-law, using a borrowed dictionary. He is now an empanelled copy editor with Indian publishers and IIM Ahmedabad. *Delhi: A Soliloquy* is his first published translation from Malayalam. He lives and works in Dubai. Nandakumar is the grandson of Mahakavi Vallathol Narayana Menon.

M. MUKUNDAN

DELHI

A SOLILOQUY

TRANSLATED BY
FATHIMA E.V. & NANDAKUMAR K.

eka

eka

First published in Malayalam as *Delhi Gathakal* in 2011

First published in English as *Delhi: A Soliloquy* in 2020 by Eka, an imprint of Westland Publications Private Limited

Published in 2023 by Eka, an imprint of Westland Books, a division of Nasadiya Technologies Private Limited

No. 269/2B, First Floor, 'Irai Arul', Vimalraj Street, Nethaji Nagar, Allappakkam Main Road, Maduravoyal, Chennai 600095

ISBN: 9789395767736

10 9 8 7 6 5 4 3 2 1

This is a work of fiction. Names, characters, organisations, places, events and incidents are either products of the author's imagination or used fictitiously.

Typeset by Jojy Philip, New Delhi 110 015

Printed at Nutech Print Services-India

To Sreeja, my wife,
from whom I learnt the joy of togetherness.

Part One

Times of War

We have been travelling through the cloud.
The sky has been dark ever since the war began.
—Black Kettle (1803–1868)

1

A HUNDRED WITHERED FLOWERS

It was on a Saturday, 13 June 1959, that Sahadevan arrived in Delhi for the first time. He was twenty years old. That was the day he spoke the most he ever had. All to himself.

Sahadevan would live in Delhi, the Indian capital, for a long time, growing old there. He would accomplish many things during this time, and would fail at a lot more. One of the important things he would continue to do was to keep talking to himself. It was a dialogue that would go on for four decades. For instance, when he alighted from the train at Delhi for the first time, he said to himself, 'Sahadeva, do you know where you're standing now? In the land where Gandhiji fell after he was shot …'

Sahadevan turned voluble and talked to himself every time something momentous happened—not necessarily in his own life. 21 October 1961 was one such day. He was exhausted from having talked to himself the whole day. When he talked to himself, he also smoked continuously. The constant chatter and smoking wore him out.

Around 9 a.m. that day, in his one-room government quarters at Sewa Nagar, Shreedharanunni had left the world of the living.

Sahadevan had great respect and affection for Shreedharanunni, to whom he owed a great deal. Shreedharanunni was thirty-nine years old when he died. He did not suffer from any ailment serious enough to cause death. It had happened as he scanned the headlines of his favourite English newspaper, which he had got into the habit of reading from the day he arrived in Delhi to start his new job. Shreedharanunni's heart just stopped beating ('His fuse blew', as Inder Bhatia put it).

The previous day had held no premonition of the impending tragedy. He had left for his office in the Central Secretariat as usual, at 9.15 a.m., having pulled on a pair of slightly dishevelled white cotton trousers and a half-sleeve shirt. The tiffin carrier containing his lunch dangled from the handlebar of his bicycle. He had worn these same trousers the previous day and cycled for two hours. A great majority of mid-level babus—the slightly pejorative term for the non-officer grade government staff—employed at the Secretariat had similarly wrinkled trouser seats, as bicycles were their primary mode of transport.

The second milk-train from Rewari was to arrive by 9.30 a.m.; the first one came before dawn. Shreedharanunni had to cross the railway gate before that. By the time the train passed and the gates opened, the place would be clogged with buses, cycles, tongas and pedestrians, making movement impossible. To be caught in the mêlée meant being late for office by at least half an hour.

'You wear your shirt and pants for one day and they're wrinkled. Do you go to office to work or to roll on the ground with some children?'

Shreedharanunni laughed away Devi's grumbling. 'Do you want me to get any vegetables in the evening?' he asked.

'Buy some cauliflower. A small one will do. Just yesterday, Vidya asked me why I don't make cauliflower curry anymore.'

Their daughter was very fond of cauliflower. She normally ate two chapatis, but would polish off at least four when cauliflower and tomato curry was cooked in the house.

The cauliflower season was just beginning; the prices were still high. Once the cold season set in, the market in Kotla would flood with cauliflowers, carrots and radishes, making the prices drop steadily. Then, every day, it would be chapati and cauliflower curry. Sometimes Devi cooked the vegetable dry, without any gravy. Sometimes she added masala and made it taste like meat. Except for Vidya, no one was particularly fond of these curries.

Before he mounted the bicycle, Shreedharanunni used Devi's saree pallu to wipe the seat clean. Its cover was split right through the middle. The leather on his shoes was also wrinkled and had cracked in places. The heels were worn out. He should get a new pair this Diwali, Devi thought, and made a mental note. She had planned to buy them last Diwali, but it didn't happen. By the time the children's things were purchased, the father's pockets had gone empty.

'Don't worry, I can manage with this for one more year,' Shreedharanunni had consoled her.

Shreedharanunni wore shoes only to the office; everywhere else, he wore rubber flip-flops. Inside the house, he walked barefoot. Even in January, when the cemented floor was cold enough to numb one's feet, he had no problem walking about without even a pair of socks.

'Arrey, Shreedharji, make haste, the milk-train will be here any moment,' Sukhram, who was riding behind him in the service lane, called out as he pedalled past. Sukhram was Shreedharanunni's colleague. He stayed in the government quarters at Andrews Ganj, where the city itself ended. Beyond it were wheat fields, interspersed with cabbage and radish patches.

Everyone was pedalling furiously to get through the railway gate in time. Shreedharanunni was punctilious—he aimed to make it through just minutes before the train arrived. His calculation never failed.

However, his return trip in the evening could never be as precise. There would be some errand to run on the way, someone to meet. If nothing else, there would be a union meeting to attend.

Shreedharanunni was an active member of the union. In the past twelve years, he had participated in seven strikes, big and small. The union leaders made the most of his organisational skills. When a strike was on, he would reach home late, often past midnight. There were days when he did not come home at all. Devi had no misgivings about this. She knew that he would spend the night at Karbala, where the Class IV employees—peons and messengers—had their quarters.

'Never surrender' was the fierce encouragement she offered when he came back in the morning before rushing off again on his cycle, unshaven, barely managing a hasty bath, and grabbing two chapatis for breakfast.

'If you have to be on a hunger strike till you die, do it, but don't surrender.'

'Oh, that won't be necessary, Devi. We've never lost. Don't you know that?'

Shreedharanunni often glanced at the photo of S.A. Dange that hung on the wall of his room, which remained dark even during the daytime. Each time, his mind grew robust in response; the longing for resistance rose within him.

There was another photo beside that of Dange—of the Chinese Premier, Zhou Enlai. A hundred red flowers adorned its borders. He had bought the picture outside Parassinikadavu Temple during one of his visits to Kerala. The official deity of Parassinikadavu was Muthappan, but photographs of Zhou Enlai and AKG* outnumbered Muthappan's in sales.

---

*A.K. Gopalan, a leader of the Communist Party of India and later of the Marxist party, universally known by his initials, AKG.

In his unwashed shirt and trousers, with his face unshaven, Shreedharanunni disappeared from his wife's sight, pedalling between the old buildings and into the distance.

In this manner, forgoing food and sleep, he had worked hard for the success of several strikes. He had only tales of victory to narrate; till date, none of their strikes had failed. Nor would they ever lose. He believed in unity; if they stood united, no power, worldly or divine, could defeat them. He was a rationalist and a communist.

It was that evening, in the parking lot of the Secretariat, that he heard the gloomy news. He was about to get on his bicycle after hanging his freshly washed tiffin carrier on the handle, when Bansilal came up and said, 'Bhaisaab, did you hear? War has started on the border.'

'What war?'

He hadn't heard any talk of war. Why would there be a war at this point? He was confused. Starvation deaths in villages, herds of cattle killed by draught, epidemics of plague and cholera … these were the things that usually figured in the news. All of these could be endured. But it was unbearable to listen to news about an impending war. How many would perish …

The first war was for Azad Kashmir. In October 1947, when war broke out in Poonch, Shreedharanunni hadn't yet reached Delhi. In those days, he was working as an accountant in a warehouse owned by a Konkani, after completing his tenth standard. But the war was still fresh in the memory of Bansilal, who had grown up in Punjab. He used to narrate stories to his colleagues while they ate their chapatis and dal on the India Gate lawns on cool, sunny winter afternoons. Bansilal's brother, Krishanlal, was one of the 1580 soldiers who had sacrificed their lives for their motherland. His youthful body still lay frozen in the snowdrifts of Uri. Perhaps it would remain there for thousands of years.

'Why would Pakistan need a war now? To annex the rest of Kashmir as well?'

In the 1947 war, Pakistan had seized two-fifths of Kashmir.

'Arrey bhaisaab, the war is not against Pakistan. It's with China.'

Shreedharanunni felt a prick, as if a bedbug had bitten him on his buttocks. He realised in a flash that Bansilal was pulling his leg.

He laughed and started to pedal. There was a sea of bicycles in front of him. People were streaming out from their offices in the various ministries and the Secretariat. Tiffin carriers or bags dangled from handlebars. Bus No. 41, which terminated at Lajpat Nagar, cut through the tide of bicycles, emitting fumes. He thought of Kunhikrishnan, his journalist friend, who also hailed from his village in Kerala. He now lived in the New Double Storey building in Guru Nanak Market in Lajpat Nagar.

Cyclists seldom take the route that buses and cars frequent. They know shortcuts. Avoiding the main thoroughfares buzzing with vehicular traffic, they ride through residential areas, parks and markets to get home faster. Having lived in Delhi for thirteen years, Shreedharanunni knew all the alleys and shortcuts along his way like the back of his hand.

A throng of cyclists appeared at the end of the road. They had turned from Janpath into Ratendone Road, taking the shorter route. The rays of the evening sun bounced off their handlebars. Like competitors in the Olympic velodrome, the government employees streamed past Ratendone Road onto a path that cut through Lodhi Gardens. A chameleon that had emerged from the trees and onto the path saw the procession and scampered back, frightened.

Though it was only 5.30 p.m., Lodhi Gardens was already turning dark. The squabble of roosting birds could be heard. The place was a veritable den of foxes right in the heart of the city. No one stepped in there once dusk fell. Wild animals were known to live amidst the trees, as were ghosts and ghouls.

Sukhram claimed to have seen a phantom cavalry brigade there one wintry night, while he was on his way home to Andrews Ganj after a late-night movie at the Race Course cinema. None of those horsemen of the Lodi king had heads on their shoulders, he said. Shreedharanunni had laughed when he heard this.

He fell behind the other cyclists. Though he had tried to dismiss Bansilal's words as a joke, a doubt had started to grow within him. Earlier, when he was in the vicinity of India Gate, he had noticed the cars of high-ranking military officials rushing towards South Block, the flags on their bonnets fluttering in the breeze. Defence Minister V.K. Krishna Menon's office was in South Block. The thought made him anxious.

Cutting through Lodhi Gardens, the cyclists entered Block 21 of Lodhi Colony. Shreedharanunni's legs slackened further on the pedals, and the rest of the cyclists rode past. Suddenly, he was all alone.

He cycled slowly towards Sewa Nagar. From Khanna Market, the grating sounds of the milling machine grinding wheat could be heard. Though Diwali was a few weeks away, two shops selling fireworks had already opened and were doing brisk business. He rode on, along Dhobi Ghat. Just as he reached the railway crossing, the gate closed. On the other side, horse-drawn carriages and bicycles swarmed. Only local trains and goods trains passed through here. Yet the gate remained closed most of the time. There was a coolness in the air, presaging winter. But he was sweating. He pushed the bicycle to the side of the road and squatted there. Cattle returning from the vegetable market in Kotla Mubarakpur after feasting on rotting cauliflowers and radishes brushed past him.

By the time he reached home, it was 7 p.m. As she took the tiffin carrier off the handle and stepped back into the house, Devi asked him, 'Where's the cauliflower?'

Shreedharanunni just stood there, silent. He had taken the route close to Kotla Mubarakpur. Riding through the railway gate, he had seen the kerosene lamps of the vegetable vendors inside the market. Even then, he had not remembered. His mind had been preoccupied with more important things than buying a cauliflower.

'I forgot, Devi.'

'Didn't you come via the vegetable market? And you still forgot? Are you going to begin a new strike?'

Devi had told Vidya that her father would be bringing cauliflower. She was already salivating at the thought of eating warm chapatis with cauliflower curry.

'Devi, I need to go to Lajpat Nagar.'

'Have some tea then. I'll just take a moment to make it.'

'No need, Devi.'

He didn't usually go out until after he'd had a bath and a cup of tea. She wondered what had happened today.

'Why are you off to Lajpat Nagar?'

'I need to meet Kunhikrishnan urgently. I have to ask him something.'

Kunhikrishnan would tell him exactly what was going on. He was, after all, a member of the press.

Shreedharanunni was already on his bicycle, moving swiftly. It was dark outside, and cold too. Night falls early as winter approaches. Dussehra was over. Next up was Diwali. Once that was over, the cold would set in over Delhi. In the mornings, the mist would pass through the jamun trees at Sewa Nagar like rain clouds. The days would pass quickly, without meeting the sun. And the nights would be long and chilly.

It was to Kunhikrishnan's apartment in Lajpat Nagar that Shreedharanunni cycled. Kunhikrishnan worked for one of the leading English dailies in the city. He would have all the latest updates. Was there a war? With whom? Was it with Pakistan?

If only he had a radio at home, he mused wistfully. Not for listening to the songs broadcast by Radio Ceylon, but for the news. But there was no way he could afford a radio. Even among his colleagues, only three or four had a radio at home. A Murphy radio was the dream of every middle-class family.

Shreedharanunni reached the Ring Road. He saw the tongas headed towards Safdarjung. They would stop plying after eight. After that, the only mode of transport was the bicycle, wherever one wanted to go.

He pedalled on in the dim light. He passed Andrews Ganj, then turned right at Moolchand Hospital and entered Guru Nanak Market. The area beyond lay in complete darkness. The cauliflower patches on the right side of the narrow road leading to Kalkaji were also in darkness. No one went there after nightfall because it teemed with robbers and thugs.

The tiny, double-storey tenements at Lajpat Nagar had been built by the government for refugees after the bloodletting of Partition. Kunhikrishnan stayed in one of these as a tenant, paying a monthly rent of ninety rupees. Electricity and water cost extra. He often said that he could not afford such a high rent.

'Kunh'ishnaaa …' he called from the shadows.

Shreedharanunni could see the dim light from the matchbox-like houses around him. He leaned his bicycle against the wall and went into the yard. There was a calling-bell, but the switch was non-functional. He knocked on the door. Someone switched on the light inside and the pale yellow glow from a low-voltage forty-watt bulb filled the entranceway.

'Who's that?' a woman asked through the half-open door.

'It's me, Shreedharanunni, Lalitha. Isn't Kunh'ishnan here?'

'Come in and sit down, Shreedharetta. Where are you coming from at this hour?'

He stood at the door and looked around.

'I was sleeping,' she said. 'What else am I to do? I'm bored stiff.'

'Where is Kunh'ishnan?'

'He's on night duty. It'll be dawn by the time he gets home. When we got married, he promised me he wouldn't do it anymore. But he is always on night duty. I don't believe him these days, whatever he says.'

'It isn't his fault, Lalitha. For newspaper employees, there's no difference between day and night. Every morning, the paper has to be brought out, no?'

Shreedharanunni was disappointed. He had cycled all that distance for some news. Now where would he find it? Who could he check with? All the main dailies were located on Bahadur Shah Zafar Marg. There were no buses at this late hour and he didn't have the energy to cycle all the way there, he thought despondently.

He could go back to Sewa Nagar and find a house that had a radio. But when was the next broadcast? Was there a news broadcast at all tonight? Would he have to wait till dawn for one?

The only other person he could approach was Sahadevan, who was knowledgeable and up-to-date about everything. He lived only half a kilometre away, in Amritpuri, a village next to Dayanand Colony. But would Sahadevan be in his room? He was the type who always got home late.

'Come in, Shreedharetta. Why are you standing outside?'

That was when Shreedharanunni's eyes fell on the aerial inside the room. He stepped in quickly. Ordinarily, he would never have entered a house where a lady sat alone.

The room was bare, except for two steel chairs and a cane mooda. A radio sat on a small stool set against the wall. Just now, the most valuable thing in the world for him was that Murphy radio. Kunhikrishnan had got married barely two months ago. He was yet to buy household furniture. But for a journalist, a radio was a necessity, not a luxury; he had bought this one under an instalment scheme.

Shreedharanunni sat on the mooda and switched on the radio. There was no sound.

'It takes some time to warm up, Shreedharetta.'

After two minutes, the radio had warmed up fully; the valves started blinking one by one. Spluttering sounds came from within. Then the opening bars of a Hindi song crackled through: '*Kisi ki muskuraahaton pe ...*'

'Please find the news, Lalitha.'

She fiddled with the knob and found the All India Radio station. A programme on agriculture seemed to be on, but nothing else.

Once again, he was disheartened. After sitting in front of the radio for a little longer, he bade her goodbye. The lights of Guru Nanak Market had gone out. The roadside corner that was usually occupied by Kallu, the cobbler—whom everyone called Kallu mochi—was deserted. He must have left for the day. Dim lights could be seen only in the windows of the tenements called New Double Storey. The cauliflower patches were completely submerged in the inky darkness.

By the time he reached home, Shreedharanunni was exhausted, both mentally and physically.

That night, he could not sleep. He kept tossing and turning on the charpoy. Every now and then, he got up to drink water from the earthen pot kept outside. Next to him, mother and daughter slept on another charpoy. Sathyanathan usually slept on the narrow veranda at the back, lulled by the breeze that blew through the neem trees. He did his homework there too. It was only when the days and nights became cold in November that he moved inside.

It was close to dawn when Shreedharanunni finally fell asleep. Almost immediately, he woke up to the rumble of Delhi Milk Scheme vans filled with milk bottles driving past the house. The DMS milk booth was two blocks away. He went to the toilet, then pulled on a woollen cap, picked up the card and the empty bottles, and walked along the deserted path leading to the booth. He had permits for two half-litre bottles since they were a family of four. Usually, Devi gave Vidya a full glass of milk from one of the bottles; the rest of the milk was used for their tea. The second bottle of milk was for making curd. In summer, she would make lassi instead, with ice, for her husband and kids.

After fetching the milk, Shreedharanunni pulled out a chair and sat outside, doing nothing, his eyes fixed on the road. Every day, at 6.30 a.m., the newspaper delivery man arrived on his bicycle. But not today. It was already 7.30 a.m. Eight o'clock, and there was still no sign of him. Eight-thirty turned to nine. Then in the distance, his bicycle appeared near Sewa Nagar Market. People were waiting impatiently for him in front of their houses.

Shreedharanunni did not ask the man why he had been delayed. He took the paper and opened it with trembling hands. His eyes scanned the headlines on the front page.

China had attacked India. There were massive troop movements at the borders. Sixty-five thousand Chinese soldiers were moving towards India. The Chinese had already entered Aksai Chin on the west and NEFA on the east.

Shreedharanunni felt as if someone had kicked him in the chest. He felt breathless. With great effort, he turned his head and looked at the portrait of Zhou Enlai inside the house.

Hindi Chini bhai bhai. Indians and Chinese are brothers.

Let a hundred flowers bloom.

The newspaper slipped from his nerveless fingers and down to the floor. His eyes rolled up. Gently, his head fell to one side.

2

WRITING IN TIMES OF WAR

Comrade Zhou Enlai, why have you done this terrible thing? We have an inexhaustible list of gods we can call upon. We have Guruvayurappan, and Ayyappan at Sabarimala. We have Paramashivan, Subrahmaniaswami and Vighneswaran. We have Parassinikadavu Muthappan, Kaadampuzha Bhagawathi, Muchilottu Bhagawathi and Koyyodan Koroth Sasthappan. Vishnumoorthi, Ghantakarnan, Karinkuttichchaathan and Gulikan are present in the countless shrines and sacred groves from Kasaragod to Vadakara. Despite that, it's your photo that Shreedharanunni chose to hang on his wall. And yet, you betrayed him. Why, Zhou Enlai?

Still muttering to himself, Sahadevan stood in front of the photo.

He was hot and panting from all the walking and running, and the tonga ride that he'd had to brave to reach Shreedharanunni's house.

Shreedharanunni was stretched out on the same bed on which he had once lain with Devi and on which Devi had breastfed Vidya. His nostrils were stuffed with cotton balls. Sahadevan went and stood next to him. His face had the look of someone who had died not just once but many times at once.

Like aftershocks following an earthquake, maybe death too has after-deaths, Sahadevan thought.

Vidya was nowhere to be seen.

Several people had gathered in the front yard. The first one to arrive was Banwarilal, the union leader. Sukhram had come from Andrews Ganj, panting. A few other Secretariat employees who lived in Sewa Nagar had arrived. All their faces reflected anxiety and fear. The arrival of the newspaper had broken the news about the war. Was it this or the premature death of Shreedharanunni that shook them the most?

'What happened to bhaisaab?'

'Heart attack. Enough, what else?'

'Ram, Ram.'

The neighbours whispered among themselves.

Only the union workers from Andrews Ganj, Karbala and Lodhi Colony managed to make it to Sewa Nagar. People staying further away could not come since the buses weren't plying. War had spread a pall of fear everywhere.

Abdullah Bawa Khan, the tea and lassi seller in Khan Market, came from Karbala. His shop lay on Shreedharanunni's route to office. He used to stop his bicycle beside Khan's shop and have a cup of hot tea when the cold January breeze turned his hands and face blue. On hot days, he would ask for chilled lassi.

Kunhikrishnan and Lalitha arrived soon afterwards. Sleep hung heavy on Kunhikrishnan's eyelids. He had not bathed or shaved. He left for his office while Lalitha remained behind. Until the war was over, he wouldn't have time to eat or sleep. He would only have time to listen to the indistinct, crackling phone messages relayed over bad connections from the news agencies, transcribe them, and make copy from them.

There was no one to wait for. In any case, who would come from Kerala? It would take a four-day journey to reach Delhi, changing trains twice. And there was no assurance that the trains would run during war time.

And so, the arrangements were made for Shreedharanunni's last journey. Banwarilal was in charge. The materials needed for the cremation were available at Yusuf Sarai Market, but all the markets were closed. It was with great difficulty that some union members managed to arrange for a bier on bamboo poles, an earthen pot, incense, oil, flowers and other paraphernalia. His body was bathed and laid on the bier. His colleagues wrapped the body in a red flag and placed a wreath on it. An unfamiliar masculine beauty radiated from his face.

'My children have no one ...'

'Don't cry, Devi.'

Banwarilal's wife Kanta caressed Devi's head. Sukhram's wife had also reached by then.

'We're all here, aren't we, Deviyechi?' Lalitha said.

'My life is over, Lalitha ...'

'No, no ... don't cry.'

The funeral procession, resonating with chants of 'Ram Ram ...' moved along the deserted roads towards the cremation ground. Sathyanathan walked holding Sahadevan's hand. There were only about twenty people, and the majority of them were local union workers.

As the procession neared the Nizamuddin dargah, Kunhikrishnan arrived in a taxi. He and Sahadevan walked side-by-side with bowed heads. Sathyanathan walked alongside, dressed in the obligatory *mundu*. Unaccustomed to its length, he kept tripping on its edge and stumbled a couple of times. Seeing this, Sahadevan put an arm around him. His body was frigid, as if he had been left on ice.

'Are we going to burn father?'

'Umm.'

'Why don't we bury him?'

'Hindus usually cremate their dead.'

'Father isn't a Hindu. He is a Communist.'

Sathyanathan had once heard his father telling Banwarilal that Communists had neither religion nor caste.

Sahadevan didn't say anything, only held him closer as they walked behind the bier. He told himself that when the kid grew up, he would be a bigger Communist than his father.

Kunhikrishnan listened quietly to the child's words. What a great burden Shreedharanunni had placed on his tiny shoulders when he died ...

They could see only the top of Shreedharanunni's head; his face and body were covered by the red flag. His black hair, with no grey in it, had rice grains entangled in the strands. When the pall-bearers shifted the weight from one shoulder to the other, his head wobbled from side to side, and a couple of grains fell to the ground.

Someone else's pyre was already burning in the cremation ground. Shreedharanunni's pyre was being readied. The priest was waiting, with vetiver, water, incense and other materials. Sathyanathan sprinkled water over his father's body, which now lay on the cement floor, and followed the instructions of the priest, who was also simultaneously chanting mantras in a language no one understood.

'Enough has been done. Hurry up, panditji.'

Banwarilal did not believe in funeral rites. Nor did Shreedharanunni. He would have stopped it if he had witnessed any of this.

Finally, all of them came together to lift the body, now wet with water and oil, and placed it on the pyre. Holding the wick in his damp hand, Sathyanathan lit his father's pyre. He didn't bother to wipe the tears that welled up and rolled down his eyes. He stood and watched his father turn into fire and smoke—his father, the sweet, gentle person who had sat him on his lap and taught him 'aa' for *amma* and 'aaa' for *aana*.

The crowd dispersed before the pyre had burnt down completely. It was wartime. The city itself seemed to wear an air of mourning, with fewer people moving about and minimal traffic. A taxi from his office was waiting for Kunhikrishnan at the gate of the cremation ground.

After dropping Sahadevan and Sathyanathan at Sewa Nagar, Kunhikrishnan left for his office.

Sathyanathan's damp body was shivering in the cold. It was afternoon, but the sun's rays on the government quarters had already turned cool.

The house seemed empty. Except for Lalitha and a couple of union workers, everyone else had left. Devi was lying on the same cot on which Shreedharanunni's corpse had lain earlier. Her tear glands had run dry. Her dishevelled hair and bloodshot eyes made Sathyanathan feel even sadder.

'Where's my daughter?' Devi asked when she saw Sahadevan and Sathyanathan.

'She's at our place, bhabhiji. Let her stay there for three or four days,' Banwarilal said.

Vidya was a child. She shouldn't have to see her dead father. Her tender heart wouldn't be able to bear it. So, he had whisked her away.

'No, bhaisaab,' Devi said, 'bring her here. Let her see it all, and seeing it, let her mind become stronger. She'll grow up as a fatherless child. Let her start building the strength for that.'

'Deviyechi, here, drink this.'

Lalitha had brought a glass of tea. Her hand was smeared with soot from the kerosene stove. She poured the tea from the glass into a steel bowl, and then back and forth a few times to cool it, before placing it in front of Devi.

'Where will I go with these little ones? How will we live?'

Devi held her head between her hands, but not a single tear fell from her eyes on to her ashen cheeks. Though they were poor, Shreedharanunni and his family had led a contented life. Now everything had come to an end. Life stretched out in front of them like an endless sea. She had no idea how to get across to the other side. The very thought made her head spin.

'There's always a way, Deviyechi. Now drink the tea. Then try to get some sleep. We can sit and plan the rest tomorrow,' said Sahadevan.

Devi sat up on the cot, took a couple of sips and put the glass down. She gathered up her hair and tied it back. She wiped her eyes with her palm. She tugged her blouse into place and adjusted her saree pallu. She knew there was nothing to be gained by grieving in this fashion. Life had to be lived. She had to move on.

She stepped out of the house with her gaze trained straight ahead. For the first time, she saw a world without Shreedharanunni. His Hercules bicycle leaned against the half-wall. On the terraces above the row of government quarters, sarees, salwar-kameez and pyjamas fluttered in the breeze as they dried. The alleys between the quarters were deserted.

'Deviyechi, you shouldn't sleep alone today. I'm staying back.'

'I'll stay too.'

Sahadevan had never stayed over when Shreedharanunni wasn't at home. After Devi went to sleep, he paced the yard late into the night. The ground was littered with moringa flowers. When his legs wearied and he stepped back into the house, he saw Devi sitting on the chair with Lalitha by her side.

'Let Banwarilal come, I'll ask him to get me a job, any job. Even a sweeper's job will do. I won't leave Delhi till Sathyanathan completes his studies. He's only in the eighth standard.'

She was not ready to go back with two little children to her family in Kerala, who already struggled for one square meal a day. It seemed to Sahadevan that she had thought it through before making the decision.

'Why aren't you saying anything, Sahadeva?'

'Don't leave. We'll find a way. I'll go and talk to Banwarilal.'

'No. I'll tell him what I need.'

At 2 a.m., a taxi arrived at the unlit gate. An exhausted Kunhikrishnan came in. Devi was lying with her eyes closed, her arms around Sathyanathan. Lalitha sat on a chair, nodding off. On another chair, Sahadevan sat sleepless. The room was suffused with smoke from the many cigarettes he had chain-smoked.

'Sahadeva, the Chinese have entered Assam. They are now forty kilometres inside our territory. They won't have a problem reaching Delhi if they want to. There's no one to stop them. Our army is just a sham. It's doubtful if they even have bullets in their guns. If two cats were to breach our border, they still wouldn't be able to stop them. It's bad times for our Krishna Menon. Poor guy, he's answerable for everything.'

'How many more Malayalis like Shreedharettan will die of a broken heart?'

'When will this war end?' Devi asked.

'Who knows? It has just started, Deviyechi!'

'How many are going to die at the border? When I think of that, my heart bleeds.'

Devi sighed. How many more women would become widows, their desire to live a full life wrested away from them ...

In the cremation ground on Link Road, Shreedharanunni's body had burnt to ashes. The smoke was still rising from his bones. Only two days ago, the man had been walking briskly through Delhi, swinging his arms, and now he was no more.

The nation was entering a new period; its history was being redrawn, revised. It was clear now that the dreams that had travelled from across the snow-covered mountains were counterfeit; they only announced a false dawn. It would take many years for the wounds to heal.

Like the country, Shreedharanunni's family was also starting a new life.

The shabad kirtan could be heard from the gurdwara. It was past the hour when the DMS truck usually arrived. However, the villagers from Kotla Mubarakpur came as usual, leading buffaloes with full, bloated udders. The old-timers wouldn't dream of drinking anything other than the fresh, slightly warm milk from buffaloes milked in front of them. They did not approve of milk filled by machines and delivered in sealed bottles.

On that cool October morning, Kunhikrishnan, Lalitha and Sathyanathan lay on the floor of Shreedharanunni's house. Sahadevan couldn't sleep. He had finished his cigarettes the previous night. He worried that the shops would not open in the morning.

He got up slowly, walked up to the photo of Zhou Enlai and stood in front of it. He stretched his hand out and tried to take the photo from the wall. It was fixed with a strong cord. He used all his strength to yank it out along with the nail that held it in place. It was like extracting a decayed tooth. He deposited the photo on top of the accumulated rubbish in the backyard.

He lay down again. As he lay there sleepless, he heard the sound of Devi sweeping the yard. Moringa leaves and flowers littered the ground. The flowers that had fallen from the wreath placed on Shreedharanunni's body by the union members lay wilted on the ground. She swept it all up and deposited it at the foot of the neem tree in the backyard. Her resilience and mental fortitude amazed him—there had been no wailing, no tears.

'Has the newspaper come?' Kunhikrishnan asked as soon as he opened his eyes.

A little later, Banwarilal arrived in a tonga. Vidya was with him. Her small, round face was dark, as if she had walked in the sun for a long time. Her hair was tousled.

'I want to see my father,' she cried. No one said anything. Devi wanted to tell her that it was not possible to see dead people. But looking at Vidya's face, she didn't have the heart to say it.

Two men from Banwarilal's village arrived from Karol Bagh. Some of the Secretariat staff who had not been able to visit the previous day also came. In silence, they sat on the hired chairs placed in the yard swept clean by Devi. After sitting there for a little while, they left.

In the evening, Kunhikrishnan left for his office on Bahadur Shah Zafar Marg. Lalitha decided to keep Devi company that night as well.

Sahadevan had been yearning to go home. As soon as he entered his house, he lit a Charminar, picked up a sheet of paper and a pen, and sat down to write his novel. He sat late into the night, scribbling.

All wars end. The war of 1962 also ended. The Chinese army started to withdraw on 21 November. But by that time, the peace and amity which had prevailed in the snow-capped mountains for centuries had disintegrated forever. More than 1500 soldiers lost their lives. Their families were orphaned.

Devi didn't have to appeal to Banwarilal. The union leaders had already discussed the matter and did what was required. Devi was given a job as a lower-grade government servant. From now on, she would fetch and carry files between capacious rooms with high ceilings, which were home to noisy fans and overflowing papers. She would fetch tea, cigarettes and paan for the babus.

And thus, Devi and her children started a new life in Delhi. That was forty years ago.

3

AN AUSPICIOUS JOURNEY

His full name on his school leaving certificate was Mataparambu Sahadevan Nambiar. Before leaving for Delhi, he shortened it to M. Sahadevan and placed a notice in the newspapers to this effect. The relief he felt was like the astonishing relief of an aching tooth pulled out once and for all.

The Malayalis who arrived in Delhi in the 1950s were familiar with poverty. Malayalis such as V.K. Krishna Menon, Sardar K.M. Panikkar and K.P.S. Menon, who occupied powerful positions in Delhi, did not of course come from poor families. But people like Shreedharanunni and Sahadevan had suffered poverty and hardship before they reached Delhi. When their story is told, the opening chapters can only be about privation and misery.

Back home in Kerala, the image that Sahadevan had of Delhi centred on Jawaharlal Nehru in his white sherwani with a red rose in its buttonhole, looking more like a white man than an Indian. A picture of Indira, holding her father's hand while standing in the gardens of Teen Murti Bhawan, also came to mind. Magnificent buildings of the colonial era; gleaming cars flowing down wide, imperial roads; the circular Connaught Place filled with nattily dressed men in suits—this was the vision of Delhi that Sahadevan carried in his head.

He had hoped his miseries would vanish once he reached the capital. After all, the first sunrise of independent India was seen in Delhi. The national flag was raised there for the first time. New India's journey towards prosperity and plenitude began in Delhi. So, as a young man, he told himself—'It's in Delhi that your life will begin. There, everyone will be employed. Their homes will contain every possible amenity. Every child will attend school. After school hours, they'll go to the parks to play. In case they fall sick, they'll have access to free or inexpensive treatment in hospitals. These are my only expectations. A dignified city occupied by people who lead dignified lives. An independent nation should guarantee its citizens a life of dignity.'

His younger sister Shyamala said, 'Will you also be suited and booted once you are in Delhi? If so, you should send me a photo. I want to show it to my friends.'

'What will you tell them when you show it to them?'

'This is my brother. He's in Delhi now. He's an important officer there. He goes to office on a gleaming bicycle. He smokes cigarettes too.'

This was her dream for her brother. Everyone back home smoked beedis. Only the gentry and the rich, like doctors, smoked cigarettes.

Sahadevan was tempted to smoke. But he was the eldest male member of a starving family that could not make both ends meet. Fate had placed a heavy burden on him at a relatively young age. So, he had nipped all such desires in the bud. No cigarettes. No romantic pursuits. No movies. His youth was barren like fallow earth.

Before leaving on a long journey, tradition demanded that he bid adieu to every relative, near and far. He visited one house after another, on foot or by bus. It took more than a week.

'Don't leave anyone out. You did go to Kunjiraman uncle's place, didn't you?' his mother asked him. Whoever he might overlook, he could not afford to forget this man, or else he was sure to come and stand in front of the house and gripe. And so he visited his maternal and paternal uncles, and even acquaintances, and bid them goodbye.

'What's up, why are you here at noon?'

'I'm going away ...'

'To Madras?'

'No.'

'Must be to Bombay then ...?'

'No, Nanu uncle. To Delhi.'

Nanumama's cataract-dulled eyes gleamed. All the young men went to Bombay and Madras to seek their fortunes. Why was this boy going to Delhi? The mention of Delhi made everyone's eyes sparkle like Nanumama's. Wasn't it the domain of Nehru? Only a few like Sahadevan recalled that it was also the city where Gandhiji was killed.

'Then go and prosper, young man. All the best. When you come back, I may not be here. My sight is gone. Can't walk either. I'm past fifty; don't know when the summons from heaven will come.'

Nanumama raised his creased hand and blessed him. He also gave him half a rupee. By the time he had finished the rounds of thirty homes, Sahadevan's legs were tired. That he had so many relatives and such a large, extended family, was a revelation to him.

When young men headed out to Madras and Bombay in search of a livelihood, they usually wore trousers. But Sahadevan started his journey in a mundu—he had no money to buy trousers. Before the start of the monsoon that year, his father had borrowed money to rethatch their hut, and to buy rations, medicines and liniments. He was ready to step out and borrow more.

There was a time when Shekharan Nambiar wore an elaborately wrought coiled-snake gold ring on his finger and ear studs made of gold. Poverty had forced him to sell these, one by one. But if he asked for a loan, anyone would lend him money, he had such a sterling reputation. Also, they knew he would ask only when he was in dire need.

'There's no need, achcha,' Sahadevan said. 'There's no need at all for trousers now. We'll do all that once I get a job. I'll get them stitched after I reach Delhi.'

'As soon as you reach Delhi, you should go to Nehru's house and meet him,' his mother said. 'But don't go there wearing a mundu. Go only after you get trousers.'

His mother felt extremely proud that her son was going to the place where Nehru lived. In the newsreels screened before every movie, she had seen Nehru and Krishna Menon arriving in black cars to view the Republic Day parade. She used to gaze unblinking at the screen, with her head tilted and her mouth slightly open, as imposing cannons, tanks and fighter planes glided forward on Rajpath and soldiers marched past. Schoolchildren in salwar-kameez and dupatta danced as they moved along. It was to that Delhi her son was going ... he could meet Nehru every day. In her heart, she thanked Shreedharanunni many times.

'What nonsense is this, Sharada? Why should Sahadevan meet Nehru? Even if he does go to meet him, do you think Nehru will see him? He is our prime minister!'

'Why shouldn't Nehru meet our son? What does he lack? We may be poor, but we come from a reputed family, a respectable tharavad.'

It was with the burden of fending for his father, mother and two sisters that Sahadevan started his journey to Delhi. Once he reached the city, he would write a novel. It was a dream he had shared with no one else.

Shekharan Nambiar and Unnikuttan came to see him off at the railway station. Unnikuttan was Sahadevan's friend. Sahadevan didn't have many—solitude was his best friend.

The sky was overcast when they left home. It started to rain as they waited at the station. The monsoon was yet to run its course.

'Hey man, so you are going to Delhi, eh? Once you are in Delhi, you'll change completely. Then don't forget this old friend,' Unnikuttan said. Unknown even to himself, in Unnikuttan's mind an image of a Delhiwallah Sahadevan had begun to form. It was similar to the one in Shyamala's imagination. A slim, suit- and hat-wearing Sahadevan, with his prominent Adam's apple, sitting astride a new bicycle with the toes of one foot touching the ground. Unnikuttan had seen a black and white photo of someone, somewhere, sitting jauntily like that. He had merely replaced that person with Sahadevan.

Eventually, the rain stopped. All the moisture receded from the leaves and the soil. Emaciated cattle foraged on cracked earth. The train had crossed Palghat and entered Erode.

The train to Delhi was hauled by a steam engine. All along the way, it spewed smoke and soot. The soot entered the bogie and his eyes through the open shutters of the windows. The shutters were jammed and could not be closed. He crouched in the third-class compartment. In those days, trains had three classes; the lowest was third class, which the majority of travellers used.

By the time the train reached Madras, Sahadevan was covered in engine soot and sweat. All through the journey, he had tasted the salt of his own sweat. Since he had not brought any water to drink, his throat was parched.

It was sweltering hot in Madras. The Central Station and its surroundings were aflame. But this was only a hint of the torrid heat he would face in Delhi.

He spent the evening wandering about in Moore Market. When he looked at the satin and georgette dresses on display, he thought of his sisters. At night, he slept on the platform. He didn't have money to rent a room in a lodge. He knew he would have to eat something to keep his hunger at bay until he reached Delhi. He wasn't sure if the money he had would suffice even for that.

As the Grand Trunk Express sped towards Delhi, passing through the Chambal ravines, Gwalior and Agra, he kept looking out through the window. He was impatient to reach Delhi. What magical sights awaited him—dreamy fantasies and images of prosperity, opulence …

A minor transformation took place within him during that train journey that lasted no more than three days. Till he got on the train, all his concerns were about getting a job. He was ready to do any work. He would have no complaints, whatever the salary he was able to secure. He should be able to send his father twenty-five or thirty rupees every month—that was all. But once the journey commenced, he started thinking about other things. He was curious about what the city looked like. The biggest town he had seen so far was Kozhikode. Delhi, with more than three million residents, was many times the size of Kozhikode.

What would he see first, he asked himself with the curiosity and eagerness of a child. Bungalows with gardens in the front, on either side of Rajpath? Tall buildings that touched the sky? Countless legs wearing shiny shoes, striding noisily towards office complexes? Girls with bobbed hair and lipstick, gliding like swans along the tree-lined avenues? Pandit Jawaharlal Nehru, on his way to Parliament in a gleaming black limousine? Whatever the first, beautiful spectacle he saw as the train entered Delhi would be etched indelibly in his mind, for him to recall all his life. Maybe it would be the starting point of his novel.

After Faridabad came Delhi. Sahadevan was to get down at New Delhi. Only the trains from the northern parts of India terminated at Old Delhi station. His train waited at Faridabad for a long time for a green signal. Most of the passengers got down and bought cardamom-laced tea, which they sipped from earthen mugs. A lame man selling poori-bhaji stood at Sahadevan's window, looking at him piteously. It was twenty hours since he'd had his last meal, but Sahadevan was not hungry. His face and hands were covered with soot. The first thing he wanted to do after reaching Delhi was to take an elaborate bath, pouring water over and over again on his head. Not just his skin and bones, even his liver, intestines and bladder needed cooling down. The heat, soot and smoke had exhausted him. But he didn't mind, cheered as he was by the proximity of the great city.

When the signal turned green, the train shuddered and started to move. After it had travelled for a while along the tangled tracks, he read the Hindi words—'Nayi Dilli'—written on the railway cabin in yellow paint which had begun to peel. The air was hot against his face. Outside, parallel to the train, which was crawling now, there was a puddle of black water. Gradually, it widened into what looked like a blocked drain and then into a big cesspool. The hot air wafting over the black film covering the cesspool brought a fetid smell into the train. He saw pigs wallowing in the sludge. Beyond the cesspool was a slum with rows of lean-tos and shelters made of tarpaulins and hessian. In front of the shelters, women were washing babies and clothes in the stinking water. Farther away, an old man squatted, defecating, with his genitals on display ... Sahadevan retched.

The train slowed down. He saw a vegetable market near the railway crossing. Vegetables had fallen out of their bundles and lay scattered on either side of the tracks. Pigs with their snipped tails curling back towards their own bodies scurried about, sniffing. Crows wheeled overhead. Some of them landed on the pigs. As the wind blew in his direction, the smell of the rotting vegetables assaulted him.

The train crawled past Nizamuddin and New Delhi railway station limped into view. The trembling of the wheels on the rails subsided. A hot, dusty wind swirled above. It was the loo, which habitually descends on Delhi with its heat and dust after gathering sands from the deserts of Rajasthan. In the withering heat, the path of the loo in the sky was the colour of fire.

As the Grand Trunk Express, one of the longest trains in the country, drew onto the platform in that hellish June heat, Shreedharanunni was waiting for Sahadevan. He wore a wrinkled white shirt and trousers. His oiled black hair was combed back neatly.

Shreedharanunni: his saviour.

The temperature was 44 degrees centigrade. Sahadevan would always remember that. He was finally in this big city. He felt an unnamed fear. After having been born and brought up in a village, and not even twenty years of age yet, he wondered how he would survive in this place. Separated from his family, relatives, his land and its people, he felt orphaned.

But simultaneously, his hopes rose—this great city would greet him with new experiences and help him learn about life. He would come to know the various ways of men, the many colours that men's dreams took on; how many yards long and how many kilos were men's sorrows? There were so many things he needed to understand.

'It's burning hot in Delhi,' Shreedharanunni said. 'When I first got here, it was hot, just like this. Let five or six months pass. Then you'll experience the winter. Even your bones will shiver here in winter.'

Burning hot. Freezing cold. What kind of a place was this?

Shreedharanunni insisted that Sahadevan let go of his small steel trunk, and walked out of the station with it. The road in front of the station was full of tongas, the horse-drawn carriages that ferried people to and fro between Ajmeri Gate and Connaught Place. He saw villagers carrying big bundles on their head. Hawkers were camped on the pavement on either side of the narrow road. Among them were masseurs who specialised in oil head massages and others who cleaned ears for a fee.

'Where are we going?'

'To my quarters, where else?'

'Won't it be inconvenient for you, Shreedharetta?'

'What inconvenience? If that was the case, would I have asked you to come to Delhi?'

Sahadevan was oblivious to the difficulties of getting a bed in Delhi. He was under the impression that everyone here lived in houses with many rooms and spacious grounds, the way it was back home. He was quite taken aback when he saw Shreedharanunni's quarters. There was one room which no light could penetrate, a kitchen and a bathroom. Shreedharanunni, his wife and two children lived here. Where would they all sleep? Wouldn't his presence be a burden for them?

'You don't trouble yourself about that,' Devi told him, reading Sahadevan's mind. 'You sleep where there's space. You won't be bothering us.'

'Till you manage to get a job, you shall stay with us. When you land a job, we'll look for another place, alright?' Shreedharanunni said.

Both husband and wife were loving and compassionate. Why else would they have invited him to Delhi? Shreedharanunni knew that Shekharan Nambiar's family was subsisting on the income from a meagre paddy field and some coconut trees. The returns from the crops sufficed only to pay back their loans. Then they would borrow some more money. They would only be able to escape the debt trap once Sahadevan got a job.

Sahadevan opened his steel trunk and took out a packet tied with fibres torn off dried plantain sheaths. The smell of dried fish made Vidya pinch her nose in revulsion.

'What's this, Sahadeva?'

'Mother sent it for you.'

Dried butterfish and mackerel; spicy yam pickle in locally made vinegar; pappadam; broken rice for kanji and a string of palm-sugar discs.

'Amma sent it specially for the children.'

Looking at the yam pickled in vinegar that had been distilled from toddy, Sathyanathan started salivating.

'Sathyanathan loves fish. This girl hates it. Look at her standing there, pinching her nose.'

Five-year-old Vidya looked at her mother crossly.

'Which class is Shyamala in?'

'Eighth standard.'

'Right. When I went back home to deliver Vidya, she was in the third standard. Does she study hard, Sahadeva?'

'Much more than I did. She ranks first or second in her class all the time. My fear is that when she grows up, she'll want to be an engineer or a doctor,' Sahadevan said, only half in jest.

He continued, 'Amma told me that as soon as I reach here, I should visit Nehru.' He laughed.

'Why should you see him? You should meet the Opposition leader, our AKG.'

Shreedharanunni stayed home that day. He sat and chatted with Sahadevan, who gave him all the news back home. Devi dozed off in the heat of the afternoon.

'You lie down awhile. You look fatigued from the journey,' Shreedharanunni said. He wanted to rest for some time too.

'I think I'll take a walk outside.'

Devi forbade him. 'Ayyo, no. You don't know the way around here. Where can you go?'

She said to Shreedharanunni, 'He doesn't know the place, nor the language. He'll lose his way and end up in some other place.'

'Deviyechi, I won't go far.'

'Let Sathyanathan come home from school. Take him along.'

'Deviyechi thinks I'm a child. I'm twenty.'

He combed his hair in front of the mirror and changed his shirt. He rolled up the sleeves a little above his elbows and stepped out. He was the only man on the street wearing a mundu.

A cow eating a rotten radish by the railway line tilted its head and looked quizzically at the young man walking along, talking to himself.

It was past seven in the evening when the sunlight started dimming. Charpoys started appearing in front of houses. People sat and chatted. Many of them wielded hand-held fans. All of them were government servants and so their discussions revolved around office matters. Words such as promotion and service rules came up regularly.

Once again, before sunset, a dust storm blew. The hot sand that rose up from Rajasthan flew over Delhi, enveloping the city in darkness and dumping sand in the river, on buildings, trees, vehicles and people.

A few drops of rain fell from the sand-laden clouds scudding across the skies. They sent up the enticing smell of wet earth, the seduction of petrichor rising to suffuse the air. It abated the heat of the night.

Sahadevan could not sleep. It was the first night he was sleeping away from home. The whirring of the overhead fan bothered him. He had to get up several times in the night to drink water, pouring it out into a glass from the earthen pot. The taste of chlorine made him nauseous.

It was late when, with much difficulty, he fell asleep. In his dreams, his mother appeared many times.

4

THE SOLITUDE OF WAR

Three years had passed since the death of Shreedharanunni. Once again, war came. This time, it wasn't Comrade Zhou Enlai but Ayub Khan who pulled the trigger. Since there was no photo of Ayub Khan in Shreedharanunni's home, Sahadevan didn't have to pull it off and fling it out of the house.

'Why are the Chinese and the Pakistanis going to war against us? Are we bad people?' eleven-year-old Vidya asked. Even the word 'war' scared her. It had taken away her father, who used to bathe her, feed her morsels of rice and teach her arithmetic with so much love. By then, she knew that news of the war had caused him to die of heartbreak. But she was not aware of China's role in it. She was a child after all.

The thirty-two-year-old Devi, who was certainly not a child, was perfectly aware of it. Still, she had not been pleased by Sahadevan's intervention.

'Flinging Zhou Enlai's photo into the rubbish bin! What have you done, Sahadeva? Hooliganism.'

'Where else should I throw the photo of the man who murdered Shreedharettan?'

'Edo, that's a photo Vidya's father hung on the wall. We shouldn't be taking it down. He would never forgive that.'

'My dear Deviyechi, Shreedharettan is dead. He doesn't have to bear any pain anymore. It's those of us who are left behind who'll bear the pain for the rest of our lives. The Chinese have destroyed the dreams of millions of our countrymen.'

'I know. Still, you shouldn't have done that.'

They never talked about it after that.

Devi and Sathyanathan reconciled to their loss with determination and a strong mental resolve. But Vidya couldn't. Often, as she bathed, her tears mixed with the chlorinated water and flowed down her chin. She was the one who grieved the most in her father's memory. She was reluctant to open up to anyone, and so no one could see inside her reticent mind.

Three years slipped away thus.

In the span of these three long years between the two wars, what has happened to me? Sahadevan asked himself. He strolled around with a lit cigarette, musing.

For the first few months, you wandered about doing nothing in particular, he reminded himself. Then, Shreedharanunni arranged a small job for you at Wadhwa & Sons. In the beginning, you were under the impression that all of Gulshan Wadhwa's children were sons. But soon you realised that he had no sons. All his three children were daughters. You began to wonder why his company was called 'Wadhwa & Sons' instead of 'Wadhwa & Daughters'. When you finally understood the reason, you were shocked. The people of Delhi didn't care for daughters; they detested them. When girls were born, the atmosphere at home turned funereal. The parents were ashamed to acknowledge their daughters and call them 'beti', so they used the masculine 'beta' instead.

Gulshan Wadhwa was bringing up his third daughter, Shailee, as though she were a boy. Her hair was cropped; she always wore shorts and shirts. No one had seen her in a frock.

Sahadevan said to himself: Your parents have three children. You, the eldest; Shyamala, the youngest; and Vanaja, in the middle. Your mother gave birth to Vanaja five years after you were born. How delighted your father was. And when you heard that your mother had given birth to a girl, you too were overjoyed, like your father.

Thank goodness Vidya was born into a Malayali family. Had she been born a Punjabi, her father would have called her beta.

When he got the job at Wadhwa & Sons, Sahadevan moved out of Shreedharanunni's house, to a mess in Yusuf Sarai. For a monthly payment of seventy-five rupees, he was given a charpoy to use as a bed, and breakfast and dinner. Breakfast consisted of three chapatis and cooked vegetables; on Sundays, it was aloo paratha or poori-bhaji. On Sundays, he didn't eat anything after breakfast till he got back to the mess at night. It was not that food wasn't available—he didn't have the money to buy anything.

Poverty had become a habit with him by then.

Before the war of 1965, Sahadevan moved again. In Delhi, only those who lived in government quarters managed to stay in one place for any length of time. Most migrants kept moving homes. Their landlords never allowed them to put down roots. The only exception was Uttam Singh. From the mess at Yusuf Sarai, Sahadevan moved into Uttam Singh's house in Amritpuri, adjacent to Dayanand Colony. Decrepit buildings were scattered on either side of narrow alleys. The spaces in between were monopolised by stray cattle. They ate, shat and slept there.

He was given a separate room. In the noisy mess, it had been very difficult for him to sit down to think, to talk to himself or write his novel. Though Amritpuri was a part of Delhi, it gave the impression of being far removed from the bustle of the city.

This was where Sahadevan stayed in 1965.

His room was in a tiny house by the side of a pond that buffaloes frequented for drinking water. Apart from him, there were two other tenants, who shared the room adjacent to his. Like Sahadevan, they too were Malayali bachelors. Uttam Singh and his family lived in the same building. He was a carpenter in a furniture shop in Palam Colony.

Amritpuri had its own distinct smell. When the city roasted in the burning heat of May and June, the buffaloes wallowed in the murky pond. Their boy-herders would frolic in the fetid, stinking water. The distinct smell of Amritpuri was the stench of that reeking, green water.

Electricity was yet to reach many parts of Amritpuri. There were no street lights either. Fortunately, Sahadevan's building had electricity. Every time the electricity bills came, a dispute broke out between the landlord and the other two tenants about the sharing of charges. Sometimes Sahadevan thought it would have been better if they had no electricity at all.

Though there was electricity, it was forbidden to switch on the lights. If any light was seen coming out of any of the buildings, gruff shouts would rise from the streets: '*Band karo batti*, switch off the lights.'

Those lights could guide bombers headed for the city. That was why they were banned.

People switched off the lights when they heard the bellowing commands of the policemen. Those who had lamps would blow them out. The glass panes of windows had newspaper sheets stuck on them. So, even if a forty-watt bulb was switched on, the light could not be seen outside. Nevertheless, once dusk fell, lights were not allowed. It was after the bombing of the Agra Cantonment that this nightly rule began to be observed strictly. Soldiers patrolled the streets; their footsteps could be heard throughout the dark night.

The night the bombs fell on Agra Cantonment, Sahadevan was sleeping on the open terrace. The sky was right above him. He liked to sleep there, with the breeze on him. Usually, it was the landlord and his family who occupied the barsati. The landlord had two daughters, Jaswinder and Pinky. Pinky, the younger one, studied in the neighbouring Khalsa School that was run by Sikhs.

The older girl was about twenty-five years of age. The four of them slept on three charpoys pulled close together. Every fifth or sixth day, at midnight, Uttam Singh and his wife would climb down silently and go into their room on the ground floor. After ten minutes or so, they would return to the barsati, equally silent, and sleep on separate charpoys like strangers. Through all this, the girls would remain in deep slumber. Their heads had only to hit the pillow for them to fall asleep.

It was on 5 August 1965 that the skirmishes at the border began. Gradually, they escalated into war. With that, Uttam Singh and his family stopped favouring the barsati. Sahadevan made the most of the opportunity. That first night, he lay there gazing up at the sky for a long time. It was past midnight when he fell asleep. Almost immediately, he was startled awake by the wail of sirens.

'Bhaiya, have you gone deaf? Come down,' Gunjan bhabhi, Uttam Singh's wife, shouted from below. 'Make haste. The Pakistani bastards are coming to bomb us.'

She hawked and spat viciously to show her contempt. It was while they were living a happy life in Gurdaspur as wheat farmers that Gunjan bhabhi's parents and siblings had been put to the sword by Muslims during the Partition riots. Her father had been wearing a sword at his waist, as was the Sikh practice. They had used it to decapitate him. It was said that the head lay separated from the torso with a smile still on its face. You have seen how the corpses of people who never smiled in their lives smile after they are dead, haven't you, Sahadeva? Eda, didn't you see the rictus of the decapitated camel in Lawrence Durrell's *Alexandria Quartet*?

On hearing the siren, people sleeping on charpoys by the side of the road or in the yard would scramble up, bewildered, and race back into their homes.

'Bhabhiji, I'll sleep here. You please go and get some sleep,' Sahadevan said to her.

'Scoundrel,' Uttam Singh bellowed. 'Are you asking us to sleep while the enemies come to bomb us?'

Before he could complete the sentence, anti-aircraft guns started spitting fire into the darkness. Fighter jets from the Hindon airbase split the skies as they roared away, making Amritpuri tremble beneath. Sahadevan felt as if his intestines had leaped out of his stomach and smashed into smithereens. In the darkness, cries of distress arose. Many, in their bewildered state, switched on the lights inside.

'Bastards, sons-of-bitches, are you trying to help the enemy by putting on lights?' The soldiers roared from the streets. They sprinted towards the closed doors and kicked them with their booted legs and hit them with the butts of their rifles. The lights went off, it was pitch-dark again. People could be heard running on the street and dogs howled.

'Help,' Jaswinder, Uttam Singh's elder daughter, called out. 'Maa, someone is touching me.'

She tried to throw off the man, but the groping continued and little could be seen in the gloom. The grip on her body was tightening even as she slapped the hands away.

'What, what's happening?' Uttam Singh roared. 'Who is that pig?'

Someone ran away under the cover of darkness. Into a room inside the house. Uttam Singh didn't catch that.

'Ohhh, my chunni.'

Had the man run away with her dupatta?

A Gnat fighter plane roared overhead. Its afterburners let out smoke and red sparks that flew like embers in its wake.

The people who ran out in terror were driven back into their houses by the soldiers. 'Get in, get in and lock the doors.'

The soldiers slashed the air with the butts of their rifles. The ruckus woke up the buffaloes dozing near the pond. The roar of the fighter jets startled them and they ran in all directions, their heavy bodies crashing into each other. Stumbling and falling over invisible obstacles, they ran, bellowing loudly.

The fiery trails the fighter planes left in their wake remained suspended in the sky. The buildings continued to shake with tremors for a few minutes. The doors trembled. The fire trails in the sky burned bright.

Gradually, the anti-aircraft guns fell silent. The planes returned to the Hindon base.

All this while, Sahadevan had been lying alone on his charpoy on the terrace, looking up at the sky. The thoughts that passed through his mind were not those a citizen should entertain when his country is at war. He wanted to scream aloud that he had no connection with this war. Not even three years had passed since the war with China. And here was another war come knocking. How many more were to spill their blood and die? He knew he was not being patriotic. If other people could read his mind, he would be arrested immediately, dragged off and shot in the chest. Why? Because it was wartime.

Patriotism *needs* wars every now and then, Sahadevan reminded himself. Humanism is against all wars. Which one is paramount then? Love for the country or love for our fellow human beings? Patriotism or humanism? He felt torn between the two. He wanted to shout that he was on the side of humanity and not guns. He lay there sleepless, gazing at the sky, hit by an acute loneliness. The loneliness of wartime.

The next morning, a military jeep arrived, driving through the narrow alleys of Dayanand Colony. An announcement was made over a megaphone: The siren will be sounded when the enemy bombers approach; no one should run out of their houses when the sirens go off; people should stay indoors and shut their doors. If it's night time, all lights should be put out. There may be more attacks by the enemy's bombers. Therefore, everyone should dig trenches close to their residence. When the bombers approach, everyone should get into the trenches.

Whenever war planes appeared on the radar at Palam airport, the sirens wailed in the city. The sound filled everyone with dread.

Uttam Singh began digging trenches in front of his house immediately after the announcement. Two big trenches for himself and his wife. A narrower one for Jaswinder. A tiny one for Pinky.

'Arrey Madrasi bhai, aren't you digging one? When the bombs start falling, where are you going to hide?' Uttam Singh demanded. He dug another trench. Sahadevan stood staring at it. He fancied that it was his grave.

Within a day, trenches yawned in front of every house. Thousands of trenches appeared in Amritpuri. They looked like graves waiting for corpses. Graves dug by the living for themselves. Dayanand Colony and Amritpuri became a borderless graveyard. It was when he saw those trenches that Sahadevan realised how many people Amritpuri was home to.

Since the start of the war, life in the city had ground to a standstill. Vegetables stopped arriving at the subzi mandis. Buses and tongas stopped running. The government offices functioned only nominally—no one did any actual work. Many institutions were shut down. On the day the war started, the airport was closed. Trains continued to arrive at New Delhi and Old Delhi railway stations, but they were off schedule and often took detours. They had lost their sense of direction.

When the trains were delayed, Sahadevan was left with nothing to do. Though the clearing agency was located in Paharganj, all his work was either at the air cargo terminal or at the cargo yards of the railway station. He left the office early and started walking to Connaught Place. Though he waited for over an hour, no bus showed up. Finally, when one did turn up, it was empty. It upset him to see the empty seats in buses that were normally jam-packed, with hardly any standing room.

He got into a bus that was headed for Sewa Nagar from Regal Cinema. The two men sitting in front of him were discussing death. During war, everything else ceases to be of consequence. War unites people through thoughts of death.

Getting off the bus, he walked along the deserted street towards Devi's house. He pushed open the gate which was fastened to the post with a rope. That instantly brought to mind an image he could not forget.

Shreedharanunni's body lay on the bamboo bier placed in the yard. His mouth was slightly open. His eyes were shut tight, as if he didn't want to see anything anymore. His face, shaved clean by the barber moments earlier, looked pale and yellow. The body was covered with a red flag. The majority of the people crowding around the yard and outside the gate were union workers.

Vidya was sitting outside, reading. She wore a blue kameez and a white salwar, her school uniform. Whenever the fabric started fraying, it was repaired and designated for home wear, so this meant that she was always in uniform. When she went to school, her hair was plaited in two, one plait on either side of her head. Was she turning every place she went to into her school?

'Will Pakistan drop the bomb on us, etta?'

Her eyes were full of fear. She was always afraid of something or the other. After Shreedharanunni's death, her fear only increased.

'They can't reach Delhi, molae. Our air force is strong.'

'How did they bomb Agra then?'

'Now they won't be able to bomb Agra either. Our anti-aircraft guns are everywhere. Our army and air force are both very strong.'

He said this only to console her. He had his own doubts. In the last war, China could have easily attacked Delhi. Today, even Pakistan might be able to achieve that. How much could India's defence capabilities have grown in three years? He had no faith in what the leaders were saying. But he didn't openly speak his mind. If he did, it would amount to treason.

War had declared a state of emergency in the minds of people. There was no room for justice any more. War emasculates the public, Sahadevan reflected.

'Hasn't amma reached?'

'Where will I go? I'm here.' Devi was kneading flour in the kitchen. He could smell potatoes and radish cooking on the kerosene stove. Devi was trying to finish her chores while there was still light. She could suffer anything but darkness. After Shreedharanunni's death, there was only darkness in her life. Every time the lights went off, she saw her husband's face. The darkness was now a mirror that reflected his face.

'Where's Sathyanathan?'

'He's loitering around somewhere. He doesn't listen to me, Sahadeva. I'm worried that the police or the army will take him into custody.' Devi's face reflected her anxiety.

Sathyanathan was an intelligent sixteen-year-old boy; he knew what war entailed. Nevertheless, he needed to be careful. Anyone found wandering the streets in a suspicious manner could be arrested by the police or the soldiers.

Sahadevan stepped into the house. A photograph of Shreedharanunni looked at him from the wall—an old photo that had been enlarged. Devi herself had hammered in the nail and hung it there. Not only that, even as the whole country was cursing Zhou Enlai, she had retrieved his photo from the place that Sahadevan had flung it in, dusted it and hung it in its old place. True, China had robbed Shreedharanunni of his life. But hadn't it also also kept him alive?

If Shreedharanunni were alive, who would he be with today? With the Communist Party of India or the Communist Party of India (Marxist)? Sahadevan wondered.

Shreedharanunni hadn't lived long enough to witness the split in the Communist Party. If he were alive, he would have died of a broken heart, once again.

'When do you think this war will end?'

'It's just started ...'

The war would end only after killing many and wounding the Earth. Every war pans out this way. Even when it's over, it leaves open wounds and scars in its wake. What else is war for?

That night, Sahadevan stayed back in Sewa Nagar. The siren wailed twice before dusk. Vidya clutched him each time, terrified. Seating her next to him in the darkness, he told her stories from Kottaraththil Sankunni's *Aythihyamala*. The small, white strip he saw in the darkness was her smile. Darkness was also a mirror in which one could see the reflection of an innocent little girl.

'Etta, you should live here, don't go anywhere.'

'Till the war ends? You're a scared mouse, Vidya. You haven't inherited your amma's strength of mind.'

'My strength wasn't inherited. I created it.'

Devi burnt her hand as she made chapatis in the dark. By the time the war ended, how many more would have their hands and legs burnt? How many lives would wilt and perish?

Early the next morning, Sahadevan left for Amritpuri. He was eager to write. He had started his novel in 1959. He had been a mere twenty-year-old then. A good-looking young man with a pencil-line moustache and hair parted in the middle. The only detraction was his prominent Adam's apple.

Six years had passed since he started living in this city.

Every war must come to an end, sometime or the other. The Indo-Pak war of 1965 finally ended after five weeks. One day of fighting was enough to kill innocent people; to turn women into widows; to raze houses. And this one had gone on for thirty-five days.

Sahadevan knew that the war hadn't really ended. It would return. It usually did. One war is ended to start another one.

Three thousand two hundred soldiers lost their lives. Punjab and Delhi turned into a land of widows. Thousands of faceless, unnamed, ordinary men and women perished in Sialkot, Pathankot and Kashmir. Countless wheat fields were burnt to the ground. Trains, buildings and bridges were reduced to rubble.

But we won the war, didn't we?

The end of the war coincided with the arrival of winter in Delhi. The air carried a chill. Winter rains filled the yawning trenches of Amritpuri with water. Uttam Singh, returning at night from his Palam Vihar furniture shop with his chisel and mallet in a bag, fell straight into one of his own trenches.

'Sister-fucker!' he swore as he raised himself out of the muddy water, holding on to the wet sides of the trench. It was the only kind of protest that a harmless carpenter in Delhi could raise against the war.

5

MEMORIES OF ROMANCE

With the advent of December, the winter deepened. Even in the afternoon sunshine, glass walls of cold rose up between the government quarters of Sewa Nagar, Guru Nanak Market and the centuries-old alleyways of Amritpuri. The Lajpat Nagar and Lodhi Colony branches of Band Box Dry Cleaning Company became crowded. The shops filled up with jackets, sweaters and children's school uniforms brought in for dry cleaning.

Devi sent Sathyanathan's school jacket to the dry cleaners because it could not be washed at home—it would lose its shape. The rest of their woollen clothes were washed by her, with soap powder. She washed Vidya's blue school sweater with care and hung it to dry in the shade of the jamun tree. Woollens tend to fade when exposed too long to sunlight. But luxuries such as dry cleaning were not meant for people like her.

She didn't know exactly how she managed to run her household with the meagre wages of a Class IV employee. Despite their straitened circumstances, Shreedharanunni had wanted to give both his children a good education. While most of the government servants residing in Sewa Nagar sent their wards to municipal schools, he had admitted Sathyanathan and Vidya to good private schools. Their uniforms and the ride on the school bus cost money. Tuition fees had to be paid. When

Shreedharanunni was alive, he had managed everything. But she was forced to start borrowing money from her colleagues at the Secretariat. She hated doing it, but not a month passed without her having to borrow money from someone. Both Sathyanathan's and Vidya's socks were full of holes. It wasn't possible to darn them anymore. Would she have to borrow money the following month as well?

'Accha, will you buy me a watch?'

'Molae, kids don't wear watches. You are a child.'

'All my friends wear watches. Rina has one, Mamta has one. A small one will do.'

'They are all rich children, molae.'

'Why are we not getting rich?'

Shreedharanunni had remained silent. He didn't own a good watch either. The old Roamer watch he wore had stopped working a while ago. However hard he tried to wind it, the hands wouldn't move. Yet, when he left for office, he picked it up and tied it around his wrist like a ritual. Every now and then, he would peer at others' watches to read the time and adjust the time on his. He used to wonder why he bothered to wear it at all. One day, he would fling it into the Yamuna. Let the river repair it and check the time.

The day before Diwali, Sahadevan arrived, holding a packet. He placed it firmly in Devi's hands.

'What is this, Sahadeva?'

'Oh, nothing. It's a shirt for Sathyanathan.'

That was not all there was. There was also a saree for Devi and a watch for Vidya.

'You shouldn't have bought all this. It's really too much. I know how it is with you. This month, you didn't have enough money to send to your mother, no?'

Devi felt disquieted, looking at the gifts.

During Diwali, Gulshan Wadhwa used to distribute one kilo of sweetmeats and hundred rupees to every employee.

Sahadevan knew that cheap watches were available in Chandni Chowk in Old Delhi. Sometimes they were duplicates, but it was believed that the duplicates of Chandni Chowk were better than the originals. After scouring several shops, he had managed to get a ladies' watch that looked good, for twenty-five rupees. He bought a reasonably good saree for twenty rupees from one of the hawkers on the pavement. He faced no trouble finding a shirt for Sathyanathan; from a shop near Birds' Hospital, he got a terylene shirt that would look good on him. With that, his Diwali shopping was over. The Diwali baksheesh Wadhwa saab had given him was also exhausted. But his heart was joyous.

He gave the sweetmeats to Lalitha. Wadhwa usually bought them from the famous Haldiram Sweets, which had outlets in Old Delhi.

It was Shreedharanunni who had arranged for him to get a job at Wadhwa & Sons International Clearing Agency in 1959, when Sahadevan had come to Delhi. While his earnings were not great, he could afford to send thirty rupees home by money order every month. That was sufficient for buying rations and kashayam for his father's asthma, and liniment for his backache. From this amount, his mother regularly put away three or four rupees without his father's knowledge, into a chit fund. When she got sixty rupees after bidding for the kitty, she had a gold necklace weighing one sovereign made for Vanaja.

Gulshan Wadhwa was a relative of Som Dev, a colleague of Shreedharanunni at the Secretariat.

'Bhaisaab, ours is a small operation. We only have work for two people. There are already three men with me. I'm employing this boy only because Som Dev requested me to,' Wadhwa said.

'God bless you for your great kindness, bhaisaab,' Shreedharanunni had replied.

The office of Wadhwa & Sons was in Paharganj. Wadhwa and three employees sat in a dark room untouched by sunlight. When Sahadevan joined, Wadhwa saab had difficulty in finding a seat for him. Most of the staff had to go out on work. As soon as one of them left, Sahadevan would perch himself on that seat. Wadhwa saab himself explained to him what a bill of lading was, and a consignment note, etc. On his second day on the job, Sahadevan cleaned up the whole room. He dusted all the old files that lay scattered on the window sills and on the shelves placed against the wall. Most of them were old Customs documents, now useless. Most of Wadhwa saab's clients were small-time exporters from Chandni Chowk.

'If I can get two or three embassy staff as clients, I'll be saved. Right now, I don't have money even to pay your salary,' Wadhwa told Sahadevan. The employees at the many foreign embassies in Delhi did not haggle about rates. Neither did they delay payments.

Wadhwa stayed with his family in a two-room house in Sant Nagar, a locality that reeked of buffaloes. He would require a lot of money when his daughters grew old enough to be married. His dream was to give each of them a flat and conduct their weddings with pomp. Three flats for three daughters. Wadhwa knew that this was impossible to achieve in his current state. Yet, that was what he dreamt of. You don't need anyone's permission to dream.

Whatever his own difficulties, Wadhwa never failed to pay the staff their salaries. At worst, they might get delayed by four or five days, nothing beyond that. Wadhwa was squat and fat, but Sahadevan quickly realised he had a big heart.

Sahadevan thought of Delhi as a city of goodness and generosity. Despite his own difficult circumstances, Shreedharan-unni had brought Sahadevan to Delhi and found him a job. Though he had adequate staff and financial liabilities, Wadhwa saab had given him a job. During Partition, these people had suffered enormously and lived through terrible times. Perhaps that was what had cleansed them of turpitude.

He began to feel towards the city of Delhi the kind of tenderness that he felt for Vidya.

Devi loved Delhi too. She was seventeen when she married Shreedharanunni. She had felt as if she had landed in an alien world; Delhi did not belong on Earth. She didn't know Hindi, and no one spoke Malayalam. For a few months, she had to live without language. For the first time in her life, she understood what it meant to be isolated.

On Rajpath, which she was yet to see, Independence Day was celebrated like it was done every year. Occasionally, from a great distance, she caught the sound of musical bands playing. She could also hear, indistinctly, voices shouting '*Bharat Mata ki jai*' and '*Mahatma Gandhi ki jai*'.

Fifteen years had passed since her arrival in Delhi. She had given birth to two children. Many summers and winters had come and gone. She was no longer that thin seventeen-year-old with a full bosom and filled out body; she was now a wife, mother and housewife. And she loved Delhi.

Many happy memories of the city lay dormant within her and she enjoyed calling them back to mind. On this chilly evening, when both her children were inside the house, busy with their homework, she sat outside and reminisced about those happy times.

The gentle sunshine passed through the trees and settled over the streets and backyards. Winter sunshine was precious. When the sun shone through the greyness of December, people pulled out their charpoys and sat on them, munching groundnuts. Street vendors had a field day doing business from their pushcarts, on which unshelled groundnuts were heaped over small earthen pots filled with burning charcoal.

It was also the time for neighbours to catch up on the local gossip. The women knitted sweaters as they talked, stopping occasionally to shell groundnuts and pop them into their mouths. When she was pregnant with Sathyanathan, Devi too had knitted a tiny sweater for him. She remembered those times. Riding pillion on Shreedharanunni's bicycle, she would go to Sarojini Nagar to buy wool and knitting needles. Though Sewa Nagar had many shops that sold wool, only Sarojini Nagar could be relied on for a wide selection of brands and colours. One such day, Shreedharanunni had stopped the bicycle after they had gone some way from home.

'Why did you stop? Do you have a puncture?'

Dismounting from the bicycle, he looked at her and smiled.

'Here, sit here,' he said, touching the bar that connected the front seat to the handle of the bicycle.

'Ayyo, isn't that where children sit?'

'You are my child now. My molu.'

Devi hesitated. What if they ran into an acquaintance? The thought made her blush.

But Shreedharanunni insisted. He made her sit in the front. As he pedalled, her hair, fragrant with coconut oil, brushed his face. Devi had thick, long tresses. As the cool breeze caressed them, he leaned forward and nestled her against his chest. *'Soja rajkumari ...'* he sang, astonishing her. She had never heard him sing before. Even a Communist can turn into a romantic, it seemed.

With winter setting in, Sarojini Nagar Market was flooded with multicoloured woollen yarn balls. Every corner of the market looked like it had been splashed with Holi colours. They tried many shops. Shreedharanunni prayed that Devi would not go for the expensive yarns. As if she had read his mind, she picked some inexpensive but very soft yarn. When she touched it, she felt like she was caressing the soft wool of a live lamb.

'Which one should I choose?' she asked, looking at the bewildering variety of colours.

'Shall I take blue?'

'No, red is better.'

After buying the wool and needles, they had hot, spicy aloo tikki and tea from a roadside vendor and rode back to Sewa Nagar on the bicycle.

In no time, Devi had learnt to knit sweaters. Her neighbour Preetam behen helped. Each day, the length of the sweater increased by at least an inch. By the time the baby in the womb was four months old, it was almost done. But the neck hadn't come out right. She undid it, and with the help of Preetam behen, knitted it again properly. By the fifth month of her term, the sweater was ready. In her impatience to put it on the child, she would spread it on her distended stomach and sit looking at it. Did her child feel the warmth of the sweater made from lamb's wool?

How time flies ...

'Amma, I'll be back soon.'

Sathyanathan wheeled out Shreedharanunni's old cycle, the one she and he had ridden to Sarojini Nagar and back. The old Hercules was still in good condition. Sathyanathan kept it clean and greased the chain and sprocket regularly.

A week after Shreedharanunni's death, Inder Bhatia, their neighbour, had come to their door.

'Beti, what do you need the cycle for now? Give it to me. I'll give you whatever you want for it,' he said.

Why did the seventy-year-old Inder Bhatia need a bicycle? Devi had never seen him ride one. As for his son, he had bought himself a Lambretta scooter last Diwali—not a second-hand model, but a brand new one.

'Shall I take the cycle then?'

Devi, still teary-eyed, didn't look at him. How many memories hovered around that cycle, did this man not know?

'Beti, why are you not saying anything?'

'Chacha, this is my father's cycle. Please don't take it from me. I wouldn't give it to you even if you paid me a thousand rupees.'

The firm, determined voice of a thirteen-year-old. The boundless love of a son for his father. Inder Bhatia left without another word.

Inder Bhatia no longer lived in the neighbourhood. When his son got promoted, they had moved to a bigger house in Moti Bagh.

She sat there for a long time, lost in her thoughts. She rode long distances on the Hercules cycle of her memories. She wished she could do it more often, but where was the time to indulge? She woke up at 5 a.m. and rarely went to bed before 11 p.m. She had to sweep the house and the yard; fetch the milk; make chapatis and curry for the children's lunch; wash and press clothes; run to the bus stop; work at the Secretariat. After returning home, she would go out and buy vegetables, then cook rice and curry. Sundays were even worse. She had to stand in queue for rations; had to take wheat to the mill to get it ground ...

Sathyanathan and Vidya were growing up. After a while, they would start helping their mother, Sahadevan told himself. It was difficult to find such loving and obedient children in this time and age. He thought: Though she is unlucky with her husband, she is lucky with her children.

6

THE PISSING OLYMPICS

The war with China ended. After that, a war with Pakistan also came and went.

Sahadevan was remembering the hardships imposed on Devi and her children by the 1962 war. What also came to mind was a funny story that Sathyanathan had told him once.

Sathyanathan was no longer a child. It would be more appropriate to call him a grown-up boy. He was birthed on the cold, dark, cracked floor of Netaji Hospital, in a ward that even the midday sun couldn't penetrate. Since all the beds were occupied when Devi went into labour, she was forced to lie on the floor. The drops of blood that dripped from the umbilical cord pooled into a line that did not dry up for quite a while. Ants led a procession down that red path.

Even after all these years, Sathyanathan was unable to make peace with his father's death. Like a bird with a broken wing struggling to fly, he encountered difficulties at every turn. He was aware of his mother's difficulties and worries. Their main problem was the lack of money. Shreedharanunni had left no savings at all; on top of that, there were loans and liabilities. Within three months of his father's demise, Sathyanathan noticed that one of the two gold bangles on his mother's hand had disappeared. The initial difficulties with money soon turned into dire poverty.

A vegetable market was held every Saturday in Sewa Nagar. By afternoon, bullock carts laden with potatoes, onions, radishes, cauliflowers and tomatoes arrived from villages on the outskirts of Delhi. Till late in the night, vegetable sellers conducted their business in the light of petromaxes, bundled up against the cold. Not just the people from Karbala and Lodhi Colony, but even rich people from posh colonies like Defence Colony came to Sewa Nagar to buy vegetables.

'Amma, shouldn't we be going to Sewa Nagar to buy vegetables?'

'We should, monae, but we'll go a little later.'

'It's going to be so cold then, amma.'

The cold set in as soon as the sun went down. By 10 or 11 p.m., it would begin to drill into their bones, numb their face. Sathyanathan could hear a booming sound in his ears.

People would hurriedly retreat into their homes. The alleyways would be deserted. The rush hour at the Saturday market would come to an end. It was then that Devi would head for the market, a cloth bag in hand and Sathyanathan in tow.

'Can't we go a little earlier?'

Sathyanathan always had a lot of studying to do. He would start after dinner and continue till midnight.

Devi didn't respond to Sathyanathan's question. As the night progressed, the prices went down in the market. The farmers didn't want to return to their villages with unsold goods. So they would start reducing the prices after 9 p.m. By 10 p.m., they were ready to sell for whatever they could get. That's when Devi did her shopping.

Market day was also a day of feasting for the cattle in and around Sewa Nagar. As the farmers doused their petromaxes, loaded their carts with empty jute bags and started for their villages, herds of cattle took over. Crushed tomatoes, aubergines, carrots, bottle gourds and white gourds lay scattered everywhere. By midnight, all of it would be gobbled up. One night, Sathyanathan saw a hare eating radish leaves. He wondered where it had come from; he had never seen any in the vicinity. When hungry, humans and animals are the same, he thought. They will forage anywhere.

One Saturday night, as the petromaxes were being extinguished, Sathyanathan saw Devi going down the alley with her cloth bag in hand. She walked slowly, between the cattle, peering down into the darkness. Every now and then, she stopped and picked up a potato or a tomato and assessed the damage. If it wasn't too severe, she put it into her bag. When she spotted a fairly big cauliflower crushed on one side but still intact on the other, her face became radiant. A cow was approaching with its mouth open. She practically snatched the vegetable away from its mouth. Another cow stood by, its mouth filled with rotting radish.

'What are you doing here, amma?'

Devi did not reply. Sathyanathan walked back with her to their house.

What was his mother doing alone in the dark, deserted vegetable market? It didn't take him long to work it out. And it broke his heart.

As soon as they reached home, Devi went into the bathroom and shut the door. Sathyanathan heard her blowing her nose. For a while, no sound could be heard. Then she emerged from the bathroom, her eyes bloodshot. She took out the cauliflower, tomato and radish from the bag, lopped off the damaged parts, cleaned them and kept them aside. They would be cooked the next day, to accompany the dry chapatis she made for her children's lunch. How her heart ached to have some ghee or butter to slather on them. But the appetising aroma of desi ghee applied on hot chapatis just off the tawa was now a distant memory.

After the death of their father, the children and their mother led a life of torturous deprivation. Sathyanathan wanted to grow up double-quick, with a moustache and all the other markers of adulthood. Only then could he begin to support his mother and become her protector. And end the poverty in their home.

Every day, he stood in front of the mirror, searching for incipient hair sprouting on his upper lip.

'Etta, why are you so stuck on being stylish these days?' Vidya would tease him.

What did she know about the anguish in his mind? She was still a child. Though not yet out of his own childhood, Sathyanathan had started thinking like an adult.

Radish was the cheapest winter vegetable. This meant that every day, their curry had radish in it. Vidya started to complain. Some days, she would get angry. Sathyanathan bore it all in silence.

At school, the students ate lunch in the playground. In summer they congregated under the trees, and in winter they sat in the pale sunshine. Since it was a boys' school, they were free to indulge in any mischief that caught their fancy. The Pissing Olympics was one of their main pastimes. Standing in a row, the boys would piss into the distance. Whoever hit the farthest point won the Pissing Olympics and the big prize: he could pick whatever he wanted from the lunch boxes of the other children. Some of the boys brought palak paneer, shahi paneer, mutton korma, egg curry and such delicacies.

One day, after the pissing competition was over, everyone opened their lunch boxes in front of the victorious Olympian. He pinched his nose with distaste.

'What a stench, yaar,' Jagdish Sahi, who sat beside Sathyanathan in class, said. He too covered his nose.

The disgusting odour that rose up from the tiffin box was that of radish.

Sathyanathan usually didn't take part in the Pissing Olympics. He was a loner. One day, out of curiosity, he stood beneath a tree and urinated, willing it to go as far as possible. He was astonished by the distance his pee travelled. Even if a little late, he was happy to have discovered this talent. Many people went through life without ever discovering their talents, and died still ignorant.

One Friday, as the children were getting ready for school, they saw their mother sitting still, looking despondent.

'What happened, amma?'

'There's no flour. What will I make the chapatis with?'

It was not that she had forgotten to buy flour. She hadn't had a single paisa to buy it with. Ration shops don't give anyone credit.

She emptied the flour at the bottom of the container into an aluminium vessel. She added salt and kneaded it. It was enough for two chapatis, no more.

'Give them to Vidya, amma.'

'What will you eat? Won't you feel hungry?'

'I'll buy Nathuram's poori-chole.'

Devi didn't ask him where he would get the money for that. Some questions were better not asked.

When Shreedharanunni was alive, on the day he got his salary, he would tell Devi, 'Give something to the children as well. They too have their needs.'

Devi used to give them a rupee each.

With his death, that practice had stopped. Nor did the children demand anything.

Nathuram would be at the school gate at lunchtime, selling poori and chole. His chickpea curry was always warm and had a special taste. Not only the students but also the teachers queued up for Nathuram's chole-poori.

Devi made the two chapatis and packed them in Vidya's lunch box with some potato curry left over from the previous night. She filled her bottle with water boiled with dried ginger. Vidya left for school in a hurry.

Perhaps it was because he had not carried his lunch with him that Sathyanathan started feeling hungry early. Half an hour before the lunch break, Nathuram had begun to heat up the chole and knead the dough for the pooris. The oil was already on the boil. He diced onions and sprinkled them on the chole; he split long green chillies lengthwise and arranged them around the dish. He squeezed a lemon and sprinkled the juice on top. The chole was ready. His arrival at the school gate was announced with loud taps of the steel ladle on the copper container.

Sathyanathan had no money. Nathuram didn't give anyone credit. 'Children, don't ask for that. Five lives depend on these pooris; five tummies have to be filled with this money,' he would say. No one ever asked whose tummies they were.

The students were standing in a row under the tree to start the Pissing Olympics. He walked up to them and declared, 'I'm in too.'

His classmates could not believe their ears. Sathyanathan had never been chummy with them. Nor did he join any of their games.

When everyone loosened their belts and pulled down their trousers, Sathyanathan did the same. They looked at him curiously, pleased that he was joining in. They detested the reek of the radish from his lunch box, but they had no other quarrel with him.

When referee Amit Pahwa inserted his fingers in his mouth and whistled, everyone let loose. And watched disbelievingly at the arc and distance that Sathyanathan's pee travelled.

They ran and fetched their lunch boxes. Eleven lunch boxes in various shapes and sizes opened in front of Sathyanathan in a trice. They were filled with pooris, chapatis, parathas, dosas, idlis, upma, sandwiches and lemon rice. A Bengali lad called Subodh Sarkar had brought rice, vegetables and fish cooked in groundnut oil.

Sathyanathan had never eaten such a sumptuous lunch. He looked down and offered a silent thanks to his pissing partner.

7

WHOOPING COUGH AND NOSTALGIA

Four years into his life in Delhi, Sahadevan fell prey to a new disease.

There was hardly any disease that had not afflicted him in the twenty years that he lived in Kerala. He was six when he contracted whooping cough, locally known as *villanchuma*, with aliases like hook-cough, *kokkakura* and ninety-day-cough. He coughed so much that the tissues in his throat tore and started bleeding. It was as if M.N. Nambiar, the arch villain of Tamil movies, had appeared in front of the six-year-old in his tasselled silk shirt, booted legs and wig, swishing his sword mercilessly. Sahadevan was under the treatment of Kunjappoo vaidyar. The apothecary, like MGR, confronted Nambiar with a sword in one hand and a pistol in the other. It still took three months for the cough to abate. He could not sleep at night or during the day. He coughed all the time.

In his eleventh year, he had measles. His whole body was covered in rashes. It was Kunjappoo vaidyar who again came to heal him. He observed that even his eyelids had rashes. Using a ladle made from a leaf of the jackfruit tree, his mother irrigated his eyes gently, dousing them with cool water infused with coriander seeds. The bitterness of the kashayam prescribed for him made Sahadevan vomit. He refused to take the concoction again. Whenever his mother approached him with a bowl of kashayam, he would turn his face away. Once, when his mother insisted that he take the medicine, he lashed out with his hand and sent the bowl flying. It fell and broke into pieces and the kashayam spread everywhere. His mother gave him a hard slap on his buttocks.

The disease that consumed him now was different. It was nostalgia—much worse and more terrifying than whooping cough and measles. And there was no Kunjappoo vaidyar to treat him. Sahadevan knew that even if he were around, this was not a disease that could be cured with herbal pastes and ayurvedic decoctions.

On his first night in Delhi, he had dreamt of his mother several times. These days, not just in his dreams, but even when awake and with his eyes wide open, he saw her face as if in a vision. His amma, oiling his hair and body with coconut oil and giving him a bath by the side of the well. Amma, who went around the whole neighbourhood cadging eggs to feed her son as he lay exhausted by the fever. Amma, who picked him up and ran to the vaidyar's house when a bursting firecracker burnt his hand during the festivities on Vishu. The mother who put chilli paste in his eyes for touching his classmate Rema's breast. The mother who used a spoon to feed him mutthari pudding made with ground millet, ripe bananas and jaggery. The mother who plucked the leaves of the Malabar nut, then heated and applied them on his feet when he developed scurvy. His amma, who took him to the astrologer and had a black thread tied on his wrist as a talisman to ward off evil when he had nightmares two nights consecutively, causing him to wake up and cry. His amma, who held him close as they slept on a palmyra mat inside the house while the monsoon rain came down in torrents outside. Amma, who used to walk behind her ten-year-old boy, entreating him to eat rice and fish and feeding him with her own hand. His amma, who used to seat him in her lap and cry for reasons he didn't understand as she caressed his head.

His mother haunted him in the form of a keen, ineffable nostalgia. He could neither eat nor sleep. His novel-writing came to a halt. If he took up a book to read, her face would appear on the pages. Except for his cigarettes, he lost interest in everything else.

'Arrey yaar, what's happening to you? What's the problem?'

Gulshan Wadhwa came up to him and patted him on his shoulder. He had been observing Sahadevan for a while now.

'I want to go home. I want to see my mother.'

'Why aren't you going then? Bhai, you haven't taken any leave for the last two years. Go and meet your mother and come back quickly.'

Sahadevan just sat there without saying anything.

'Do you need money? How much?'

'No sir, No need, saab.'

'I don't like you pussy-footing around me like this. If you want the money, why don't you tell me frankly, yaar?'

Without saying anything more, Wadhwa saab opened his bag, took out some money and gave it to Sahadevan. Sahadevan took it hesitantly and, without even counting the notes, put them in his pocket.

'This is very kind of you, sir. I'll repay it quickly.'

His mother's face flashed in front of him, as if on a wide cinemascope screen.

Sahadevan didn't bother to reserve a ticket in advance. There was only one train to Madras: the Grand Trunk Express. Much ahead of the arrival of the train, with his steel trunk in tow, he waited on platform No. 1 at the New Delhi railway station. It was the same platform that he had got down at when he first arrived in Delhi. That day, Shreedharanunni was waiting for him.

Now, all around were portents of another imminent war with Pakistan. Pakistan needs us and we need Pakistan. When they fight each other, only the lives of people like Shreedharanunni are sacrificed, he thought.

Sahadevan disembarked at platform No. 3 of Madras Central Station, looking like a headlamp-toting miner emerging from the depths of a coal-mine. His face, clothes and limbs were coated with coal dust. His eyes were bloodshot from the dark fumes of the engine.

The poori-bhaaji and dosa-sambar that he had managed to buy by leaping out of the train at Nagpur and Vijayawada stations had, instead of settling his hunger, unsettled his stomach and deepened his thirst. There were times when he thought that hunger and starvation would have been better than this.

Toddy sellers bearing earthen pots of palmyra toddy had got into the bogie at different stations in Andhra Pradesh. Soldiers returning from Kashmir on furlough, now squeezed together in the compartment, drank deep from these pots. When they offered them to Sahadevan, he declined politely. He smoked often, though. He bought cigarettes at Gwalior, Amala, Balharshah and Gudalur. His favourite brand was Charminar; if that was not available, he settled for Scissors.

He took a room in a lodge very close to the railway station. He had a bath and a meal, then set off for Moore Market. The market was suffused with the cloying smell of jasmine. He could not see a single Tamilian woman without jasmine or kanakambaram flowers in her hair. He bought a saree for Vanaja and fabric for a long skirt for Shyamala. He was fulfilling a long-cherished dream. But he asked himself an inconvenient question that day. He was headed home with borrowed money. Was he buying expensive gifts from Moore Market for the happiness of his sisters or for his own gratification?

Many years later, he would see something on Pusa Road that reminded him of this day. A schoolchild was crossing the road and a speeding bus was headed in her direction. Seeing this, an old man dressed in loose trousers, who was walking on the pavement with the help of a walking stick, threw away his stick, dashed across the road, plucked up the child and carried her to safety. If he had not done that, the bus would have crushed the child. The incident brought back to him the old conundrum: Did the old man do it for the child or for his own sake? The correct answer was that he had done it for his own happiness. Sahadevan, the delivery clerk at Wadhwa Clearing Agency, was often lost in such irrelevant thoughts. But then, he was not a mere delivery clerk, he was a novelist too.

At Moore Market, Sahadevan also bought a clothes iron, a walking stick for his father, and one kilogram each of jalebi and laddoo. The iron was heavy, but he knew that Vanaja had always wanted to have one. She used to borrow the iron from their neighbour Raman Registrar's house and fill it with charcoal embers to press her clothes. Now she could have her own iron box and press her clothes anytime.

When he had packed everything, the steel trunk was almost too heavy to lift. It was already half full with the stuff Lalitha and Devi had sent for their respective homes: Lalitha had bought clothes, plastic sandals, flasks, a folding umbrella and kaju barfi. Also, a woollen cap and a muffler for her father. He could wear them while taking a walk in the cold month of Makaram. Devi had given him three or four aluminium vessels and a blanket to carry. Aluminium vessels were very expensive back home.

He left the lodge at 8 p.m. and headed for the station, lugging the heavy trunk. His hand hurt. Red-uniformed porters swarmed around him like house flies. But he had no money to pay them. Panting and switching the heavy trunk from hand to hand, he walked up the platform. He somehow managed to get into the Mangalore Mail and sat cramped, without room to even wiggle his legs. He did not dare go to the toilet, worried that he would return to find that he had no leg room, let alone space to sit. His bladder became swollen and his lower abdomen felt distended.

It was in such a condition that he reached home.

One month flew by very quickly. The sojourn at home refreshed him like a bath in a cool pond. He felt energised, as if he had swallowed a handful of multivitamin pills. *Aage chal*, Sahadevan said to himself. Should one not live a long life? Achieve something significant? Go, man, go!

Two or three years passed. Vidya had her first period. Gulshan Wadhwa found new clients in two African embassy employees. His company slowly started to prosper. These days, Sahadevan worked mostly outside the office. He could be spotted walking around the goods yards at the railway station or at the cargo terminal at the airport, sweating profusely, his hands loaded with Customs declarations. His stomach was always upset from the unhygienic food that he ate from roadside vendors or on railway platforms on hot afternoons. The sun had turned the skin on his face, neck and outer arms very dark.

Then came the new war, which resulted in the founding of Bangladesh.

The day the war started, Sahadevan and Lalitha were on a bus journey. It was 3 December 1971, and bitingly cold. He was returning early from office since he had a throat infection and fever. When the bus reached INA Market, he noticed a Malayali lady standing at the bus stop. She wore a blue sweater; a silk scarf was wrapped around her head. She had a bag in her hand. Some distance away from the bus stop, he noticed a young woman in an eye-hurting bright yellow saree. She had the figure of a Punjabi and the face of a Malayali. Perhaps because of her looks and her deportment, she was attracting many admiring looks.

Lalitha's eyes fell on Sahadevan as his bus stopped right in front of her. He had a blue muffler wrapped around his neck. He had bought it from a Tibetan hawker selling woollen clothes and blankets on the pavement in Queensway.

Although Lalitha had lived in the city for nine years now, she was still afraid to travel alone. But anytime she heard that sardines or mackerels were available in the market, her fear would vanish. She would change into a fresh saree at once, pick up her bag, put on her sandals, and set out to buy fish.

She got into the bus and sat next to Sahadevan. Unlike in Kerala, there was no segregated seating here. The city granted its citizens many such freedoms, which did not exist in the villages of India.

'Where are you coming from?'

'I went to buy fish. There were sardines in INA Market. Good sardines with a lot of oil. Deviyechi called and told me.'

They all waited for winter, to enjoy rice with sardine curry. In November and December, sea fish arrived in Delhi from Gujarat and Orissa—pomfret, seer fish, sardines and mackerel. The pleasure of eating fish curry helped them forget the inconveniences of the cold season.

'There are sardines, but the prices are on fire. How can people like me buy fish, dear Lalitha?' Devi had asked her.

Sathyanathan seemed to have taken after his father—if there was fish curry, he didn't need anything else. Vidya was the exact opposite. Her favourites were cauliflower, spinach, aubergine and okra. When she went with Devi to INA Market to buy fish, she would stand far away. 'I don't want to see.' She crinkled her face and blocked her nose with her chunni.

'I'll have to find you a pattar husband when you grow up. No boy from the thiyya caste will cohabit with you.'

The thiyyas of North Kerala loved their fish. Boiled fish wrapped in banana leaf was the oblation handed out to devotees in the matappura, the congregation room of the Parassinikadavu Temple. Devi had gone there on many occasions and accepted the offering. Shreedharanunni never visited temples. However, he had no objection to others doing so.

'Sahadeva, if Deviyechi hadn't called me, I wouldn't have known about the sardines. It would have been such a grievous loss,' Lalitha said with a shudder.

She clutched the bag close as if she expected someone to snatch it away. It was moist from the melting ice on the fish. The bag was from Shankunni & Sons at Thalassery bus stand, he saw. While they were packing a saree and blouse-piece into this bag, did any member of the family, the elder Shankunni or his sons or anyone else, ever imagine that one day, it would reach Delhi and travel in a DTC bus bearing fish? Predestination is not just limited to humans; bags too have their destinies.

'Have you had any letters from home?'

'Amma writes every week. She gets very worried if I don't reply promptly and has someone send me a telegram: "No news. Mother extremely worried. Please send telegram."'

He smiled. He had received such telegrams many times. It must be Shyamala who dispatched them, after taking a bus to the telegraph office in the town six miles away. These days, he replied promptly. Not solely out of affection for his mother but also to save on the expense of sending those telegrams.

'When you write home, please convey my regards to amma, Vanaja and Shyamala.'

He nodded his assent. When he heard Vanaja's name, he felt a searing pain shoot through him, burning up his insides. She was past the marriageable age. And still single ...

The bus went past Andrews Ganj. Sukhram was standing at the bus stop with a bag in hand. Lalitha had to get off at Gupta Market, which was the stop after Moolchand. Sahadevan could get off there and go on to Amritpuri, but it would be a longer walk.

'Why are you going home early today?'

'I have fever and a sore throat too. I'll go to my room and rest a bit.'

Only then did she notice that his eyes were bloodshot and the veins on his temple were distended. He must be running a high-grade fever. She touched his hand; it was burning hot, like a pan on the fire. A cold, debilitating wind blew into the bus. She tried to close the glass window, but to no avail.

'Come with me. Don't sleep alone when you have fever. Kunh'ishnettan doesn't have night duty today. He'll be home before dusk.'

'No, Lalitha. I'm not feeling well. I want to lie down.'

'Which is what I'm telling you. Sleep at our place and you can go home tomorrow morning.' She laughed and continued, 'Your fever will vanish if you have steaming hot rice and sardine curry. I'll make some rasam too.'

She knew Sahadevan loved rasam.

Sahadevan's room was cold and damp, but quiet. His plan was to lie down and cover himself with a thick razai. He could ruminate over many things and talk to himself.

Everyone claimed that life as a bachelor was difficult. Sahadevan never felt that way.

The bus reached Gupta Market, where Lalitha had to get off.

'Come, we've reached our stop.' Lalitha got up, still clutching her bag.

'I'm not coming.'

He was fantasising about lying alone, toying with his memories and tickling himself into laughter under the warmth of the razai. He had a lot of things to tell himself. He could spend any number of days without talking to another person. But he could not survive a single day without talking to himself.

Lalitha wouldn't give up. She pulled him up by his hand. Other people tried to push ahead, also trying to alight. '*Behenji, aage chalo, utarne do,*' they grumbled.

Earlier, Sahadevan used to get off at the stop after Gupta Market. When he was in the mood to stretch his legs, he would get off at Gupta Market. It was a ten-minute walk from there to Dayanand Colony. Another ten minutes of walking and he would be in Amritpuri.

But these days, he lived on the upper floor of an old building in Jangpura. His rooms looked out into the backyard. It was his fourth home after coming to Delhi. The first one was Shreedharanunni's quarters in Sewa Nagar. Then there was the mess at Yusuf Sarai, followed by Amritpuri. The new place was convenient, even though the entrance was located at the rear of the building. There was a big living room, a kitchen and a store room. And also a veranda. The best thing was that the bathroom was attached to the bedroom. During the bone-chilling winter nights, he didn't have to go outside to pee, shivering in the cold. Also, the rent for the accommodation at the rear was lower. From the veranda one could see Eros, the movie theatre. Under the jamun tree, the barber Dasappan stood, cutting hair and shaving beards. He was the poor man's naii. Sahadevan had always wondered who cut Dasappan's hair. Does one naii go to another naii to have his hair cut?

Having dropped Lalitha and Sahadevan at their stop, the No. 41 bus proceeded to Jangpura.

Sahadevan walked silently with Lalitha. He was very tired and had a headache. His face reflected his annoyance at being forced to do something he didn't want to.

All around them, the road seemed to be emptying out. Those who had been waiting for their bus to arrive were rushing back to their homes. The guy at the cigarette kiosk and the aloo-tikki vendor seemed to be closing their businesses in a hurry. Kallu mochi, the cobbler, had already left. There was a pervading sense of disquiet. Sahadevan, who was normally alert to things around him, didn't seem to notice. Maybe it was the fever; maybe it was his sour mood.

It was rare for Sahadevan to be off-colour. Even when the lights went off, his mood usually remained bright.

'Here, sit for a moment. I'll make you some tea with crushed ginger. Drink it hot and your throat will stop hurting. Then lie down for a while. Kunh'ishnettan will be back soon.'

Kunhikrishnan's house had a telephone, the only one on the entire street. Since he was a journalist, the connection had come through very quickly. Everyone else had to curry favours with an MP or a minister. Even then, the waiting time was three or four years. Several years had passed since Sahadevan made his booking and he was yet to get it; there was no information on whether he would ever get it. Anyway, who would he talk to? One doesn't need a phone to talk to oneself.

Lalitha made tea for Sahadevan, then went into the kitchen and started slicing the sardines with a sickle. The extra-sharp sickle had been specially made by a blacksmith back home. One nick was enough to slice the head off. She had also brought a flat-bottomed clay pot from home to cook fish in. 'To be able to savour fish, it has to be cooked in a clay pot,' she often said.

'The fish is full of ice. Hmm ... can't help it though. It has come all the way from Gujarat.'

She sliced the belly of the fish along its length and pulled out is entrails. That's when the phone rang. She washed her hands, wiped them on her saree, and crossed the room to pick it up.

'Where were you, Lalitha? I must have called at least ten times.'

'I went to INA to buy fish; I've got sardines. How do you want it cooked? Shall I make it with tamarind and chilli? Or with raw mango? I also bought mango from INA.'

There was a moment's silence from the other end.

'I'll be late today, perhaps I might come only tomorrow.' There was anxiety in Kunhikrishnan's voice. 'Lalitha, the war has started. Pakistan dropped bombs on nine of our airbases this evening ...'

'My Muthappa ...'

'Shut the door and windows and switch off the light. Don't be afraid. I'll be home as soon as I'm through here.'

Kunhikrishnan hung up in a hurry. In the background, she could hear the clacking of teleprinters.

All of a sudden, the night was split by the piercing wail of sirens. The power went off. The city was enveloped in darkness. Lalitha sat there, feeling numb. Memories of the wars of 1962 and 1965 came surging back. One war ends and another starts. She felt like weeping. She shouldn't have married Kunhikrishnan and come to Delhi. It would have been better if she had married a clerk or a school teacher and stayed back in the village peacefully. But in those days, it was a pretty big deal, moving to a big city. When she heard from her mother that Kunhikrishnan was employed in Delhi, she was so happy that she pranced around like a goat kid. Now, she hated Delhi.

She got up to search for a candle. She lit the candle and pulled the curtains closed to prevent the light from going out.

'Sahadeva ...'

He was sleeping on the settee and only groaned in response.

'It was Kunh'ishnettan on the phone. The war has started.'

He opened his eyes with great effort. In the dim light of the candle, he could see nothing. Even if there was a petromax in the room, he wouldn't have discerned anything. His eyesight had dimmed.

'I don't know when Kunh'ishnettan will reach home. It's a good thing that you are here. Otherwise, I would be half dead with fear.'

Even if he was down and out with fever, at least there was someone else in the house.

She lit another candle and went to the kitchen. She made some kanji. There was dal left over from the afternoon. She took a spoonful, checked the smell first and then tasted it; it wasn't spoilt.

She poured the kanji into a bowl and woke Sahadevan. He only managed to down three or four spoons of the hot kanji. His body was on fire. He returned to the settee with its loose springs.

She waited up for Kunhikrishnan till 11 p.m.

Then she woke Sahadevan again. 'Sahadeva, you go inside and sleep on the bed. I'll sit here till Kunh'ishnettan comes back.'

Sahadevan only groaned again.

The third candle also died out. There were no more candles left. Only darkness remained.

Curled up on the settee like a millipede, Sahadevan moaned aloud. But the wailing of the sirens drowned out his voice.

Enticed by the smell of the fish, the neighbour's cat made a stealthy entry into the kitchen and, having snatched a big sardine from the pot, dashed out of the house. Stop, cat, stop, there's a raw mango in the bag, take that too, she shouted after it.

It was past 2 a.m. when Lalitha broke out in sobs. Sahadevan tried to speak, but could only moan. He couldn't remember ever running such a high temperature, not since he had become an adult. Perhaps, during times of war, fevers run on high heat too.

Does one become more sensual during wartime? Sahadevan's view was that war does awaken libido. When his temperature crossed 104 degrees Fahrenheit, he remembered an episode from his past. He was then in the first standard at school.

The temple pond of Thiruvettoor had started overflowing in the monsoons, going past the highest step. Everyone who had seen the pond dry out to its bottom in March–April wanted to have a bath in it. Lakshmiyechi, Santhayechi and their daughters made six-year-old Sahadevan stand guard: 'Son, stand here and warn us if any man approaches,' they told him. There was a path near the pond that was often used as a thoroughfare. Leaving him there as a sentry, Lakshmiyechi and Santhayechi undressed and got into the water wearing only a thin cotton towel each. They seemed to have forgotten that he was a male too. As he rested on that settee with broken springs, images of the two women stepping into the temple pond, clad only in narrow towels, repeatedly flashed through his febrile mind.

The theatre of war has everything. It has collapsing buildings and bridges. It has patriotism. It has death. It has soldiers who martyr themselves. It has loneliness. Separation. Memories. It has mature women wearing towels. It has fever. It has sardines carried away by roving cats. War is the comprehensive human experience.

Kunhikrishnan reached home at 4 a.m. He came in a van that belonged to the newspaper and had 'PRESS' in bold letters pasted on the windscreen for all to see. It was packed with the day's newspapers carrying the piping hot news of the war.

'Is Sahadevan's fever better?' Kunhikrishnan asked as soon as he came in. He felt Sahadevan's temple with his palm. The fever was down; it was almost gone. His body was bathed in sweat.

After eating the kanji that Lalitha had heated up for him, Kunhikrishnan fell on the bed. He did not hear the wail of the sirens or the boom of the anti-aircraft guns. He was dead tired.

'I'm going home.'

'Ayyo, don't, Sahadeva.'

With a war on, how would he manage his fever all by himself? Who would give him some gruel or a cup of tea?

It's all right to boast that bachelors lead a merry life. But if you are suffering from diarrhoea or fever, you need a wife to make a bowl of kanji and give you arrowroot porridge.

'The fever is gone, Lalitha. It won't come back.'

Sahadevan walked to his house in Jangpura. He hadn't realised there would be no buses and that he would have to walk all the way. Did his legs have the strength to carry him such a long distance? A single night's fever had drained him completely. He walked along the railway line. The road was deserted. The space under the tree where Dasappan used to cut his customers' hair and shave their beards was also desolate. There wasn't a soul in sight.

War is also loneliness.

8

THE HERALDS OF WAR

By the time he had walked from Kunhikrishnan's home to his house in Jangpura, Sahadevan was exhausted. He lay down once more, feeling like his tiredness would never leave him, even if he were to lie there for the rest of his life. He suspected that tiredness wasn't the only thing affecting him.

Eda, Sahadeva, this tiredness that you are feeling is not yours, it's the fatigue of the soldiers on the battleground, he told himself. You have invoked the weariness of those hungry and sleep-deprived soldiers who have had to traverse deserts and mountains to guard the nation's boundaries. You cannot fight in a war, so you are trying to share the plight of the fighters, at least in your mind. The fever is only an omen. This fever is only to acquaint you with the state of the soldiers who are lying in the freezing deserts, bereft of all energy, helpless and mortally wounded, waiting for death. What more can you do, Sahadeva?

He switched on the radio to listen to the news. In all the other houses, packed cheek by jowl along the narrow alley, radios were switched on too. Today was not like the first day of the Chinese attack in 1962. Shreedharanunni had struggled to get the news then. He had needed to go to so many places, cycling through the darkness. Now, the radio was ubiquitous.

Earlier, the aerials were on top of buildings, strung between two bamboo poles fixed far apart. But now there were internal aerials. Sahadevan had driven two nails into opposite walls and strung the aerial across his room, tethering the ends to the nails. He had no faith in the news broadcast by All India Radio. Yet, he listened, alternating between the English and Hindi news which came on AIR A and AIR B respectively. Listening to AIR news bulletins was a demanding activity. He was unable to digest them without continually crossing out and correcting the facts and the language. The listener had to fill in the bits that the editor who prepared the bulletin had left out. He straightened out the segments that had been twisted out of shape.

While listening to the news, the memory of a mini-war came back to him.

It had happened two or three years ago.

A minor incident that served as a harbinger of bigger events.

In the shrine near his house, before the supreme and potent theyyams like Theechaamundi and Sasthappan appeared in their full panoply and their magnificent headdress and crown, their minor versions—vellaattukal—appeared to dance.

This was exactly like that.

The incident took place while he was still with Wadhwa & Sons International Clearing Agency. He had gone to clear a consignment at the airport. The consignee, an employee of an African embassy, was a new client.

Among Gulshan Wadhwa's staff, the only one who could speak English fluently was Sahadevan. Even their senior-most employee, Kiran Bagga, could speak only halting English. Therefore, for all the work involving foreigners, Wadhwa saab always deputed Sahadevan.

Sahadevan improved his conversation and language skills by speaking to himself. He spoke in many languages, stringing together English, Hindi and Malayalam words in the same sentence: 'You good-for-nothing, *badmash, eda ente peru Sahadevan ennanenkil njaan ithinu ninnodu pakaram chodikkum.'*

Wadhwa & Sons possessed a scooter for use outside the office. But Sahadevan did not use it. He liked to travel by bus. Bus journeys strengthened human relationships. Passengers sat side by side, brushing against one another and catching the odour of the other person. Sometimes he felt the warm breath of the person beside him on his face. It could be the smell of beedi or ghutka or it could be the stench of halitosis. He had seen Om Prakash Jain, his landlord, cleaning his teeth with a neem stick. The old-timers in Delhi used these to clean their teeth, and neem was as effective as charcoal dentifrice. But even then, when passengers in DTC buses opened their mouths, Sahadevan had to turn his face away.

As his surname indicated, Om Prakash Jain was a follower of Jainism. There was a Jain temple close to their place where naked munis held religious discourses and blessed those who came to worship at the temple. Sahadevan used to go there to listen to the discourses. He used to wish that he could walk around stark naked like the digambara. Giving up everything and owning nothing—even the cloth around one's waist—symbolised total freedom. Mahatma Gandhi had exhorted everyone to lead a simple life, shorn of luxuries and ostentation. Jainism wanted people to not merely shun luxuries but live a life in which every material convenience could be renounced. He knew he was incapable of such abstention. Instead of renouncing the world, he was trying to suck up everything. He used to marvel at the gluttony of his own pen.

The minor, heraldic performance of war took place at Golf Links. The national flag of the African nation fluttered in front of the embassy. The high-net-worth individuals of Delhi lived in that area. Sahadevan took the entry pass at the gate and entered the consul's room. He had been there many times before and knew his way around. All the staff knew him well too. The receptionist was a good-looking girl called Damayanti Talwar. You could see the most beautiful Indian female staff of Delhi in the African embassies. These fair-skinned Indian beauties were said to be the weakness of the African dignitaries. The diplomatic staff would scour Delhi for them and appoint them as receptionists, secretaries, social secretaries and public relations officers.

The sight that greeted Sahadevan when he opened the door to the consul's room was a tableau of the ambassador and the consul facing each other, guns pointing at one another. He thought he was watching a movie.

The ambassador was a young man. He resembled Patrice Lumumba. The consul was elderly. Both were black as night.

'*Viens*,' the consul said, gesturing towards himself. '*Viens salaud*.'*

The ambassador lunged forward, his gun aimed at the consul, his junior staff member. '*Bouge pas. Sinon je tire sûr toi*.'†

Sahadevan stood there, stunned. It took him a while to realise that he was not inside a movie theatre.

Suddenly, a shot was fired. The young ambassador ducked and ran into his room. Firing still, the consul pursued him. Though he was an elderly man, he was fitter than his younger adversary.

'*Tu veux coucher avec ma copine? Pas possible, salaud. Elle est a moi, Damayanti. Tu m'écoutes? Je suis amoureux d'elle, tu vois? Tu es jaloux de moi salaud ma pote. Que tu me laisse en paix. Sinon je t'envoies en enfer*,'‡ the consul shouted.

---

*'Come, come to me, bastard.'

† 'Don't move, or else, I'll shoot for sure.'

‡ 'You want to sleep with my girlfriend? Won't happen, you bastard. She is mine, Damayanti. Do you hear me? I'm in love with her, do you see? You are jealous of me, my slutty bastard friend. Leave me in peace. Otherwise, I'll send you to hell.'

The ambassador's response was a deafening shot from his gun. The staff scurried off in different directions and slammed the self-closing doors after them. By the time Sahadevan emerged from the building, a crowd had gathered in the front. Smoke could be seen coming out from the windows. Within a short while, a jeep from the Police Control Room arrived. But the police were not permitted to step into diplomatic missions.

Sahadevan slunk out of the embassy like a cat.

All that he had needed was a signature and the stamp of the consul on a bill of lading. As he was leaving, he heard another shot from behind him.

He was happy that even if his work was unfinished, he had been a witness to a heraldic performance of the real war.

The next day, Sahadevan went to the embassy again to get his papers signed. There was no sign that anything untoward had happened there. He went into the consul's room with some trepidation. The ambassador and the consul, who had been shooting at each other the previous day, were chatting amicably like friends. In their hands were glasses of white rum. A thick cigar smouldered between the fingers of the consul. During their conversation, they stood up often, shook hands, clinked glasses and laughed loudly.

Sahadevan got the signatures. He put the stamp under the signatures himself. Neither the consul nor the ambassador glanced at what he was doing. They clinked glasses once more, laughing loudly.

How good it would be if India and Pakistan were like them, Sahadevan mused.

Soon after that incident, Sahadevan left Wadhwa & Sons, the company he had worked at since coming to Delhi. He joined a travel agency.

'It was the job that Shreedharettan got me ...'

'Just think that the new job is God's blessing,' Devi said. 'Those who had to leave us have left. What's the point of thinking about them now?'

Devi's hair showed signs of greying. There were dark circles under her eyes. Nine years had passed since Shreedharanunni had passed away. But she was not the least bit sentimental.

'It's a good thing that you have changed jobs. Now make some money and go home and bring a wife.'

'There's time enough for that. I'm not that old.'

'Are you thirty or thirty-two? Old enough to be the father of two children. If you are not going to marry now, then when? After you've become old and infirm?'

'There's still time, Deviyechi,' Sahadevan repeated. 'Before I die, I'll marry and invite you all to the feast.'

'Will the feast include chapatis and cauliflower curry?' Vidya, who had been listening silently, piped up.

Sahadevan never spared a thought for his own marriage. His worries revolved around getting his sister Vanaja married. He had never thought of marriage as essential. If the circumstances were favourable, perhaps he would marry. It could happen the other way too.

He lay in his room in Jangpura, tired. He had experienced two wars. He could imagine what would happen next. He wished, though, that Pakistan and India could be made to sit on either side of a table. Both would be handed a glass each of white rum. Water would be added, and a squeeze of lemon. Let them converse loudly, embrace each other and laugh aloud. Let them occasionally lean forward and clink their glasses together.

How could one make this happen?

9

JOURNEYS IN WARTIME

Danger lurks in wartime travel. Soldiers lose their lives. Homes are bombed. Even ordinary folk, in no way connected with the war, may lose their life and limbs anytime or anywhere—aboard a train, while strolling or sitting at home, eating or listening to music on the radio with their families. Besides, people lose their common sense about not travelling during times of war. It was because of this slip of common sense that Nenmanda Vasava Panicker set off from Pathankot for Delhi in December 1971. It was when the war was at its peak. Why did he leave for Delhi at that time?

Vasu was not the only one who lost his good sense. Sathyanathan and Rosily also lost theirs. They too undertook a short journey. A wartime journey.

'Amma, I'm stepping out for a short while.'

'Where are you going? There isn't a soul on the streets. Only policemen and soldiers. This is not the time to loiter. Don't go anywhere, come, stay at home. If you are feeling hungry, amma will make you parippuvada.'

'I'm not going far. Just walking up to Kotla. Don't worry too much. Who's going to arrest us? We are not Muslims.'

Abdullah Bawa, a resident of Karbala, was in jail. As soon as the war broke out, policemen from the Tughlak Road police station had come to his house and hauled him away.

'Where are you taking me? What crime have I committed?'

'You are a Muslim.'

Later, the policemen at the station had accused him of being a Pakistani spy.

The innocent Abdullah Bawa, who used to provide for his family of nine by selling lassi and masala tea at Khan Market, was branded as a spy and locked up. He was from Uttar Pradesh. When Shreedharanunni was alive, Abdullah Bawa used to tell him about his poverty. The trade union worker used to go to Khan Market regularly to drink tea.

Shreedharanunni was no more. Abdullah Bawa's poverty was alive and kicking.

Sathyanathan was growing up to be a strong-willed young man. Like father, like son. While on strike, Shreedharanunni had been threatened many times. He had been told that his arms and legs would be hacked off and that he would be thrown in the gutter. Policemen used to come and knock on his door at night. But he remained steadfast and did not change his views. Sathyanathan was his father's son all right.

'You and your fears, amma,' he laughed.

'Come back quickly.'

Devi acquiesced, but her anxiety didn't abate.

After reassuring his mother, Sathyanathan set out on a cycle ride in the cool sunshine of winter. He wore a faded brown sweater that was two sizes small for him. It was his old school uniform. His trousers stopped short of his ankles.

'Eda, if you shoot up like an areca nut tree, what will I do? Where do I have the money to buy trousers for you every second month?' Devi used to say.

The previous day, the Indian Navy had attacked Karachi and sunk the warship PNS *Khaibar*. There were conjectures that US warships had started moving towards the Bay of Bengal. There was a palpable sense of fear everywhere. You could hear the footsteps of danger approaching. Trenches had been dug in front of every house, just like Uttam Singh had done in 1965. Most of the shops remained closed and the roads were deserted. There was no vehicular traffic. Every place was silent and bereft of movement. Even the flocks of birds that flew overhead were silent. The still and lifeless city annoyed Sathyanathan.

Sahadevan enjoyed solitude and silence, while Sathyanathan liked crowds and noise. He was a regular at the Ramlila Maidan where hundreds of thousands of people congregated to witness the Dussehra celebrations.

For a while after Shreedharanunni's death, Sathyanathan had become silent and introverted. But he soon rediscovered the energetic boy inside him. He concentrated on his studies, and though he was a child, he did the household chores and involved himself in domestic matters.

Nine years had passed thus.

Another war had broken out. It was also the third war Sahadevan was witnessing.

Vasava Panicker alighted from the Pathankot Express at Old Delhi railway station with a cloth bag slung over his shoulder. His long hair flew in the cold breeze. The train had reached its destination four days after the scheduled date. Two coaches at the train's rear had been hit by bombs and destroyed. It had gone some distance with the coaches on fire. Desperate cries and wails rose from within. The majority of the passengers were burnt to death. A few lost their limbs. Some others were turned into black lumps in the intense heat of the exploding bombs. The bombed bogies were detached only after the train had travelled almost two hundred kilometres from Pathankot. They were filled with unidentifiable corpses and half-burnt survivors.

Vasava Panicker had survived because his coach was in the middle of the train.

He thought he shouldn't have survived.

The train, which continued to roll along, contained no supplies. There was nothing for people to eat or drink. Fortunately, since it was severely cold, no one felt thirsty. But the cold heightened their hunger. Their empty, growling stomachs yearned for a poori or a chapati. The train, moving at a crawl, had to stop often, for hours together, for a green signal. The passengers got off then and trekked to nearby villages and drank water from the wells. They went into sugarcane fields and pulled out sticks of cane and chewed on them. In some places, the villagers fed them dry chapatis and onions.

Occasionally, bombers and fighter planes flew over the train. Each time this happened, the passengers wailed collectively. Once, a bomb fell into a nearby field and detonated. Vasu watched as the wheat fields went up in flames. He had a momentary vision of himself catching fire and being blown to pieces. He thought he would never reach Delhi. His ashes would leach into the soil of Punjab, the sweet-as-sugarcane soil.

This long-haired young man, not yet nineteen years of age, had left without a single rupee in his pocket, with just a cotton sling bag. That was a year ago. Apart from his clothes, his bag contained a sketchbook and pencils. No toothbrush or razor or blades. He had no need for such things. He neither shaved nor cut his hair. Even a bath was rare. He took pleasure in travelling and sketching the things he saw. Hunger or thirst didn't bother him. He slept at railway stations. He had slept for two nights at the Gurdaspur railway station, unmolested. His aim was to proceed to Dharamshala from Pathankot. That was when the war broke out. And so, Vasu turned his route map upside down. Instead of Dharamshala, he travelled to Delhi on the Pathankot Express. Since he had left home, he had been continuously travelling on trains. He never bought tickets, for he had no money. He did not like taking buses as ticketless travel was not so easy. Once, in Bhatinda, a bus conductor had beaten him up for travelling without a ticket. Nevertheless, he liked Punjab. There were gurdwaras everywhere. In every gurdwara, chapati and dal were handed out for free; sometimes there was also halwa made from semolina. It was not leftover food flung at beggars. These were chapatis made of the dough milled from the crop of wheat that the villagers harvested for themselves. They were smeared with ghee made from buffalo milk. Vasu loved the Sikhs who fed the hungry with nutritious and tasty food. He liked to sit for hours together in their gurdwaras, meditating. The gurdwaras filled his stomach and his mind. It was the only religion that showed concern for people's hunger.

The day he landed in Delhi, Vasu slept on the railway platform. There were no trains or travellers anywhere in sight. No vendors of aloo-tikki or rajma-chawal. As far as the eye could see, all the signals along the railway lines were red. Using his bag as a pillow, he curled up on the frozen stone bench. However, the soldiers and the policemen on duty would not let him sleep. Every now and then, someone would poke him with the butt of a rifle and awaken him.

'Who are you? Are you a Muslim?'

'I'm an artist.'

Artist. They had not heard of a religion by that name. They knew the followers of only two religions—Hinduism and Islam. They troubled him all through the night, interrogating, questioning. He was not allowed to sleep at all. Once, he lost his patience and screamed: 'Get lost, you bourgeoisie ... won't let a man sleep ...'

He shouted this in Malayalam, which neither the policemen nor the soldiers understood.

'He's a lunatic,' they decided.

Close to dawn, a train arrived. It disgorged hundreds of soldiers. When they stepped out of the coaches, their boots made a noise like flocks of birds taking off together, startled by the sound of gunfire. For the first time, Vasu saw a train that carried only soldiers. Military trucks were waiting outside to ferry them away.

He didn't have a place to stay. Not that he ever felt the need for such a place. In Pathankot, he had spent his nights in one of the long-distance trains that had been washed and shunted to the outer yard. He did not think he would have any difficulty finding a similar place in Delhi. But then, these were times of war.

And this was the time when Vasava Panicker, Sathyanathan and Rosily ran into one another.

Sathyanathan, who had left for a cycle ride on that cool, sunny, wartime afternoon, did not return home even after darkness had fallen. Devi's eyes were strained from staring unblinkingly at the road for hours together. Anxiety surged in the mind of the forty-year-old widow who had lost her husband at such a young age. It was wartime; where could she go and look for her son? Who would she seek help from? Sahadevan was the one who came to her aid in times of crisis. He was the only man who would answer her call, irrespective of which corner of the city he was in. But how would she contact him in Jangpura? How could her voice reach his ears? No one had a phone in Sewa Nagar. She sat there frozen, unable to decide what to do. Every now and then, the sirens wailed. All the neighbours had shut themselves into their homes, with all the lights switched off. Vidya sat beside her for a while, sniffling. Then, putting her head on her mother's lap, she fell asleep.

It was a night full of anxiety, fear and pain, like no other she had undergone and one she would never forget for the rest of her life.

After Shreedharanunni's death, she had struggled to bring up their young children on her own. Poverty was not the only problem. Her young, shapely body was also a curse. During the cold nights of December, men used to lurk in the darkness, tapping on the windows of her house. They robbed her of her sleep. Even at the Secretariat, she encountered such people, who seemed to think—she's a widow, who's going to challenge us?

Somehow, her children needed to grow up and become independent. Till then, Devi would not rest.

The glass panes of the windows at the Defence Colony police station had been painted black. Inside, the light from a small lantern flickered. Its yellowish light fell on the wall at an angle. In that light, one could see seven people sitting hunched on the floor. They were of different ages and spoke many tongues. There was only one female in that group. Sathyanathan's face reflected deep outrage. His eyes blazed with anger. Vasu sat there peacefully, his head filled with indecipherable thoughts. Occasionally, shadows of anxiety and apprehension flitted across his face. Then, slowly, a smile would bloom to replace them. Rosily's eyes betrayed the fretfulness of a fawn caught in a trap. She sat with her back to the wall, avoiding everyone's eyes and looking at the floor.

'Chokri, what's your name?'

'Rosily.'

'Are you a Muslim?'

'Rosily is not a Muslim name.'

'So, you are a Hindu?'

'No.'

'Then what the hell are you?'

The policeman swung his lathi in her direction. She pulled out the crucifix from under her woollen pullover and kissed it.

'Tell me, which religion do you belong to?'

She did not answer him. Despite seeing the crucifix, they had not understood that she was a Christian. In their limited understanding, there were only two religions: Hinduism and Islam.

'Please give me some water,' Sathyanathan said. He had been sitting on the floor for nearly eight hours.

'What do you need water for? To wash your ass? But you haven't even shat for that!'

The policeman took a drag of the beedi in his hand, and exhaled.

'Mind your words,' Sathyanathan said in English.

'Oh, you are a gora. You will only speak in angrezi, is it? *Theek hai, angrezi mein bolo, yeh kya hai?*'

The policeman started to unbutton his fly. Rosily averted her face. Sathyanathan ground his teeth and controlled himself.

'Answer me, you bastard,' the policeman roared.

Suddenly sirens began to wail. All the street lights went off. The policemen blew out the lantern and ran out. There was complete darkness everywhere. They lowered themselves into the trenches and crouched there like bandicoots.

It was his chance to escape. Amma and Vidya would be frightened. If he didn't get away now, there was no knowing how many days he would be detained at the station. There would be no one to challenge the detention; it was wartime.

Sathyanathan went out and found his cycle. He slipped away into the darkness. The policemen crouching in the trenches did not see him. Even if they had seen him, they would have done nothing. They were praying to Bajrang Bali with their eyes tightly shut, that there should be no more fighter planes overhead and no bombs would fall on them.

When the sirens tailed off, they went in and lit the lamp once more.

'Where's that bastard?'

Vasu, Rosily and the others kept silent. They could also have run away under the cover of darkness. But Rosily didn't have the courage. Vasu didn't have the inclination. To go where? Inside the police station, it was not cold. Warmth was spreading from the angeethi fired by burning coal lumps.

It was 11 p.m.

'Give me something to eat,' Rosily said, gathering up her courage.

'This is not a hotel, this is a police station,' the policeman said.

'A war is on, and all you are worried about is filling your tummy,' another policeman said scornfully.

'Don't people feel hungry during war?' she retorted.

She had not eaten anything since the morning. Once the war had started, she's had no work. She had been picked up from the Ring Road. Pulling her into the jeep, they had brought her directly to the Defence Colony police station. She still wore the blinding yellow saree.

'You are not fashionable enough, you should wear a miniskirt like Zeenat Aman,' the Station House Officer said, surveying Rosily as she leaned against the wall. 'If you swaddle yourself in a six-metre saree like this, who's going to come behind you?'

'Hey, guruji,' a policeman asked Vasu. 'How are you? Quite well?'

Vasu sat without speaking, stroking his long hair. The policemen had grabbed him while he stood outside the barbed-wire fence of Safdarjung airport, sketching the Dakota airplane parked on the runway. He was seeing the inside of a police station for the first time in his life. He found it invigorating.

'What's your name, man?'

'Nenmanda Vasava Panicker.'

'What?'

'Nenmanda Vasava Panicker.'

Perplexed, the policeman stared at him.

'What do you do?'

'I'm a painter.'

'Very good. Once the war is over, you should come and paint this station. Look, all the walls are dirty.'

The walls of the station were indeed shabby.

Vasu was let off the next morning.

'Can I also go?'

'Scoot, make yourself scarce.'

Vasu and Rosily emerged together from the police station.

'*Tu Kerala ki hai*?' Vasu asked her. She didn't reply. She didn't talk about herself to anyone.

'Why are you wearing such a bright saree that hurts the eyes? You have no sense of colour.'

'Let alone colour, I have no sense at all. What do you know about me?'

Their worlds were equally impermanent and unpredictable. Vasu wanted to invite Rosily home. Then he remembered that he didn't have a house. He had no regrets about that. But he did need a place to sit and paint.

I shall be brief now, Sahadevan told himself. The intensity of the war increased in the next few days. Millions of refugees from Bangladesh entered India. The US warship USS Enterprise entered the Bay of Bengal. The Soviet Union, on its part, sent warships fitted with nuclear warheads. On 16 December, the Pakistani forces in Bangladesh surrendered. A new nation called Bangladesh was born.

All this happened within a span of thirteen days.

The staff at the telegraph office were busy. Messengers dressed in khaki cycled through the alleys and shortcuts of Delhi, delivering telegrams to housewives. They were the intimations of death, of brave soldiers martyred on the battlefield, who had sacrificed their lives for their motherland. In each house that the telegram was delivered to, a widow was made.

Then it was the turn of military vehicles to get busy. They travelled on the capital's roads, bearing ceremonially draped bodies of soldiers. Corpses without arms, corpses without legs, corpses with parts of the torso missing, corpses with one side of their heads missing,

How quickly you have summarised it, Sahadevan said to himself, continuing his monologue. And how easily. Though the war is over, its aftershocks will continue for a long time. You will be witness to the agonies brought on by the war. Will you have enough ink in your pen to record all that?

That was also the day he recovered from his thirteen-day fever and left the house after a bath. He had written a little. He had written about war.

But he had left some ink in his pen. Wars always return, don't they?

Part Two

The Republic of Hunger

So long as you have food in your mouth, you have solved all questions for the time being.

—Franz Kafka (1883–1924)

1

HUNGER, LINES, COLOURS

Vasava Panicker shivered like a man with ague. He was leaning on the metal fence between the pavement and the road near Regal Cinema. People passed by, dressed in sweaters and jackets. Many had mufflers wrapped round their neck and woollen socks on their feet. Women wore knee-length coats over their sarees and silk scarves around their heads. Vasu shivered uncontrollably in his cotton shirt and trousers. His fingers and face had become numb with cold. It had been twenty-four hours since he had eaten anything. He hadn't even had a glass of tea that day. Though it was noon, the sun was missing in action. The spot in the sky which hid the sun was a little paler, but that was all. It was a typical December in Delhi.

For a man with no money, hunger is a real problem. But Vasu was one of those who believed that one doesn't need money to get food or end hunger. How did birds and animals eat? Did they have money?

When he was hungry, he would find a way to satisfy his hunger. According to him, the god who gave man a mouth would also provide food for him to eat. If not, someone else would invite him in for a meal. It could be Sathyanathan. Or Harilal Shukla. Or the gurdwaras of Punjab and Delhi. Visiting the Hanuman Mandir near Rivoli Cinema on Tuesdays could get him food. On Fridays, Baba Balak Mandir in Krishna Nagar offered devotees rice and rajma, served on a leaf. The literary meet at Kerala Club in Connaught Place also took place on Friday evenings. He would get parippuvada and piping hot tea there. The vada came from the Navakerala Restaurant nearby. Vasu had been there once, to eat dosa and spicy beef curry.

One day, while Vasu was walking through Refugee Market in Lodhi Colony, a bicycle stopped beside him. Sathyanathan was returning after buying fish. You couldn't get the sardines and mackerel of INA Market here, but round the year, you could get rohu from the Yamuna River.

Sathyanathan was now a college student and took care of all household matters. Shreedharanunni had been like that—even when union activities took up all his free hours, he found the time to take care of his wife and children.

'Looks as if the kerosene in the stove is over,' Sathyanathan said, as he pumped the stove before lighting it. 'Do we have any more, amma?'

'Not a drop, eda,' Devi said. After the war, there was a shortage of everything. Kerosene had vanished from the market. Sugar was not available. Lentils and onion prices were on fire. For the poor, all these were essentials. What did the rich need kerosene for? They had gas stoves in their kitchens. What did they need lentils and onions for? They ate their chapatis with chicken and paneer tikka. That must be why the prices did not rise for these.

Devi did her cooking on a kerosene stove and used the angeethi to heat water. To save on kerosene, she would boil the water for tea on the angeethi, so the tea always smelled of smoke. Fortunately, there was no shortage of coal. They could get as much as they wanted from the coal depot in Sewa Nagar. These days, it was Sathyanathan who weighed the coal and heaped it into the gunny sack reserved for it, then heaved the sack onto the cycle's carrier. Looking at him, Kanta behn would say, 'So what if you have lost your husband? You have an able son.'

But can a son take the place of a husband?

'Where can we get some kerosene, amma?'

'Lalitha should have some to spare. Pick it up from her place on your way back from college.'

Recently, during one of their phone calls, Lalitha had told Devi, 'Tell me if you need any sugar or wheat, Deviyechi. I'll give you my ration card. You can buy your entire ration; I only need a little sugar. All the wheat and kerosene, you can take.'

So, while returning from college in the evening, Sathyanathan went to Lajpat Nagar. Kunhikrishnan and Lalitha were still living in the New Double Storey building. A man called Ouseph had started a South Indian store in the nearby Guru Nanak Market. Lalitha was boiling tapioca with coconut and shallots bought from this shop. The aroma of tapioca reached his nose even as he entered the yard.

'What's cooking, Lalithechi?'

'I'm boiling some tapioca. Sahadevan will be here soon; he loves tapioca.'

Sathyanathan didn't wait for Sahadevan's arrival. He ate some tapioca and left for Sewa Nagar with a canister of kerosene. It was not easy travelling in the crowded bus holding both his books and the canister. But he was untroubled by the inconvenience—and euphoric at having got the kerosene.

Sathyanathan recognised Vasu at first glance, when he saw him walking in Refugee Market with his long mane flying in the wind. How could anyone not recognise Vasu after having seen him once?

'Don't you remember me?'

Sathyanathan sat on the bicycle with one foot on the ground.

Vasu gave him a wide-eyed look. His eyes drooped; he was sleep-deprived after having sketched all through the night.

He didn't recognise Sathyanathan. He was forgetful like that. Except, he never forgot shapes and colours. He still remembered the shape of the rainclouds he had seen in his childhood and the colours and designs on the sarees Kamala teacher wore to school. Almost everything else, he forgot. Sometimes he even forgot the way he looked, the shape and features of his own face. Someday, he would look in the mirror and not recognise himself.

'Don't you remember? We met at the Defence Colony police station. During the war. You were picked up from outside Safdarjung airport.'

Faint memories of him trying to sketch the Dakota planes on the tarmac and being interrogated by the policemen who had whisked him away surfaced in Vasu's mind. Yet, he could not remember Sathyanathan. He was missing some memories.

'My house is in Sewa Nagar; not far from here. Would you like to come?'

'Who else is at home?'

'My mother and sister. My father is no more.'

'Why did he die?'

Sathyanathan did not understand Vasu's question. Often, Vasu's questions were incomprehensible even to himself.

Vasu was excited. If he went to Sathyanathan's house, he would get some rice or chapati. Or tea and biscuits, at the very least.

They walked along Dhobi Ghat and turned into Sewa Nagar. The clothes hung out to dry on the clotheslines by the side of the railway line billowed in the breeze. The level crossing was not crowded: there were no trains at this time.

'What do you do?'

'I study in St. Stephen's College. What do you do?'

'Nothing.'

'Not found a job yet?'

'No.'

'Are you looking for one?'

'No.'

Vasu had carried vegetable loads in Okhla. Washed dishes at Madras Hotel. Bent reinforcing bars for concrete workers. He didn't look for jobs. When he needed one, he would do some odd job somewhere, anywhere. He would sleep in a park or in a railway station or in front of a store. He didn't worry about where he would sleep when the cold became worse. He always found some way, some place.

He wanted to travel for two or three years more, to see new places and sights. Then he would start the life of a full-time artist. These were the future plans of Vasava Panicker.

Sathyanathan looked at him closely. His way of talking and his behaviour were as droll as his appearance. But it piqued Sathyanathan's curiosity. All said and done, he was a Malayali, wasn't he?

Sathyanathan pushed open the gate to his house. The yard now had a curry leaf plant and a guava tree that was heavy with fruit. Devi had planted it after returning from her second confinement. There were roses in bloom, tenderly cared for by Vidya, this second child of hers. The old moringa tree was still there.

'Son, who is this?' Devi asked in a low voice. Sathyanathan didn't usually bring people home. Hemmed in by poverty and hardship, they led a quiet life with few social contacts.

'Sit down, son,' Devi said. She didn't like his unkempt look, the long hair and beard. But she noticed the tenderness in his eyes, the innocence, and couldn't help but like him. With his long face, broad forehead and sharp nose, he could be easily mistaken for a Sikh.

'What is your name?'

'Vasava Panicker.'

'Where is your home in Kerala?'

'In the south.'

'Have you been in Delhi for long?'

He glanced towards the kitchen without answering. The hollow feeling in his stomach was spreading to his limbs. He felt weak. The only place on earth his eyes were attracted to now was the kitchen. All else—from the Rashtrapati Bhawan to Parliament—was irrelevant.

'Do you want some water?'

'Tea would be fine.'

Devi looked at his face closely. She was quick to recognise hunger. Shreedharanunni had instructed her well in many matters. 'Don't ask who or why. When someone is hungry, just offer them whatever is in the kitchen. Doesn't matter if we don't eat,' he used to say. She went into the kitchen with a deep sigh.

Vasu had a glass of tea and biscuits. He waited for the rice to boil and watched as Devi ground coriander and made fish curry. He left late at night, having eaten his fill.

'Poor man,' said Devi. 'How did you get acquainted with him?'

'At the Defence Colony police station.'

Vasu was often at Connaught Place, where he put his sketches on display on the metal fence bordering the pavement near Regal Cinema. In front of him were spread out rolls of paper, drawing pens, pencils, crayons, erasers and blades.

A tonga parked in a deserted street. Sweepers warming themselves around a small fire on the pavement. A schoolgirl with a bag on her shoulder, headed to school. There were also many portraits—of women, children and old people. In their midst was an oil painting. Of two legs running into emptiness. From a very young age, Vasu had developed a style of painting that showed the subject up close and, in the same frame, a deconstructed view of it.

Possibly due to the cold, few came to the noon show at Regal Cinema. The pavements were crowded with hawkers of woollen clothes. One could see tongas drawn by half-dead nags making slow progress along the outer circle of Connaught Place. Occasionally, a bus or a car came along.

Vasu didn't travel by bus. He covered the whole city on foot. Barefoot at that. Feet are meant to touch the ground, he would say. It's with the invention of footwear that we started to lose contact with the earth.

'Mister, did you draw this?'

Vasu woke with a start. He had dozed off, leaning against the iron fence. A man with black hair and a white moustache was standing in front of him. He wore an expensive shirt tailored in the latest fashion.

He hunkered down to examine each of Vasu's pictures. He paid great attention to the painting of the running legs and the scattered parts drawn around it. He stood up and nodded his head as if he approved of Vasu's work. It might be easy to work this style in acrylic but it was very difficult to execute with oils.

'Is this for sale?'

Vasu jumped to his feet when he heard that question. The stranger observed that he had the face of an adolescent. His long hair danced in the breeze. His beard had not yet achieved the stiffness that comes with maturity. If he cut his hair, had a bath, and wore a clean shirt and trousers, he would look no different from a college student.

Vasu looked at the man with rising hope. He was very fair, with ruddy cheeks.

'I'm interested. But I don't have the time now. I'll come later.'

Vasu felt a howl escape his empty stomach. Instinctively, he stretched his hand towards the man.

'What? What do you want?'

It took the man a moment to understand. His eyes filled with sympathy. He took out two or three ten-rupee notes from his pocket and put them in Vasu's hand. His breath smelt strongly of tobacco.

'My name is Harilal Shukla. You can meet me at Dhoomimal Gallery. I'm there every evening.'

Harilal walked on, puffing on his pipe. Vasu stood perplexed, clueless about what to do with the money. He had not seen such a princely sum for a long time. It would be more than enough to feed him for the next fifteen days since he ate only once a day.

The previous day, he had gone to Bangla Sahib in search of food. There was a long queue. The cobblers from Connaught Place, the flower sellers of Hanuman Mandir, the prostitutes and the hippies from Shankar Market were all there. When his turn came, after waiting for two hours, there was nothing left. The time for langar was over, and the supply of aloo-pooris was exhausted. He had walked back dejected, cursing his stomach. Without hunger, how cheerful his life would have been. In front of him lay the shadow of the gold-covered dome of the gurdwara. He swerved to avoid stepping on its sacred shadow.

It was after coming to Delhi that his stomach had begun to pose problems for Vasu. In Punjab, there was no dearth of food. There were gurdwaras everywhere, even in the villages. Anyone could go in as long as they covered their head. Sardarnis from wealthy families served everyone chapati and dal made with their own hands. During his travels through Punjab, his body had started filling out from eating the wholesome food at the gurdwaras. His sunken cheeks had filled out. His neck became thicker. He smoked weed all the time. There was no shortage of that either in Punjab.

It was because of the 1971 war that he had fled Punjab for Delhi. The Golden Temple and Jallianwala Bagh had been his favourite haunts. Covering his head with a cloth, he would sit beside the Amrit Sarovar inside the temple for hours together, meditating. It had been an indescribably intense and deeply spiritual experience. He felt sorry now that no sardar or sardarni so much as glanced at his paintings. Even when he offered to sketch their portraits free of charge, not one of them posed for him.

Vasu bought a pint of Old Monk rum, got some water from the toilet at the Kerala Club to add to it, and got gloriously drunk. Someone else must have been in the toilet earlier, drinking rum or brandy, for a strong smell of liquor emanated from the walls with their peeling plasters and from the cracked, dirty doors. After finishing the rum, he bought four chapatis and a vegetable curry from a roadside stall and ate till his heart and belly were contented. His stomach stopped wailing. Poor thing, Vasu told himself. Why blame it? It's only doing its job. Just like I'm doing mine.

He returned to Regal and, once again, sat down and leaned back against the metal fence. The sun peeped out. Its tender light spread over the melancholia of winter-time Connaught Place. He drifted off to sleep. Like Sahadevan, he saw his mother in his dreams. He had no idea if she was even alive still.

The next morning saw him near Jama Masjid. In an alley near Turkman Gate, he saw an old Muslim man with a hennaed beard, who was selling used clothes. Most of them had holes or were torn. Amidst them Vasu saw a thick khaki-coloured shirt in fairly good condition. It was part of a soldier's uniform. Though a couple of buttons were missing, and it was a size too big for him, he bought it for four and a half rupees. Now he needn't fear the cold. He put on the ill-fitting khaki shirt standing right there and started walking through Turkman Gate. He thought he could hear the boom of cannons and the roar of tanks coming from valleys covered with snow and ice. The shirt probably belonged to a soldier who had died a valorous death in the last war. The ghost of the war walked with him now.

The money Harilal had given him was soon over. He began to display his paintings again, dangling them from the metal fence near Regal. He sat in front of them with paper, drawing pens and other accoutrements. But no one approached him to have their portraits drawn.

In the days that followed, the cold intensified. It rained intermittently. A thick fog enveloped the city. Visibility was zero and, in the dense fog, even people and objects that were right in front remained hidden. The days became shorter and the nights longer. After dusk, the streets became deserted and lifeless. Delhi became like a black and white photo in the fog.

Very soon, Republic Day would be upon them.

2

THE POLITICS OF HUNGER

Until he began living there, Sahadevan had thought of Delhi as a city of love, heartbreak, separation and melancholy. It was the novelist in him that made him believe that. For the journalist Kunhikrishnan, Delhi was a city of death and starvation. Where the novelist sees separation, the journalist sees death. Where the novelist perceives love, the journalist perceives lust.

Before he quit Wadhwa & Sons, Gulshan Wadhwa had once asked Sahadevan, 'Arrey yaar, you look like you haven't eaten for two days. Come, let me buy you a grand meal. Have you been to Karim's?'

'No.'

Karim's Restaurant in Kababiyan Gali near Jama Masjid was famous for its Mughlai food. It was more than a century old, Wadhwa told him, and was run by the family of Haji Zaheeruddin, a descendant of cooks from the time of Akbar the Great. Once upon a time, nawabs and lords went to Karim's to eat tandoori roti and makhni murg. Later, when actors like Raj Kapoor visited from Bombay, they would go to Karim's and eat murg jahangiri and butter naan. These days, it was the diplomatic staff and foreign tourists who were the main clientele of Karim's. There was a saying that anyone who has tasted the badshahi badam pasanda at Karim's would go there again and again, till the end of their lives. As Wadhwa continued raving about it, Sahadevan was sceptical for a moment. Was Wadhwa saab actually going to take him to such a place? Let's go, he told himself, one should experience everything.

'Chal, yaar.'

Wadhwa saab put on his jacket. Though it was afternoon, a cold breeze had sprung up. Most pedestrians were fully covered. Even the women who displayed their fair, blue-tinted armpits and navels during the summer were swathed from head to toe in woollen clothes. The men used to joke among themselves that when the winter got over and Holi came around, the women would divest themselves of their shawls and sweaters, coats and woollen shawls—and lo and behold, everyone's tummy was big. Dilliwaalis get pregnant collectively, Wadhwa saab said, cracking up with Punjabi ribaldry.

Wadhwa saab had his own scooter. But knowing Sahadevan's distaste for two-wheelers, he walked to New Delhi station with him. At Paharganj, they boarded a phut-phut for Jama Masjid. It would cost them only half a rupee per head.

Alighting from the phut-phut, they entered gate No.1 of Jama Masjid and walked through, into the alley. Kababiyan Gali was full of men with red, hennaed beards and white skull caps, and women in burqas. Child beggars, pickpockets and prostitutes lurked in corners. They heard the heart-rending bleat of a goat whose neck had just been slashed by a butcher's knife.

All the leftover food from the restaurants nearby was dropped off here. From all directions of the alley, famished humans in dirty, torn clothes converged at the rubbish heap. Old people as well as children rummaged in it. Two kids fought over a single bone that had some flesh left on it. They sifted through the rubbish, pulling out pieces of discarded parathas, butter naans, chicken and mutton bones. The next moment, they were joined by cattle and birds of prey. When the children tried to pelt stones at the eagles, the birds attacked with pointed beaks. Humans, animals and birds fought over every scrap of chapati.

One religion and one caste for the hungry man, Sahadevan mused sorrowfully.

If any tourists appeared in these alleys, hungry scarecrow-like effigies rushed towards them with outstretched hands. The tourists snapped photos of them. Along with the Taj Mahal and the Qutub Minar, abject, grinding poverty was also part of the tourist package.

Wadhwa saab was oblivious to it all and prattled on about the seekh kababs and ras malai at Karim's. In the cool sunlight of the afternoon, Jama Masjid glowed fluorescent. On its minarets, hundreds of pigeons flapped their wings. On the tallest point of the minaret, two pigeons were billing and cooing.

'I have also been to Karim's. To watch, not to eat,' Kunhikrishnan said when Sahadevan reminisced to him about that afternoon.

Kunhikrishnan had pitched the idea of publishing a series of articles on hunger and poverty in Delhi, and his editor had okayed it. Kunhikrishnan was bored with the daily routine of tearing off despatches from the teleprinter, sent by various agencies and reporters from all corners of the country, and copy-editing them at the desk. The idea of writing something different enthused him. He planned to take leave and focus on the project.

One Sunday evening, Sahadevan went to Kunhikrishnan's house in Lajpat Nagar. There were only two homes that Sahadevan visited regularly: Lalitha's and Devi's. Since he had no family of his own here, he took a special interest in Devi's. She was like a sister to him, and Sathyanathan a younger brother. As for Vidya, he thought of her in the same way as he thought of his younger sister, Shyamala. He would rush to their place when they had the littlest of problems. Devi, on her part, relied on him as the one person she could talk to openly about all her concerns and fears. That was how she ended up telling him something she was loath to discuss with anyone else.

One bitterly cold evening in January, someone had rung the doorbell at about 10.30 p.m. Sathyanathan and Vidya were already asleep. Devi had got under the razai and was lying sleepless in its warmth, thinking of Shreedharanunni. She had become a widow before she turned thirty-two. Despite the poverty and hardships, she had many memories to nurse in the loneliness of the cold nights. One of them was the memory of their trip to Sarojini Nagar to buy wool, on Shreedharanunni's bicycle. He had sung Kundan Lal Saigal's '*Soja rajkumari*' in her ears as he cycled. She lay there teary-eyed, thinking of the past. That's when the doorbell rang.

Devi switched on the light and opened the door.

A young man stood in the front yard, swaddled in woollen clothes. Two others stood on the road behind him, in the darkness. They had come by taxi. Sewa Nagar was dead to the world. The lights were off in all the houses. From Bansilal's quarters, a Mohammed Rafi song could be heard playing on Radio Ceylon. There was no sound from anywhere else.

'Who are you?' Devi asked.

'We are Malayalis,' the young man said.

'What do you want?'

The young man looked hesitant and unsure.

Devi couldn't understand what he had come for. Whether he was a Malayali or not, it was not proper for him to come at this hour and ring the bell. She didn't try to hide her irritation.

'Sathyanathan is sleeping, come tomorrow morning.'

'We've come to see you.'

'Me? For what?'

The young man didn't say anything for a while. Then, lowering his voice, he urged, 'The taxi is waiting outside. Come with us. Even if your rate is high, don't worry. We'll pay.'

Devi thought of waking Sathyanathan. He was buried under the razai, even his head wasn't visible outside. He had the strength to take on anyone. His physique was not like that of his father. He was six feet tall. But she restrained herself. Her son should not know what others thought of his mother.

'Boys, you are mistaking me for someone else. You'd better leave quickly. Otherwise, I'll call my son.' She tried to close the door.

'Don't shut the door, sister, please. We'll pay whatever you want. And we'll drop you back here in two hours.'

The two young men waiting in the shadows also came into the yard.

'You are mistaken; I'm the mother of two children.'

'What do we lack? We are Malayalis. We are ready to pay whatever you want. What else do you need? Stop acting like a Sheelavathi,' he snapped. '*Phthooo!*'

'Come with us, you slut!'

Devi latched the iron grill door of the veranda from the inside. For the first time, she wondered if it was strong enough.

Devi's eyes didn't well up easily. Citing rules and regulations, the real estate department had tried to evict her from the government quarters that had been originally allocated to Shreedharanunni. Devi had fought them tooth and nail. Since then, she had been forced to fight on numerous other occasions. She never quailed or showed any weakness. But that night, she felt destroyed from the inside. She lay weeping silently till 3 a.m.

'You should have called me. I would have taught those sons-of-bitches a lesson,' Sahadevan said.

'It doesn't bother me anymore, Sahadeva.'

Strangely, she found herself worrying about those young men. The one who had stood before her in the moonlit night was only as old as Sathyanathan. He wanted me; I am old enough to be his mother.

There must be rumours floating around about her. Otherwise they would not have approached her. They may have gone on to someone else afterwards. Perhaps to Rosily, mused Sahadevan.

After meeting Devi, Sahadevan left for Lajpat Nagar.

'Where have you been all this time, Sahadeva?'

Lalitha came into the living room, smiling. She was no longer the woman Sahadevan had known in 1971, when, laid low by fever, he had spent the night at their house. She had put on weight; there were dark circles under her eyes. Sahadevan knew her secret sorrow. She would never open up to anyone about it, not even to Devi. But Devi too knew the source of her anguish.

Although she and Kunhikrishnan had been married for over a decade, Lalitha's womb was still hungry. If someone had told her many years ago that the hunger of the womb is harder to suffer than the hunger of the stomach, she would not have believed them. But that's how she felt now. A handful of rice can take care of the stomach's hunger. The womb's hunger only causes anxiety and a sense of futility. It can make one feel as if the purpose of life has been lost. Lalitha prayed a lot, and made a lot of offerings to the deities. When she heard that there was a holy man in Rohtak who could transform barren wombs into fertile ones, she went there too.

She and Kunhikrishnan quarrelled over it.

'No holy man is going to gift us a child. The fault is mine; my sperm count is low. Godmen and holy men can't do anything about that—can they increase the count?'

'You don't know anything about Rohtak Baba. The Maharani of Saipur had a daughter thirty years after she got married. How? If Baba blesses you, you can have a child anytime. I'm going to see him.'

'You shouldn't. I don't like it. And it's against my beliefs.'

'I need a baby. I can't live without a baby.'

'Lalitha, how many times have I told you? Let's adopt a child. A beautiful little girl. We'll bring her up like our own child. So many people adopt children. Why are you so against it? Thousands of children starve to death in our country. If we take one child and give it a good life, what greater happiness can there be for us?'

'An adopted child can never be our own. However much we love it, it's still someone else's. I can't bring up another man's child.'

It was not enough for Lalitha to mother a child. She had to bring it into the world. She was aching to experience pregnancy, to watch her lower abdomen fill out, to feel exhausted by the labour pains in the tenth month, and to have her own baby girl—or, better still, a boy—emerge from her belly along with a potful of amniotic fluid and blood. And before that, like Devi, she wanted to go to Sarojini Nagar and buy balls of wool and knit a tiny sweater.

God, such a beautiful dream ...

'I'm going to see Baba.'

Kunhikrishnan thought for a while and said, 'Okay, then, go.'

'You have to come too.'

'No way.'

'How will I go alone?'

Lalitha could make it till Connaught Place. And to INA Market to buy fish. Rohtak was in another state, in Haryana. Moreover, for a trip like this, a woman has to be accompanied by her husband, she said to herself.

'You have to come,' she insisted.

'No, I won't come.'

'Heartless man.'

That was how Lalitha ended up asking Sahadevan to accompany her to Rohtak. He, who tried to be a crutch for everyone all the time, was a little taken aback at this request. However, after some reflection, he agreed. He saw it as a humanitarian task. He was providing succour to a sorrowing sister.

Baba's ashram in Rohtak was green and peaceful. He did no work apart from infertility treatment. Outside the ashram, rows of jeeps, cars, auto rickshaws and tongas were parked. Sahadevan found it hard to believe that all of these women who came here from different cities and villages, by bus and auto rickshaw, were barren.

There were women from other states too. Photographs of women and the children they'd had through divine intervention were displayed in the ashram. Some of these women were from the erstwhile royal families of North India. With eyes wide open, Lalitha dreamt that someday, amidst these, there would also be a photo of her with her son.

'Why doesn't Baba display photos of the husbands?'

'Who wants to see those worthless fellows?'

Lalitha's turn came after a two-hour wait. Baba was seated on a throne-like chair, wearing a white dhoti and shawl. Lalitha joined her hands in supplication and bent low in obeisance to him. Baba was reportedly a hundred and forty years old. With his jet-black hair and beard, and smooth, glistening forehead and nose, he didn't look like he was even forty. As she narrated her litany of woes, tears rolled down her cheeks, enough to melt any baba's heart.

'Beti, don't cry,' he consoled her. 'You will become pregnant within sixteen months from today.'

That was the prophecy of Baba. She bowed low again and joined her hands.

'Boy or girl, Baba?'

'That I'll decide when it's time.'

Baba gave her a framed photograph of himself, in colour. In those days, colour photos were rare and costly. She looked at it with awe and reverence. Baba instructed her to keep the photo in her bedroom, in a spot where it could be seen from the bed. All that you do should be done within my sight, he told her. As you reach orgasm, you should look directly at me. You should imagine that I am the one who is giving you pleasure. At that moment, your mind should be free of everyone except me. Even your husband should not be present, he explained.

Lalitha felt a shiver rise up inside her. She didn't know what to say or do. From her eyes, tears flowed in a continuous stream. She took off all the gold bangles on her hand and placed them at his feet. This pleased Baba.

'Daughter, you won't require sixteen months, you will be pregnant in twelve,' he said, giving her a rebate of four months.

All this while, Sahadevan had been waiting outside. He had wandered around the ashram and tried to make conversation with a few devotees of Baba. All the women, except Lalitha, had come with their husbands. Among them were wealthy landowners and some political leaders.

Lalitha came out and stood holding the oblation and the photo Baba had given her close to her chest. She seemed lost in some fantasy world.

'What did he say, Lalitha?'

'I'll become a mother. You'll see, Sahadeva. If Baba says so, it will happen. For sure.'

When they reached the gate, Sahadevan did an about turn and marched back towards the ashram. He entered the audience hall where only women were allowed. Some people tried to hold him back. But he strode along the aisle between the rows of aggrieved women, and up to Baba's throne.

'Baba,' he called out.

'We don't need a rebate. My sister should become pregnant within sixteen months. If not, I'll come and take back all the gold bangles. They were bought with money earned by a poor journalist who spends every night in front of a teleprinter.'

When he returned to Lalitha, she was still in a trance, a kind of hypnotic daze.

He was silent during the journey back. But he was solicitous about her needs. When she was thirsty, he brought her jal jeera. When she was hungry, he bought bread pakoda and tea.

'Thanks, Sahadeva,' said Kunhikrishnan, when they reached home.

Kunhikrishnan and Sahadevan had done the same thing: they had enabled something they didn't believe in. For many days after that, Sahadevan could not look Lalitha in the eye. She had no such qualms. Her mind was filled with thoughts of Rohtak Baba and the baby she was going to have with his blessings.

'All the women who met Baba were in a trance,' Sahadevan told Kunhikrishnan.

The night Lalitha returned from Baba's ashram, she became a personification of desire. She left the light on so she could look at Baba's photograph on the wall. The thought of making love in the brightness of a sixty-watt bulb cooled Kunhikrishnan's ardour somewhat. Even more deflating was the Eastman color stare of Baba. Later, when she was asleep, he saw her eyelids and the skin on her cheeks twitch as she dreamed. He didn't know that it was Baba who filled her mind.

Kunhikrishnan sat before his Remington typewriter and continued his conversation with Sahadevan about poverty and hunger.

'We should think about the poverty in India in two parts—poverty before Independence and poverty after Independence. They are not the same. The pre-Independence poverty was created by the local rulers and colonialists. Religion also had a part to play in it. Look at Kashi and Rishikesh. They are crawling with beggars, amputees and starving humans ... like ants. Even the places of worship and the prayer halls have been colonised by them. It's astounding that India has so many starving people. Dear Sahadeva, someday, on a Friday, go and visit the Ghantakarna temple near Purana Qila. You can see lepers on their carts, begging along an extended stretch of road.

'Now, let's forget the poverty created by this alliance of local rulers, colonialists—and religion. We had no control over that. But we cannot say the same about post-Independence poverty. Someone has to take the responsibility for that. But who? A quarter century has passed since we won Independence. What has the government done to remove poverty and hunger? Zilch. The number of poor people who are starving has only increased. The responsibility for that should rest with the government which was elected to power by the citizens. That is, the Nehru family, which has been governing independent India for a quarter century ...'

Kunhikrishnan stopped speaking and went back to typing.

The sixteen months stipulated by Baba had gone by. As Sahadevan and Kunhikrishnan had expected, nothing happened.

'Let's adopt a child.'

'No,' she snarled. 'If you can't produce one, I'd rather live like this forever.'

Kunhikrishnan sympathised with her. At the same time, he did not feel any guilt. According to him, men were born with many shortcomings. If he was supposed to feel guilty, what about Shreedharanunni? He had presented Devi with widowhood at the age of thirty-two. But then, Kunhikrishnan was not into comparative studies or calculations. He believed that human life transcends all such things. He trusted in an ideology. His dream was the eventual realisation of that ideology.

'Sahadeva, I've made arrowroot payasam with bananas and jaggery, would you like some?'

Sahadevan left before dusk for his Jangpura residence after having the payasam. Work on his novel had been languishing for many days. I'll write something tonight, he promised himself.

3

THE NAKED POOR

What was Rosily's real name? Or was it possible that she didn't have a real name? Even if they have nothing to eat and drink, or a place to sleep, every Indian has a name of his or her own. Not abbreviated names, but lengthy ones. The long names of gods, emperors or prophets. Rosily also had a name of her own—it was Rosakutty. How did Rosakutty turn into Rosily? There was a story behind that too.

In the Delhi of 1975, only famous people like Indiraji and Sanjayji had stories attached to them. The city itself was about unending stories. But most of its residents did not have a story worth telling. What kind of history was available to a poor girl from Kerala's hill district, who had come to the capital to earn enough money for her dowry?

When Rosily arrived in Delhi, she was not yet nineteen. She had waited for some time after finishing school, but it was a futile wait. Her father, Pathrosekutty, didn't have money to buy even silver, let alone gold. Jomon's father was not amenable to an alliance unless there was gold in the picture. So, she decided to make some money all by herself, and set about exploring ways to do that.

It was in the early seventies that a new kind of restaurant opened in South Extension; it was called Shagufa. They used to have jam sessions in the mornings. A band from Goa would perform on the drums, saxophone and clarinet till lunch time. The cabaret started at 8 p.m. The dancers were also from Goa. Shagufa was the first restaurant in Delhi where middle-class men could watch a cabaret while dining.

On 24 December, there was a Christmas Special cabaret and dinner on offer at Shagufa. Photographs of the cabaret dancers were displayed in front of the restaurant. The men passing by, irrespective of age, cast furtive glances at them. A few sighed deeply. Some fled, abashed.

No one had any objection to making the girls strip on the holy night of Lord Jesus's birth. It was because Lord Jesus was a Christian. If he was Hindu, the glass panes of the restaurant would have been shattered, Sahadevan assured himself. The plates filled with matar pulao and tandoori chicken would have been thrown out.

One could get to South Extension from Sewa Nagar in fifteen to twenty minutes via the village of Kotla Mubarakpur. When Sahadevan had first arrived in Delhi, it was a city of villages. The villagers used to grow crops, breed buffaloes and engage in small-time trade. During the summer, they peddled clay water pots on their donkeys. During Diwali, they sold earthen lamps. When Holi arrived, they sold water-guns and coloured powders. During Dussehra, they went about with bows and arrows for demolishing Ravana. It was quite likely that they were ignorant of much that was happening outside their immediate world: India winning freedom, Gandhiji falling prey to an assassin's bullets, Indira Gandhi becoming the prime minister. Maybe they were unaware of Yuri Gagarin orbiting the earth and Neil Armstrong landing on the moon. They had lived in villages like Rajokri and Najafgarh for hundreds of years, bathing and milking their buffaloes, sowing and reaping wheat, and celebrating Holi and Diwali.

On Christmas Eve, Sahadevan went to Sewa Nagar to meet Devi and her children. He had two days off.

When he reached there, he found that all was going well. No new problem had raised its head. There were no fresh anxieties or sorrows to deal with.

'Deviyechi, I'm leaving,' he said to her, relieved.

'What's the hurry, Sahadeva? Sit for a while and talk to the children.'

'I have some work.'

'You always have work. You are busier than Indira Gandhi.'

He laughed. What did Devi know of a bachelor's tangled life?

Every morning, as soon as he woke up, he needed a cup of tea. Only then could he get started. That morning, he had poured kerosene in the stove, pumped it, then fired it up and put the water on to boil, with milk. When he opened the Horlicks bottle in which he stored sugar, it was crawling with ants. Dejected, he sat on the floor of the veranda for a while. Then he left the house and had to wait outside Chandni restaurant until it opened ...

'Have some tea and go.'

'What's for breakfast?'

'Upma. If you want, I can make two chapatis for you.'

'Is there some vegetable curry?'

'There's brinjal curry from last night.'

He had started to leave, but now he came back in and sat down. Vidya came and stood next to him.

'Will you tell me a story, etta?'

'Once upon a time, there was a Kungkiyamma who used to make appams,' he began immediately. 'Her appams were legendary, not just in this world, but in heaven as well.'

'What does legendary mean? Can't you tell me the story in Hindi?'

'Don't be silly, edi. We are Malayalis. We should tell our stories in Malayalam,' Sathyanathan chided his young sister.

At home, Vidya always spoke in Hindi. Or Malayalam mixed with Hindi. Sathyanathan, on the other hand, spoke in chaste Malayalam.

By the time Sahadevan was through with the story of Kungkiyamma, upma, steamed bananas and tea were ready. Happy after the meal, he lit a Charminar, exhaled, and stepped out.

He walked to South Extension through Kotla Mubarakpur. By the time he arrived, he was beginning to feel a bit despondent. The pleasures of a good breakfast and a story-telling session had dissipated completely.

The alleys that he walked through had women and children lined up on either side, defecating. There was the bracing smell of fresh, steaming shit everywhere. What he could have done was make some casual remark and walk on. One needs a little humour to counter the harsh realities of the city. But Sahadevan was not that kind of man. As he walked along, the shabbily dressed village women squatting on the ground with beer bottles filled with water next to them, didn't even acknowledge his presence. He remembered the day he had gone to Dasappan's house, when the sight of tongawalla Lallu's wife bathing stark naked on the road outside had similarly shocked him. Hunger could trigger indifference, he knew. But was this indifference that he was witnessing? You don't give us a roof over our head or a couple of chapatis when we are hungry, so now agonise over the sight of our emaciated nakedness—that was the kind of statement the villagers were making, thought Sahadevan. The open, unabashed display of nakedness by men and women shitting by the side of the railway lines, the alleys and dirty pools of water, in any open space, was but the defiance of the poor.

Sahadevan kept walking, talking to himself.

He had been following the rise of nudity as a language of protest and defiance in Europe. They called it 'streaking'. Taking off their clothes, people streaked through football stadiums and busy streets. The heroes and heroines of Jean-Luc Godard and Alain Robbe-Grillet appeared in their movies stark naked. Were they also poor? Yes, he said to himself, nodding his head. The only difference was that their hunger did not manifest in their alimentary canal but in their brains. Hunger, whether of the alimentary canal or the brain, is hunger.

What about Rosily, aka Rosakutty? Wasn't she the naked queen of Christmas Eve?

He imagined her bathing with Rexona soap, using strongly scented Tata hair oil to style her hair, then dabbing Afghan Snow on her face, patting it with Lakmé talcum powder, and setting off with her handbag on her arm. Where did she go, and why?

He had to find out more about her. Why did she leave her family in a hilly district of Kerala to come to Delhi and why was she working here?

For the Christmas Eve Extravaganza, we introduce
the captivating dancer from Bombay—
Rosily!

Rosakutty, who lived in poverty and hunger in the hilly tracts of Kerala, was brought to Delhi by Georgekutty, who sold nurses' uniforms, brassieres and briefs at INA Market. He had enticed her there during his vacation in Kerala. A bottle of Hercules XXX rum for her father, fifty rupees, and a bottle of Waterbury's Compound for her mother. That was all. Enough to take Rosakutty from their midst as easily as plucking a rose.

Though her father and mother had acquiesced quite quickly, Rosakutty had been adamant. She needed money to marry Jomon, but she was not ready to go with Georgekutty for that.

'I won't come. Kill me if you want, I still won't come,' she snapped at him.

'Your father has agreed.'

'Then take my father.'

'Georgekutty, what are you taking her for? Will she be paid a salary?'

'She'll get a salary. She'll get a commission too. Be a dear, ammachi, get her to agree.'

'She is ready to come a hundred times over.'

'Do you hear, Rosakutty, what your ammachi is saying? Now, don't say you won't come.'

'No, I won't come.'

'If you won't come, you and the kids will starve to death.'

The kids were not hers. They were her father's and mother's. Rosakutty and her siblings—her three sisters and two brothers—had grown up with hunger. One day, fed up with their life of hardship and grinding poverty, Rosakutty's mother had leapt into the river from the boat. Because she was a strong swimmer, she did not die. She reached the shore by employing the crawl and the backstroke. That was the day she realised that the poor and the hungry ought not to learn swimming.

'No one will come to marry you. Who's going to marry Pathrosekutty's daughter?'

Rosakutty remained silent.

She broke her silence by transforming herself into Rosily.

From the time she was twelve and reading serialised novels in the magazines, a boy had crept into her heart. Jomon worked in the rubber estate across the river. He went to work in a boat. He was six years older than her.

On moonlit nights, when the wavelets stirred by the cool breeze turned into golden folds in the river, she would sit with Jomon on the boat. One night, the moon had not risen and it was dark on the bank; under the starlit sky, they sat close, leaning against the side of the boat. Their hearts heavy with the sorrow of the impending separation, they remained silent for a long time.

'Will you forget me?'

'Till this earth is here, I won't forget you, Rosakutty.'

'Swear upon your father and mother.'

'Upon my mother and upon my father, I'll never forget Rosakutty.'

'We should visit the Taj Mahal after we get married.'

Jomon embraced Rosakutty like Shah Jahan might have embraced Mumtaz.

'We'll have two children, a girl and a boy.'

She convulsed in his arms as if she were in labour.

It was Sathyanathan and not Georgekutty who narrated Rosily's story to Sahadevan. She refused to open up to anyone. Sahadevan had approached her many times, his pen lusting after her life story, greedy to suck up her life and transcribe it on paper. At first, he had broached the subject with the humility of a Dalit from Govind Puri and then with the threatening bluster of a brahmin from Arya Samaj Road. But she wouldn't utter a word.

What did a life story even mean to Rosily? For those with no life, what story remains to be told?

I'll tell you briefly. After all, Sahadevan spoke and wrote with brevity.

Rosily accompanied Georgekutty to Delhi. It was Vinod Duggal, the manager of Shagufa, who invented the name Rosily. She welcomed it with open arms.

'You should not have allowed your name to be changed, Rosakutty. Our name is our identity. Even for a hundred thousand rupees, we should not change our name.'

'In Delhi, I'm not the old Rosakutty. Isn't Rosakutty still back there, seated on the river bank, waiting for the boat? One day, I'll return home. Then I'll become Rosakutty again.'

The aroma of coffee wafted in from the kitchen. Rosily appeared with two glasses of hot coffee. The coffee powder was from the Indian Coffee House in Connaught Place. When it was stirred into boiling water, its aroma spread to the yard.

The Indian Coffee House opened in Connaught Place in 1957. It was AKG who had inaugurated it and Shreedharanunni had attended the function.

Sahadevan drank the coffee quickly before it became cold. Vasu, meditating under the neem tree, had forgotten about the glass he was holding in his hand. He was as forgetful as the proverbial salamander. Sahadevan worried that he would misplace his own life somewhere and forget it forever.

Rosily bobbed up and down inside Sahadevan's mind as if she were sitting on the boat in the river. Like Shreedharanunni and Kunhikrishnan, she too had come in search of a livelihood. But life had short-changed her and her hand was now off the tiller. Poor Rosily. One day, she would repossess and reclaim her life, and become Rosakutty again, or so he hoped.

Never lose hope, Sahadevan told himself. Hold onto life firmly and battle with one's circumstances. That's what Devi has been doing since Shreedharanunni's death. Devi should be a model for everyone. To me as well.

Goodnight.

He capped his pen.

4

THE UNWED

Sahadevan moved from Amritpuri to Jangpura after leaving Wadhwa & Sons. He needed solitude to read and write. When Uttam Singh's family came to know he was moving, there was an uproar. They couldn't believe it. For them, he was a member of their family.

'*Bewakoof, tu idhar se kyon ja raha hei? Tujhe kya kami hei idhar?*' Uttam Singh asked angrily.

'I need to be alone, sardarji.'

'Isn't it enough that you lock yourself up in your room? *Jhooth, tu jhooth bol raha hei.*'

'*Nahi beta, nahi. Mat jao,*' Gunjan bhabhi pleaded.

'Don't give us any rent. Live here for free,' Uttam Singh said.

After Uttam Singh had let go of his other two tenants after the night-time incident during the war, his income had come down. Working as a carpenter in Palam Village, his finances were in a worse state than Sahadevan's. His daughters used to clamour for new salwar-kameez and sandals and to be taken to the movies. Aware of Uttam Singh's hardships, and despite his own difficulties, Sahadevan used to pay him rent every month without fail. It was only during the war that he had fallen behind.

There was no trading during that time; Wadhwa's company had no business.

'Where should I give you salaries from? My pockets are empty. *Meri jeb bilkul khaali hai.*' Wadhwa opened his palms to express his helplessness.

When Sahadevan started living in Amritpuri, Pinky was a small child. Her complexion matched her name. A fair, roly-poly, ruddy-cheeked girl, she was big for her age. When he was young, back when he wore short pants with suspenders, Sahadevan used to put his youngest sister Shyamala on his lap and tell her stories. Now he told Pinky those same stories, in Hindi. She would sit by his side, listening, while Uttam Singh and his sardarni snored on the terrace, dead to the world. Below them, all along the street, men, women, children and old people slept on charpoys. Clay pots filled with water were kept on the compound walls, with brass tumblers atop them. During the summer, the inhabitants of Amritpuri slept on the roof or by the roadside. Even those who chose to sleep inside could be found sitting on the road, fanning themselves, late into the night.

Sahadevan would accompany Uttam Singh when he dropped Pinky to her school. The school building, with a colour picture of Guru Nanak Singh at its entrance, was very old. Its front yard, bereft of trees, used to be leased out during the wedding season. With a shamiana erected in the yard, aglow with decorative lights, it became a baraat ghar.

Some days, it was Sahadevan alone who dropped her off at school. She would walk with him in her blue kameez with her hair braided in plaits on either side of her head. Spotting the shamiana in the yard, he used to tease her, 'Your wedding will take place here. And I'll bring Bhangra dancers from Punjab.'

She would laugh at that, dimpling prettily. Uttam Singh didn't even know his daughter had dimples. He didn't know how to look closely. He was a take-it-all-in-one-look sort of person.

'Bhaiya, does everyone get married when they grow up?'

'Yes, beti.'

'Then why isn't bhaiyaji getting married?'

He had walked in silence, holding her hand. You don't need to know of my poverty and how I juggle with life. It's the only thing your father and I have in common—poverty. That's where both our horoscopes match.

Most of the salwar-kameez suits Pinky wore had been bought by him. The clips she wore in her hair and the colourful bangles on her wrist were also gifts from him.

As Sahadevan left with his box, bedding and books, Pinky sobbed uncontrollably. She could not contain her anguish. For two days, she did not eat. She was no longer the child he used to entertain with stories; she was a grown-up girl.

'I don't need food anymore. I won't go to school either,' she declared angrily.

Uttam Singh was pleased that Sahadevan was starting his own business. Like every carpenter, he too dreamt of owning a furniture shop of his own. 'How else am I going to get my daughters married? Who will give me money for the dowry?' he used to tell Sahadevan.

As he said his goodbyes, Sahadevan consoled Pinky and told her he would come often to see her. But that was not enough to alleviate her anger and grief.

Sahadevan kept his promise. He went back very often to meet Uttam Singh and his family, with a gift of apples or a kilo of soan papdi. On one of those visits, he saw Gunjan bhabhi applying mustard oil to Jaswinder's flowing tresses, running her fingers through them to untangle the knots. It was a winter's day and the sun's rays were cool on the ground. Wheat lay scattered and drying on a piece of cloth spread on the charpoy. When it dried, Gunjan bhabhi would take it to the mill to have it ground. Earlier, their relatives in Gurdaspur and Faridkot used to bring them sacks full of wheat grown and threshed locally, along with aroma-rich cow's ghee. Gurcharan Singh used to come from Faridkot with a canister full of sugarcane juice. Now, they came empty-handed, and every time they visited, it meant more expenses for Uttam Singh, for the guests could not be hosted without chicken and brandy. On Guru Purnima every year, Uttam Singh's house would be filled with sardars and their families from Punjab.

'*Bhabhiji, kaisi hain aap? Sab theek hai na?*' Sahadevan shooed away a brace of pigeons which had swooped down to peck at the wheat.

'Is this wheat from the ration shop?'

'Who else will give us wheat? We don't sow or reap any more. Those were the good old days. Now everything is lost. Except penury.'

Sahadevan could see that Gunjan bhabhi was reliving old memories of a carefree childhood spent frolicking in the wheat fields, playing hide-and-seek amidst the tall sugarcane, and herding the cows home. Now she had to pay money to get wheat from the shop.

The sardarni combed her daughter's richly oiled hair with her fingers and tied it up tightly. Sunlight fell on the glorious knot of hair and made it glisten. Jaswinder's femininity was in full bloom. Her wheat-complexioned cheeks and arms were full and round. Her eyes flashed like lightning. When she stood up after the ritual oiling, Sahadevan felt as if the whole earth had risen.

Uttam Singh's and his wife's hearts ached when they looked at their eldest daughter. They were losing sleep over her. Sardarni was even loath to go out of the house. The questions shot at them by their neighbours pierced their hearts like arrows.

'Your Baba can't do anything. After all, he is just a carpenter. You go and find a man for yourself. Go, seduce someone. Doesn't matter if he's blind. Get away from here.'

The sardarni's words were like harpoons that stabbed Uttam Singh where it hurt. Everyone got their daughters married when they came of age. Not just carpenters, but also people who roped charpoys; those who lead-plated copper vessels; those who sold ice-water in summer and groundnuts during winter; rickshaw-pullers; tonga-drivers; hawkers who sold moth-eaten books on the pavements of Daryaganj; even the used army uniform seller at Turkman Gate from whom Vasava Panicker had bought his thick khaki shirt. Uttam Singh couldn't do it because he was honest. He didn't know how to cheat or inveigle.

He had only one weakness—chicken. Some days, when there was no money to buy chicken and he was unable to control his craving, Uttam Singh set off for Jama Masjid. The biggest abattoirs and meat shops of Delhi were here. Heads of dead goats were arrayed in every shop, staring at passers-by with fixed, unblinking eyes. Apart from that, there were heaps of offal—head, spleen, liver and kidneys of goats dumped together. Those who couldn't afford goat meat bought the heads and cooked them with garam masala.

Uttam Singh preferred the taste of chicken. Unfortunately, unlike goats, chicken don't have big heads. In the chicken shops, there were heaps of chicken shank and feet. Uttam Singh hunted among the chicken feet with their curved toes and picked those with some flesh left on them. For three rupees, he got 25 shrivelled chicken feet with sharp claws. Neither his sardarni nor his daughters were willing to cook chicken feet. But that wasn't an issue. Uttam Singh heated desi ghee in a wok, stir-fried garlic, ginger, cardamom and tomato, then deposited the chicken feet in the mixture. He added coriander powder, chilli powder, salt and water, and cooked it on a low flame. He polished off the entire dish of chicken feet with the five phulkas his sardarni had made for him. He didn't leave even a tiny bit of flesh on the feet, gnawing each one clean. After letting out a satisfied burp, he relaxed on the charpoy placed in his front yard. He had only one regret then—along with the chicken-feet curry there should have been some moonshine too …

Today, Sahadevan noticed an unusual brightness on the faces of the sardarni and Jaswinder.

When she saw him, Jaswinder tossed back her well-oiled plaits and smiled at him.

'*Muh meetha karo.*'

Sardarni came up to him with barfi in a small bowl that shone from a recent buffing. She herself broke a piece off and put it in his mouth.

'What's the good news, bhabhiji?'

'*Iski shaadi pakki ho gayi.*'

Jaswinder's marriage had been fixed! Sahadevan could not believe his ears.

'*Sachch?*'

She smiled sweetly. Though he was not fond of sweets, he reached for another piece of barfi and dropped it into his mouth. It melted on his tongue and the sweetness spread in his mouth and throat. Even the air tasted sweet.

Shortly thereafter, Uttam Singh turned up at Sahadevan's home in Jangpura bearing half a kilo of sweetmeats in a gold-coloured box. It had Aggarwal Sweets, Amar Colony, written on it.

'Who's the boy?'

'He's from a good family. He runs a footwear shop in Tilak Nagar market. He has his own house too.'

To own a two-room residence in Delhi was not a small thing. What more could a carpenter's daughter hope for? Not just that, the boy had said he didn't want any dowry.

A wedding with no dowry. Sending a daughter to her sasural empty-handed ...

It was unthinkable. No self-respecting Punjabi family would send their daughter to her in-laws' house empty-handed. Just as poverty had rendered the women of Kotla shameless, it had divested Uttam Singh of self-respect.

None of Uttam Singh's relatives could believe it.

Uttam Singh was silent for some time, then he sighed and continued, 'I could not find a boy for my daughter. She had to do it herself.'

That was what her mother had demanded of her. Go, find someone! It didn't take her long to bring Joginder Singh, the footwear seller of Tilak Nagar, under her spell. When he heard the news, Uttam Singh had stood with his head bowed, mortified.

'What is your shoe size?'

She laughed. A laugh redolent with the aroma of desi ghee and whole-wheat rotis.

'I don't know.'

'Are you buying footwear for the first time?' Joginder Singh asked.

She didn't back off.

'Measure it.'

She stretched out her leg. The hem of her pastel yellow salwar rode up, revealing a slim ankle. When she bent over, the sight of her milk-white breasts nestled in her white kameez caused Joginder to miss his step. And that was it. He didn't betray his lack of control, however. He assumed a grave expression. A young Sikh who would not quail before a sword, would he bow before a mere girl? Never!

One week later, Jaswinder came back to the store. Inside the shop which was not big enough to swing a bat, she made the salesman pull out chappal after chappal. She tried on some of them, then decided she liked the one with thin black straps and a blue flower where the straps met. Sitting behind the cash counter, Joginder cast sidelong glances at her.

On Monday, when Tilak Nagar Market remained closed, Jaswinder and Joginder went for a noon show at Delite Talkies in Old Delhi and lunched on kadhai chicken and phulkas at the century-old Moti Mahal restaurant.

Uttam Singh unburdened his humiliation where he would be unobserved by others. After that, he threw himself into the arrangements for his daughter's wedding. He went to Bhatinda and Gurdaspur and took as many loans and donations as possible from his siblings there. After that, everything proceeded smoothly, without any roadblocks.

For the wedding, they followed both Hindu and Sikh traditions. Joginder Singh's forebears had been Hindus. One of them was childless and made an offering with the promise that if a child was born to him, he would be brought up as a Sikh. Sure enough, a child was born and it was a boy. His hair was left unshorn and he was brought up wearing a turban. When he was a young man, he grew a beard too.

Uttam Singh organised a grand shagun ceremony before the wedding. In the morning, he sent a platter with an offering of a coconut, almonds, sugar, and one thousand and one rupees to Joginder's house. Sardarni looked at the money and asked, 'Should we give that much?'

'Let there be no complaints.'

At the rokka ceremony preceding the shagun, Jaswinder and Joginder wore new clothes and exchanged flowers and sweetmeats. They made a vow to live as one soul in two bodies.

Earlier, Joginder's uncle and a few other relatives had come to Uttam Singh's place, to discuss the specifics of the shagun.

'We agree,' Joginder's uncle said, without looking at Uttam Singh's face. Uttam Singh knew in his heart that they did not agree at all. Joginder's uncle was wearing a sword at his waist. It seemed to be whispering to Uttam Singh that it would slice him in half.

'I cannot give anything as per the accepted custom of the community. But I shall take care that the ceremony is conducted well ...'

'We know that.'

The uncle still did not look at Uttam Singh. His hand was on the hilt of the sword.

'My daughter is a good girl. Though we are poor, I have brought her up with discipline and decorum.'

Joginder's father and uncle would not meet Uttam Singh's eyes. A marriage broker had brought an alliance where a DDA flat and a Fiat car were on offer as dowry. The marriage could not take place because of this carpenter's girl. He had won for now. But they would bring him to his knees. He would be taught a lesson.

Joginder had presented his case casually at first. But when he saw that none of his elders was amenable, he changed tack. He threatened that he would snatch his uncle's sword and slash his own throat with it. With this threat, he forced his family to accept the alliance. But the car and the flat now lost to them forever would never fade from their minds. Never.

The chura ceremony followed the shagun at Jaswinder's home. Sahadevan arrived early that day. He watched with interest as Jaswinder's uncle and aunt put red- and ivory-coloured bangles on both her hands and hung kaliras from these.

After the ceremony, Sahadevan blessed Jaswinder and headed for Kunhikrishnan's home. He and Lalitha were to leave for Kerala the next day.

Sahadevan had gifted Jaswinder a bangle that weighed a tola. He had bought it with borrowed money on which he would have to pay interest. He thought of Vanaja and Shyamala and sighed deeply. Vidya came to mind too. She didn't have any gold on her hands or ears. The small earrings she wore to school were gold plated.

On the morning of the wedding, Sahadevan arrived at the gurdwara wearing a kurta-pyjama he had bought from Khadi Bhandar. In his pocket was a clean white handkerchief for covering his head. Though it was winter, the sun was out. All over the city, old men and stay-at-home women pulled their charpoys out and sat enjoying the sun, shelling and eating groundnuts and gossiping. By the time Sahadevan reached the gurdwara, the milni ceremony had commenced. He left his footwear outside and covered his head with the white handkerchief, then entered the Darbar Sahib. The place was full of sardars wearing colourful pagris and sardarnis in flashy salwar-kameez. Pinky was running around, her hands decorated with mehndi, much like Jaswinder's. The sevadars were fanning the holy Guru Granth Sahib with chaurs. When the shabad kirtans, the hymns from the Guru Granth Sahib sung by the ragis, ended, the anand karaj began.

Jaswinder was dressed in a bright blue lehenga. She appeared to be standing in the middle of a heaving blue ocean under the blazing sun. Her fair, shapely hands and feet were covered with mehndi. Her kohl-lined eyes danced in anticipation. Holding a sword aloft, Joginder led his bride in circumambulation of the Guru Granth Sahib.

Soon, the doli, accompanied by appropriately dolorous music played by the band, was ready to leave for the bridegroom's house. Jaswinder took a handful of rice and threw it over her shoulder in the direction of her parents. She was bidding goodbye forever to the two people who had brought her into this world and looked after her. Her hands trembled, and she whimpered.

'My daughter, this carpenter could not give you anything,' Uttam Singh lamented. 'You are so beautiful and good-natured. A girl like you should have been sent off with a DDA flat or a Fiat car. And what did I give you? One Godrej almirah, a cot I made with my own hands, and twenty-five thousand rupees. This father is ashamed, my daughter. How undignified was your wedding, my daughter.'

Sahadevan left for his residence in Jangpura soon afterwards. He was happy that Jaswinder was married, even if the wedding had been somewhat delayed. At the same time, he felt a strange sense of disquiet grow within him. He blessed her in his heart: Let only good things come to you, my dear.

5

THE PARADE OF HUNGER

On 26 January 1973, the nation celebrated its twenty-third Republic Day with great pomp.

'A Republic of Hunger'.

That was the headline of the article Kunhikrishnan wrote for his newspaper's Republic Day edition. Sahadevan tried translating it into Malayalam, but he just couldn't get it right. It doesn't matter, he consoled himself. How can there be any poetic beauty in hunger?

On 26 January 1950, our country got a unique constitution; it was the dawn of a republic of hope, Kunhikrishnan wrote. Not just Indians, but even the then British prime minister, Sir Anthony Eden, and others like Granville Austin, the American expert on the Indian Constitution, saw it as a historic manifestation of liberty and democracy. Kunhikrishnan quoted Sir Anthony Eden: 'Of all the experiments in government which have been attempted since the beginning of time, I believe that the Indian venture into parliamentary government is the most exciting. A vast subcontinent is attempting to apply to its tens and hundreds of millions, a system of free democracy which has been slowly evolved over centuries in this small island. It's a brave thing to try to do and has been so far remarkably successful. The Indian venture is not a pale imitation of our practice at home, but a magnified and multiplied reproduction on a scale we have never dreamt of. If it succeeds, its influence on Asia is incalculably for good. Whatever the outcome, we must honour those who attempt it.'

But was this really the dawn of a republic of hope, Kunhikrishnan asked, going on to describe how Adivasi children in Madhya Pradesh were driven by hunger to eat soil mixed with water. The question echoed in Sahadevan's mind too.

After a dinner of kanji and puzhukku, Sahadevan sat down to read Kunhikrishnan's article. It was a veritable map of hunger. Rivers of hunger. Forests of hunger. Villages of hunger. Cities of hunger ... When he thought of the children who had to eat soil moistened with water, his stomach churned. Half-digested kanji and puzhukku burned in his throat. He went to the sink and vomited. His nose and mouth felt as if they were on fire. With his eyes closed, he stuck his head under the tap and let the water run over his head.

That night, dense black rainclouds hung over the city. The little imps must have travelled from the neighbouring states of Uttar Pradesh, Rajasthan and Haryana to witness the Republic Day celebrations. Groups of villagers on their way to Rajpath had begun to trickle in the previous evening. They had started a day earlier in order to occupy the front rows. At the India Gate lawns, under the open skies, it was freezing cold. Many of the women, children and old folk had wrapped themselves in blankets which had holes. On their heads, they carried bronze and earthen vessels filled with foodstuff for that night and the next day. Many of the young men were carrying charpoys to sleep on. Old men were carrying hookahs. That whole night, unmindful of the chill, the crowd moved towards India Gate, in the heart of the city. The flow did not cease even at dawn.

If you had a pass, you could sit inside the enclosures, not far from where the VIPs were seated, and watch the parade from the shade. It was not easy to get a pass, however. Except for a journalist like Kunhikrishnan.

'Here's a pass, Lalitha. Go and see the Republic Day parade.' He had three or four passes with parking stickers. Real VIP passes.

'You are not coming?'

'Don't you know that I don't like these things?'

'For once, can't you do something for your wife's sake? It has been ten years since I came to Delhi. I'm yet to see the Republic Day parade. No one will believe me if I tell them this. I feel ashamed.'

'I haven't seen it either.'

'That's because you have decided you don't want to see it. You wouldn't face any difficulty if you were to go. You have VIP passes. The office will send you a car. Don't make excuses. This year, you have to take me. I have to see the parade. For sure.'

'It's not that I don't want to take you, Lalitha. I cannot suffer through it. That's why I'm not coming.'

'Hundreds of thousands go to India Gate to watch the parade. More than hundreds of thousands listen to the live commentary on radio. What is it that you alone can't see and stomach? You just don't like what ordinary people like.'

Kunhikrishnan replied, 'Go with Sahadevan. He'll take you.'

'Why are you always tagging me with Sahadevan? You are my husband. I'll go only with you.'

'Don't be mule-headed, Lalitha.'

But she dug in her heels. She said she would not go. She gave all the passes away to Sahadevan. And he, in turn, decided to take Vidya, Sathyanathan and Pinky to see the parade.

He took a taxi in the morning to Uttam Singh's house. People were streaming towards Janpath on foot, on cycles and on scooters. None of the shops were open. But he could see that

Dasappan had arrived early and was ready to ply his trade with his mirror hung on the jamun tree.

'What ho, Dasappa, aren't you going to watch the Republic Day parade?'

Sahadevan stuck his head out of the car window to hail Dasappan. Once every month, he went to Dasappan to have his hair cut. Each time, he would scan his face in the mirror and note every change with astonishment. His thinning hair was now sticking to his scalp. His face was fleshier, but fairer. Perhaps the skin did get lighter in chilly Delhi. There were bags under his eyes and dark rings, as though he had not slept for several days. His hairstyle was different too. He used to part it in the middle, but now it was brushed back and slicked to one side. His Adam's apple was not as prominent as it once was.

A man was sitting in front of Dasappan with his face covered in lather. A shabby cloth was tucked under his chin.

'Sir, you go and watch the parade. Today is when I can earn a few rupees.'

The previous Republic Day, Dasappan had shaved the faces of seventeen villagers. They liked to be spruced up and have Himalaya Snow cream applied to their faces for that special glow as they watched the parade. He hoped to make it twenty this year.

The taxi turned towards Uttam Singh's house in Amritpuri. Pinky was waiting for him, all dressed up and ready to leave. On her feet were sandals with red and black straps and high heels. Where the straps joined, there was a flower with five petals. With Jaswinder's marriage to Joginder, Uttam Singh's footwear-poverty at least had ended. He went to work wearing the kind of shoes that college-going boys favoured. Once, while passing through Tilak Nagar in a bus, Sahadevan had seen Jaswinder sitting behind the counter in Joginder's shop. If he had gone into the store, Jaswinder would no doubt have given him a bag full of footwear too.

'We should marry off our Pinky to a ration shop owner, then we'll get rice, wheat and desi ghee to our hearts' content,' Uttam Singh said one day, after coming home sozzled.

The poor carpenter was finding his nirvana in chicken and army supply rum. If he didn't have enough money for rum, he looked for moonshine.

Gunjan bhabhi gave Sahadevan a tall glass of hot, steaming milk boiled with sugar and cardamom. She was always trying to fatten him up. If he'd had the physique of a sardar, unshorn hair and beard, and a turban on his head, she might even have given her daughter in marriage to him, the vast difference in their age notwithstanding.

After picking up Pinky, Sahadevan headed for Sewa Nagar. He had to pick up Vidya and Sathyanathan next. Devi was dusting the windows and walls of the veranda using a broom, her nose and mouth covered with a piece of cloth torn from an old petticoat. Dust flew up wherever she touched her broom. Only on holidays did she have time to clean the house. Sahadevan could see the grey strands glinting in her hair. Time was passing swiftly.

'Come, Vidya, hurry, we have to leave. Where is Sathyanathan?' Sahadevan asked as he got down from the taxi.

'Don't come in. The place is full of dust, your clothes will get dirty.'

Sahadevan was dressed in a kurta-pyjama he had bought at Khadi Bhandar. As Republic Day drew close, Khadi Bhandar usually saw big crowds drawn by the forty to fifty per cent discount.

'Sathyanathan left early in the morning with his friends,' Devi said. 'Who's in the car, Sahadeva?'

'It's me,' Pinky said, getting out of the car and running in. 'Where is Vidya didi?'

Pinky was bursting with eagerness to show off her midi and sandals to Vidya.

Vidya emerged from the house wearing a white salwar-kameez and pale yellow dupatta. She was not a fashionable girl.

Her classmates used to make fun of her dowdiness and call her Vidya aunty. She was not good at studies either. But she was the most beautiful girl in her class.

'Vidya, come. Let's go. If we get there late, we won't get seats,' Sahadevan said. 'Deviyechi, there's going to be a big crowd. I don't know why everyone is so enthusiastic about the parade this year.'

Was the Republic Day in Delhi turning patriotism into a carnival?

People from the government quarters in Sewa Nagar were moving towards India Gate with their children and foodstuff.

'I'm going with a friend. Sahadevettan can drop me in front of the zoo. She'll be waiting for me there.'

'How will you come back, Vidya?' Devi asked her anxiously. The crowds would be so intense that if you threw some sand into the air, the grains wouldn't reach the ground. If someone got separated from their companions, they would not be able to find them again. It was usual for children to get lost at the parade.

'My friend has a car.'

The daughter of a peon in the Secretariat has a friend who has a car. Devi sighed.

'Why can't you put some powder on your face?'

'This is enough, amma.'

She didn't use talcum powder. She didn't even wear the watch Sahadevan had bought for her. Both her children were like that. Perhaps they were only too aware of the fact that they were fatherless children.

'Sahadeva, you must have lunch with us. I've managed to get some dried prawns from Gol Market. Lalitha gave me some jackfruit seeds. I'll be making dried prawns and jackfruit-seed curry.'

A real meal with dried prawns and jackfruit-seed curry. Could Republic Day be celebrated more joyously?

Sahadevan agreed with alacrity.

The dust raised by army vehicles on their way to Rajpath lingered like mini clouds above the roads.

Vidya got off at the bus stop in front of the zoo. Though no buses were running, there were large groups of people moving about. Sahadevan looked out of the window and saw Vidya walking up to a boy in a blue pullover. They disappeared into the crowd.

Not bad, Vidya! Sahadevan observed to himself.

They let go of the taxi in front of the Supreme Court building, which was shaped like a weighing scale. Holding Pinky's hand, he made his way through the ocean of human beings headed towards India Gate. The pavements were colonised by hawkers selling balloons, peanuts, bananas, jal jeera, aloo chaat and golgappa.

By the time Sahadevan and Pinky reached the outer circle of India Gate, Prime Minister Indira Gandhi was offering flowers at the Amar Jawan Jyoti, the memorial for the unknown soldier, where the flame burned eternal. This was followed by two minutes of silence.

It was a struggle to reach the VIP enclosure, like crossing the Yamuna during high tide. Sahadevan and Pinky managed to find seats behind the journalists, senior officers and party leaders who were already seated inside.

'There, look, look … Indiraji.'

Pinky was an ardent admirer of the prime minister. She watched wide-eyed as Indira Gandhi stepped down to receive the President of India and the chief guest, Mobotu Sese Seko. Sahadevan remembered that the chief guest for the previous year's Republic Day parade had been Seewoosagur Ramgoolam, the prime minister of Mauritius. It had been only one month since the war ended. The citizens of Delhi had not yet recovered from it.

The parade mainly had war memorials wrought in iron and steel. When the Gnat fighters that Flight Lieutenant

R. Massey and Flying Officer D. Lazarus had used to destroy Pakistan's F-86 Sabre fighters in the air rolled down Rajpath, Pinky clapped her hands vigorously, forgetting where she was. It was, after all, Sikh blood that coursed through her tender veins. As the endless procession of tanks, cannons and fighter planes continued, the spectators applauded with a keen patriotism. Sahadevan imagined he could smell blood in the air. The day's festivities ended with a flypast by fighter jets that made the ground tremble.

That day, Sahadevan asked himself a question: While people like Kunhikrishnan contemplate and write about issues like hunger, what are you doing? You feckless man, you took your friend's wife to meet a godman. And now you have brought Uttam Singh's daughter to watch the Republic Day carnival. Is this what you should be doing? Can't you also live an expansive, purposeful life? Can't you spend your time doing something creative and meaningful?

He had forgotten that he was writing a novel. And God didn't bother to remind him either. After the war, ten million refugees had entered India. God's eyes must be on those miserable humans wracked by illness and poverty, Sahadevan told himself. They can't be looking at my novel. Sahadevan knew that when great human tragedies were taking place elsewhere, a half-baked novel by someone as insignificant as him had no relevance. His life, like his novel, was half-baked.

6

THE SIGHS OF OLD DELHI

Sahadevan was running a small firm of his own—V.P. Agencies. He undertook small jobs such as booking air and train tickets, arranging guides for tourists, doing import and export documentation, etc. His income was higher now than when he had been employed. But there were expenses too. He had to pay the rent for his dark, airless office room in an alley near Turkman Gate. He employed a boy to take care of the office and to help him with other things while he was dealing with Customs in Palam airport and at the cargo terminal. The boy's name was Abdul Ameen, and he lived nearby, close to the Dargah Faiz-e-Ilahi. At the end of every month, he would be tipped some money. Another big expense was the telephone. He had managed to get a telephone connection quickly with the help of Kunhikrishnan. As a journalist, he could walk into any MP's or minister's office. Sahadevan had gathered up the courage to start the firm only after Kunhikrishnan's assurance that he would help him secure a connection. Getting one was like winning a lottery. And if you had it, many kinds of businesses could be attempted.

Today, he decided, he would get a haircut before going to the office. Long hair was the fashion among young men these days.

Sathyanathan wore his hair long, and since he was tall, it looked good on him. Vasava Panicker had started growing his hair a long time back; it fell below his shoulders now. As an artist, he had the freedom to walk around in any garb, anywhere. But could Sahadevan, the owner of a new business, behave that way? If he were to grow his hair long like a hippie, what would his clients think? In any case, he had no interest in fashion.

Sahadevan had got up at 4 a.m. in the morning, made tea, and sat down to write. The newspaper was delivered at 6 a.m. Once it arrived, he couldn't concentrate on any other work. He pored over it with a fine-tooth comb, from the first to the last page. One of his sorrows was that he could not get his hands on a Malayalam newspaper every day. Even at the Kerala Club, they were usually four or five days old, having arrived late through the post.

It was as he was reading a newspaper at the Kerala Club one day that, quite accidentally, his eyes fell on a photograph and the words below it.

The face in the poorly lit photograph looked familiar. When he peered closely at it, he realised that it was none other than Vasava Panicker. There were some small differences. His hair was short and his face looked younger. Under the photo was the caption: 'Missing'. There were some details: 'This youngster is missing since 12 June 1970. If anyone has any information or sees him, contact the address given below and you will be rewarded adequately.' His father's name was given on top. Nenmada Shreekanta Panicker, Retired District Collector, Vasava Vilasam ...

Sahadevan felt as if lightning had struck his image of Vasu. In that bright light he saw Vasu walking in darkness. A collector's son ... and such a man was queuing up along with beggars for two rotis and dal at the gurdwara, unable to contain his hunger?

Sahadevan decided that he would get in touch with the retired collector. Not for the 'adequate reward'. Only to let him know that his son was living happily in Delhi and that he should not worry. But before that, he had to think a few things over. First of all, should he or should he not tell Vasu about this advertisement?

Sahadevan only ever stole one thing in his life. It was that newspaper. As he left Kerala Club after reading to his heart's content, no one noticed that he was holding a rolled-up newspaper in his hand.

From that day, Vasu was transformed in Sahadevan's eyes.

As he walked towards Dasappan, wearing an old blue shirt and a mundu torn at its selvedge, Sahadevan was thinking about that day at the Kerala Club. He had set aside this old blue shirt with missing buttons especially for wearing on haircut day. He passed by Dasappan's little corner on his way to the bus stop every day. But whenever Dasappan spotted him in the distance, wearing his blue shirt, he instantly knew he was coming for a haircut. And his unshaven, dark face would light up. Sahadevan always paid up after a haircut and never demanded credit. Dasappan knew he wouldn't have to starve that day.

'What, Dasappa, you are early today?' Sahadevan asked.

Jangpura was yet to wake up. The streets were practically deserted. Only a few school-going children could be seen. The neighbourhood had one municipal school. Only the children of poor people studied there. Looking at the faded, wrinkled and shrunken uniforms, the dishevelled, unwashed hair, and sandals worn down to only a suggestion, one could gauge their state of poverty. There were Dalits among them, daughters of sweepers and scavengers. None of them would complete their studies; their poverty would not allow them to.

'Sir, I always reach before seven o'clock,' Dasappan said. Every minute was valuable for him—it was time spent in anticipation of customers. Dasappan would see people queuing up in front of Eros Cinema. One afternoon, when he had dozed off in the warm haze of summer, he dreamt that customers were queuing up in front of him for haircuts and shaves. Worn down by the tedium of waiting for customers, he would sit beneath the jamun tree and doze off.

Every morning, the head-load workers, cart-pushers and rickshaw-pullers would set off from Jangpura for the truck-hub, timber market and vegetable market in Bhogal. If even one of them came to get a shave, Dasappan would earn enough money for a cup of tea. But those men were worse off than him. Just a glance at the head-load workers would tell you that they were going about on empty stomachs.

'Would you like to have a shave?'

'No, Dasappa, a haircut will do.'

The mirror was nailed to the jamun tree by the side of the road. In front of it was a seat made of two old softwood crates arranged one on top of the other. Between the crates and the tree was a wooden plank, held up by a stack of bricks on both sides. A pair of scissors, machine clippers, a soap stick, a brush and a towel were placed on the plank, which was grubby with congealed soap and hair. Sahadevan balanced himself with difficulty on the crate. Dasappan took the old mundu Sahadevan had brought with him and deftly wrapped it around his neck. He would not allow Dasappan to use his scruffy, dirty towel for this purpose.

Like Uttam Singh's dream of owning a furniture shop, Dasappan dreamt of starting a salon in Delhi. There would be large mirrors in the front and behind the seats. In front of the swivel-chair and under the mirror, all his implements would be arranged—scissors, hair clippers, leather strop belt, water spray bottle, V-John soap stick, lathering brush, Afghan Snow cream, Lakmé talcum powder, and the whitish alum stone used as an antiseptic after-shave. Photographs of Comrade Krishnapillai and Comrade AKG hung on the wall. Beside them, a framed photograph of Vyjayanthimala in a swimsuit, cut out from a calendar. Raj Kapoor's movie, *Sangam,* had run for months on end at Eros Cinema in Jangpura. There were huge posters of

Vyjayanthimala emerging from a swimming pool. Dasappan had been desperate to watch *Sangam*. But he mercilessly plucked out that wish too from his mind and flung it away. A man who doesn't have the means to eat wants to watch movies, he ridiculed himself.

Sahadevan sat looking at his image in the mirror, as was his habit. His face seemed to change every month. The months and the years were flying by ...

How had he spent all those years? What had he gained?

No, he calmed himself: I'm not in a mood to tote up gains and losses. Moreover, a life is not to be measured in terms of gains and losses.

Dasappan sprayed water from the bottle on his head and massaged it, reverse-cupping both hands. Sahadevan's eyes closed—what a feeling! He used to pay Dasappan five rupees for a haircut. His usual rate was two rupees.

'Sir, should I make it short?'

'No, Dasappa. Not too short.'

The scissors and comb in Dasappan's hand began their work. He used the comb to pull the hair up straight and then snipped the bits poking out between its teeth. Wet snippets of hair fell in quick succession and stuck to the old mundu that covered Sahadevan. With a slight shake of his head, Sahadevan dislodged the strands caught behind his ears.

'No one is coming to cut their hair. All the boys are walking around with long hair. I'm half-starved already; if everyone decides to grow their hair, what will we barbers do? We'll starve, that's what we'll do. Why are the youngsters growing their hair like this, sir? It's not like they don't have the money for a haircut, right? Even those travelling by cars and scooters are growing their hair. What is all this?'

'Those who are growing their hair are rebels. They want to live as they please, not according to the diktats of others.'

'Let them live any way they want, sir. As long as they don't hit us where it hurts—in our tummies.'

Dasappan's scissors, which had long lost their sharpness, continued to move in and out of Sahadevan's slick, oily hair.

'You have dandruff in your hair, sir. Squeeze out the jelly of aloe vera and apply it on your scalp, let it remain for some time before bathing, and you'll be rid of it.'

Where would he find aloe vera in Delhi? It grew luxuriantly in rings around the well back home. But that home was not in Delhi.

There were days when Dasappan would spend the whole morning waiting in the blazing sun, with his eyes peeled for a customer. Dejected, he would stay back in his room and not go to work for a few days. Sitting for long hours in his room in a dark, gloomy alley near the Nizamuddin dargah, he felt like his soul was rotting. He shared the room with two Biharis whose job was to clean the municipal drains. The drain-cleaners returned in the night with dried patches of sewage on their bodies. With their arrival, the room would reek of sewage. In the beginning, Dasappan used to retch. Now he was able to tolerate it.

The road Dasappan took in the morning to reach Jangpura was also nauseating. In every nook and corner, men and women squatted with a bottle of water in their hands. He had to thread his way between them. Shit-eating pigs waited behind the squatting forms, sniffing and waiting for them to get up and leave. These days, he didn't cover his nose. He was immune to such sights and smells.

'Dasappa, why are you suffering like this, just in order to live here? Why don't you go home? Since the Communists have come to power, the life of workers has improved. Barbers like you go to work wearing a watch around their wrist and sandals on their feet.'

Dasappan remained silent.

Sahadevan realised that he should not have asked the question. Dasappan could well ask him the same thing. Why was he struggling in Delhi? Everyone had their reasons for leaving behind their land of birth. Vasu had his reason. Rosily had hers.

'*Bas, ho gaya*.'

Dasappan put the comb and scissors down. He took the mirror off the jamun tree and handed it to Sahadevan. Sahadevan saw in it the face of a healthy man. His face and neck looked thicker with his hair trimmed. Dasappan removed the cloth from around his neck, flicked it once, folded it, then gave it back to Sahadevan.

'Dasappa, here's the money.'

'Ayyo! This is too much.'

'Keep it.'

After a breakfast of dosa with coconut chutney and tea, Sahadevan set off for Turkman Gate.

In Delhi, the realities of life pulsate not at Rajpath where the Republic Day parade takes place, or in Connaught Place which is a shopping heaven, or in Chanakya Puri with its rows of embassies and the fluttering flags of different nationalities, but in Old Delhi. The precincts of Jama Masjid crawled with people, teeming like ants in an ant-colony. One could not walk without stumbling or brushing against someone. In that throng, an old man sat, having his ear cleaned with a long needle, cotton, and some solution. For fifty paise, you could get both ears cleaned. A head massage cost fifty paise too. A whole-body massage would set you back by two rupees. As men emerged after namaz into the dark, foreboding alleys around the Jama Masjid, beggars and hawkers lay in wait for them. A crazed-looking woman limped through the crowd, dark blood clots between her legs. No one noticed her. No one gave her a scrap of cloth to cover her nakedness. A beggar without legs and arms propelled himself forward on his back, wriggling between the wheels of rickshaws and the legs of pedestrians, balancing his begging bowl on his chest.

On the pavement, a row of vendors sat ready with their lunchtime fare. The yellow-tinged mutton-rice inside big copper pots was covered with flies. Mutton-rice or fly-coated rice? A man with a henna-coloured beard stood eating his rice from an aluminium plate, watched hungrily by a beggar. Once he had sucked out all the marrow from the bones, he discarded them into the waiting hands of the beggar, who gnawed hungrily at the bits of flesh still left on them. A child was caught pickpocketing someone and was flung to the ground. The crowd began to kick him in his chest and stomach. Blood spurted from his nose. His howls of pain set the hearts of the doves on the minaret of Jama Masjid aflutter with fear ...

These were daily sights for Sahadevan. Each day, they underscored his certainty that he was indeed a citizen of independent India.

His workload was light that day. Three or four bills of lading had to be readied, and he had to go to Chawri Bazaar to collect a payment. He went out again, leaving Abdul Ameen to take care of the office. He could have sent Ameen to collect the payment, but he liked his solitary walks. He used to pray to God that nothing should ever happen to his legs and that he should never be paralysed by a stroke or in an accident.

It was then that he saw Vidya passing by in a cycle rickshaw.

Was it Vidya? He was suddenly uncertain. She had no reason to come to Old Delhi. But he couldn't possibly have made a mistake—every chapter of her growth was etched in his mind.

'If I didn't commit suicide even when I was fed up with life, it was only because I worried about my children,' Devi used to tell him. The children would never do anything to hurt their mother or to make her sad. They never troubled her or demanded new clothes or footwear. Sahadevan knew all this better than anyone else.

The rickshaw was stuck in a sea of tongas, handcarts and pedestrians, unable to move forward or reverse. He pushed his way through to it. Inside the rickshaw, a boy sat next to Vidya. He had long hair and sideburns. His left hand rested on her shoulder.

When the rickshaw started moving, he followed it. It headed towards Red Fort. The driver swerved suddenly to one side and the boy pulled her close. Sahadevan could see only part of his face, but it was enough for him to know that he was not a Malayali. After leaving Chandni Chowk, the rickshaw forged ahead. He saw them getting off in front of the tall gate under the arched portals of Red Fort. He saw them strolling hand in hand near the tall red wall, standing where Pandit Nehru addressed the nation on every Independence Day. He stood at a distance, watching them walk away and become shadows. Eventually, they disappeared from his sight.

He was distraught all through that day and night. He knew that Devi could not keep an eye on Vidya. Was God entrusting him with that charge then?

Vasu.

Vidya.

Worrying about them gave him sleepless nights.

7

FRIENDS AND REFUGEES

The refugee influx from Bangladesh which had started before the 1971 war continued after the war too. Hungry, sick and exhausted, they moved to various parts of the country through multiple entry points in the north-east. It was like the overflow of sludge and rocks that follows a landslide. Journeys that began as a flight from death turned into funeral processions of poverty and hunger.

Sahadevan saw them for the first time near the Nizamuddin dargah. The settlement lay on the route from the eastern part of Delhi to the city centre. The road from Sundar Nagar, home to the rich, to Chanakya Puri, home to diplomats, also passed through this area. Beside the road, and below the trees, they appeared as sores and grew like pustules. Little children with misshapen torsos, pale yellow skin and sunken eyes thrust their arms out at pedestrians and passing cars. Most of them were naked, and the boys were circumcised.

As he watched, a middle-aged man in a pristine white kurta-pyjama, probably on his way back from the Shiva temple on Humayun Road, with no provocation whatsoever from anyone, got down from his cycle, picked up some stones from the pavement and threw them at the children. One of the stones found its mark. It hit the thing he had aimed at—a circumcised penis. For a moment, the child stood with his mouth agape, numb like a statue. Then, convulsing in pain, he screamed and ran. The women who were cooking on makeshift stoves under the trees, using rotten fish scrounged from the rubbish bins of Jama Masjid and rice bought with money cadged through begging, started wailing too. No one could understand why the man had stoned the children.

Like in Nizamuddin, termite hills of refugee camps began to spring up all over the city.

'Why are you silent? What happened to you?' Kunhikrishnan asked him. Sahadevan had been silent for a long time. He looked as if something was stuck in his throat.

'It's something like depression. My mood is off.'

'That's because you are not getting married. You are old enough to be a father of two children,' Lalitha said.

'Are all unmarried people depressed, Lalitha?'

'Only when you are down with some ailment will you realise the importance of a woman in your life.'

Sahadevan didn't mean to remain a bachelor all his life, like V.K. Krishna Menon. But he had two younger sisters to think of. Vanaja was of a marriageable age now. Despite several years of hard work, he still had no savings. If things did not improve, both Vanaja and Shyamala would become old spinsters, greying and wrinkled. He too would grow grey and wrinkled in Delhi.

One evening, as he exited the British Council Library and started walking towards Central Secretariat Bus Terminal to take a bus to Jangpura, he saw Devi waiting for her bus. She had put on weight. More than half of her hair was grey.

Instead of going to Jangpura, he tagged along with Devi and went to Sewa Nagar.

Sitting next to each other in the bus, they talked about many things. Shreedharanunni did not come into the conversation even once. These days, even the children had little to say about their father. Two days before Shreedharanunni's death anniversary, Sathyanathan had reminded his mother, 'Shouldn't we be taking food to the orphanage, amma?'

Mother and children followed the ritual every year without fail. The day before the anniversary, Devi and Sathyanathan would go to Kotla Mubarakpur and buy potatoes, onions and green chillies. At night, the three of them would peel and dice the vegetables. Sathyanathan helped his mother knead the dough, which they left covered with a damp cloth. Early next morning, Devi would light the stove and make the potato curry. Sathyanathan and Vidya would roll the dough into thin, round pooris, which Devi would deep-fry in boiling oil. When the cooking was done, they bathed and quickly changed into fresh clothes. Sathyanathan would hail an auto, they would load the vessels containing the still-hot curry and pooris, and leave for the orphanage.

By the time the widow and her children got there, Sahadevan would be waiting with a big packet in his hand, of laddoo or jalebi. Last year, he had bought some bananas too.

The children in the orphanage would not go hungry that day.

Some days later, Sahadevan and Kunhikrishnan were walking towards the Press Club when they saw Vasu coming out of the AIFACS Art Gallery. The edges of his bell-bottom trousers swept the ground like an elephant's legs. Two buttons were missing from his shirt, which was two sizes small for him. As usual, on his shoulder was a sling bag bought at Khadi Bhandar.

'I thought you wouldn't come.'

'Who wouldn't, if they're invited to the Press Club?' Vasu said. Kunhikrishnan had invited Vasu to his home many times. But he had not visited even once. Maybe he wasn't comfortable inside a home, with a family. Wasn't that why he had cut off relations with his own parents?

The three of them walked towards the Press Club. From the time he began work as a newspaper man, Kunhikrishnan had been a member of the club. It was early still, and the place was near empty. Only after sundown would the tables get taken, as journalists from the many newspaper offices on Rafi Marg and Bahadur Shah Zafar Marg found their way there. Then, till midnight, it could get boisterous.

As soon as they sat down, Kunhikrishnan lit his pipe. Seeing that, Sahadevan took out a pack of his favourite Charminar cigarettes from his pocket.

'Do you want one, Vasu?'

'He doesn't like our Charminar, Players, etc.'

As Sahadevan and Kunhikrishnan let out puffs of smoke, as if to show solidarity with them, Vasu took out a cigarette from his bag. It was a misshapen one with bulges here and there. In some places, the paper was torn and the tobacco lay exposed. He had removed some of the tobacco, mixed it with something else and refilled the cigarette. He lit it and inhaled deeply with closed eyes before exhaling a large plume of smoke. The smell of cannabis spread through the room.

'Will she come, Vasu?'

'She said she would.'

But Vasu knew she might not turn up if she found a customer on the way.

Sahadevan couldn't help noticing that Vasu's face looked prematurely aged. Perhaps it was because of the lack of nutritious food and proper sleep. Bits of dried grass from the lawns of India Gate were trapped in his hair. His teeth were the colour of the tobacco in Charminar cigarettes.

The son of a retired district collector.

He let out a deep sigh.

'Shall I get your drinks?' Ramchand appeared with a scrap of paper and a stub of pencil in his hand.

Vodka for Kunhikrishnan and Vasu. His favourite Old Monk rum for Sahadevan.

Kunhikrishnan told him that they would order the food later. She might turn up by then.

Vasu inhaled deeply. Then he drank a mouthful of vodka, without adding water. Then another drag. Followed by another drink. Another puff. Yet another drink ...

By the time Sahadevan finished a large peg, he had started thinking in English. Wadhwa saab used to say he could speak fluently in English. Old Monk decreed that he could also think in English. His nightmares were in English; his sweetest dreams were in Malayalam.

It was dark outside, but the lights were bright inside the club. The number of empty chairs rapidly diminished. K.K. Nair, the art critic at *Hindustan Times*, walked in, his teeth clamped around a glowing cigar.

'Vasu, are you painting anything new these days?'

'Yes, I can't live without painting.'

'Where are they then, these paintings? I want to take a look at them. I haven't seen your work so far. The reviews are good.'

'Rosily also thinks highly of them.'

'So, where have you stashed them?'

Vasu laughed. He himself didn't know where his work could be found. When the weed and the vodka hit, he laughed without any reason.

'How old are you?'

'Why, are you thinking of an alliance for me?'

'I'd just like to know. Anyone can ask a man his age.'

'I don't know.'

'You don't know your own age? What nonsense!'

'I swear on my father, it's the truth. I don't know.'

'What does your father do? What's his name?'

Retired District Collector Nenmanda Shreekanta Panicker, Sahadevan thought to himself.

Vasu said nothing.

'You don't know your father's name either, Vasu?'

'Nenmanda Shreekanta Panicker,' Vasu said, as if he had suddenly remembered.

Just as Kunhikrishnan was about to say something, Rosily appeared at the door, like a bird landing on a branch. Behind her was darkness, in front were the bright electric lights of the club. She stood at the door, hesitating. A dove fluttered in her heart.

'Dee, Rosily, come here.'

Recognising the sound of Malayalam shouted aloud, some ten or twelve heads swivelled to look at Vasu. There were a lot of Malayali journalists there.

Kunhikrishnan got up.

'Come, Rosily. We were all waiting for you.'

'Should I? I've never been to such places. I don't know how to hold a conversation or anything like that.'

She stood there, nervous, looking at the long-haired journalists with their full glasses, smouldering pipes and cigars between their fingers. She was only familiar with cheap hotel rooms and barsatis that reeked of stale sweat from unwashed clothes and days-old food.

Kunhikrishnan took her by the hand and led her to their table. Nobody at the other tables paid her any attention. They were too busy chatting, drinking and smoking. That settled her nerves and made her a little less afraid.

'What will you drink?'

'A Bloody Mary.'

'You little sneak. So, you have drunk alcohol before. Right?'

She laughed uncertainly.

She wiped the salt from the rim of the glass and drank a mouthful of the tomato-coloured Bloody Mary as soon as it reached her.

'I have a complaint. Why do you always wear such brightly coloured sarees?'

'No one will look at me otherwise, chetta.'

'Why don't you stop doing this work, Rosily? I'll get you a job somewhere.'

Rosily was silent.

'Rosily doesn't like discussing her personal matters,' Vasu said. He was the closest to her in that group.

'I'm telling you this in all seriousness. You should stop doing this.'

'Have you called me all the way here to tell me this?' She was visibly annoyed.

'I'm only saying it out of concern for you.'

'I can look after myself. No one needs to interfere.'

Ramchand appeared again with his scrap of paper and pencil stub.

Kunhikrishnan ordered makki ki roti, jeera aloo and murg masala.

'Rosily likes dal makhni.'

'Okay, Vasu.'

By now, the club was full. There wasn't a single empty table. With no place to sit, men stood around drinking and talking. Occasionally, the booming laughter of K.K. Nair could be heard above the din. Star editors like Mangekar and Durga Das were also present.

Ramchand brought plates and bowls. The spicy smell of steaming hot murg masala rose into the air.

'We could have called Sathyanathan too, chetta.'

'No, he shouldn't learn to drink so soon. He has big responsibilities. He has to look after his mother and sister,' Kunhikrishnan said.

Don't I have responsibilities too? Don't I, too, have two sisters? Sahadevan asked himself.

Vasu asked for a refill of vodka. Rosily broke off a roti and ate it contentedly with dal makhni. Sitting among them, she looked happy. She was not alone in Delhi.

When she got up to leave, it was past 9.30 p.m.

'I have to go.'

'What's the hurry? I'll drop you off in a taxi.'

'No, chetta. I have a customer,' she said nonchalantly.

'Can't you not do it, this one day?'

The only day in the week that she refused to work was Sunday. She would bathe in the morning and, wearing a colourless saree and blouse, set off for the Sacred Heart Cathedral on Bhai Vir Singh Marg. She didn't socialise with the other Malayalis there. Most of them thought she was from Goa and would make comments about her in Malayalam.

After Rosily left the club, the men continued talking. The most voluble among them was Vasu. At one point, he started to sing. When the others shushed him with fingers on their lips, he quietened down.

Smoking weed did not make Vasu garrulous. But when he drank vodka or rum in excess, he would start singing.

When they stepped out into the cold at 11 p.m., a thin hand stretched out from under the darkness of a tree in front of the Press Club. The young woman was holding a circumcised child. Sahadevan took out all the money he could find in his pocket and dropped it into her outstretched palm. Then he walked on to the taxi stand in the company of Kunhikrishnan and Vasu.

8

LETTERS FROM HOME

A letter arrived from Vanaja.

It had been a long time since he went home. The last time was when his father was on his deathbed. He had reached home after an exhausting journey, barely making it before his father died. He had travelled without a reservation, alternating between sitting and standing for three days. By the time he reached home, both his ankles were swollen with oedema.

'I'm leaving. At least there's one less person to spend on now,' his father said as soon as he saw Sahadevan.

He did not understand why his father said that, but the words remained stuck in his heart like hooks.

Sahadevan would have liked to go home once every year. At the start of the thirayutsavam season in the Mundiyattu kaavu near his house, he would become restless. Even while walking in broad daylight on Delhi's streets, he would hear the bells on the anklets of the chaamundi theyyam. He would feel the heat from the flambeaus in the hands and around the waist of the ghantakarnan. Only the paucity of funds held him back from getting on the train. But he managed to send money for new clothes to his parents and sisters before the festival flag was raised in the kaavu—that was one thing he never failed to do.

The postal authorities had recently installed a post box near Muttanparambu Lower Primary School. Vanaja was the one who wrote long, detailed letters to him. Shyamala wrote too, but rarely. More often than not, she added a postscript to her sister's letter: 'Hope etten is keeping well. Amma says you should drink your milk every day without fail' or something like that. Vanaja's letters were as beautiful as her handwriting. She described in detail all the news at home and in their locality. But she never wrote about herself. Her letters always gave the impression that she lived a happy life, ensconced in comfort and with all possible conveniences. She wrote about others' trials and tribulations. But she was missing in her own letters.

Yesterday, a long letter from her had arrived. He put it in his pocket while leaving for work so that he could read it later, at leisure. When he returned, there was one more letter in the letterbox.

> Brother,
>
> I am no longer of a marriagable age. How come you, who always worry your head off over other people's problems, do not think about me? Should I not give birth to a child? Should I not become a wife and a mother?

He could not read any more. He felt like a bomb had exploded in his hands. Once he got over the initial bewilderment, he tried telling himself that someone was playing a prank on him. But how could he not recognise Vanaja's handwriting? He sat numb for a long time.

On his deathbed, his father had said, 'One less person to spend on.'

Now his younger sister had sent this letter.

Where had he gone wrong? Not just that night, but for many nights after, he found it hard to fall asleep. Something had happened to Vanaja. The letter was uncharacteristic of her, and it frightened him. He considered taking the next train home.

But his common sense stopped him. He must practise patience. He had to learn what was in her heart, slowly, ever so slowly, he told himself.

He could have told Vanaja—I'm turning thirty-six; shouldn't I become a husband and a father? Why are you all not on my case? But Sahadevan was not the argumentative type. He would never seek answers to his problems from others. He believed that one should find them all by oneself. A notion that was reinforced by some of the books on Western philosophy that he had read recently.

He read the letter again and again, whenever he was on a bus, and even while walking. Something must be hidden between those words and lines. He tried to get to the root of it—to discover the new Vanaja, the one who had undergone such a sea change.

After three or four days, he wrote back:

> I have not forgotten. You are always on my mind. It looks as if there is no end to my deprivations. That is the only reason for the delay. Anyway, before it's too late, both of us could start a new life. You as someone's wife and I as someone's husband. Then, if God wills it, you will become a mother and I, a father.

After this, his primary priority became money. He had changed jobs. He had started his own business. But nothing seemed to bring an end to his state of poverty.

Gradually, he calmed down. He bought a second-hand copy of Simone de Beauvoir's *The Second Sex* from a used-books seller in the Sunday market at Daryaganj for five rupees. The new paperback edition cost thirty rupees. The cover was a bit shabby, but otherwise, the book was in good condition. On the first page was a long but indecipherable signature in green ink. The pages still had the smell of a new book. The very next day, he sent it by registered post to Vanaja.

A few months passed. He didn't visit Uttam Singh on Guru Purnima because he couldn't afford to buy a gift for Pinky. He was squirrelling away every paisa for Vanaja. He knew that if he continued to save like he had been doing till now, he wouldn't be able to get her married before she touched sixty.

It was at this time that Rosily made her entry into his mind, thanks to Sathyanathan. Sahadevan was exhausted from carrying the burden of so many people. Yet, the doors of his mind would not slam shut. They remained open, always, and anyone was free to enter. Devi and her children had been parked there for a long time. Vasu had also found a spot. And now, Rosily.

Sahadevan was returning from Jangpura after visiting Kunhikrishnan and Lalitha. He visited them at least once a week, to make sure all was well. If they didn't see him for a week, they would call his office to speak to him. Devi would also call from her office. Lalitha had a telephone at home. She didn't have to bother about the bill either; it was paid by Kunhikrishnan's office.

Kunhikrishnan was no longer satisfied with his work at the newspaper. His series on poverty had triggered a lot of criticism. Even the editor who had approved it was in a bit of a spot. He now looked at Kunhikrishnan as if he was the wrongdoer. Kunhikrishnan's liberties had been curtailed. An article he had written, critiquing the Nehru dynasty, was rejected by the editor.

Yet, he worked hard and was engaged all twenty-four hours. Lalitha became increasingly lonely at home. Though she had paid obeisance to many godmen and saints since the encounter with Rohtak Baba, her wish for a child remained unfulfilled.

Kunhikrishnan often wondered why he had such a low sperm count. He was a creative person. His reports on party politics and the financial bill presented in the Lower House read like poetry. Even his speech was creative. While smoking, he blew smoke rings with exquisite ease. Like some super god, he blew planets and satellites into existence. How could it be that in the case of Lalitha alone, he was unable to be creative? The nights were barren. On chilly nights, lying under the razai beside her, he was assailed by a sense of futility. He was frustrated both at home and at work. He should change his job. He should adopt a child. Only then could he get his life working again and back on track, repaired, maintained, oiled and greased.

'Even if you kill me, I won't allow it,' Lalitha had said.

To be honest, he had no great regrets about living a childless life. It was her unhappiness that caused him to be unhappy.

In October, at the beginning of the Durga Puja season, into the cool, sunlit air redolent with the fragrance of frankincense and flowers, unexpectedly, rain began to fall. Hailstones lay scattered on the ground. They brought down the purple jamun from the spreading branches of the tree which stood near the gate and both fruit and hailstones tumbled down into the yard. Standing on the veranda, Sahadevan drank in the sight. Lalitha bunched up her saree pallu and ran into the yard to gather up the hailstones and the jamun. 'Ayyo, my hands are frozen numb, Sahadeva!' She threw down the hailstones and shook her hands vigorously. Sitting on the veranda, Lalitha and Sahadevan let the cold jamuns melt slowly in their mouths. All this while, Kunhikrishnan sat inside, clacking away on his Remington typewriter.

As Sahadevan walked towards the bus stop after crossing the Ring Road, he saw Sathyanathan cycling down Shaheed Mohan Dutta Road. Sathyanathan bicycled everywhere, except to college. A belief was growing in him that once he mounted his father's old bicycle, it would take him to his destination without straying. With age, the rear rim of the cycle had started to go out of shape. He had got it repaired. He changed the worn-out tyres for new ones. Now, even though it looked old, it was still robust. All these expenses were met with money he earned teaching classes in social sciences and economics, thrice a week, to students at the tuition centre on Feroze Gandhi Road.

He ran into Sahadevan just as he was heading towards Govind Puri after classes.

'Where are you going? Are you going to Lalitha's place? I'm coming from there.'

'I'm going to Govind Puri.'

'To Govind Puri? Why?'

The place was known for its dire poverty and attendant squalor. It didn't even have footpaths; the ground was swampy and full of potholes. Pigs could be seen wallowing in the little pools of thick, dark, fetid water, and cows from Kalkaji gathered to eat the rotting vegetables. Sahadevan had gone there once, retching as he stepped on shit. The next moment he was cross with himself. People lived in this place too. When you step on their land, you should not retch, you should shed tears.

'Vasu lives there now.'

'Shall I come too?'

Without waiting for Sathyanathan's response, Sahadevan jumped on to the carrier of the cycle. He was no longer a lean man. He had put on weight. Sathyanathan started pedalling. The cycle moved along the ridges beside cauliflower fields. Once they got past the fields and reached the dirt road in the village, they had to get off the cycle and walk. There were more buffaloes and swine than human beings on the path.

It was a single-storey house with a compound wall around it. Cow-dung cakes were stuck on the wall to dry. There were cows and buffaloes inside the yard. The house-owner, Lalaji, was sitting on a charpoy, smoking a hookah. He was an old man, with a face that had deep furrows etched into it by the sun and the heat.

'Lalaji, is Vasu here?'

'No, beta.'

'What about Rosily?'

'Yes, she is inside.'

Dodging the cattle, they went around the yard and reached the rear entrance. Rosily sat on a stool in front of a dark room, applying nail polish to her toes. A bright yellow saree hung on a clothesline inside—the same saree she had worn while waiting at the INA bus stop. Sahadevan recognised it.

She brought out the lone chair inside the room and placed it in the yard. The house had only one room and a kitchen. The bathroom and toilet were outside. A large old neem tree gave Sahadevan some solace. The ground was littered with its fruit.

'When will Vasu be back, Rosily?'

'It has been three days since he left.'

Vasu was like that; she didn't know when and where he went. Nobody knew. On Guru Gobind Singh Jayanti, amidst the procession of sword-bearing gyanis and dancing children headed towards the gurdwara, Vasu could be seen walking along Baba Kharak Singh Marg. When the Ramlila festivities started, he would be sitting at midnight among the countless devotees who had come to hear the dramatised glories of Rama's life. On 15 August, he would be at Red Fort, nodding along to Indira Gandhi's speech, which always started with 'brothers and sisters' and ended with 'victory to India'. On the last day of Durga Puja, he would stand on the bank of the Yamuna, witnessing the immersion of thousands of Durga idols brought in a procession from various points in the city.

Vasu did not inconvenience Rosily in any way. During summer, he slept under the neem tree. In winter, he shifted inside and slept in the kitchen. Between the bedroom and the kitchen, an old, torn saree hung as a curtain. He spent most of his time outside. When he was in the house, he would spend all his time sketching and painting.

Sahadevan and Sathyanathan sat on the charpoy under the neem tree. Inside, Rosily was getting ready. She was more experienced now; she knew where in the city to wait. Usually, she stepped out by late afternoon. It was not easy to get customers before that. College students would give her sidelong glances and come and stand close to her. Their problem was that they had no place to take her. Sometimes they made lewd comments. She usually found customers around sunset, as dusk approached.

These days, she didn't go to INA Market. The place was full of Malayali men. They came in the evening from the air force bases at Palam and Race Course Road, to ogle at the nurses from Safdarjung Hospital. Some of them would approach her, assuming she was also a nurse. When they realised they had got it wrong, they would walk away contemptuously. As a rule, Rosily avoided Malayali customers. They usually had a litany of complaints. And they asked her about her family. Some would sing the songs of Yesudas. Some asked for credit. She didn't like any of that. North Indian men didn't trouble her. They didn't say a word, they paid, did their bit, and went away quietly. That was professionalism. She sought out such customers.

She came out of the house now, wearing a dark green saree and matching glass bangles, with kohl-lined eyes, a bindi on her forehead and a handbag.

'I'm leaving. If you want tea, make some. There are some sesame laddoos in an old Horlicks bottle in the kitchen,' she said, looking at Sathyanathan. She hurried off, trailing the scent of Rexona soap and Lakmé talcum powder behind her.

'Poor girl,' Sathyanathan said. 'We have to rescue her from this life, Sahadevetta.'

'That would be good. But can we do it?'

'Nothing is impossible, Sahadevetta. Do you know, her name is not Rosily. Her real name is Rosakutty. She claims that Rosakutty is dead. She is from a family of settlers in the high ranges.'

'I've read *Vishakanyaka* by S.K. Pottekkat.'

Sahadevan's own life was a novel that was being written every day.

Sathyanathan made some strong tea. From the old Horlicks bottle, he took out two sesame laddoos, one for each of them. Rosily used to buy these, as well as lime pickle and pappadom, from the South Indian store in Karol Bagh. Also, mixture and murukku from the UNI canteen.

They sat there and talked for some more time. Vasu did not turn up.

Nenmanda Vasava Panicker was a young man who only knew how to leave, not how to arrive.

Sahadevan knew that in this capital city, poverty and hunger grew faster than anything else. He was accustomed to heartrending sights of demeaning poverty and mind-numbing hunger at the Nizamuddin dargah, Jama Masjid, Govind Puri, Mangolpuri, Pappan Kala and Harijan Colony.

He rarely saw a Malayali who did not crib about his life. Even for the occupants of the government quarters in Netaji Nagar and Sewa Nagar, salary day was not a happy day, it was full of stress. Apportioning the money for milk, electricity, medicines, bus passes, school fees, for sending back home ... even if one sat with a paper and a pen toting it all up, it could not be stretched enough.

With her salary in front of her, Devi sat with a paper and pen to do the calculations. Sathyanathan helped her. The income and expenses never matched. They would exhaust themselves doing the sums over and over again.

'We should keep a goat, amma.'

'A goat? Whatever for?'

'Haven't you read *Pathummayude Aadu* by Basheer? We can give the salary to the goat as its feed. Then we don't have to break our heads over these calculations.'

Goats were available near Jama Masjid in Old Delhi. They were also always famished. If they could dream, they would dream about filling their bellies at least once with oil cakes and cotton seeds dissolved in water, before the butcher's knife slashed their throats.

Sahadevan asked himself: When will we ever find deliverance from poverty?

Part Three

Of Crypts, Religion and Caste

One man's theology is another man's belly laugh.
—Robert A. Heinlein (1907–1988)

1

WHAT IS IT WITH VANAJA AND ABDUNNISSAR?

On the inland letter on which was superscribed URGENT in red ink, just above the address, Vanaja had written: My friend Abdul Abdunnissar is arriving in Delhi for a training programme. Perhaps you remember him. Please extend all possible help to him. Also, please book a return ticket for him for the eighteenth of next month. Don't forget.

Sahadevan rummaged through his memory bank from twenty years before he had arrived in Delhi. It felt like a huge haystack. He wormed his way into it, his eyes closed, punching through with his head, but all he saw was darkness. If he opened his eyes, the stiff ends of the straw poked them painfully. Sometimes they tickled his nostrils, making him sneeze repeatedly. When he crawled out from the darkness after much sneezing and with his eyes burning, he had a bundle of memories with him. In none of them could he see a person called Abdul Abdunnissar. He must be someone he had known closely. Otherwise, Vanaja would not have written the way she did. Yet, however much he tried, he could not locate him in his memories.

Later that evening, Sahadevan went to meet Kunhikrishnan. He was at home, relaxing in a mundu and singlet, a book in his hand, his eyes and ears glued to the radio. A smouldering pipe was balanced on the ashtray. Sahadevan told him about Abdul Abdunnissar.

'Give me his name and age. I'll get the reservation done.'

Sahadevan handed over the slip of paper on which he had noted the details. Kunhikrishnan placed it on the table and put a pen on it to prevent it from flying away in the breeze from the fan. His full attention was on the radio news. There were repeated mentions of the Allahabad High Court and Indira Gandhi. When the news bulletin was over, Kunhikrishnan switched off the radio.

'Will Indira Gandhi get trapped?'

'No one needs to be trapped. All that is required is that justice be done. Let's wait to see what will happen.'

He took the slip of paper from the table and ran his eyes over it.

'Who's this Abdunnissar? A friend of yours?'

'No. I've never met him. He's Vanaja's friend.'

'That's a sign of progress. Now girls have boys as friends. That's a good thing, no?'

Lalitha joined the conversation.

'When is he coming? Ask him to bring some mussel pickle. Moplahs are caring folk. If you ask them, they'll get you anything.'

Despite Lalitha's insistence, Sahadevan didn't stay for dinner. He was in the mood to walk alone, smoking a cigarette. He reached Jangpura in fifty minutes, walking slowly. He knew the shortcuts between Lajpat Nagar and Jangpura quite well.

What was it with Vanaja and Abdul Abdunnissar? He pushed open the door to his home, still thinking about it.

2

THE SLIP-UPS OF A THIYYA GIRL

Even before Indira Gandhi declared Emergency in the country, a state of emergency descended on Shreedharanunni's home.

No one had noticed the changes taking place in the normally taciturn and soft-footed Vidya.

'Vidya ...'

Devi called out through the half-open, rather decrepit bathroom door. The upper frame had already fallen off from age and decay. There was no latch; in its place was a piece of electrical cable. Before using the bathroom, you had to first hook the ring at the end of the cable to a nail driven into the wall. Sathyanathan had set up the contrivance.

'Vidyae ...' Devi called out again. Vidya, daydreaming in front of her open book, did not hear the summons.

That was the first time.

The second time, Devi raised her voice as much as she could. Vidya remained oblivious, adrift in daydreams.

Sathyanathan's and Vidya's books were stacked on the same table. They sat next to each other while studying. Sometimes, when they had a tiff, there was pushing and shoving. Vidya only fought with Sathyanathan. In front of everyone else, she was like a dove with a quivering heart. Devi fretted about how this faint-hearted girl would survive in a big city like Delhi. Sahadevan shared her anxiety.

Vidya was short-statured like her mother. Her hair was long and fell to her waist. Devi cared for it tenderly, massaging Vidya's scalp with fortified coconut oil as though she was still a baby, washing it with aloe vera extract, and removing the knots and tangles. Devi used to say that a Malayali girl's fortune was her hair.

Sahadevan heard her say this once and asked, 'Echi, then where does the fortune of the boys reside?'

'Boys don't need good fortune, they need masculinity,' she had replied tartly.

Vidya was now in her first year of college. Sathyanathan had completed his master's degree in economics and wanted to do a PhD. He was interested in economics and sociology, but was no less interested in the arts and in literature. He devoured all the books he could get his hands on, in English and Malayalam. Though he and Vidya had lived in Delhi all their lives, Shreedharanunni and Devi had brought them up as Malayalis. Sathyanathan even spoke in the patois of North Malabar. Most of his friends were Malayalis.

Unlike Sathyanathan, Vidya had only scored 54 per cent in her final exams at school. Even with Kunhikrishnan's influence, she could only get admission to the BA (Pass) course in Dyal Singh College. None of the better-known colleges would have her.

'What has happened to my daughter?' a heartbroken Devi asked herself.

Vidya had always been a good student, never falling below the fourth or fifth rank in her class. In the ICSE exams, she had scored Grade 1 in Mathematics, Grade 2 in Science and Grade 3 in English. It was only after she had joined the eleventh standard that she started becoming indifferent towards her studies. By that time, she had grown to be a beautiful girl with a shy smile.

Vidya did not respond to Devi's calls from the bathroom. Finally, Devi ran out, still wet, with only her petticoat on. The kitchen was filled with the smell of burnt lentils. The curry was burnt and blackened; there was no water left and everything was stuck to the bottom of the aluminium vessel. Before going in for her bath, Devi had reminded Vidya several times that she should take it off the stove after five minutes. Lost in her daydreams, Vidya had forgotten. She was even oblivious to the burnt smell from the kitchen.

When Devi went in to check on Vidya, she found her sitting with her head bowed, staring at the open book and smiling. Suddenly, her face became grave. She moved her eyes from the book and looked out of the open window. Though it was close to noon, the sun was missing. The neem trees stood shivering in the smokescreen-like fog. They could see the shadowy forms of people walking through the fog, wrapped in shawls and blankets.

'Baby ...' Devi went up to her daughter. On hearing Devi's voice, she looked up. There was a dull light in her eyes, shadows of unhappiness on her cheeks.

Devi looked closely at her daughter's face. The next moment, she lost her patience and exploded, 'Which world are you in? Even the vessel is burnt, and you are oblivious! You didn't even hear me shout. You are useless to me. I have to sweep the yard and the house before I leave for office. I have to wash all the clothes before the water supply stops. I have to make chapatis and curry for breakfast. I'm tired. How long can I go on like this? You wait, one day I'll hang myself and go join your father. Then you'll learn your lesson.'

Vidya was terrified by her mother's tirade. She tried to speak, but the words got stuck in her throat. She just gaped at her mother standing there, her heavy body exposed without her blouse and with water dripping from her thinning hair.

Devi could feel her strength ebbing away. She was still in her mid-forties, but more than half of her hair had turned grey.

There were dark circles under her eyes. Till now, she had lived with courage and self-confidence. She had brought up her children without allowing them to see how hard it was on her. She had no life outside of her own house and her job as a peon in the Secretariat. Suddenly, she felt like she couldn't go on any longer.

Vidya was shivering in fright. After some time, she asked, 'Shall I knead the dough for you and cut the vegetables?'

'You don't have to do anything. All you need to do is study well. And think about your mother, who toils day and night for her children. I don't need anyone's help, not until my limbs are paralysed. I'll do everything.'

Vidya teared up. She didn't know how to cry aloud. Tears welled up and brimmed in her eyes, without spilling over on to her cheeks. She stood at the bathroom door till Devi emerged after washing her clothes and finishing her bath. It was a Sunday, so neither of them had to go anywhere.

Devi's heart melted at the sight of her teary-eyed daughter standing there meekly. She touched her on the shoulder.

'Molae, you don't have a father. You should never forget that. If I fall, if I become bedridden, who's there for you both? Can I do everything? It's a fire that burns constantly in my mind. Only when I'm able to marry you off after your studies will I have some peace of mind. Till then, please don't cause me any more pain. Don't get any fancy thoughts into your head or stray from the path. You should always pray to Muthappan.'

Devi had never sought God's help for anything, but here she was, invoking Parassinikadavu Muthappan.

Sahadevan arrived in the evening, holding a Charminar cigarette between his fingers. His lips, darkened from smoking, were chapped by the dry winter breeze.

'Have you had lunch, Sahadeva? Otherwise, I can make chapatis for you. There's some dough.'

'No, Deviyechi,' he said, 'I made rice and rajma in the afternoon. I've had enough of eating in restaurants, can't do it anymore.'

'Edo, why are you going to restaurants anyway? Why don't you come here whenever you are hungry? Though we are poor, we don't starve. If nothing else, there'll be some rice and curry. Even otherwise, do you think it's such a problem for me to make you a couple of chapatis?'

'It's not as if it's a huge task, making rice and curry. But sometimes I feel terribly lazy. I don't even feel like stepping into the kitchen.'

'If it's difficult for you, don't come daily. Eat with us on Saturdays and Sundays. It's no trouble at all for me.'

Lalitha also often said this to him too.

'Lalitha, if anyone were to hear you and Deviyechi, they'd think my biggest problem is food,' he would laugh.

'Then what is your problem?'

'Every human being has some problem or the other. It's the same with me, nothing more.'

'Sahadeva, you are going past the age for marriage. Don't delay it any more. Everything needs to be done at the right time. I can find you a lovely girl.'

When Vidya saw Sahadevan, she turned pale. 'Are you not well, molae?' Sahadevan asked.

Vidya had started looking at him differently since the long talk he'd had with her, that day, near Dyal Singh College. He had not spoken a single harsh word to her. He had not threatened her. Every word was filled with affection and compassion. And yet ...

Sahadevan had spotted Vidya standing in front of Dyal Singh College from afar. She would take a bus to Lodhi Colony and walk down to Sewa Nagar, a fifteen- to twenty-minute walk. She was usually accompanied by two other students who turned off near Dhobi Ghat for their homes. Vidya would walk the rest of the way on her own, head bowed, not looking at anyone, just as her mother had told her to.

When she saw Sahadevan, her face registered uneasiness. Was she really waiting for the bus?

'I'm also going to Sewa Nagar. Come, let's go together.'

She didn't say anything. His eyes followed her gaze. He had no difficulty in picking out a young man with broad sideburns, standing beneath one of the large-canopied trees in Lodhi Estate and staring in their direction. He wore flared bell-bottoms.

'Vidya, come, let's walk for a while. We'll take an auto then and go home.'

She accompanied him obediently. When they got to the young man, he smiled indulgently at him and said, 'Son, what is your name?'

'Rahul Sharma.'

'I'm Vidya's uncle. I stay in Jangpura. Where do you stay?'

'In Kamla Nagar. I know of you, Sahadevan uncle. Vidya has spoken about you.'

'Come, Rahul. Let's take a short walk.'

They walked through Lodhi Estate, with Vidya on Sahadevan's right and Rahul to his left. He felt like smoking; he took out a Charminar from his shirt pocket and lit it.

'Shall we have tea?'

'Vidya likes tea. I prefer Limca.'

They went into Jor Bagh Market, which had some good bookshops and eateries. They chose a restaurant near the Chinese footwear shop. He noticed that Vidya's face had become paler. He smiled to reduce her stress. But it only seemed to make her more anxious. Rahul remained baby-faced and calm.

'Where are you studying?'

'I'm done, I'm not studying any longer. I failed twice in the examinations.' Rahul smiled.

When the tea and Limca were brought to their table, Vidya stared at her cup without drinking.

Sahadevan and Rahul quickly became friends. Rahul started off by calling him uncle, switched to bhaisaab, and then to bhaiya. He chatted about films and music. Boney M. was his favourite pop band. He owned a Philips LP record player, which he kept in his bedroom. The drumbeats of Osibisa reverberated in his room even after midnight. His father was a rich man. Though they lived in Kamla Nagar, he had a big mansion and farm lands in Gurgaon, and three tractors. He had been born into a high caste; Sharmas were traditionally priests in Hindu temples. 'My uncle is the chief priest of the Radhakrishna Temple in Mathura,' he said.

Sahadevan wasn't keen on discussing caste. He had snipped off his own caste name, Nambiar, before leaving for Delhi. But now, placed between Vidya and Rahul, he felt that it was essential to discuss caste.

'Vidya doesn't know anything. She's clueless. Even about her caste,' Rahul said.

'Did you ask her?'

'I did. She doesn't know.'

His uncle, the head priest of the Mathura temple, had drilled it into Rahul from his childhood that, before breaking bread with strangers, he should find out their caste.

Vidya didn't know she was a thiyya girl. She didn't even know what caste was.

Sahadevan realised it was time to have a serious talk with the youngsters.

'I need to know a few things. Consider me a friend. If that is difficult, think of me as a brother.'

'All right. What do you want to know, bhaiya?'

Sahadevan stubbed out his cigarette in the ashtray and sat up. Unintentionally, his face had taken on the expression of a schoolmaster with a cane in his hand.

'Are you in love?'

'Yes, bhaiya.'

'You are not old enough to fall in love. Nor do you have the maturity for it.'

'I like her. I want her very much.'

'Rahul, have you considered what will happen if your father comes to know of this? You are of a higher caste.'

There was a brief moment when Rahul appeared to be startled. Collecting himself, he averred, 'Baba will never get to know of this.'

'He will. I found out, didn't I?'

Rahul started again. 'Irrespective of whoever opposes me, I'll marry her.'

'No one will let you live in peace. My advice to you is this: Consider this an infatuation and go your separate ways. I have only your welfare in mind when I tell you this.'

Returning home with Sahadevan, Vidya was still unaware that she was a thiyya girl in love with a brahmin boy. She wasn't angry with Sahadevan, though it hadn't been pleasant listening to the things he had to say. At least, even after seeing Rahul and her strolling through Old Delhi, he had not tipped off her mother. If she ever came to know of this …

Vidya felt faint.

I am fed up with these two kids, Sahadevan told himself. It was not an ordinary tiger he had by the tail; this one was feral and ferocious. In this big city, it was dangerous for a thiyya girl to go astray. There would be hell to pay.

He couldn't open up to Devi, nor could he hide it from her. It would be a sin to split up the lovebirds. His heart wouldn't allow him to separate them. But he couldn't afford not to separate them. It was the same with Vasu. He couldn't bring himself to inform Nenmanda Shreekanta Panicker about his son. But he couldn't keep it from him either. Delhi was teeming with people. Why did the tiger have to place its tail squarely in his hand?

3

ABDUNNISSAR IN DELHI

On his way to New Delhi railway station to meet Abdul Abdunnissar, Sahadevan saw Joginder Singh and Jaswinder waiting at the turn on Panchkuian Road. From his side seat on the bus, he got a good look at them. She was wearing a flashy blue saree and a sleeveless blouse and leaning very close against him. Tall and long-limbed, and with a bright red turban on his head, he had the majesty of the proverbial Punjabi lion. The couple were still swimming in the euphoria of their honeymoon.

It gladdened him to see them.

As his train drew up at the New Delhi railway station, Abdul Abdunnissar witnessed the same sights that Sahadevan had seen when he first arrived in 1959. Watching the scenes of poverty, the piled-up garbage and bare male bodies, Sahadevan had wondered how long he would be able to stay in this city. And yet, he had survived. He had seen no major improvements in his life. But he had no desire to return home either.

If material comforts had been the purpose of life, by now Sahadevan would have gone back to Kerala. The only two problems there were unemployment and poverty. And even if there was poverty, there was cleanliness and hygiene. Even if there was hunger, people were socially conscious. He saw nothing of that in Delhi. The Rashtriya Swayamsevak Sangh or RSS was a powerful organisation in Delhi, but they helped the cows more than human beings. 'It's better to be born as a cow in Delhi than as a painter,' the normally reticent Vasava Panicker had pointed out one day.

The villages of Madhya Pradesh and Uttar Pradesh through which Abdunissar's train passed had remained unchanged through the years. The villages that Mahatma Gandhi saw were the ones that Jawaharlal Nehru saw. And they were the same that Indira Gandhi was seeing now. The clocks in North Indian villages have no hands, Kunhikrishnan had written in one of his articles. However, the city was certainly changing. The city that Shreedharanunni saw was not the one his children Sathyanathan and Vidya lived in.

Abdul Abdunnissar alighted from the train at New Delhi railway station and looked around. For a moment, as an army of red-shirted porters swarmed into the bogie, he wondered if he had reached the Red Square in Moscow. The first thing he noticed was the stench. Beneath the train and between the rails, freshly dropped faeces lay splattered. Passengers poured out of the bogies as if the train was excreting them. The majority of them were Tamilians and Malayalis. They heaved big suitcases and bundles on to the platform. Cartons with the Horlicks logo on them were packed with mangoes, coconuts, bananas and pickles. Some had brought jackfruits wrapped in gunny bags. Wherever Malayalis go, they take their food with them.

In the milling crowd around him, Abdunnissar could not recognise Sahadevan. One of the identifiers he had been given was that Sahadevan had thinning hair. Seeing a person who fit this description, he walked towards him, lugging his bag.

'Are you Vanaja's brother?'

'Yes, I'm Sahadevan.'

'I'm Abdunnissar,' he said. 'I'm bothering you, aren't I?' he said in apology.

Sahadevan would not normally have left his office in Turkman Gate on such a warm afternoon to receive a stranger. He had a lot of work to complete. An urgent consignment of one lakh kites had to be despatched before the end of the day. A trader in Lal Kuan exported these every year to the Netherlands.

He had come to the station only because of Vanaja's letter to him. When Abdunnissar arrived, he had to be met at the station; his lodging had to be arranged; whatever his other needs, they should be taken care of. Those were her orders.

As soon as he boarded the train at Kannur, she had sent Sahadevan a telegram: Meet Abdunnissar at New Delhi railway station.

While taking the bus that plied between Turkman Gate and Paharganj, and walking towards the railway station afterwards, he had asked himself that old question: What is with Vanaja and Abdunnissar?

Amidst that throng that reeked of stale sweat, Sahadevan looked closely at Abdunnissar. He sported a beard in the orthodox Muslim fashion. He wore black trousers and a white shirt and spectacles with a golden frame. He was tall and fair.

'Do you recognise me?'

'No. I only know that you are Abdunnissar.'

'I'm from a village close to yours. I studied in Muttanparambu Lower Primary School. After I completed my studies there, my father packed me off to Kasaragod. I studied there till my tenth. I got my Bachelor's from S.N. College in Kannur.'

'What do you do now?'

'I'm a schoolteacher.'

Abdunnissar described the topography of his tharavad, as well as the routes leading to it. Sahadevan couldn't remember anything about him or his family members. His memory was losing its edge. He was more than willing to concede that not just his memory, perhaps he himself had lost his edge.

'I'll leave now. You must have work to do,' Abdunnissar said. 'I'm thinking of taking a room in some lodge in Paharganj. It's just for a one month, after all.'

Sahadevan had thought at first of having him stay at his home in Jangpura, but had changed his mind. He needed his privacy. He couldn't predict when the mood to write would hit him. When it did, he had to be able to sit down and write undisturbed. And even when he was not writing, he liked to be alone. Cook alone, eat alone, walk alone, sleep alone.

'Don't stay in Paharganj. It's not safe. I've booked a room for you at the South Indian Lodge in Karol Bagh. It's safe there. If nothing else, you'll get fresh food.'

'You've gone to a great deal of trouble for my sake.'

'Come now, this is not too much, Abdunnissar.'

Is this too much trouble, Vanaja? That was what he was thinking.

They took an auto rickshaw to Karol Bagh. The room in the South Indian Lodge smelled of sambar.

'Winter has not started yet. But it can get chilly in the night. Here, take this sweater.'

Sahadevan gave Abdunnissar a warm Tibetan sweater he had picked up from Chandni Chowk. Abdunnissar also had a package for Sahadevan. It contained mussel pickle, which Lalitha had asked for.

After leaving Abdunnissar at the lodge, Sahadevan took a bus to Chandni Chowk. Before that, he picked up some moringa and curry leaves, and yellow cucumber for Kunhikrishnan. Late in the evening, he went to Lalitha's house to hand these over along with the pickle.

'Why did you buy so much moringa and curry leaves? Won't the moringa go bad, Sahadeva?'

'Give some to Deviyechi.'

'Who's going to go all the way to Sewa Nagar?'

'Sathyanathan will come and take it. I called Deviyechi and told her.'

As Sahadevan watched, Lalitha divided the leaves into two portions. She wrapped one and kept it aside. Then she filled an empty Horlicks bottle with pickle for Devi.

'How's the moplah kid doing? He sounds like a good guy.'

'He's no kid. He looks around forty.'

'In that case, he must be married. Don't worry so much. Your mind is full of all sorts of imaginary fears. There's probably nothing between them. Times have changed, Sahadeva. Nowadays, men and women can chat and stroll together. When I was in school, if a man even looked at a woman and smiled, the village would have quaked. One day, a guy happened to smile at me as he passed by our street. I smiled back. For that, my mother practically flayed the skin off my bottom. My God! What terrible times those were!'

'Why should I worry? She can choose anyone she likes as her partner. There's no need to seek my permission either. But I need to know. Nothing should be kept hidden from me. That's all!'

'Bring Abdunnissar here one day. Where is he staying?'

'The South Indian Lodge in Karol Bagh.'

'Ayyo, isn't that a vegetarian hotel? Rice won't go down a moplah's throat without meat or fish. Don't you know that? Why would you put a moplah in a brahmin lodge?'

Sahadevan hadn't thought of that.

Abdunnissar didn't like the South Indian Lodge one bit. Everywhere, there was dampness and the smell of sambar. He wanted to stay in a place that had a North Indian ambience. He couldn't sleep at night. The sound of the grinding stone from the next room did not cease even past midnight. He could hear the thuds and grating sounds of dal and rice being ground for the next day's idli and dosa till 2 a.m.

The next day, as soon as she reached the Secretariat, Devi called Sahadevan to ask about Abdunnissar. She too was anxious.

In the evening, after leaving Turkman Gate, Sahadevan headed to Karol Bagh. If Abdunnissar was free, he would take him to Lalitha's house for dinner.

Abdunnissar wasn't at the lodge. Nor was his bag. He had left the place some time back. No one knew where he had gone.

'Sorry, Sahadeva,' Abdunnissar apologised when they met after two days. 'I moved to a friend's place.'

Abdunnissar noticed Sahadevan's face darken. His office in Turkman Gate resounded with the clacking of typewriters. But that did not affect Abdunnissar like the sound of the grinder. Sahadevan ordered in two cups of tea and a packet of glucose biscuits. Usually, he lit a cigarette only after having tea. But today, even before the tea arrived, a Charminar had started to smoulder between his fingers. Abdunnissar drank the tea and ate the biscuits. He was a pious Muslim who neither smoked nor drank.

'There's an old acquaintance of mine called Raghunathan. He's from Palghat. His wife has gone home for her delivery. When he asked me, I went off to his home. It's company for him as well.'

'Good.'

'It's a little far. But the house has all the amenities. There are two bedrooms too.'

'Where is it?'

'On Arya Samaj Road.'

Was it only a couple of days since Abdunnissar had arrived in Delhi? Even after all these years, Sahadevan knew little about the parts of the city he didn't have to frequent for work. Where was Arya Samaj Road? He had no clue what kind of people lived there. And he had no way of knowing about the lathi-wielding men clad in knee-length khaki trousers, doing their drills in the plot of land behind the temple.

Raghunathan lived in a spacious flat. It had a living room and two bedrooms, with lace-trimmed, light-blue curtains on the windows, bolsters on the sofa, and a green carpet in the living room. There was a radio antenna strung across the length of the living room. He owned a new Philips LP record player. He travelled to his office on a Lambretta scooter. He lived a life of luxury, enough to make anyone envious.

'Why didn't you let me know of your plan before coming? Why stay at a lodge when you can stay with me?'

'Aren't you staying with your family?'

The first night, they sat up late, chatting about their families and all the news back home.

'How old is your son now? He must be close to twelve?'

'You have a good memory. But you only saw him once, right?'

'Niyaz. Isn't that his name?'

'I have to grant you this—your memory is first-rate.'

Abdunnissar stood up and shook Raghunathan's hand. The next moment, they burst out laughing. Raghunathan had remembered the name of Abdunnissar's son whom he had met once, many years ago. And Abdunnissar? Try as he might, he could not recall Raghunathan's wife's name.

In the morning, Abdunnissar rode pillion to the Central Secretariat bus stop on Raghunathan's scooter. Employees coming from various places were being thrown out from the buses, ejected by the crowd. People streamed into the magnificent Secretariat building as if they were coming to attend some festival. Devi got down from her bus and entered the Secretariat, bag in hand. Abdunnissar boarded the bus that would take him to his destination. From the window, he gazed at the circular Parliament building that he had seen only in photos. He reminded himself to buy some postcards with the Parliament, the Qutub Minar and the Jama Masjid on them before he left Delhi. Niyaz's hobby was collecting picture postcards.

Ten days passed. Now Abdunnissar knew the bus numbers and routes of all the buses which plied between Arya Samaj Road and the main terminals such as Connaught Place, Central Secretariat and Jangpura.

One evening, Abdunnissar returned to the house at around 9 p.m. Raghunathan wasn't back yet. He opened the door using the duplicate key, and entered the house. He bathed and changed into a lungi and singlet, and sat near the radio, listening to music. The maid had come in earlier, to clean the house and cook. She was an Oriya woman and had left a dinner of rice, vegetables and fish fried in mustard oil for them in the kitchen. Though he was hungry, he decided to wait till Raghunathan returned. That was when the doorbell rang.

'*Kaun*?'

'*Tera baap*.'

Before Abdunnissar could get up and go to the door, the intruder had stepped into the house, a corpulent figure wearing a dhoti. Behind him was an equally massive figure, wrought in the same image. Their hair was cropped close to the scalp, except for a wisp at the back of the head, which hung down like a rat's tail.

'Who are you? Raghunathan is not here,' Abdunnissar said.

The man acted as if he hadn't heard him.

'*Kya naam hai tera*?'

'Abdul Abdunnissar. Who are you?'

'You want to know who I am? I'm the owner of this building.'

Abdunnissar knew that Raghunathan's landlord owned two buildings on Arya Samaj Road, in addition to seven buffaloes.

'Please sit. Raghunathan should be coming soon.'

'Are you a Muslim?'

'Yes, why do you ask?'

Abdunnissar stroked his long black beard.

'*Baahar nikaalo saale ko*.'

The other man, who looked like a bouncer, moved towards Abdunnissar.

'What do you want?'

'*Chup kar badmash.*'

The man pulled Abdunnissar up from his chair and pushed him out of the front door. Abdunnissar didn't understand what was happening and why. He stumbled into the yard and fell face down, his nose scraping the ground. He got back up, repeating that he was Raghunathan's friend, and tried to re-enter the house.

The house owner screamed at him: '*Bhaag jaa yahaan se. Nahi toh mein tujhhe kaat doonga.*'

During Partition, his father Narayanji had cut open the chests of three Muslims, one of them a seven-year-old child.

The bouncer pushed Abdunnissar out of the gate and on to the road. On hearing the altercation, people emerged from the neighbouring houses.

'*Baat kya hai, chor hai kya?*'

'*Kya ho gaya, Shivshankarji?*'

'*Yeh musalman hai.*'

Shivshankarji pointed at Abdunnissar. Torch lights were beamed on him from all directions.

More people started coming out of their homes with torches. Abdunnissar's blood started boiling. He drew himself up and started to say something, then stopped. He controlled himself. He was alone in a place that was alien to him.

Abdunnissar could hear footsteps behind him. He sensed the presence of several men closing in on him. He didn't look back. He walked along the dark Arya Samaj Road. It was deserted. He walked the streets for many hours, burning with fury and humiliation, but thankful that he had kept his cool despite the extreme provocation. At least he was still alive. Niyaz would not have to grow up as an orphan.

He found himself recalling images from a different time and place. There was a locality in Malappuram, in Kerala, called Changuvetty. On either side of the road, people were lying on the ground, without even rags to spread over the dirt. Men, women, infants, even old people. One old man looked at him and cried, '*Beta, bhookh lagi hai.*'

In the light from a passing jeep, Abdunnissar saw the long beard of the man. Naked little children were curled up like centipedes on the cold earth. Seeing him, they started crying. He stood there, unable to move, listening to the wailing of the famished children. He couldn't understand anything they said. They were speaking in Bengali.

Everywhere he turned, he saw starving people, barely covered by their tattered and torn clothes, begging pedestrians for money. When the traffic signal turned red, they swarmed around the stalled cars and scooters with outstretched hands. If someone was walking on the pavement, they followed, whining and wheedling.

'Children, listen carefully. Till last year, a part of Pakistan was in Bengal. It used to be called East Bengal. The people there were Bengalis. Sheikh Mujibur Rahman was the leader of their Awami League Party. Awami League won the elections—167 of the total 169 seats in East Bengal. Majlis Shura had a total of 313 seats. Since his party had won a majority, Mujibur Rahman claimed the right to form the government. But would President Yahya Khan agree? Instead, he banned the Awami League. He jailed Mujibur Rahman and other Awami leaders. The Pakistan Army tried to obliterate the Mukti Bahini, who were fighting for freedom. They butchered old men, women and children. They set fire to houses. They kidnapped girls ...'

'Dear Allah!'

One little girl, who had her head covered, wept openly in the class.

'Bangladesh was burning. Its green fields turned into pools of blood. The heinous atrocities of the Pakistani army were worse than what Genghis Khan did in Baghdad. To save their lives, Bangladeshis left their homes and sought refuge in Assam,

Tripura and Meghalaya. Children, it was the largest refugee exodus seen by the world. More than one crore escapees entered India. Later, they dispersed to various parts of our country. Tens of thousands of them reached Delhi. They subsist there, begging and starving. No one wants them. Pakistan doesn't want them, nor does India, nor does Bangladesh …'

A year ago, Abdul Abdunnissar had explained all this to his students. Now, he was seeing it with his own eyes; he was experiencing it first-hand.

Into the outstretched, emaciated hands in front of dargahs, pavements and traffic signals, he dropped coins. Sahadevan also used to give money to the Bangladeshi refugees who crowded around the Baba Abdullah Gate of Jama Masjid. Their shrunken bellies and the wretched look in their eyes urged Vasava Panicker too, to help them. But he was poorer than the Bangladeshis. The one who helped them the most was Rosily. Around midnight, when Abdunnissar was walking along the deserted, cold roads, his heart wounded, she passed him by in an auto rickshaw; she was going back home after the day's business. Had she been acquainted with Abdunnissar, she would have taken him to her place in Govind Puri. He too could have spent the night there, like Vasu.

That night, for the first time, Abdul Abdunnissar knew he was alone in the magnificent land of India, not merely in Delhi.

4

THE CASTE OF ART

On Sunday, Sahadevan went with Abdunnissar to see the museums and art galleries of Delhi. When they reached Dhoomimal Art Gallery, Harilal Shukla was there, smoking a cigarette and discussing the art market with a foreigner. Sahadevan often ran into him at various exhibitions in the city.

After the incident in Raghunathan's flat, Abdunnissar had moved into a cheap hotel in Paharganj. On the pavement in front of the hotel, an emaciated man sold birds whose feathers were dyed in bright colours. Some of the birds were coloured dark red.

Though many days had passed, Abdunnissar still could not forget the trauma of that night. He remained wounded and humiliated. After Ameenath died, he had imagined that if he were to marry again, he would marry a Hindu woman. Even that belief was shaken now.

The hotels in Paharganj were full of Western tourists and hippies. Drug peddlers and pimps of underage girls lurked in the busy side lanes. Older women weren't as interesting for the tourists who stayed in the tiny rooms in these hotels. Perhaps, in their own countries, there was no dearth of adult women to have sex with. But one inappropriate gesture towards a minor could result in ten or even twenty years of imprisonment. So, the girls of Delhi were in great demand. Many of the tourists were in India only for this, under the pretext of seeing the Taj Mahal and the Qutub Minar. The traffickers brought innocent, pre-teen girls from the tribal areas of Madhya Pradesh, the remote villages of Nepal, the oppressed Dalit villages of Bihar, and served them to Western tourists in the dark, dingy hotel rooms.

Abdunnissar reflected that the smells of real life and temporality emanated stronger from the dilapidated hotels of Paharganj than the lodges of Karol Bagh. His nose was learning to sense many things. He would have so much to tell her when he returned.

Their first stop was the National Museum on Janpath. Sahadevan had been there many times. It was full of visitors from different countries. Among them were Muslims, Jews and Buddhists. Fortunately, there were no considerations of religion or caste here. Else, Abdunnissar may not have been able to enter.

They spent a long time at the National Gallery of Modern Art, which was next door to the museum. It was the erstwhile winter residence of the Maharaja of Jaipur, Sahadevan told Abdunnissar. The main attractions there were the paintings of Tagore. Abdunnissar purchased the prints of a few paintings. When he went to the counter to pay for them, a salesman noticed his long beard and suggested, 'Shall I show you the works of Husain saab?'

'No.'

The insinuation in that question enraged Abdunnissar.

Instead of M.F. Husain's paintings, he picked out two prints of a tantric painting by Sayed Haider Raza. The salesman probably didn't know that Raza was Muslim. And thus, the Muslim Abdunnissar stepped out of the gallery with a rolled-up painting of Hindu tantric emblems made by a Muslim artist. It was his response to Shivshankarji of Arya Samaj Road, owner of two buildings and seven buffaloes.

'I'm a Muslim who does namaz without fail, five times a day. On the wall of my house hangs a Thanjavur painting of Krishna,' said Abdunnissar. 'My wish is to marry a Hindu woman.'

A bulb flashed in Sahadevan's mind.

'I was under the impression that you were married.'

'I was married, Sahadeva. But Ameenath is not with me now.'

'You gave her talaq? That's not a difficult thing for you guys, I suppose. As easy as changing a garment, isn't it?'

'True, what you have said is true,' Abdunnissar said after a moment's reflection. 'Yes, we die when God gives us talaq.'

Sahadevan stopped smack in the middle of Janpath.

'Ameenath is not alive?'

God had taken Ameenath away a long time ago, giving up on her early. Without uttering a word, Abdunnissar crossed to the other side of the road, not waiting for Sahadevan. In the distance, the Rashtrapati Bhavan glowed in the afternoon sun, as if bathed in gold.

After Ameenath had passed away, he had been under pressure to marry her sister, Raihanath. She was very young; younger to him by seven or eight years.

'Marry Raihanath? No way,' he had said, his aggressive rejection meant to fend off any further pleas.

Is Vanaja fated to marry a forty-plus non-Hindu widower with a twelve-year-old son? Like Jaswinder ensnared Joginder, has my own sister too … Sahadevan felt as if he was about to pee his pants with anxiety.

How did you get acquainted with my sister? What is your relationship with her? Sahadevan felt suffocated as the questions welled up in him. Still, he said nothing. Nor did Abdunnissar mention Vanaja's name.

Their next destination was Triveni Art Gallery. That was where they met Nenmanda Vasava Panicker. He was sleeping on his side on one of the steps leading into the lawn, his head cushioned by his arm. He wore trousers with frayed hems and a loose, ill-fitting shirt. Beside him was a shoulder bag stuffed with a drawing book, sheets of paper, books and colour pencils. His long, feminine, dandruff-powdered tresses were tangled with dirt and dust. Sahadevan wanted to drag him to the bathroom and stand him under the tap with the water running.

'Vasu, eda, Vasu …'

Vasava Panicker opened his eyes. He looked around him, bewildered.

'Where am I?'

'Right here, on this earth.'

'Who is this?'

'Abdul Abdunnissar. He has come to attend a training programme. We've been going around visiting museums and art galleries. Would you like to come with us?'

'Why should I come with you?'

'Well, it would be interesting for us to look at paintings in the company of a painter.'

'I'm not a painter.'

'I want to see the Didarganj Yakshi. Where is that?' Abdunnissar asked.

'In the Patna museum. Why are you so keen on seeing it?'

'It's just a wish. That's all.'

'Most people who stand in front of the Didarganj Yakshi only want to see her nakedness. Is that what you also want to see?'

'My friend, I was married at the age of twenty-five and have a grown-up son. I have no interest in seeing nudity in stone. It's the sculpture that I want to see.'

'Then you certainly must visit Patna.'

'I won't have time for that, unfortunately. I'm here for a training programme.'

'Everyone has time for everything. But they have no time to see works of art,' Vasu replied.

Before stepping into Triveni to see the exhibition, they decided to have tea at the nearby Bengali Market. It was

Sahadevan's idea. It was time for his tea and smoke. Abdunnissar and Vasu talked to each other as they walked along. Although Vasu was right next to him, Sahadevan felt like he was far away, in some other place.

Once, Sathyanathan had said something similar to him.

'Vasu doesn't live among the rest of us. He is somewhere very far away.'

Sathyanathan was closer to Vasu than to Sahadevan. They were approximately of the same age. Rosily too was more in harmony with Sathyanathan. She was fond of Vasu, but these days, she didn't bother discussing serious matters with him. She had realised it was a waste of time. After listening to her attentively, he would ask, 'What were you saying, Rosily?' Furious, Rosily would walk away.

Rosily shared with Sathyanathan secrets that she told no one else. They had, after all, spent a few hours together that first night, at the Defence Colony police station. It was from there that their friendship took off. When Devi heard about it, frigid winds had blown through their home.

'Call girls are human beings too, I know. That doesn't mean you should keep their company. Do you hear me?'

'Why are you saying that, amma?'

'I don't know. But you can't be with her.'

Which mother would like to see her son in the company of a girl like Rosily?

Seated at the tea shop in Bengali Market, they had hot samosas and cardamom-laced tea. Abdunnissar and Vasu got into a lively conversation on art. As they talked, Sahadevan's mind wandered back to an evening in Govind Puri.

After a recent bout of rain, Govind Puri was dirtier than usual. The shit that used to lie by the side of the road was now mixed with the rainwater. Sahadevan took out a handkerchief from his pocket and covered his nose with it. The next moment, he put it away, assailed by guilt. I am not able to tolerate this smell even for a moment. But there are people here who suffer it twenty-four hours.

Pushing open the door, he entered the front yard of Lalaji's house. The cows and buffaloes were missing; they had gone out to graze. Wet piles of dung lay scattered all around. Sitting on a broken, one-armed chair under the neem tree, Vasu was engrossed in drawing in his sketchbook, his brow furrowed in concentration. On the table in front of him were unopened oil colour tubes. He wore a brand-new khadi kurta. It was a Christmas gift from Rosily. Total silence prevailed.

Even when Sahadevan went up close to him, Vasu didn't wake from his meditative state.

'I won't trouble you, I'll leave quickly.'

'Who's asking you to leave?'

Small birds babbled atop the neem tree. Sahadevan recognised the mood of a person engaged in an intensely creative activity—the helpless state of an artist struggling to arrive at the desired combination of colours or imagery. He tried to find the right word for it. Even if he wasn't yet a novelist, he was attempting to write a novel. When he sat down to write, he didn't like anyone approaching him. However, Vasava Panicker could draw even in a crowd. No sound could distract him. He listened to his own, inner silence. Even if the whole world crashed around him, he would be oblivious.

Sahadevan sat on a mooda under the neem tree.

'I've come to talk to you.'

'I don't want to listen to anything.'

'Did you leave home after a fight with your father?'

Vasu lifted his head and looked at Sahadevan. His gaze was missing rhyme and metre.

'To leave home, is it necessary to fight with one's father?'

'You left home without telling anyone, didn't you? That's why I asked.'

'Should one put an advertisement in a newspaper about leaving one's home?'

'No, but couldn't you have said a word to your father before leaving?'

'Why? Did he ask my permission before he gave me life?' Vasu said. 'My greatest enemies are my father and mother. They gave me this damned life because they wanted two or three minutes of pleasure. Couldn't they have bought a packet of Nirodh and kept it under the pillow before deciding to indulge their lust?'

'Is that what you'll do when you are married? Don't you want kids?'

'I don't want to get married or have children.'

'How long can you live without a partner?'

'When I need company, isn't drawing enough?'

Sahadevan smiled. He too had no mate. He felt happy in the knowledge that he and Vasu were oxen under the same yoke. Come, my partner ox, together we'll pull this cart called life, filled with rice and salt bags, panting and palpitating all the way. Sahadevan's smile became broader.

Then, wiping the smile from his face, he broached the subject. It was after much contemplation that he had decided to speak to Vasu about the advertisement placed by his father. He had the newspaper under his arm.

'Have you seen this newspaper?'

'I don't read newspapers.'

'There's some news about you in it.'

'In the obituaries?'

Sahadevan showed Vasu the page with his photograph. Vasu glanced at it; an anxious look crossed his face.

'Did you inform my father?'

'No.'

'Have you told anyone?'

'No.'

'Not that it bothers me. Anyway, thanks.'

Sahadevan could have sent a telegram to Shreekanta Panicker. 'Vasava Panicker in Delhi. Staying at House 8/124, Govind Puri.' But he hadn't.

None of the other questions Sahadevan shot at him got any response from Vasu. He just changed the subject. 'Don't you want to see my new work?'

He went inside and fetched three oil paintings. He lined them up outside, in the light. They were amplified versions of the remarkable painting that had caught the attention of Harilal Shukla, on the pavement in front of Regal Cinema. Decapitated torsos that entered the frame from unforeseen, unlikely directions. Heads with no bodies. All the humans, animals, objects depicted in the paintings were amputated or incomplete, as if they had been sawed into pieces. He had named them Fragmentation One, Fragmentation Two and Fragmentation Three.

Vasu was developing a distinct style of his own. In his use of colours, he was a minimalist. Harilal Shukla used to say that one of the drawbacks of Malayali painters was their obsession with colours.

'You should be consistent. Stand steadfast. One of the problems with the new generation is their lack of consistency,' Shukla had said after viewing Vasu's work. He didn't go to Govind Puri to look at the paintings. When he heard that the way to Lalaji's bungalow was through the Harijan colony, he had scowled.

'What is your caste?'

'I don't know.'

Harilal stepped back in shock.

'Are you a low-caste?'

They were standing in front of Dhoomimal Art Gallery in Connaught Place. In the throng on the pavement, a hippie girl who had not washed her hair for ages brushed past them, trailing an unpleasant smell behind her.

Vasu's reply to the second question was the same: He didn't know. He had transported his paintings to the gallery in a taxi. Harilal had paid the fare for it. Vasu didn't have enough money even to take a bus. As he looked at the paintings, Harilal's face brightened. A secretive smile appeared on the right corner of his mouth, which was red from chewing paan.

Harilal Shukla lived in a mansion in Rana Pratap Bagh near Kamla Nagar, where Rahul Sharma lived. Its outhouse was lying unoccupied. He wanted Vasava Panicker to move in there and paint. Vasu needed a well-lit place where people like Harilal Shukla could visit him. But Harilal couldn't take Vasu there without knowing his caste. Though he had questioned him many times, and in many ways, he could not get anything out of Vasu. Eventually, he reached the conclusion that Vasu was from a lower caste and was trying to hide it from him. After that, he took care not to stand too close to Vasu and ensured that he didn't touch him even by mistake.

Once, when Harilal Shukla met a Malayali at the Rabindra Bhawan Gallery, he asked him if Panicker was a lower-caste name. The young man, who had come to see the exhibition and was dressed like a hippie, looked him in the face and spat out an explosive '*phthoo*' before walking away without another word.

By now the better paintings that Vasu had done were in Harilal Shukla's custody.

'Do you know how to make tea? If so, make two cups. I need just black tea,' said Vasu.

Strange, for a painter to be asking a novelist this. But Sahadevan was happy to do it. He went into the house, lit the stove, and put the water on to boil. This was something he had been doing regularly. He could make a mean cup of tea, blindfolded.

The dimly lit room was suffused with the smell of Tata coconut oil and Lakmé talcum powder, both of which Rosily used every day. The yellow saree she had worn in 1971 while waiting at INA Market was on the clothesline. Three or four months ago, he had seen her walking near Gol Dak Khana, clad in the same saree. Poor thing, he thought, she must not have enough sarees to wear. Sahadevan had a dream; when his business began to flourish, he would appoint her as the receptionist in his office. He could not think of any other way to rescue her.

Kunhikrishnan also had a similar thought. Like Sahadevan, he too desired to lead Rosily onto the path of righteousness.

Sitting beneath the neem tree and enjoying its medicinal breeze, Sahadevan and Vasu sipped tea and chatted. Vasu was certain that he would not return to his native place in the near future. Artists often prefer to migrate to places which are home to other people, rather than stay in the place of their birth.

'Do you paint?'

'No.'

'Do you write?'

'No.'

He hadn't written anything worth mentioning. He had not published anything either. He had no desire to be known as a writer.

'Good. Someone like you should not paint. Nor should you write.'

'Why? Why do you say that?'

'You are very normal.'

The next day, Sahadevan sent a letter to Shreekanta Panicker. Vasu is alive and well; he is drawing and painting well; you should not be worried about your son. If there's anything important, I'll keep you informed. He did not include his own name or address in the letter. That night, after a long while, he slept peacefully.

There was one other thing that continued to bother him, though. The affair between Vidya and Rahul Sharma. He hadn't spoken to anyone about it. He knew it was not right to keep it hidden from Devi. But his heart did not permit him to rat on two young people and their love. He was in the grip of a moral dilemma he did not have an answer to.

After finishing their tea and samosas at Bengali Market, the three men walked back to Triveni Gallery. Though it was nearing sunset, the light was clear. Abdunnissar was pleased to have met an artist like Vasu in Delhi. Once he was back home, he would tell her all about it.

Standing under the streetlamp, Abdunnissar said, 'The days have gone by swiftly. I feel sad. Whatever it is, I like Delhi.'

Abdunnissar was to leave soon. Sahadevan had wanted to ask him so many things before he left. But, in the meantime, he had received an inland letter from Vanaja. Don't ask Abdul Abdunnissar anything, she wrote. When it's time, I'll tell you everything.

What more was there to say?

Hadn't she already said everything there was to be said?

5

RIOTS IN SEWA NAGAR

'Ammae ...'

Sathyanathan called out from the road, even before he had walked through the gate. His lanky form was silhouetted against the shadowy yard. The house was in a state of utter disrepair. The plaster was falling off the walls. The steel frames of the windows were corroded.

Sathyanathan rang the doorbell. Vidya appeared to let him in. They always kept the door opening into the small veranda closed. Otherwise, beggars and hawkers passing by could get in and ring the bell. They lived an impoverished life, driven by adversity. There was nothing worth stealing in their house. And yet, one day, in broad daylight, the house had been burgled.

Only Devi's sarees were stolen. The thief was not interested in Vidya's salwar-kameez suits or Sathyanathan's trousers. Possibly because they were too old and threadbare.

'Great God, what will I wear to the office?'

Earlier, Devi used to wear cotton sarees. When nylex sarees came into the market, she reluctantly gave up wearing cotton. Nylex sarees were cheap, they didn't get dirty quickly, and even if they did, they were easy to wash. A simple soak and a rinse got rid of all the dirt. On rainy winter days, when most clothes wouldn't dry, all you had to do with a nylex saree was to wash and spread it under the fan for a little while.

Lalitha gave her two sarees. After coming home in the evening, Devi would wash the saree she had worn that day and hang it in the back veranda to dry. Sathyanathan used to read and sleep there, smelling the dampness of Lalitha's—now his amma's—saree. There had been penury in their home for as long as he could remember. It had become worse after he joined college. It was one of the finest colleges in the city. Even after so many years, the thrill of getting admission there remained fresh in his mind.

Getting into St. Stephen's was the dream of Delhi's upper classes. His achievement was something that even rich kids from affluent families could not match. The son of a lowest grade employee getting admitted to St. Stephen's—no one in Devi's office could believe it. When he heard the news, Banwarilal, Shreedharanunni's old colleague, came to their house after a long time. He was retired now. He wore an old white cotton shirt and trousers, neatly starched and ironed. He always dressed smartly and stepped out in style, whether it was to his neighbour's house right across the street or to the office.

'*Bahut achcha hai, behen. Achchi baat hai. Dukh iss baat ka hai ki Shreedharanunni nahi rahe yeh dekhne ke liye.*'

The old union leader handed over a package he was holding under his arm.

'Give this to your son.'

It was a handloom shirt he had purchased from the pavement at Queensway. For a long time, till it faded and shrank, Sathyanathan wore that shirt to college. He was the only poor student in his class. During the summer, when his classmates arrived in air-conditioned cars, he used to reach the classroom bathed in sweat, his shirt crumpled, having changed two buses on the way. The slippers on his feet had straps that had been mended multiple times. His classmates kept their distance from him because of his poverty and the body odour from all that sweat. However, with each exam, his grades kept climbing. Gradually, he acquired more friends than he could have asked for, both boys and girls. They were the smart kids, with clear views and opinions. A radical left-leaning group was putting down roots in the college. One day, a fashionable girl wearing a sleeveless top and trousers talked to Sathyanathan about politics for long hours, sitting in the canteen, and when they said goodbye, she gave him a copy of Mao's Red Book.

'It isn't enough for you to browse through the book. You must feel it,' Kunhikrishnan told him. 'And then I want to discuss certain things with you.'

Sathyanathan tried to read and understand the book. For someone studying economics at St. Stephen's, it wasn't that difficult.

How could Devi, only a peon, educate two grown-up children and run the household? Every night, she would note down the day's expenses in a small notebook. A long sigh would escape her. Once, Sathyanathan noticed his mother's eyes well up with tears as she sat with the notebook in her hand. Devi never lost her composure in front of her children, nor did she show any anxiety. She doubled as their father and mother. If she let her mind weaken, how would she keep it all going?

Sometime after Shreedharanunni passed, there had been another major strike at the Secretariat, and Devi had actively participated in it. Leaving her children at home, she went for the union meeting in the company of Banwarilal. When she returned close to midnight, Vidya was waiting for her, looking scared. Sathyanathan was in the rear veranda, engrossed in a book.

'Haven't you slept yet?'

'I'm scared, amma.'

Her voice trembled. The mother held her daughter close and stroked her head.

'Why should you be afraid? Isn't your brother here?'

'Amma, like father, you … please don't do it, amma … don't go for meetings and strikes.'

Vidya leaned into her mother's body. She was always afraid. Of even a slight breeze.

Sathyanathan put down his book and came over. 'Vidya, amma should go. We are Shreedharanunni's children. We shouldn't stop our amma.'

'I'm scared …'

'What are you so scared of?'

'I don't know.'

Vidya stayed close to her mother. She had grown up scared. She had realised before anyone else that Delhi was a city of fear.

During the Emergency, Kunhikrishnan had written an article titled 'The City of Fear'. It had been published in a magazine in England.

'Ammae …' Sathyanathan called out again as he entered the house. In that moment, he wanted to see his mother more than anybody else in the world.

'Amma is having a bath,' Vidya told him. The water supply had stopped earlier than usual that day. Devi usually got up at 5 a.m. and began her chores. She had to complete everything before the taps ran dry, and no one could predict when that would happen. In any case, before 7 a.m., she would wash the dishes and clothes, clean the toilet, bathe, and fill water in the copper pots and steel containers. Shreedharanunni had bought these in 1950 at Kotla Market, before the birth of their children. Even in Lalitha's New Double Storey building in Lajpat Nagar, there was a shortage of water. But she had big 100-litre plastic buckets to store it in. Devi used to feel envious looking at those bright-coloured, clean buckets. She dreamed of owning one like that.

By the time Devi was ready to leave for the Secretariat, Vidya would be done with her bath too. Sathyanathan slept late and woke up late. His college education was over; he had passed his MA examination. Still, he never slept before 2 a.m. During winter, Sewa Nagar and its surroundings fell silent early in the evening; there were few people on the roads. The sweepers, with no place of their own to sleep, lit small fires on the pavements and huddled close. The street dogs, attracted by the warmth, also came to curl up nearby. After an early dinner, most people got into bed and under their razais. In the back veranda of Devi's house, however, a forty-watt bulb would still be burning.

Sathyanathan waited for his mother near the bathroom door.

'Why this urgency to meet amma?'

'I have some special news.'

'Why aren't you telling me?'

'First amma. After that, I'll tell you.'

'Yeah, I know, you don't love me.'

The only person Vidya allowed herself to be irritated by was Sathyanathan. Sometime ago, she had begun to speak freely with Sahadevan too. She would vent to him whenever she was upset about something. That was until Sahadevan had caught her and Rahul red-handed. She had not closed her eyes the whole night after Sahadevan spoke to her. She was afraid he would go to her mother's office the next day and tell her everything. She didn't know that Sahadevan never went to the Secretariat to meet Devi. It was not easy to meet a Class IV employee in their office. He was aware of the impropriety.

The next day, after darkness fell, Vidya waited with bated breath till her mother got home. But, other than fatigue, she could read nothing on her mother's face. She let out the breath she had been holding all day. Sahadevan had not told her mother anything. She felt respect and affection for him well up inside her.

Vidya could not have imagined the stress Sahadevan was under, ever since the day he had seen them together in the maroon shadows of the Red Fort. He was aware that it was his duty to inform Devi. If anything were to happen to Vidya, God forbid, it would be a matter of great regret for him. On the other hand, if Devi were to hear of it, there would be an uproar in the house …

One day, Vidya sidled up to him when no one else was around and told him, 'Etta, please don't tell anyone.'

'No, I won't tell anyone.'

'Swear upon Muthappan.'

She went inside and fetched a small picture of Parassinikadavu Muthappan from inside her English textbook.

'Now, promise.'

She placed the picture on his clammy palm. When he looked into her fearful eyes, all sense of propriety and caution flew out of his head. He didn't have to think after that.

'I swear upon Muthappan. I won't tell anyone.'

'After this, if you tell anyone, you'll become blind.'

She took back the picture and put it between the pages of her book. He had never seen her so happy before.

The picture of Muthappan had been gifted to Vidya by Lalitha, when she returned from her last holiday in Kerala. Though Kunhikrishnan was a rationalist, she believed in all the gods. She had once told Kunhikrishnan that she had not been blessed with a child because he was an atheist.

That night, Vidya slept peacefully without her mother's thunderous face appearing in her dreams.

'Ammae,' Sathyanathan called again.

Devi stepped out of the bathroom with her body still damp.

'I got a job.'

Devi's eyes, wet from the chlorine infused water, gleamed.

'As a trainee at *The Economic Times*.'

An appropriate job for someone who had completed his post-graduation in economics at St. Stephen's College. Kunhikrishnan had swung it for him.

All of Delhi's youth was hunting for jobs at this time. Every day, trains from Kerala would bring hundreds of educated youth in search of jobs. They wandered about in the capital like unmoored souls not yet freed from their earthly sins. The young men, stressed and frustrated at not being able to find work, sought refuge in drugs and alcohol. Many committed suicide. Devi used to read about them in the Malayalam papers that Sathyanathan brought home for her to read. She had been worried that he too would remain unemployed. She didn't have to worry about that any more. She was unsure whom to thank. Parassinikadavu Muthappan or Kunhikrishnan? Or the spirit of Shreedharanunni watching over them from the heavens?

On hearing the news, Banwarilal turned up with half a kilo of gulab jamun from Aggarwal Sweets. He seemed to have aged a great deal in a short period of time. But, as usual, he was smartly dressed.

'*Muh meetha karo, beta*.'

He took out a gulab jamun and extended it towards Sathyanathan. Flicking off a dead fly that lay on top of it, Sathyanathan put the gulab jamun in his mouth. The relentless trade union work had taken its toll on Banwarilal. Fatigue had taken over his body. Even after retiring from his job, he continued to organise the truck drivers and headload workers of Bhogal and Badarpur. One day, a red flag was seen fluttering from the dusty peepal tree near the junction in Badarpur where the trucks parked. A vermillion mark that Banwarilal applied on the forehead of the city in which he lived and where he would die.

'The salary isn't much, amma. I'm a trainee.'

'Doesn't matter. Whatever it is, you have found a job. Your father, sitting in the heavens, must be happy.'

She looked up instinctively. The old fan continued to whirr above, making a racket.

Hearing the news, Sahadevan arrived with a small box of kaju barfi he had picked up in Chandni Chowk. It cost twice as much as the gulab jamun that Banwarilal had brought. Sahadevan's earnings were going up. Business had improved after he opened the office in Turkman Gate. If he could continue like this for three or four years more, Shyamala wouldn't have to face the same fate as Vanaja. He could marry her off in style.

Sathyanathan was to join work on the following Monday. Sahadevan visited their house the day before. He managed to come by almost every Sunday. Sometimes he came for lunch. Sometimes it was in the afternoon or late at night. He was unaffected by the weather. He and Vasava Panicker were alike in that. For Vasu, day and night were no different. He didn't know the difference between summer and winter either. Which was why, at the height of winter, during Christmas time, when the rest of Delhi went around swaddled in woollen clothes, woollen caps and two pairs of socks, one on top of the other, he would sit in the yard and paint, dressed only in a cotton shirt, not even slippers on his feet.

'Eda, Vasu, go wear a sweater. If you sit in the cold like this, you'll get pneumonia,' Rosily would admonish him.

When the air started getting chilly after Diwali, she bought Vasu a woollen sweater in Shankar Market. But she rarely saw him wear it. He preferred to wear ill-fitting and faded clothes. Most of his shirts were extra large. They ended below his knees; his hands couldn't be seen in the long sleeves. Rosily used to wonder why he never wore the right size.

Sahadevan reached Sewa Nagar at noon. He had brought ripe nenthran bananas and dried mackerel from the Malayali store in Gol Market. When he saw the dried fish, Sathyanathan's face lit up. Fish, whether dried or fresh, was his weakness.

'You and your lust for fish! Were you a Bengali in your last birth?' Devi would tease him. The Bengali obsession with fish was well known. 'Amma, if you don't make fish curry this

Sunday, I'm going to marry a Bengali girl and bring her home,' he would retort.

'Eda, have you found someone without telling me?'

'I wouldn't do anything without your knowledge.'

Vidya burst into tears.

'What is it, baby?'

She wiped her eyes. Devi let out a deep sigh. She was not able to fathom her daughter. She only knew there were many things on her mind. Why did she suddenly burst into tears or laughter, for no apparent reason?

'There's no coconut for the curry,' Devi said, untying the packet of dried fish.

'I'll go get some.'

There was a Malayali store in Lodhi Colony. Though dried fish was not available there, they had pappadam, coconuts, pickle and coconut oil. There was also a restaurant where Malayalis went to eat. It would take him less than half-hour to cycle there and back.

'Let's fry the fish today.' There was not enough time to grind coconut and make a curry. It was already close to 1 p.m.

She washed the fish and prepared it. If it wasn't cleaned properly, the grit would remain. But fish that was sun-dried on a sandy beach had a special taste.

Devi scored the dried fish through its middle, smeared it with chilli paste and put it in the pan with coconut oil. The fragrance of the sizzling fish spread through the house, making their mouths salivate. The afternoon breeze carried it to the neighbour's house too. The Sewa Nagar government quarters had several vegetarian, upper-caste occupants. But as they battled poverty and privation, thoughts about caste seldom troubled their minds. Such things were for rich people. The poor had no time for them. So, the smell of fish frying in coconut oil did not bother them.

'Even the smell is enough to make the rice go down smoothly. We don't need anything else,' Sathyanathan said. Vidya didn't respond. She didn't need rice, fish curry or puttu. What she wanted was chapati and cauliflower curry. When she went out and saw girls eating hot and sour aloo chaat at the street vendors', she couldn't help looking at them greedily. She didn't have money to buy even that. Her faded dupatta and worn out chappals marked her as a girl from a poor family.

As the dried mackerel sizzled in the pan, outside the gate, a jeep roared up and screeched to a halt, emitting smoke. Two men jumped out. The middle-aged man with a shaven head wore a dhoti; the young man was in a white shirt and black trousers. The pointy, patent leather shoes on his feet gleamed like mirrors.

Since the door of the veranda was open, they didn't ring the bell. They leaped onto the veranda.

The middle-aged Virender Sharma shouted, '*Chokri ko bulao. Kidhar hai woh?*'

Hearing the commotion, Sahadevan and Sathyanathan came out.

'*Yeh kya badboo hai?*' Sharma pinched his nose, unable to withstand the smell of the fish. He retched. He looked like he was going to vomit.

'Who are you?'

'*Tera baap! Bulao ladki ko. Kidhar chupi hai?*' he bellowed.

Devi came out, hearing the ruckus.

'Who are you? What do you want?'

'*Kahan chupaya hai ladki ko? Bahar nikalo use.*'

'Whatever you want to say, say it to us. My little sister is not for exhibiting to scoundrels.'

'*Woh mere bete ke saath ghoom sakti hai. Mere se mil nahi sakti? Hat jao raste se.*'

He pushed Sathyanathan aside and entered the house. But the overpowering odour of the fried fish pushed him out again.

Sathyanathan looked at his mother, nonplussed. Sahadevan swallowed hard. Vidya was inside, hiding behind the door of her room. Sathyanathan wanted to expel the intruders and shut the door on them. But he controlled himself.

'Bhaisaab,' Sahadevan said, 'whatever the matter is, we can discuss it. Please sit down.'

'You want us to sit? This whole place is stinking of fish. Despicable dried-fish-eating lot!'

The blood rushed to Sathyanathan's head. Seeing the anxious look on Devi's face, he restrained himself.

'My son will not consort with stinking women who eat meat and fish. We are brahmins. Do you understand?'

Sathyanathan lost all control. He charged across and physically pushed the man out. Rahul Sharma's father staggered, his foot striking the threshold, and would have fallen but for the young man holding him.

'*Kutta kameena … Harami ka pilla …*'

As Virender Sharma swung hard at Sathyanathan, the young man with him held him back. Sharma then turned on Devi.

'Tell your daughter to leave my son alone. If I see her with him ever again, I'll burn her alive. I'll burn down your shanty too. I'll set your whole family on fire and burn everything to ashes.'

Virendra Sharma looked at Devi with unconcealed hatred. The brahmin's baleful stare was potent enough to turn Shreedharanunni's family into ashes in that instant.

'Come, let's go and take a bath. Move.'

Clutching his son's hand, Virender Sharma stomped out of the house, spewing expletives. By then, the neighbours had gathered near the gate.

'What is all this, Sahadeva? I don't understand.'

'Come, Deviyechi. I'll tell you everything.'

He had sworn on the picture of Parassinikadavu Muthappan that he wouldn't breathe a word to anyone. He was going to break the promise he had made to Vidya in God's name. He remembered his own mother telling him when he was a child that if you did not honour your word, you would go blind. If God wanted to punish him thus, let His will be done. It was for Vidya's sake that he had to speak up now.

Sahadevan told Devi everything.

6

THE LINGAM OF ICE

Vidya's eyes scanned both sides of the road as she walked towards Dyal Singh College in Lodhi Estate. Her eyes were red, as if she had been crying. For so many nights now, she had not been able to sleep. Her eyelids were swollen from lack of sleep.

It wasn't easy to fall asleep in the month of May. People would sit around fanning themselves, on the streets and in the colony parks, late into the night. There were brisk sales of earthen pots on the streets of Sewa Nagar and Kotla. When your mouth was parched and the veins on your temple throbbed, all you wanted was a glass of cold water, fragrant with the smell and coolness of earth. Radishes and cauliflowers had disappeared completely from Sewa Nagar's Saturday markets. In their place, watermelons were piled up everywhere. Hawkers pushed their carts through the streets of the colony, with halved watermelons covered by a damp cloth.

Would he come? Her eyes flew anxiously in all directions.

An ice-water seller had stationed himself at a little distance from the bus stop. Like the watermelon sellers, they too did brisk business this time of the year. Rain clouds could be seen beyond India Gate. The summer rains were tarrying. All it would take was a single burst of rain for people to start ignoring the ice-water seller. His day's sales would end there. He would have to go across the Yamuna, pushing his cart of water. Most of the pedlars and hawkers here lived in the slums across the river.

Her eyes widened when she spied Rahul among the customers at the ice-water cart. He had been waiting for her under the pretext of drinking water, hidden in the crowd so that he wasn't recognised by anyone.

Rahul Sharma had lost his self-confidence. He became nervous when anyone looked at him. That day in the morning, when he was combing his hair, the face that had stared back from the mirror had frightened him. He was beginning to fear his own reflection.

How could these two scaredy-cats keep their love from going out of control and disintegrating?

'I thought you wouldn't come. I waited for you yesterday and the day before. *Kya ho gaya? Kyun nahi aayi?*'

'*Tujhe meri pareshaani nahi pata.*'

Devi had been keeping a close watch on Vidya. Once she got back from the office, she wanted to know all the details of her day: exactly when she had got on the bus to college, the time when class got over, and at what time she arrived home. Since it was getting close to exam time, Vidya had to attend special classes intermittently.

One day, after she had finished for the day and was walking out of the college alone, she saw a woman who looked like her mother waiting at the gate. It was Devi. Vidya was taken aback. She knew why her amma had come for her. Even Shreedharanunni's death hadn't weakened her like this. In her dreams, Devi was hounded by the shaved head, the white dhoti and janeu of Rahul Sharma's father. She would not have agonised so much if Vidya had chosen to walk with a boy wearing a torn shirt from the Harijan colony.

'I need to drink some ice-water,' Vidya said. Her throat was parched.

'It's not clean.'

'I'm thirsty.'

'We'll go and have lassi at Khan Market.'

Skipping college, she walked along with Rahul to Khan Market, staying close to the trees on the side. She wore her faded yellow dupatta with its frayed edges looped around her neck.

They went directly to Abdullah Bawa's tea shop. He was an old acquaintance of Shreedharanunni. When Shreedharanunni died, Bawa had come to their house to pay his respects. Vidya was a little girl then. She didn't remember seeing him.

Little had changed in Abdullah Bawa's tea shop. The same old rusty chairs and wobbly, tea-stained tables. On the table at the front was an icebox, a hammer for crushing the ice, and a bronze vessel in which the lassi was prepared. The ice chunks were wrapped in a cloth and hit with the hammer to crush them. Water from the wet white cloth dripped down and formed a puddle on the floor. A line of crawling ants, their bodies wet, could be seen next to the puddle. Unaware that she was the daughter of the long-dead Shreedharanunni, Bawa placed two bronze glasses of cold, rose-scented lassi in front of Vidya and her friend. Two of his teeth were missing. He had lost them at the Tughlak Road police station during the last war.

'Why are you so quiet? *Kuch bolo*.'

'I'm scared. What if amma sees us?'

'How can she come to Khan Market? *Tum pagal ho gayi ho kya*?'

'Didn't she wait at the college gate one day?'

Her mother might appear anywhere, anytime. She was forced to stay within the boundaries set by her. If she overstepped even a little, Devi would be there in a flash.

'*Aane do tumhari mummy ko*. I'll talk to her.'

'Amma will kill herself.'

That is what Devi had told her.

'You have lost your father. You should always be conscious of that. If you continue with your wanton behaviour, I have only one option in front of me. This,' she had said, pointing towards the rattling ceiling fan.

Sitting in Abdullah Bawa's teashop in Khan Market, Vidya winced, recalling that incident.

'Vidya, let's elope. I know where my father hides his money. We can take some and run away.'

'Won't the police catch us?'

'Let's go to your Kerala. The police won't go that far, will they?'

Though he was more than twenty years old, Rahul Sharma didn't know that when a brahmin boy elopes with a thiyya girl, be it to any corner of the world, those who have to find them will find them.

Vidya picked up her bag and together, they left Khan Market and walked to Lodhi Gardens. Trees grew thickly around the grave of Sikandar Lodhi. From the thickets, the fluttering of all kinds of birds could be heard. A hare ran across the foot trail and disappeared into the tangled vines. Though it was frying hot outside, the shadows of the trees lay dense within. They sat close to each other, hidden behind the trees and vines, where no prying eyes could reach.

'It's beautiful here. *Mazaa aa gaya na*?'

'I'm feeling scared.'

'You and your fear. Who can come here?'

Rahul's own fears had vanished on seeing Vidya.

He held her close. They sat with their eyes closed. A bird that was perched on a branch above them left warm droppings on his head. But he was oblivious to it. He wouldn't have noticed even if an elephant shat on his head. He was lost in her.

'After our wedding, we'll go to the Amarnath cave and see the lingam made of ice,' Rahul said.

They would take the Delhi–Jammu Express. Inside the train, she would sit close to him, her head covered with the pallu of a zari-hemmed silk saree. Her hands and feet would be covered with henna. From Jammu, they would take a bus to Amarnath along with the other pilgrims. A two-day journey later, after taking a holy dip in the Amaravati River on the roof of the world and sprinkling their bodies with the whitish, sand-like, holy ash and chanting '*jai bhole nath, jai Shivshankar*', they would enter the hallowed cave. They would pray in silence in front of the lingam.

Holding Vidya close to him, Rahul whispered, '*Jai bolo Shivshankar ki. Jai jai bolo nathh Shivshankar.*'

Suddenly there was a flutter of wings on the branches above them. Something moved amidst the vines and thickets.

Hearing the heavy treads, both Vidya and Rahul opened their eyes.

Rahul's father Virender Sharma and his brother Inder Sharma loomed over them.

Rahul leapt to his feet. Vidya sat there immobile, frozen with fright, like the ice lingam inside the Amarnath cave. She saw a humongous figure clad in a white dhoti moving towards her.

That was the last thing she saw.

7

SWEET PARTINGS

'Are you going to leave me alone?'

'Everyone is alone in this world. You are born, you live and you die all alone. Isn't that what the writers tell us?'

'I know how to live alone. How else have I lived in Delhi till now? Yet, it makes me sad when you say you are leaving.'

'It's those syrupy, serialised stories you read that make you think like that.'

'I read those stories, but am I in love with anyone?'

'What about Jomon then?'

'That's a very old relationship, from when we were children.'

'I'm not going far. I'll come and see you often.'

'Do you know where Tilak Nagar is?'

'You are the one who knows the geography of Delhi. Is there any place you haven't visited during the night?'

'Don't hurt me with your barbed words.'

'Sorry. But you do prowl the night like a fox. Perhaps you aren't able to see all the places you go to clearly.'

'I know every place, I do things consciously.'

'I don't know where Tilak Nagar is. In Delhi, every locality is some nagar or the other. Lajpat Nagar, Sundar Nagar, Sewa Nagar, Kirti Nagar, Rabindra Nagar, Tilak Nagar, Ambedkar

Nagar. Harilal has given me a barsati to stay in. It belongs to one of his relatives and is lying vacant.'

'How much is the rent?'

'I don't know, must be free.'

'Free?' She was surprised. 'Tilak Nagar is chock-a-block with Sikhs. You'll see sardars everywhere. It's the right place for you. Whoever looks at you will take you for a sardar.'

'So, you have been to Tilak Nagar?'

'Didn't I tell you I know everything?'

'You must come with me today. It's my house-warming, isn't it? You know I don't have anyone else.'

'*You* are the one without anyone? Aren't Sathyanathan and Sahadevan your friends? I'm the one who has nobody.'

'No one knows that I'm moving there. I haven't told anyone.'

'You are secretive about everything.'

'How can you say I'm secretive? I have never even used a lock and key. And won't, ever.'

He didn't own a house to lock up when he went out. He didn't even own a suitcase. He kept telling everybody that he lived, not in a house or an apartment, but in the wide world. To the best of his knowledge, the world had no doors. No one went out or came in. Everything happened inside it. Why then did you need a lock and key?

All of that day, from the morning, he had been floating. Anyone who looked at him would think he was levitating. Perhaps he was being garrulous because of that. Sometimes, however much he inhaled, he remained silent. His moods were unpredictable.

She usually slept till afternoon, but she left her bed early that day. She had a bath and changed her saree. She went into the kitchen and peeled onions, diced potatoes, cut aubergines, chopped beans, sieved wheat flour and kneaded it after adding salt. She was going to cook a feast for him. If she could get some ice, she would make litchi custard too; she had already procured litchis and custard powder. Getting ice was the problem. Who in Govind Puri had a fridge? If she went to a cool-drinks seller in the faraway Govind Puri Market, he would break off a piece or two from the ice slabs on which he cooled Fanta and Limca, for half a rupee or a rupee. She would cover the ice with a towel to prevent it from melting and run back all the way home. Nevertheless, by the time she reached home, half the ice would have melted. Once, craving cold lime juice in the forty-four-degree heat outside, she had run home with the ice, but when she opened the towel, there was only a patch of dampness where the ice had been.

She had heard on Lalaji's radio that the temperature was forty-three degrees now. A mottled buffalo that had diarrhoea from the extreme heat was lying listlessly outside, near the compound wall of the house. Rosily had twice given it water.

'What did you give the buffalo?'

'Water. It has diarrhoea.'

'I have some medicine.'

'What kind of medicine?'

'Enterovioform tablets. The loose motions will stop immediately. It's a super drug.'

'Eda, isn't that medicine for humans?'

'How are we drinking milk meant for buffalo calves? If animal milk is suitable for us, our medicines must be suitable for them too.'

Vasu dissolved the tablets in a mug of water and took it out for the buffalo.

Then he sat back in the cane chair beneath the neem tree, smoking, dozing, waking up, then taking a couple of drags on his cigarette and nodding off again. He wore an ill-fitting camouflage shirt bought from someplace close to Jama Masjid. He wouldn't change his shirt, however much he sweated or however shabby it became. When the smell of stale sweat became overpowering and beyond sufferance, Rosily would forcibly remove the shirt and soak it in a bucketful of water, adding some drops of Dettol on top.

She spent a considerable amount of money on Dettol every month. As soon as she reached home, late in the night, she would fill the metal bucket with water and pour Dettol into it. She never felt clean, however much she washed her body with the Dettol-laced water.

'Eda, go and brush your teeth. Otherwise, you aren't getting any tea today,' she would scold him in the mornings.

Gradually, she was domesticating him. She was growing close to him without meaning to. If he went away, who could she open her heart to, at least once in a while? Sathyanathan always looked at her challengingly: one day he was going to bring her back onto the straight and narrow path. The worst was the pity in Sahadevan's eyes. She didn't need anyone's sympathy. She had chosen her own path after due deliberation. She was ready to face the consequences. Vasu was the only one who looked at her normally. Which was why she had a soft spot for him.

'I'll be here for a couple of years more. After that, I'm going back.'

'Have you saved enough money for your dowry?'

'I'm getting there …'

'What kind of man is Jomon? Isn't he your childhood playmate? How is he still able to demand dowry from you?'

'It's not Jomon. His parents have to be paid the dowry. I'm as dear to him as his own life.'

'Does Jomon know how you are earning money in Delhi?'

She had answered all his questions honestly, but now she became silent. She was selling only her body. Whenever a man had intercourse with her, she shut her eyes and prayed to Jesus and Jomon for forgiveness. Always.

Jomon should never know. He shouldn't get an inkling of what she did in Delhi. If he ever got to know, all this toil would be for nothing. She would lose him forever.

But right now, that was not her worry. Jomon was artless. He was like a rubber tree, full of sap. But the wood wasn't sturdy, unlike that of the mango or jackfruit tree. She believed she would be able to control him to a great extent. His parents were only bothered about gold and money. If enough of that was given, they would stay in line. She had thought it through and made her decision. She could handle anybody. Rosakutty was more worldly-wise than her father Pathrosekutty.

She was only scared of one man: Georgekutty. He still lived in Delhi, making a living selling nurses' uniforms and underwear. She didn't meet him anymore. If she saw him somewhere, she turned her face and walked away as if she had not noticed him. She was in this sorry state because of him.

She had already stopped going to INA Market. She avoided places where Malayalis congregated. Some of them had started recognising her. They whispered among themselves and looked at her with contempt.

She was aware that she wouldn't be able to live in Delhi much longer.

'I'll go back. Definitely.'

'Will you come back after that?'

'I'll come back with Jomon for our honeymoon.'

'Then you should come and stay with me in my barsati in Tilak Nagar.'

'I have in mind a hotel in Karol Bagh. It has AC. Jomon and I'll stay there.'

The Punjabi fare that she cooked up for Vasu was first-rate. Since they didn't have a table or chairs, she spread old newspapers on the floor and put the plates on them. Aloo parathas shallow-fried in ghee, baingan bharta, raita with chiffonaded mint leaves, and mango pickle.

'Eat. Why are you sitting and staring at the sky? I have made all this for you.'

He wiped the cigarette smoke stains around his lips with the back of his hand and sat down on the floor. She sat next to him and served him. He broke off a piece of the paratha, dipped it in raita and ate it. Raita made from buffalo's milk; thick and delicious. He'd had no idea that she was such a good cook.

'Like my food?'

'I like all kinds of food.'

'I have made all this specially because you are leaving. I couldn't make custard. There was no ice.'

Vasu ate his fill. He had not had such tasty food in the recent past. She peeled the litchis she had brought for the custard and offered them to him. Sweet, juicy ones. Litchi trees, heavy with the fruit, grew on either side of the road between Ranchi and Haridwar. Travellers stopped their cars and jeeps to pluck them. He had seen them doing it.

As promised, the jeep sent by Harilal Shukla arrived at 4 p.m.

Vasu placed his easel, paintings and paint tubes inside the vehicle. She helped him.

'Don't you need these?'

She handed over a bundles of his clothes, washed and ironed.

'Don't forget me.'

'What can I say to that? I can't promise anything.'

She knew what he meant. Sometimes he forgot himself, never mind others!

He climbed into the open-top jeep and sat amidst his paintings. If he had looked back, he would have seen her, standing motionless, looking at the departing jeep from the gate of the bungalow with its walls covered with cow-dung cakes, amidst the dust-coated, sickly trees and herd of grazing buffaloes.

8

THE ANGUISH OF A WIDOW

You only win to lose it all later, Sahadevan told himself. Youth is like that. How excited he had been when he began to wear a mundu and to shave. He had been propelled by excitement. It was neither lust nor love. He had experienced the ebullience of youth as an inner vision. A joyful vision of a land filled with youthfulness. But he had started losing his treasured youth. He got the first inkling of that from Dasappan's mirror nailed to the jamun tree.

When he thought about it, it wasn't just his youth, he had been steadily losing something or the other, all along. The HMT watch he had bought when he got a job at Wadhwa & Sons must have fallen off in a bus. He often lost money. Perhaps it was the doing of a pickpocket. Or maybe it fell out when he bent over. He also sometimes left things behind in Balbir Singh's shop, where he used to buy bread when he was living in Amritpuri. Once, he had lost the key to his room. Most commonly, he lost his pens.

But he only lost inanimate things. There were those who lost people. Devi was one such person. She had lost her husband while still young. Sometimes Sahadevan used to imagine that Shreedharanunni had not died but had been misplaced somewhere by someone.

But now, Devi was haunted by another loss. Vidya had been missing for two months.

One day, in the beginning of July, Sahadevan woke up to the enticing smell of damp soil. The rains had arrived.

The city had been toasting. The branches on the trees in Buddha Jayanti Park had started dying. Badkal Lake had dried up and its bottom was cracking. The amber sky glowed like an ember. The edges of the horizon which opened out to Rajasthan were suffused with orange sand from its deserts. Birds were dropping dead in Lodhi Gardens. The sleepless denizens of the city loitered on the streets in groups, fanning themselves.

And then came the monsoon.

Since he ran his own business, Sahadevan went to his office in Turkman Gate even on Sundays. That day, he didn't feel like going anywhere. The dhobi hadn't come for two weeks due to water scarcity. He washed his trousers, shirt, lungi, underwear and towel before the water supply stopped. He then started to cook. Once the summer started, he had stopped eating outside. The food in the restaurants was invariably stale. Two days ago, the dal makhni at Chandni Restaurant, which he used to frequent, had gone sour. Sahadevan never took ill if he ate spoiled rice and rajma or dal. All bachelors are like that. Yet, he tended to be careful. He made bottle gourd curry and lemon rice. He fried two pappadams and had a hearty meal, with Palat mango pickle on the side. Then he dozed off for a while. That's when the clapping noise of rain outside the window woke him up.

When Sahadevan opened the door, the sleet hit his face. The water drops felt like needles. Summer rains are like that—sharp. All the neighbours were out, enjoying the first rain. The most enthusiastic were the children. The two daughters of Jain, his landlord, studying in the second and fourth classes, were jumping about with abandon in the rain, along with their parents. The wet kameez of the women stuck to their bodies; water dripped from their hair. The children kicked the water, splattering it in all directions. Dasappan alone cursed the rain as he gathered up the chair and cloth he used for his customers, the Himalaya Bouquet powder, Afghan Snow cream and Vi-John shaving stick, and sought refuge in the nearby footwear shop. No one had come for a shave or a haircut all morning. Now that the rain had started, it was unlikely anyone would. Today, he would starve for sure. The summer rains made everyone else happy. To Dasappan, it signalled hunger.

Standing in his narrow veranda, Sahadevan watched the celebrations set off by the rain. Men and women came out of their homes. They had no qualms about going to the market or taking their children to school even amidst torrential rains. They didn't carry umbrellas in the rainy season. They used them only to ward off the sun. Umbrella sales were brisk during the summers.

Back home, it wasn't like this. When he played in the yard with his friends, at the first sign of a drizzle, his mother would call out, 'Enough of your games, Sahadeva. Come in. Don't catch a cold playing in the rain.'

After half an hour of washing down the dusty trees, buildings and vehicles, the rain moved north to Himachal Pradesh, along with the wind. The sunlight hung around in the city, refusing to go anywhere. Sahadevan wanted to get out of the house and walk on the wet roads. He put on trousers and a half-sleeve shirt and stepped out. He walked for a long time. Eventually, he reached Kunhikrishnan's house in Lajpat Nagar. By that time, the edges of his trousers were wet and reddened with mud.

His hope that Kunhikrishnan would be home on Sunday was not misplaced. His cheeks were grey with stubble and he had on a shirt with big black checks. He was smoking his pipe. A tall, lean man and a girl were sitting in front of him. Lalitha was busy in the kitchen. Seeing the guests, he hesitated at the door.

'Come in, Sahadeva,' Kunhikrishnan said. 'Let me introduce you to someone. Do you know this teacher?'

When he went closer, the man's face seemed familiar. Surely, he had seen him somewhere before.

'Isn't it Kunhikannan mashu?' he asked, astonished.

Sahadevan had seen photos of Kallikkandi Kunhikannan mashu in the newspapers. He was under the impression that mashu had gone underground. How did he get here? He was the last person he would have expected to meet.

'Mashu is underground,' Kunhikrishnan said, as if he had read Sahadevan's mind. 'No one knows that he is in Delhi. And no one should know.'

Sahadevan was pleased that Kunhikrishnan had introduced mashu to him.

Mashu smiled easily. In the photos, he looked quite grave; he never smiled. The gaps in his teeth were coated black. Beedi stains? He hadn't done a good job of shaving either. There were small clumps of stubble all over his face. He was wearing rather tight trousers which were short for him. Like they had been borrowed from someone else.

'Sahadevan is a close friend of mine.'

'What do you do?'

'I run a small clearing agency.'

'So, you are a businessman, eh?'

'Don't make it sound like that, mashu. It's just a job that I do to make both ends meet. I don't know how to run a big business. Nor do I have the wherewithal for that.'

Lalitha came in and placed hot tea and something to eat on the table.

'Have this, Janakikutty.'

'What is it, echi?'

'Elanji. It's a sweet we make back home. You only need four eggs, sugar, some wheat flour and a piece of coconut, and it can be made in no time.'

Janakikutty broke off a piece and tasted it. She nodded her head in approval. The round-rimmed spectacles on her nose shook like a bridge that vibrates when a bus crosses it.

'Will you be here for a few days? It's terribly hot now. Today is a little better because it rained.'

How could the heat be a problem for Kunhikannan mashu, who spent so much time hiding in the forests and hills?

'He has come to enrol Janakikutty in JNU. Mashu will be around for a few days,' said Kunhikrishnan. The smoke from his pipe was pungent. A friend who had come from Cuba had gifted him the tobacco.

Clearly, mashu hadn't come just to do that. His brilliant daughter, who had passed a national-level entrance examination to get into the university, didn't need someone to accompany her. Sahadevan knew that mashu had some other agenda. It was highly unlikely that he didn't. He travelled in secret to many places, especially in Andhra Pradesh and West Bengal.

Sahadevan himself was not particularly in favour of mashu's ideology. But that didn't bother him. He believed that one type of treatment alone cannot cure the ills of society. Allopathy, Ayurveda, Homeopathy, Unani, everything should be tried. If need be, even acupuncture and colour therapy. The question is not which method of treatment is to be followed. It's about how soon the ills of society can be cured, Sahadevan told himself.

The unexpected meeting with Kunhikannan mashu made him happy. All said and done, he had a lot of respect for mashu. Until now, he had only seen him in the newspapers.

'When do you plan to return?'

He immediately felt he shouldn't have asked that question. The arrival and departure of people like Kunhikannan mashu were well-kept secrets. The movements of those who are underground can't be made public.

'I haven't decided, my friend,' mashu told him.

After thinking for a moment, Sahadevan asked, 'Do you want me to do anything for you?'

'We need everyone's help. Without the support of the people, there's nothing we can do. When the time comes, I'll tell you.'

Sahadevan didn't want to stay there much longer. Kunhikrishnan and Kunhikannan mashu would have many things to discuss. He said, 'I'll take your leave then.'

Kunhikannan mashu stood up and shook hands with him. It surprised Sahadevan that he was so tall. He felt like a dwarf when he stood next to him.

By the time he left the house, there was no sign of the rain. The thirsty earth had greedily drunk up all the water. Heat was rising into the air from the ground.

He got into a bus headed for Safdarjung Hospital, got off at Andrews Ganj, and walked towards Sewa Nagar. To his right was Defence Colony and to the left, Kotla Mubarakpur. Though darkness was yet to fall, adults and children were squatting by the side of the road, defecating. In the dim light, they chatted about the latest news in their homes and locality. They would be visible from the houses in Defence Colony, full of rich and famous people. Most Delhiites didn't seem to mind the stink and refuse. It was a problem for Sahadevan because he still had the civic sense of a Malayali.

After walking past rows of furniture shops for about five minutes, the government quarters of Sewa Nagar came into view. The street was permeated by the damp smell of split logs lying around. For no particular reason, he thought of Uttam Singh.

Gently pushing open the unlatched door of the veranda, Sahadevan entered the house. Sathyanathan wasn't back yet.

Devi lay in bed, exhausted after the bus ride from the Secretariat. To lie down and sleep for a whole day till she got over her fatigue was something she often yearned to do. She also knew that she would not be so lucky in this lifetime. Her body might recover from the weariness, but what about her mind?

'Who is that?'

'It's me, Sahadevan.'

Devi jumped up from the bed. She gathered her hair and tied it up. She had changed beyond recognition. There were dark circles under her eyes; under her chin, there were folds. It had been two months since she had a night of peaceful sleep. She would lie awake all night, with her eyes open. Gradually, the sounds of the radio and the conversations from the neighbouring houses would die down. By midnight, the sounds of vehicles from the road outside also stopped. There was complete silence after that. At 4 a.m., when the first milk train from Rewari passed by, Devi would still be lying awake, her eyes open.

'Deviyechi ...'

'What?'

He stood in silence.

'What has to happen will happen. No one can stop it, can they? I believe in fate and God.'

'Is there no news from the police station?'

'What news can there be? It's been over two months now ...'

'Kunh'ishnettan even got the office of the Opposition leader to talk to the ACP.'

'Nothing's going to happen, whoever calls.'

'Don't say that. I'll go with Sathyanathan once more and meet the SHO.'

Their slippers had worn thin from the countless trips they made to the Defence Colony police station. Kunhikrishnan and Sahadevan had met the ACP and the SHO at least four or five times. They had got MLAs and MPs to talk to the police. Devi was right, none of that would help. Rahul Sharma's family was related to the chief priest of the Radhakrishna Temple of Mathura. Which police or criminal code from faraway Kerala was going to come to the aid of a poor widow in Sewa Nagar?

'Please eat something, Deviyechi. Don't go to bed on an empty stomach. If nothing else, you have to go to work every day. If you starve, how will you have the strength to get about?'

'How can I eat when I'm not hungry?'

'Didn't you cook anything today?'

'Who should I cook for?'

Sahadevan peeped into the kitchen. The copper and aluminium vessels which used to shine like mirrors were now lying around darkened and sooty. Milk stains covered the stove. The kitchen was filled with the mouldy smell of sour milk. Sahadevan lifted the lids off the pots. One contained some rice. Another was full of dal that was fast turning foul. A dead cockroach floated in the leftover oil in the wok used to fry pappadam.

A sigh escaped him.

'What do you feel like eating, Deviyechi? I'll go and fetch it.'

'I don't need anything. If I want something, I'll cook.'

Nevertheless, Sahadevan bought poori-chole in Defence Colony Market and placed it before her. The chickpea curry was still warm. When he saw the split green chilli on top, he salivated. He was devoted to spicy food.

'Please eat, Deviyechi. If you fall ill, we are the ones who'll have to bear the brunt. Starving is no solution for anything.'

'I'm not a child. No one needs to advise me.'

'Come, we'll eat together.'

He washed his hands, fetched plates and spoons from the kitchen, and sat down across from her. He put three pooris on a plate, then served the chole and put the plate in Devi's hands. She ate a little, much to his relief.

He sat with her till it was dark. She was silent all the while. He tried to strike up a conversation. If only she would talk for a while and unburden herself, she would feel lighter. But Devi went in and lay down again. He knew she was pretending to sleep. All she wanted was solitude.

'I'm leaving.'

He bid goodbye and headed to Jangpura, walking between the shadows cast by the neem and jamun trees in the dim light of the street lamps. Devi's sorrows had piled up because she was a low-caste thiyya. Had she belonged to a high caste, she wouldn't have lost Vidya. Did caste decide a person's destiny?

He was in a hurry to reach home. He had to work on his novel, which had been ignored for a while. Perhaps he would sit late into the night and write. Till the milk train from Rewari reached Jangpura, passing Lajpat Nagar station …

But that night, he couldn't write even one sentence. For some time now, his pen had ceased to be productive. It was weeks, even months, since he had managed to write anything.

Devi in Sewa Nagar.

Sahadevan in Jangpura.

Both lay sleepless. There was one person who featured in both their thoughts—Vidya.

Where are you, Vidya? he asked aloud. But she didn't answer.

He felt as if the darkness was entering his eyes. He had sworn upon Muthappan that he wouldn't tell anyone. But he had. Was Muthappan filling his eyes with blackness because of that? Was he being punished?

No, no god had the right to punish him. God was not watching over Vidya. It was he who had watched over her.

Part Four

Blackholes

We have, I fear, confused power with greatness.
—Stewart Udall (1920–2010)

1

JUNE, A NIGHTMARE

25 June 1975. That was when the age of nightmares began.

That day, Janakikutty, daughter of Kallikkandi Kunhikannan mashu, was walking along the bank of a river, when she suddenly slipped and fell in. Her eyes and nose burned as if they were on fire. The water was as spicy as a bird's eye chilli. She knew how to swim, so she closed her eyes tight, and using one hand to pinch her nose shut, she swam to the safety of the shore. Drops of water fell from her round spectacles.

Kanth""aripuzha—bird's-eye-chilli river.

Even after the passage of so many years, the pungency of the dream lingered in her eyes and nose.

That same day, Sahadevan had a nightmare. He woke up in a sweat. His heartbeat had become irregular. He felt like he was having a heart attack.

He had gone to sleep the previous night like a person with a toothache. There was a throbbing pain in the cavities in his teeth and the nerves in his gums. His cheeks were swollen. He couldn't open his mouth even to drink water.

Janakikutty had a burning sensation in her eyes and nose.

Sahadevan had a toothache and swollen gums and cheeks.

God, what times were these?

He had a lot of work these days. Running his own firm meant increased responsibilities. He was no longer able to reach or leave the office exactly as planned. Even after the others left, he would stay on, clinging like a raindrop to the tip of a leaf.

By 7 a.m., he was ready to leave for Turkman Gate after a cold-water bath and breakfast. As usual, his landlord, Om Prakash Jain, was seated on the balcony, reading his favourite newspaper, *The Times of India*. He must be back from feeding the ants. Seeking them out in the nearby park and along the roots of trees on the roadside, he would sprinkle wheat flour for them to feed on. If there was leftover wheat flour on the street or in the park, you would know that Om Prakash Jain had passed that way.

For Sahadevan, Jain was more of an elder brother than a landlord. Once, when Jain was setting off for the Jain mandir in Chandni Chowk, he had gone along with him. He had also sat cross-legged in front of the naked digambara muni and prayed. Just like he had snipped off his caste name before coming to Delhi, he now wanted to be liberated from his religion too.

'How are you, my friend?'

Fine, thank you. Except, those three words got stuck in his throat and refused to come out. He tried again, but it was no use. The words would not emerge. He smiled wanly and, slipping the house-key and the office-key into his pocket, walked out.

Dasappan was already stationed beneath the jamun tree. His mirror reflected a dilapidated building in the distance and the labourers headed for the truck adda in Bhogal.

'Your hair has grown, sir. Shouldn't we cut it?'

I don't have time, Dasappa. We'll do it on Sunday.

But the words wouldn't come out of his mouth. Sahadevan became agitated. He continued to say things to Dasappan, but nothing came out. He shouted some more. But all his efforts to speak failed.

I have lost my power of speech. ...

In a room that smelled strongly of phenyl, Kunhikrishnan, Sathyanathan, Uttam Singh and Pinky stood around his bed in Moolchand Hospital. Kunhikrishnan was talking to the doctor in an undertone.

'I'm sorry. There's little we can do. He has lost his voice forever.'

He would never be able to talk again. He looked piteously at Pinky's face. She was wearing a green salwar-kameez with a matching dupatta bordered with artificial silver thread. He tried calling out to her: '*Meri gudiya*!' He would never call her that again. As a last resort, he summoned all his strength and shouted, 'Ammae'. All that came out of his mouth was some air.

The man who had lost his voice writhed on the bed like a cockroach turned on its back, wiggling its legs.

It was past 2 a.m. Beyond the open windows, dust and sand hung heavy in the red-hot copper sky. He picked up the pot that was kept outside in the veranda and poured water straight into his throat. Some of it escaped and flowed down his body. He increased the fan's speed and sat on the bed till he could breathe again, without panting. He could see the silhouettes of charpoys placed haphazardly on the terraces across from his house. Men, women and children slept peacefully, unaware that, one lane away, a man sat sleepless in the darkness, having had a nightmare about losing his voice.

Sahadevan didn't try to sleep after that. He decided to make a cup of tea and try to write or read.

He went into the kitchen and switched on the light. The place smelled of boiled cauliflower. The previous night, he had made cauliflower curry with chapatis. This was not the season for cauliflowers, and it had been expensive. But he had bought it for Vidya. While he cooked it with turmeric, sliced onions, coriander and a slit green chilli, his mind had been full of her.

Sahadevan took pleasure in eating the favourite food of others.

He set the glass of steaming-hot tea on the table. Then he took out a pen and paper from the almirah. It was a Chinese-made Hero pen that had been with him from the time he had come to Delhi in 1959. After the Chinese invasion of 1962, India's relationship with China had suffered some dents and fractures. But Zhou Enlai's photo still hung on the wall in Devi's house. And Sahadevan still had his old Hero pen.

When he was in the mood to write, Sahadevan often forgot about the cup of tea in front of him. It would go cold and tasteless. That day, he finished his tea before even picking up the pen. His enthusiasm to write had vanished with the same speed with which it had arrived. The pen had lost its power to write, just like he had lost his voice.

A mouth that didn't speak and a pen that didn't write. Spicy water and an aching tooth.

Aimlessly, he paced the length of the room. It was a reasonably big room, with a large window. Om Prakash Jain's father had built the house long before India gained Independence. He had been in the employment of the British government. Though it was an old construction, the kitchen and the bathroom were neat. In Uttam Singh's place in Amritpuri, the house owner and the tenants had shared the same bathroom. It was always wet and smelt of mustard oil. Sahadevan would never go in after Jaswinder had bathed. Once, when he had gone in after her, he had found her unwashed brassiere hanging from the hook on the back of the door. The sight had made him very uncomfortable.

Jaswinder was like a sister to him, as Vanaja was. And Shyamala. And Vidya. And Lalitha …

Sahadevan lived among sisters.

He asked himself: Do you need only sisters? Don't you need a lover? A partner? How old are you? Past thirty-six. The average lifespan of an Indian is just over fifty years. You don't have many years left, and there are many things left to do. You have no desires—that's the problem with you. By giving birth to a useless fellow like you, your mother wasted an egg and the nine months and seventeen days she carried you in her womb.

The relentless tirade against himself always gave him some relief.

Sahadevan continued to visit Uttam Singh once in a while. He could see that his lot was steadily improving. During one of his visits, he heard the sound of an electric mixer from the kitchen.

'Bhaiya, did you see our Sumeet mixie? Didi bought it for us,' Pinky said with obvious delight. Joginder had bought it for them without his family's knowledge. If his father or mother came to know, there would be hell to pay. The hostility and humiliation from the time their daughter-in-law had arrived empty-handed, without any dowry, still smouldered inside them.

One day, Sahadevan had seen Pinky getting out of her school bus in front of the National Stadium with a hockey stick in hand. Before he could greet her, she had gone into the stadium, chattering loudly with her friends. Whenever he saw her, Vidya's face surfaced in his mind. Where was she? What could have happened to her? Was she alive? Every human sorrow is said to have an end, a closure, someday. This one alone had none.

Sahadevan paced the floor, deep in thought. His business was flourishing. Turkman Gate was an important node for trade. Its alleys were full of traders and businessmen. Though the rent was high, he was fortunate to have found the space. He had renovated the office; employed two assistants. He had bought the latest Remington typewriter, two new chairs, and a used Vespa scooter for the staff to visit clients and travel to Palam.

However, he was still weighed down by the thought of getting Vanaja and Shyamala married. He didn't know what Vanaja had in mind. He only knew that something was afoot there.

After Abdul Abdunnissar left Delhi, he had sent Sahadevan two or three letters. In these, he had addressed Sahadevan as 'Dear brother'. Sahadevan didn't understand why Vanaja and Abdunnissar were being so opaque. He preferred to engage with minds behind bikinis, not burqas. In his opinion, life should be like writing, or writing ought to be like life—transparent.

He made another glass of tea and began to read. At 7 a.m, the newspaper boy still hadn't turned up. He wondered what had happened. He had been living in Delhi for sixteen years, but he had not been able to shake off this Malayali habit. Without reading the day's news, he wouldn't be able to do anything else. He walked up to the window.

I won't go to the office today, I am tired, he told himself. He decided against cooking too. He would spend the day sleeping, reading, and maybe writing.

But nothing went as planned. He called a few people and chatted with them desultorily. Then he called Kunhikrishnan. He hadn't met or spoken with him for a week.

'I called your office. I was told you had not turned up. What happened, are you not well?'

'I'm very tired. Couldn't sleep a wink last night.'

'Umm, what happened? Were you drinking?'

'I had a nightmare. I dreamt I lost my voice. I couldn't speak.'

There was a long silence at the other end.

Had Kunhikrishnan also become mute?

'Kunh'ishnetta ...'

'Don't you know what has happened?'

'What?'

'We can't speak.'

Sahadevan didn't understand.

'Don't you have a radio? Why don't you listen to the news?' He was angry now. Sahadevan had never heard him raise his voice before. 'Indira Gandhi has declared an Emergency.'

'I didn't know.'

'You don't know anything, Sahadeva. You aren't interested in anything.' His voice pierced through the earpiece. Sahadevan knew that his ire was directed against someone else and not him. He had enough common sense to see that.

He went up to the window and looked out. People were strolling through Jangpura Market as usual. Cycle rickshaws, auto rickshaws and cars passed by. But there was an all-pervading silence. As though everyone had lost their voice.

Were others living through the same nightmare that he had? Could it be contagious? A communicable disease that was spread through touch?

He took off his lungi, put on his trousers, and opened the door. He felt as if his head had bumped against something hard. It throbbed painfully. There was the sleeplessness and tiredness on top of that. But he had to walk ...

2

THE CANE IN MADAM INDIRA'S HAND

Before the declaration of Emergency, a tall, bespectacled young man went to the Defence Colony police station one more time. As usual, his face reflected his disgust and anxiety.

Sahadevan had tried to stop him. 'There's no use going to the police station. It's a waste of time. I don't think they are going to do anything after all this time.'

'How can I give up on my sister?'

He had become a daily visitor to the police station. Some people thought he was a policeman in mufti. The paan seller and the charpoy-stringer near the police station took him to be one. It was not only his frequent visits, but his height and carriage that helped create that impression. What didn't go with the image were his spectacles. Bespectacled policemen were rare.

'*Arrey yaar, tum? Aao, baitho,*' said the SHO, Dhyan Chand. His tone was mocking. Dhyan Chand was not your typical policeman. He didn't have a gruff voice, a thick moustache or bloodshot eyes. He was good-looking, with a voice like a professional singer's. Sahadevan used to wonder how he had come to be a policeman.

Sahadevan often remarked on the number of people in this world who ended up in the wrong places. It was like catching the wrong train. The first person who came to mind was Rosily. When he saw women in their Sunday finery going to church with their husbands and children in tow, he would tell himself, there, that is where Rosily belongs.

And what of himself? It was by accident that he had landed up at V.P. Agencies in Turkman Gate. Was it written in the stars that he would become a clearing agent? Come rain or shine, he was destined to scramble around in the goods yards and cargo terminals of Delhi. His face and hands were sunburnt from prolonged exposure to the blazing sun.

Dhyan Chand sized them up again. 'Sit down, pal.' He pointed to the chair.

'I haven't come to sit down. Where has the investigation reached, Dhyan Chandji? It's been a year since I started coming here.'

'*Kya baat hai yaar*? Is one year that long a time? There are cases older than that here.'

'You don't understand our anguish.'

'Everyone who comes here is anguished. You are not the only one.'

'I can't come here every day like this.'

'Listen, bhaisaab. I know people like you are busy. So, there's no need for you to come here all the time. If there's any news, I'll let you know. Okay?'

'I don't trust you.'

'Friend, you need to trust in God and policemen. Otherwise, you'll find it difficult to live in this world.'

'Keep your advice to yourself. Just do your work. Find the culprits.'

He wouldn't normally have dared to talk that way. The first few times, it had been difficult to even get a meeting with the SHO. There were days when he waited for hours in the hot sun and returned without seeing him. It was only after he told him he was a journalist and gave him his visiting card that the SHO became a little more amenable. Now, he was invited inside and asked to sit. Sometimes tea was ordered in. The too-sweet, cardamom-laced tea tasted like payasam. Yellowish cream from rich buffalo's milk floated on top. He was never able to finish it.

Twice, he had gone with his mother. He wanted the policemen to see the tears in her sunken eyes, so that their hearts would melt. He had not known that the policemen of Defence Colony had bodies but no hearts.

'We have registered a case and are investigating. What more can we do, sister?' the policeman had said, scanning the case diary. It had a copy of the advertisement the police station had placed in the newspapers.

> Age 20. Height 5 feet 1 inch. Round face. Fair complexion. Last seen wearing white salwar-kameez, pale yellow dupatta. Address P/38, Block C, Sewa Nagar, New Delhi. Anyone who sees her please report to the address below:
> SHO, Defence Colony Police Station, Defence Colony, New Delhi, Phone 644821.

'I'm not blaming you. But please understand the pain of a mother.'

'Listen, sister. Every month, we get five or six missing-person complaints. Mostly children. Those kids also have mothers. But none of them pester us like you do. Look at her.' SHO waved another photograph in the newspaper in her face and continued, 'After this girl from Sant Nagar went missing, not once did her family come asking for her. They are smart. They must have thought, she's a girl, let her go. After three months, we found her body on the railway tracks in Tughlakabad. Perhaps, one day, we'll find your daughter too that way.'

A shudder rose from deep inside her and choked her.

'Dhyan Chandji, she is my only daughter. Please don't say such things.'

She tried not to show how shaken she was.

'*Jaane do beti ko*. If she's gone, let her go. Consider it your good fortune that this happened. If I were in your position, I would rejoice. If you agree, I can close this case.'

'*Tum police nahi ho, tum shaitaan ho*.'

'Sister, who doesn't become a devil after begetting a daughter?'

There was a pen stand on the table, with red and blue pens. Devi picked it up and threw the whole lot at the SHO's face.

'*Tumhari maa paagal ho gayi hai kya?*'

Dhyan Chand leapt to his feet, his hand raised. When Sathyanathan stepped in to deflect the blow, his spectacles flew off his face and fell to the floor. One of the lenses broke.

After that, he went alone to the police station. Nor did Devi have any desire to go with him. Which mother would go anywhere near Dhyan Chand after hearing what he had to say?

With Kunhikrishnan's help, Sathyanathan met the MLA, the MP, and even the LG. To what end? Those who went missing had to find their own way back home. The Delhi Police couldn't find them.

Sahadevan was also doing whatever he could, though he didn't have connections in high places like Kunhikrishnan. He managed to get a letter from a party leader from Kerala and met the Assistant Police Commissioner with it. The petition he wrote out reached Dhyan Chand two months later. The SHO summoned him to the police station. He didn't ask him to sit or offer him cardamom-laced tea.

'What is your name?'

'Sahadevan.'

On the table, he saw the petition that he had typed in his Turkman Gate office and submitted with the politician's note to the ACP.

'What is the meaning of your name?'

Sahadevan didn't understand what he was getting at.

'Sahadevan, an assistant to God, isn't it?'

Dhyan Chand burst out laughing.

'Who are you, O God, to send a written complaint to the Assistant Commissioner? You are only an assistant to God. *Ullu ka pattha*. If you have any complaint, you should have come and reported here. Why did you go and meet the Commissioner, you son of a bitch?'

He took a Gold Flake cigarette from the pack lying on his table, lit it, and blew out smoke. He said loudly, 'Scram! What a whiner you are!'

All this while, he said nothing about the status of the investigation. All he did was shower abuses.

'Why did you go and meet the commissioner?'

'I went with a letter from Chathuvettan.'

'Eda, what value does a letter from a CPM leader in Kannur have in Delhi? I didn't realise that you are so stupid.'

'I'm doing whatever is possible from my end.'

'If each of us does whatever we feel like doing, it's not going to help. We should confer with one another and do things together. Only if we can manage high-level pressure will something come of it.'

'I don't know anyone other than Chathuvettan.'

'I'm trying to get an appointment with the home minister.'

Kunhikrishnan did get an appointment, but he couldn't meet the minister. By then, the Emergency had been declared. Vidya's case mattered even less now. Many people, all around Delhi, started disappearing. No one went to police stations asking about missing people anymore. They knew that if they did, they too would disappear.

The Emergency was a time of disappearances.

But the buses ran to schedule. Not just that—the conductor patiently ensured that everyone got on board before blowing the whistle. Other passengers helped the blind and the lame onto the buses. The Lotharios who used to stand close to the women passengers and rub against their bodies now kept a respectful distance. People didn't have to repeatedly pat their pockets to make sure their wallets and cash were safe. The pickpockets disappeared. There were orderly queues at post offices, milk booths and ration shops. And no power cuts. If the power failed, a phone call was enough; the lineman came running. When girls walked about in short skirts, there were no wolf whistles. The usual eve teasers disappeared from parks and theatres and colleges. The Jayanti Janata Express and the Grand Trunk Express, which typically ran five or six hours late, started arriving on the dot. There was one hundred per cent attendance at the Secretariat. Quacks closed their clinics and vanished. The eateries in Daryaganj and Pandara Road stopped adding artificial colouring to their kadhai chicken. Smuggled goods disappeared from Chandni Chowk.

Madam Indira, with a stick in her hand, was teaching discipline to the city's inhabitants. She had converted the nation into a lower primary school. Her subjects sat in class like small, obedient children. Those who disobeyed were severely punished. Kunhikrishnan and Sathyanathan received the worst punishments; lifelong punishments. Sahadevan had a narrow escape. If everyone was punished, who would be left to write about them? he asked himself.

To write a novel is to live outside oneself. Who had said that? Some great writer whose name he could not recall. In the chapters he had written during the Emergency, Sahadevan had included that quote somewhere.

'The Emergency has only started. Who knows what will happen now?' Kunhikrishnan said.

He struck a match and lit his pipe again. There wasn't a moment when it was out of his mouth. It was like an extension of his body, an additional organ.

'Why should we fear, Kunh'ishnetta? We are not party members. Only they need to be afraid, no? It's a good thing that we didn't join any party.'

For some time now, there had been a party growing inside Kunhikrishnan, unknown even to Lalitha. Kallikkandi Kunhikannan mashu had come to see him with Janakikutty precisely for that reason.

He would have to pay a heavy price for nurturing such a party.

3

THE HEARSE OF DREAMS

Dasappan got to the jamun tree in Jangpura in the morning with all his paraphernalia in a plastic bag. He was wearing ill-fitting bell-bottom trousers and a tight shirt. He had bought them at the Sunday market in Bhogal, where they sold second-hand clothes.

The street market sold shirts, trousers, underwear, shoes, sandals, aluminium vessels, earthenware, pressure stoves, coal-fired stoves, flour sieves, anything one could think of. One of its main attractions was brassieres. The whole street was festooned with colourful brassieres of different sizes.

The poor street vendors led itinerant lives. They had no homes. On Sunday, they were in Bhogal. On Monday, in Uttam Singh's Amritpuri. On Tuesday, in Rosily's Govind Puri. Wednesdays were spent in Vasu's Tilak Nagar, Thursdays in Lalitha's Lajpat Nagar, Fridays in Sahadevan's Jangpura, Saturdays in Devi's Sewa Nagar. Thus, they went about the city with their wares. They were the travelling supermarkets of the poor.

Dasappan, who used to sleep on a charpoy next to the manual scavengers from Bihar, had had a dream the previous night. In it, he was opening a haircutting salon near the shop that sold Rose brand atta and Milkmaid ghee. Suddenly, he began to earn a lot of money. He moved into a rented place atop the workshop in Bhogal where trucks were brought for maintenance. Then he went home to Kerala and fetched his wife Leelamma and his children, and they spent the rest of their days in comfort. It was the most delightful dream he'd ever had. Like alcohol, dreams also come with hangovers. Dasappan was still in the grip of that hangover.

Earlier, he used to carry home the big mirror he hung on the jamun tree. The dirt-encrusted mirror would not shine, however much he polished it. Its frame had started to disintegrate. These days, it hung there, reflecting the light and shade of the road through the night. Who would want to pinch it? In the morning, women rushing to the Jangpura bus stop paused in front of it to rearrange their hair or apply a fresh coat of lipstick. The boys headed to the typewriting institute near Eros Cinema would stop, pull out combs from their hip pockets, and style their hair. The policeman who was on duty at the cinema would stop to turn up his moustache. One day, when Dasappan arrived in the morning, he found a cow staring at its reflection in the mirror with an unblinking stare. It was seeing its own face for the first time.

It was a Sunday, so Sahadevan might come for a haircut, Dasappan thought hopefully. More than a month had passed since the last one.

Every Sunday, the morning show at Eros featured an English movie. And it was always adults only, with unruly young men making up most of the audience. A policeman stood on duty. That day, he paid a visit to Dasappan and got a shave before the movie began. He didn't pay for it, however. And Dasappan wouldn't have accepted the money, even if he had offered to pay.

Also on Sundays, Sangam Cinema in R.K. Puram showed Malayalam movies in the morning. Sahadevan would go, not to watch the movie, but to gaze at the people gathered there. It was an all-Malayali crowd, with no visible divisions of religion, caste or political bigotry.

It was Lalitha who usually called to tell Devi and Sahadevan about the Sunday movie.

'Deviyechi, Sangam is showing *Jeevikkan Marannu Poya Sthree* on Sunday. Shall I tell Kunh'ishnettan to get tickets?'

It was the new K.S. Sethumadhavan movie starring Sheela. Lalitha was a fan.

Rajiv Makkar, who looked after the matrimonial columns in Kunhikrishnan's newspaper, stayed in Munirka, close to Sangam Cinema. He would get the tickets for them.

There were plenty of chores to finish on Sunday—washing clothes, sweeping the yard, ironing clothes, and a hundred other things. And yet, Devi would go to watch the movie with Vidya and Lalitha. Kunhikrishnan never went with them. Sahadevan was their chaperone. And he never allowed them to take the bus; he paid the taxi fare. During the intermission, he would buy Kwality vanilla ice cream for Vidya and Lalitha, and Nescafé for Devi. As for himself, he smoked a cigarette.

After the disappearance of Vidya, Devi stopped going to the movies. Perhaps she would never go again.

'When I lost her father, I managed to bear the grief. Today, I'm no longer able to do it. All my strength has drained away. Now I just want to join Vidya's father. I have no other wish left.'

Let alone the movies, Devi didn't go anywhere anymore. From the Secretariat, she came straight home. Buying the rations and going to the mill were now tasks that Sathyanathan undertook. He also bought vegetables from the Saturday market.

When Devi stopped accompanying her to the movies, Lalitha had to depend on Sahadevan for her Sunday entertainment. They would take an auto to Sangam, since it was just the two of them. Kunhikrishnan would stay home, reading or typing. Sahadevan would look at him enviously, this man who only read or typed or smoked his pipe, and ate his rice with yellow cucumber curry made with coriander paste.

At the theatre, Sahadevan would observe his fellow Malayalis. Women, children and elderly folk. The fragrance of coconut oil mixed with the smell of wet hair, Chandrika soap and Pond's talcum powder. Nurses from Safdarjung Hospital, All India Institute of Medical Sciences and Moolchand Hospital, wearing salwar-kameez bought from Sarojini Nagar Market and with Lacto-Calamine on their faces. Young soldiers with close-cropped hair from Race Course and Cantonment, hovering around them. These soldiers and nurses were the stars of the early romantic history of the Delhi Malayalis. Sahadevan remained a spectator in their midst.

Unlike Sathyanathan, Sahadevan avoided big crowds. But he did go to places where Malayalis congregated. He had forsaken his religion and his caste. But he was not prepared to forfeit his Malayaliness. He believed that Malayaliness itself should be given the protection of reservation.

Had Sahadevan given up on his religion?

Yes.

But did he cover his head with a kerchief and make an offering of chador at the Ajmer dargah? Did he cover his head and listen to shabad kirtans at gurdwaras? Did he go to Jain temples and meditate in front of naked digambaras?

Yes.

Dasappan saw Sahadevan emerge from Chandni Restaurant at around 9 a.m., after a breakfast of hot aloo parathas dipped in raita and washed down with hot tea. He knew immediately that a haircut was not on the day's agenda. Sahadevan wasn't carrying the cloth he looped around his neck before having his hair cut. And he wasn't wearing his blue shirt.

'What, Dasappa, didn't you have any customers today?'

'There, that policeman came and got a shave.' Dasappan pointed at the man standing in front of the cinema and scratching his back with his lathi.

'Did he pay?'

'Who takes money from a policeman?'

'You should. Don't you read the newspaper, Dasappa? Don't you know that an Emergency has been declared? There's no corruption now. No one is taking bribes. Policemen are not taking their monthly hafta from paan sellers and cobblers. So, you don't have to shave anyone for free from now on. All those who work have a right to their wages.'

Would such a time ever come? Dasappan couldn't believe it.

When the policemen came to collect their monthly protection money, he fell at their feet and told them of his sorry state. He was usually exempted. But the constables who passed by came to him to have their faces and armpits shaved, even if they didn't need it. He would do the work happily; at least he was spared the hafta. Bhim, who sold aloo chaat and papdi in front of the dry-cleaning store, had told him that the police took away half of his daily earnings. Perhaps these street vendors who suffered the extremes of heat and cold and were forced to live in dirty, crowded slums would be saved now.

The thrill of the dream he had seen before waking shot through his body once more. He would be able to bring his wife and children to stay with him, thanks to the Emergency.

Dasappan didn't know what an Emergency was. And yet he asked, 'Sir, why didn't this Emergency come before?'

There was despair in his tremulous voice.

Sahadevan remained silent.

In the last ten years, Dasappan had gone home only once to see Leelamma and the kids. He had travelled ticketless. On the return journey, at Vijayawada, the Travelling Ticket Examiner had caught him. He had to suffer his insults and be humiliated in front of all the other passengers. Then again, what dignity was left to a barber who had travelled over three thousand kilometres to live and work in Delhi, suffering impoverishment and hunger?

Sahadevan knew that there were many Malayalis like Dasappan in Delhi. Malayalis of every type lived here. He had seen the Malayali roadside vegetable seller in Munirka; the fish seller in Bengali Market, who spoke Bengali as fluently as his customers did; the balloon seller at India Gate; the keychain seller at the zoo, who pestered visitors who came to see the tigers, gorillas and lions; and the pimp who worked in the red-light district. There were Malayalis among the pickpockets who came from Trilokpuri to pick pockets on DTC buses. There were Malayali goondas. There were Malayali policemen who collected a monthly hafta from them. There were Malayali adulteresses who stole money from the pockets of their khaki uniforms. They, like Dasappan, got to go home only once in five or six years to meet their families. There were some who couldn't even do that.

'When are you going home next, Dasappa?'

'I'll go, sir. When I get some spare money in my hand after starting the salon.'

'Salon? What kind of salon?'

'My own haircutting salon. One day, I'll start one, sir.'

Uttam Singh, meanwhile, had given up on his dream of opening a furniture shop. He had a new dream now—he wanted to be a brewer of moonshine. Not to make money, but to be able to distil his own alcohol.

When one dream dries up, another replaces it, Sahadevan told himself.

He wondered: Just like someone may be influenced by Gandhiji or Marx, can one be held captive by one's dreams?

His dream had touched Dasappan deeply. He believed that good times were around the corner. And if the good times were coming, they'd better hurry up. His teeth were falling out one by one. His cheeks were shrunken. His already thin legs had become matchstick-like. It was on these sticks, bell-bottom trousers flailing around them, that he walked around every day.

Sahadevan knew he had to help Dasappan. Once Shyamala was married, he would be free. He would have money. Then, he would rent a shop somewhere in Jangpura or Refugee Market or Jail Road, organise some furniture and mirrors, pin AKG's and EMS's photos on its walls, and ensconce Dasappan in his salon. A barber's salon was not just Dasappan's dream, it was Sahadevan's as well. He wanted to see Dasappan living with Leelamma and his family in Delhi.

He had to help Uttam Singh too. Pinky was growing up, like Jaswinder before her. Uttam Singh was riven by anxiety these days.

'I sent Jaswinder off empty-handed. If that happens with Pinky too, Sahadev bhaiya, I swear upon Wahe Guru, I'll kill myself.'

He would do it too, by cutting his own throat with a chisel.

Uttam Singh could suffer anything but loss of face all over again. Every sardar has a kirpan tucked away. As it is, the veins of sardars, even those with low blood pressure, throb with blood that's volatile, Sahadevan mused.

Parents are usually happy and relieved after their daughter has been married off. In Uttam Singh's case, it was the reverse. Unable to face people, he did not leave his house for a long time. The fear that Joginder's family might harm Jaswinder nearly wrecked him. He lived with that dread even now. A Punjabi girl who went to her in-laws' place without any dowry could never live in peace. She would be a source of lifelong anxiety to her parents. Each time the *Punjab Kesari* carried a story about a young woman who had doused herself with kerosene and set herself on fire, Uttam Singh's spine splintered.

One day, while returning from the Jain temple near the airport at Palam, Sahadevan caught sight of Uttam Singh in the bus. He was returning from work in Palam Village. He had fallen asleep, leaning back in his seat. Drool ran down his beard from his open mouth. The turban on his head was shabby and stank. His beard still had sawdust stuck in it. The strong smell of cheap toddy emanated from him. He was unaware of Sahadevan's presence in the bus.

'I won't be like my sister,' Pinky said one day, after overhearing a conversation between her parents. 'I'll study and get a job. I'll earn good money and put together my own dowry.'

'Pinky, my daughter, it's the father's responsibility to make the money for a girl's dowry.'

Sometimes she spoke to Sahadevan about it. She expected to get into a medical college or an engineering college in the sports quota. She was a good hockey player.

'That's a good idea, Pinky.'

If Pinky were to get admission into a professional course, how was penniless Uttam Singh going to support her education?

'I'll help you. You just need to study well.'

Sahadevan was handing out dreams with gay abandon and no forethought.

He had to set up a haircutting salon for Dasappan.

He had to help Uttam Singh set up a furniture shop.

He had to see Pinky through to her graduation.

A fine mess!

Meanwhile, his mother was adamant that they would need at least fifty sovereigns for Shyamala's wedding.

His lavish distribution of dreams to others was his own dream for himself.

Dreams nestling within dreams.

'Dasappa, take a look. Someone's coming. I think he's headed this way.'

The pot-bellied man had parked his scooter in front of Aggarwal Sweets and was walking towards them. The golden bracelet of his watch glinted in the sun.

'People like him don't come to me, sir.'

Well-off people didn't come to Dasappan's shop under the tree. His customers were rickshaw- and handcart pullers, vegetable vendors, truck drivers from Bhogal, scrap collectors. The only well-off person who used his services was Sahadevan.

'Next Sunday, I'll come for a haircut, Dasappa,' the well-off man promised.

Sahadevan was getting ready to leave when the New Delhi Municipal Corporation vehicle turned the corner. It looked like a military truck, the curtain-raiser of the Emergency.

It stopped in front of the paan shop. Some policemen and men who looked like clerks got out of the truck. A fat man with a tie around his neck stayed inside. The clerks and the policemen looked around, talking among themselves. Then they walked towards Dasappan.

'Cutting or shaving, sir?' Dasappan asked expectantly.

They didn't reply. They looked at his scissors, comb, razor, and the mirror. Before Dasappan could open his mouth, they took the chair and dumped it in the back of their truck. They took the razor, scissors, soap stick, powder and everything else and threw them in the gutter. Then they turned their attention to the mirror hanging from the jamun tree.

Dasappan stepped between them and the tree and screamed, 'Please don't break my mirror.'

Sahadevan lunged forward and tried to stop them.

It was no ordinary mirror. It reflected the faces of the poor and the famished. It was a mirror that helped the barber to shave the stubble from their pitiful faces and clean them up.

'*Tu kaun hai?*'

'I'm Sahadevan. I live over there.' He pointed towards Om Prakash Jain's double-storey house. The policemen must have thought he was a rich man.

'Are you a Madrasi?'

'I'm a Malayali.'

'How are you concerned with this? Get lost!'

'He's a poor barber. He knows no other trade. Please don't trouble him. What do you need? If it's money, I'll give it to you.'

'Saala! Are you trying to bribe us and stop us from doing our duty, you bastard?'

'He has no other means of livelihood. As it is, he's starving. If this is also taken away, how will he live?'

'Policemen are not bothered about such things.'

'Then whose concern is it?'

'Don't argue with us. We'll break your legs and throw you in the gutter. Don't fuck with the police.'

'Even if you kill me, I won't allow you to touch this barber's mirror.'

Sahadevan stepped in front of the tree, blocking the police. They were fast losing patience.

The tie-wearing, corpulent form tumbled out of the NDMC truck. He had been watching everything from the truck. And listening.

'Sir, this man is crazy.'

'Gentleman, don't waste your time arguing. We are sorry for depriving this poor barber of his livelihood. But these are the orders from the top. If you want to make a representation, do it to those in power. Please don't stop us from doing our duty.'

'Who is above you? Are they above God too?' Sahadevan asked. After the Emergency was declared, even the gods were under Indiraji and Sanjayji. There was no one above them, Sahadevan knew.

'Sir, shall I throw this lunatic into the truck?'

'No.'

The man placed an arm around Sahadevan's shoulders and led him away. He took out a pack of cigarettes, Gold Flake King Size, from his pocket and offered Sahadevan one. When Sahadevan placed the cigarette between his lips, the fat man struck a match and lit it for him.

The policemen threw the mirror into the gutter. It hit the ground and broke into smithereens.

No one rushed to Dasappan's aid. The spectators stood mute. If they reacted, they would be flung into jail.

The policemen and the clerks cleaned up the area around the jamun tree. They were carrying out Sanjay Gandhi's orders to clean up the city's streets.

Whoever it was that drew the lots had chosen Dasappan to be the first victim of the Emergency in Jangpura.

The NDMC truck roared away and was soon out of sight.

Dasappan was relieved. He wouldn't have to dream anymore. He lay curled under the jamun tree like a piece of torn cloth. Gradually, he drifted off to sleep. A dreamless, happy sleep.

Dasappan the barber would never dream again. He understood that, like reality, dreams could also be painful.

4

THE CLOSING DOORS OF JUSTICE

Four days after Dasappan found himself on the streets, there was a minor incident at the Defence Colony police station.

SHO Dhyan Chand threw the papers lying in front of him at Sathyanathan's face. One of them hit his face while the others flew past on either side.

'Scram. You mustn't be seen here anymore. If I see you, I'll throw you inside the lock-up. You won't see the light of day after that. Understood?'

'I haven't come all this way to go away just like that. I want to know what you have done so far to find my sister. I'll leave only after that. Tell me, what have you done?'

'What will you do if I don't tell you?'

'There's a system of justice and law in this country.'

'Ha, ha, ha.'

'Are you mocking me?'

'Are you going to implement the laws that I'm unable to? Leave quietly now, you idiot. It'll be better for you. Or you'll be spending the rest of your days in Tihar Jail.'

'Isn't Tihar full? There won't be any space there. Don't try to threaten me, Mr Dhyan Chand. I'm not the type who gets scared.'

He pulled up a chair and made as if to sit.

'Let's go.'

Janakikutty gathered up the papers lying scattered on the floor. She was more pragmatic. What was the use of arguing with the policeman? Especially during an Emergency?

It was the power of the Emergency that allowed the SHO to behave so rudely. Even superstar journalists had had their mouths muzzled. Who would bother with a worthless journalist low down in the pecking order?

The cement floor, which had been swept and mopped clean, smelt of phenyl. The walls had been whitewashed. As soon as he heard of the Emergency, Dhyan Chand had taken some proactive steps. One of them was sprucing up the station and its surroundings. The drain in front of the police station used to be blocked with sewage and all kinds of rubbish. The children from the slums would sit and defecate around the drain. The gutter was always chock-a-block with broken bottles of DMS, Dalda tins, old clothes and torn footwear which had come floating down in the last rainy season and got stuck there.

Among the papers Janakikutty picked up, there was one with a black and white photo of Vidya stapled to it. She looked at it carefully. A schoolgirl with two plaits tied with ribbons, wearing the white salwar and dark kameez of her uniform, her school bag hanging from her shoulder.

'Who is this girl? She seems to have more sense than you do,' Dhyan Chand said.

'We are friends. Please forgive him. He spoke that way because of the pain inside him. If you were in his position, you would have said the same things.'

'Never. I would never behave irreverently with the police.'

Had he forgotten that he was a policeman himself?

Dhyan Chand gazed at Sathyanathan for some time and then got up from his seat and went to him. His uniform was starched and pressed. His boots and belt buckle were shining.

Sathyanathan had never seen him look so smart. He too had been spruced up, along with the station and its surroundings.

'Listen, my friend. I need only two days to find out what happened to your sister. Only two days. I have only a year to go before I retire. I know every nook and corner of Delhi.'

'Then why aren't you doing anything?'

His eyes were blazing with anger behind his glasses.

The SHO placed a hand on Sathyanathan's shoulder. Sathyanathan was on the point of exploding.

'You all believe that the police can do anything. But policemen don't enjoy even the freedom that you have.'

'Then why are you walking around wearing that cap?'

Dhyan Chand smiled.

'Why are you working in a newspaper? For your livelihood. I also wear this cap for the same reason. I have a family, a wife and three children, of whom two are girls.'

After a pause, Dhyan Chand continued, 'My friend, I have closed your sister's file. Forget her. Both of you may go now. Thank you.'

As he turned to leave, Dhyan Chand called out from behind, 'One more thing. Don't talk to other policemen the way you talked to me. Don't forget that it's the Emergency now. We can kill you and string you up. No one is even going to ask us. Do you understand?'

They walked through Defence Colony Market in the blazing sun.

'I want to invite you home. Will you come?'

'I'll come when your mother is there. Isn't that better?'

'Amma is home. She has taken leave.'

'Isn't she well?'

'She is unwell all the time now. It's her mind, not her body. My mother is luckless. She became a widow at thirty-two. Now she has lost her only daughter. I'm the only one she has.'

They walked towards Sewa Nagar. She pulled her pallu over her head. It was the first week of July. Twelve days since the Emergency had come into force. Looking at the sky, one might wonder if the Emergency was in force there too. There were no birds, no clouds. A blanket of dust had turned the sky into a desert. Why had Indiraji declared an Emergency in such weather? Possibly to harass the people even more.

'Someone is watching us,' she said as they walked. He had also felt it. Everywhere, red eyes were watching under curved unibrows. Every word that fell from their mouths was swept up by alert, fan-like ears.

'It has only been two weeks. Already we are unable to tolerate it. I feel suffocated. There's been an Emergency in the Soviet Union from the time of Stalin, hasn't there? How were they able to tolerate it?'

'Be careful, Sathyanatha. Comparison is an art too, and you know nothing of it. How can you compare Stalin and Indira Gandhi? Stalin is a great revolutionary who changed the course of history. Has Indira Gandhi done anything like that? What is her status in history?'

'Stalin or Indira Gandhi, it's all the same. I'm against anyone who silences the voice of a people.'

'Stalin himself has answered that.'

'What did that worthy have to say?'

'You cannot start a revolution with silk gloves.'

'Janakikutty, you just said that I'm poor at making comparisons. You're poor at quotations. What kind of a revolution are you talking about, if it killed and silenced hundreds of thousands of people?'

'Can you catch fish without getting your hands wet?'

Sathyanathan laughed.

'Why are you laughing? I don't like it when you laugh while discussing something serious.'

'You could have come up with a better riposte. "If only one man dies of hunger, that is a tragedy. If millions die, that's only statistics." That too was Stalin. That's why Stalin had hundreds of thousands of people killed. For him, it was just statistics.'

'There's no need to drag Stalin into a conversation about the Emergency,' she said testily.

They walked in silence after that. It was a time when every citizen could declare his own personal Emergency and keep silent.

Sathyanathan's mother was resting in bed when they reached. The house was filled with the aroma of rice being cooked. Though she was only forty-five years old, Devi looked sixty-five. Most of her hair had turned white. More than the hair, it was the wrinkles on her face and the folds under her chin that made her appear older.

'Did you meet that SHO?'

'I did. He claims he has expanded the investigation to UP and Bihar.'

'Didn't he say that last year? The police are liars. Ruthless.'

Sathyanathan knew his mother couldn't take the truth. She was surviving on some faint, remote hope.

Devi sat up in bed. Her saree was all crumpled. She had forgotten to put on the top hook of her blouse.

'Who's this girl?'

'Janakikutty. She's studying in JNU. She's Kallikkandi Kunhikannan mashu's daughter.'

There was flash of shocked recognition in Devi's eyes, which had lost their shine a long time ago.

'You needn't worry, amma. She isn't into Kunhikannan mashu's politics. Even if she is, what's the problem? I don't have a problem with his politics.'

'Why should I fear politics? I'm very weary. When I see the things happening in this country, I too feel like picking up a gun and joining Kunhikannan mashu.'

Why the shock in her eyes then? Sathyanathan wondered.

Devi went into the kitchen to strain the rice.

'You've come home for the first time. I'll make you some tea. I won't ask you to have lunch with us. There's nothing to offer you.'

'I'll be happy with a glass of water.'

She poured water from the pot into a copper glass and drank it. She could feel the cool water making its way through her body. In the Delhi summer, water was tastier than milk.

It was her second summer in the city. She had come to Delhi in July 1974 with her father. The Jawaharlal Nehru University campus, with its greenery and peacocks and vast spaces, was now part of her life. Her friends and she would get tea from the roadside canteen and withdraw into the recesses of the trees, to sit and chat. Around them, cigarette butts dotted the paths and the base of trees. Sometimes there were liquor bottles too.

Sathyanathan took her to the rear veranda.

'This veranda, where a charpoy just about fits, was my world. I studied here. I slept here in summer and winter.'

Once, the house had four occupants. But now, only two were left, or to be precise, one and a half. With Vidya's disappearance, Devi had dwindled to half her old self.

'I want to move to a better house. But amma won't hear of it. My father brought her here after their wedding. Vidya and I grew up here.'

Devi had been promoted once in between. She was entitled to a two-room house. But if anyone hinted at it, she would say, 'I'm not going anywhere. I want to die here.'

'Amma insists that Sewa Nagar matches her lifestyle.'

She had told Sathyanathan, 'If someone insists that I should leave Sewa Nagar, I'll go to only one place. Where your father is.'

Janakikutty spent a few hours with them. All through, she couldn't stop thinking about Shreedharanunni. It was Shreedharanunni, whom she had never laid eyes on, who had brought her close to Sathyanathan and his family. She could only think of him with respect and amazement as the man who, sitting in Sewa Nagar, had become a martyr by taking the bullets fired by Chinese soldiers in Aksai Chin directly in his chest.

Sathyanathan put her on a bus to JNU, then came back and read a book, lying on the charpoy in the veranda. It was one of the little joys he indulged in, and he had few enough of those. I don't need more, he used to think. There are so many people in Delhi who have even less.

5

THE FEAR OF CASTRATION

The Emergency affected some people like an epidemic. During his childhood, Sahadevan had seen its aftermath. Five members of a family living on the road to Muttanparambu Lower Primary School, close to Abdul Abdunnissar's ancestral home, had died one after the other, after contracting typhoid. Their heads had been shaved to stave off the heat; those were the days before electric fans. Three children, their father, and his sister had died. The eldest was old enough to be married. The barber had come to the house to shave off her hair. She was given injections daily, but she couldn't be saved. She died on the thirteenth day of the fever.

All the five died, along with their unsightly bald heads. The Kalari exponent next door, Cherai asan, survived the fever. But he remained indoors for months even after it had run its course. One day, while going to school, Sahadevan had caught a glimpse of him. With his bald head, sunken cheeks and matchstick-like limbs, he was unrecognisable.

The Emergency was similar. Those who caught it would die; those who didn't die were rendered unrecognisably infirm. Dasappan, Sitaram, Sathyanathan, Kunhikrishnan and many others suffered this fate.

Dasappan lay beneath the jamun tree, fatigued, for three days. Then, he disappeared. No one knew where he went.

During those three days, Sahadevan went to see him several times.

'Dasappa, get up. Let's go to Chandni Restaurant and eat something.'

'I'm not hungry, sir. You please go and eat.'

'Then come, let's have a glass of tea.'

'No, sir. I won't eat anything anymore. I just want to die.'

Sahadevan bought three chapatis and aloo mattar curry and offered it to Dasappan. When he refused to accept it, Sahadevan put the packet beside him and left for his office.

On the third day, when Dasappan disappeared, Sahadevan went in search of him. He went to the place where he used to live. Dasappan's world was small. He was either under the jamun tree or in his room that smelled of the drain. Where else could he go?

While he was waiting at the Jangpura bus stop, Sathyanathan came by. Janakikutty was with him.

'We are on our way to your place. Where are you off to?'

Sahadevan told them about Dasappan.

'Poor man,' Janakikutty sympathised. She wanted to see Dasappan's jamun tree.

They went and looked at the tree. Then Janakikutty went back to JNU.

Sathyanathan had to go the office because he was on night duty. He walked along with Sahadevan, smoking a cigarette. Though he went to work every day, he had little to do. What could a newspaper do during an Emergency? Besides, there were strict instructions from the management about avoiding confrontations with the government.

As usual, the shit-eating pigs along the road were having a field day. The whole place stank of faeces. Their faces hidden behind their saree pallus, the women stood in front of the houses, looking at the approaching men anxiously. All the eyes peeping out at them were filled with fear.

'Sathyanatha, why are these people looking at us with so much dread?'

'In such a political climate, each one is afraid, and they ignite more fear. Fear will soon be the only emotion left.'

'So, patriotism turns to fear, eh?'

'Exactly.'

Sathyanathan was tall and able-bodied. Perhaps, looking at him, they feared he was a policeman. But what part of Sahadevan's puny physique struck fear in them? It baffled him. Was he a virulent being, like the *Salmonella enterica* bacteria that spread typhoid and chewed up and spat out even a kalari guru like Cherai asan?

'Dasappa.'

Sahadevan called out to him from outside the building. He didn't dare enter the room. He understood that the sewage workers from Bihar still lived there.

No one answered him.

'Isn't Dasappan here?'

In the dim light inside, there was a shadowy movement. Was it Dasappan?

Before Sahadevan could say anything more, the shadow leapt out of the room. The smell of sewage hit them. The shadow started running on its spindly legs. The unexpected approach of a running form caused consternation among the shit-eating pigs. They started running too.

'*Nasbandiwale aaye hain. Bhaag jao, bhaag jao,*' the naliwala shouted as he kept running.

After running for some time, the pigs stopped. They swished their curly tails and stood panting. Though the pigs littered more profusely than human beings, Sanjayji's forced vasectomy programme did not include them. No municipal vehicles drove up with a roar to round them up and take them away by force.

'The lives of the shit-eating pigs are safer than ours,' Sahadevan said.

The shouts of the naliwala prompted other men in the slum to run away. Among those who fled were men who cleaned people's earwax for fifty paise and gave oil head massages in public places.

'Why are they running away from us? Are we snakes or what?' Sahadevan asked.

'They may be afraid that we are here to take them away, to get them vasectomised.'

'These poor people living in the slums are ignorant and superstitious. In our Kerala, it's the other way around—it's the rich who are superstitious. Where do the poor have the time to be superstitious? Hunger is their biggest problem. Only education can rid us of superstitions,' said Sahadevan.

'Education will create new superstitions.'

'That's true. Isn't that why scientists and vice chancellors flock to Mahesh Yogi and Rajneesh? Our education system is to blame, actually,' said Sahadevan.

'Recently, there was an incident at Safdarjung Hospital. A pregnant woman, nearing her term, had been brought to the hospital on a bullock cart. The doctor said that a Caesarean section needed to be performed the next day. The word "operation" alarmed her so much, she went to the third floor and jumped to her death.'

'I read about it in the paper. It's no surprise, these poor people being afraid of vasectomy,' said Sahadevan.

'Sanjay Gandhi doesn't realise that sterilisation by force is stupidity. There's no denying that the slums are teeming with children. But who are we to tell them not to reproduce? Who is he to say that?' Sathyanathan was furious.

Pinching his nose closed, Sahadevan entered the dark room. Sathyanathan followed him. There were dirty clothes strewn on the floor. A kerosene stove and some utensils lay in a corner.

There was nothing else in the room. Sahadevan hadn't realised that the manual scavengers from Bihar lived in such penury.

'Dasappan must have been taken away for forced sterilisation,' said Sathyanathan.

That was possible. Stories of such kidnappings were rife. They didn't take into consideration your age and health. They just had to make up the numbers.

'They'll do that too, if they want. They'll get hold of sixty-year-olds and perform vasectomies. They have to fill their quota. These are bad times for us Delhiites.'

Unprecedented, unheard of things were happening in Delhi. Until now, there was only hunger, poverty, and communal and caste conflict. Nowadays it was vasectomies, arrests and incarcerations. People disappearing had become a daily occurrence. It was common for parents to go to police stations on the trail of their missing children.

'The naliwala may know where Dasappan is. They are roommates after all.'

'He may be hiding somewhere. He'll emerge only after we leave,' said Sathyanathan.

They started to walk back.

'Why didn't you go to the office today?'

'Not in the mood. Also, nothing to wear.'

That was when Sathyanathan noticed that Sahadevan was wearing an old, unwashed shirt. Since he had to meet clients and interact with officials at the Customs and air cargo departments on a regular basis, he was compelled to dress smartly. Typically, he wore white cotton trousers and full-sleeve shirts when he went to the Turkman Gate office. His shoes were always polished and shining. The briefcase in his hand contained office documents, books, magazines, a comb, Saridon tablets and a plastic water bottle. He was amused at the reflection of his dressed-up self each time he caught sight of it in a mirror or a windowpane.

'Where are your clothes?'

'The washerman didn't bring them. He usually comes on Sunday. But he didn't turn up yesterday.'

Sitaram usually collected the whole week's clothes for washing on his bicycle. No matter when he took them, he returned them without fail on Sunday morning. After he had laundered and pressed them, any old garment looked as good as new. His tobacco- and paan-stained teeth, the yellow tinge from the mustard oil in his hair and his unshaven face made him look unclean. But when it came to his work, he was scrupulously clean.

'What will you do? If you come home, I can give you some clothes.'

'Long ago, when your house was burgled, Deviyechi didn't have any sarees to wear to work. Lalitha lent her two. Do you remember?'

How could one forget those days?

They could not find Dasappan or the runaway naliwala. On top of that, their presence was making the residents of the slum nervous. All the men remained inside their homes.

'Come, let's go.'

Sahadevan walked towards Sitaram's house. It was close to noon. The heat was scorching; his throat and mouth were parched. But there wasn't a drop of sweat on his skin. Delhi summers were like that—all dry heat. Sahadevan was acclimatised to it by now. It had been years since he started living in this city. Unbeknownst to him, his roots were growing into its soil. It had become a habit to say 'our Delhi' when he spoke of it.

He had to cross the railway track to reach Sitaram's house. Only local trains pulled by steam engines used these tracks—trains coming in from places such as Faridabad in Haryana and Ghaziabad in Uttar Pradesh, which lay adjacent to Delhi. As in the case of the milk train from Rewari, which went through Sewa Nagar, these trains too were full of villagers.

An image of Hanuman had been scratched into the earthen wall of Sitaram's hut, possibly during the previous year's Ramlila. Standing in knee-deep water in the long cement tank near the house, a row of men were washing clothes. They did not run away like the naliwala in Dasappan's slum. But they threw him suspicious glances.

Sahadevan stood in front of Sitaram's hut and called out his name. Loud Hindi film music could be heard from inside the hut. He could see the long table used for pressing clothes, with the iron on top. There were no burning coals inside it. The charcoal brazier lay cold.

'Arrey Sitaram, where are my clothes? Because of you, I didn't go to office today. What kind of behaviour is this? Come and ask for new clothes and shoes this Diwali, then I'll show you! I'll give you nothing. *Ullu ka pattha*!' In spite of himself, Sahadevan raised his voice.

The music stopped. In the silence that followed, he could hear Sitaram's plaintive voice.

'*Babuji, sab khatam ho gaya. Mera jeena barbaad ho gaya.*'

When he saw Sahadevan, Sitaram wailed aloud. The sound was like that of a bamboo being split end to end. He was lying on his back on the charpoy, with the thin fingers of his large hands pressed to his belly. Sahadevan deduced that his problem lay in that area.

'What happened to you? Are you not well, Sitaram?' Sahadevan's voice softened.

'Babuji, I'm going to die. My children will be orphaned.'

Sitaram sobbed. Sahadevan didn't know how many children he had; he knew that there were many. The youngest was probably the child who stood holding on to his mother's saree, leaning against the wall. The young man holding the transistor radio to his chest must be the oldest. It was still playing softly, cradled in his hands.

How had Sitaram managed to get his hands on a radio? It was the dream of every ordinary man in Delhi. When Sahadevan went to Palam airport, he used to see it in the hands of Indians returning from abroad.

'Tell me what happened to you, Sitaram. If you are not well, I'll take you to the hospital. But first stop this crying.'

'He has been weeping non-stop since the committee people brought him back. We are poor people. They think they can do anything with us. No, this can't go on. We will go and meet Indiraji,' said a washerman who had just walked in.

Sitaram moaned, his hand pressing down on his stomach.

'Is it hurting?' Phoolrani, his wife, asked with concern and sympathy.

'When did the committee guys take him?'

'It's been three or four days,' she said.

They referred to the municipality workers as committee people. When the committee people were spotted coming in their military style vehicles, it was understood that something bad was going to happen.

'He has not slept for two nights. The whole night he was crying in pain. What can I do, babuji? They might just as well have killed us.'

Phoolrani also started to cry.

'What did those men give you?'

'The radio. And a hundred rupees.'

The reward for not having children in the future.

Phoolrani dabbed her eyes with her saree pallu. The eldest son held the transistor radio close. He seemed afraid that Sahadevan would snatch it away from him.

'Didn't they give you any medicines?'

'No, babuji.'

'No painkillers either?'

'No.'

Sahadevan went back to Jangpura, met a doctor, bought a strip of painkillers, and came back to the Dhobi Colony. He gave the medicines and some sweet lime to Phoolrani.

After two days, Sitaram's condition worsened. His testicles became swollen. He could not pass urine. He could not even move his hips. He lay on the charpoy and moaned without pause.

The men who had been taken away by force were made to lie in rows on a hospital veranda, where doctors operated on them with unsterilised equipment.

Sahadevan took Sitaram—who was by now rolling on the bed in pain and delirium, running a high fever and with both his testicles and penis turned septic—in a taxi to Safdarjung Hospital and got him admitted. He was in a critical condition. Leaning against the wall of the hospital corridor, Phoolrani wailed. The wives of the other washermen cried along with her. Sahadevan tried to console her. Before leaving, he pressed a few notes into her hands.

The next day, on his way to the office, he dropped in at the hospital to meet Sitaram. No beds were available, so he was on the floor, sleeping peacefully. For a moment, Sahadevan was afraid that he was dead, not asleep.

It was after this incident that Sahadevan began to wash his own clothes. He didn't wait for the dhobi. He washed his clothes and hung them out to dry before leaving for work. At night, he would iron and keep them ready for the next morning.

He had not been writing for a while now. He hadn't stopped writing even during the war. But now, he was unable to write anything at all. Did the Emergency make writers impotent, the way it affected barbers and washermen? Did it emasculate them?

Sahadevan's pen had also been rendered sterile.

6

DISAPPEARING MEN

Once, Sahadevan went to see P.C. Sorcar Jr.'s magic show. Pinky was with him. If Vidya had been around, he would have taken her too. Sahadevan himself was seldom able to enjoy magic. When the magician performed a trick, he couldn't stop trying to work out how it was done. When the magician conjured up a pigeon from the air, he would look at the loose sleeves of his flashy costume. He was sure that the pigeon had been hidden there.

On their way to the show, they ran into Vasu. He was sleeping on the granite steps outside Garhi Artist Village.

'Vasu.'

After Sahadevan had called his name three times, Vasu opened his eyes slowly, like a chicken emerging from a newly hatched egg.

'Where am I?' It was the question he always asked. He closed his eyes again.

'Vasu, do you want to come with us to see P.C. Sorcar's magic show?'

'This whole world is a magic show. We can watch it for free. Why should we pay money to see Sorcar's magic show?' Vasu said with his eyes still closed. Was he sleeping or pretending to be asleep?

Once, Sahadevan had seen him curled up, fast asleep on the steps of Triveni Kala Sangam. There were three art galleries in Triveni. It was a place frequented by many art connoisseurs. The sight of an artist sleeping there couldn't have done his image any good.

Sahadevan didn't say anything. Vasu would have argued back.

'An artist doesn't need anyone's charity,' he would quip.

'Why are you painting then, Vasu? What do you aim to achieve through art?'

'No aim.'

'Why do you paint then?'

'I don't know. I don't think about these things.'

'We don't paint or write for ourselves. It's for society. I'm not the only one who says this. So does Kunhikrishnettan, who's wiser than I am.'

'Let him write for the sake of the society or community. I can't do all that.'

'Dear Vasu, you should read the *Chithrasoothram* at least. It's in the *Vishnudharmottara Purana*. It explains what a painting is and how it should be.'

'If I read all that, I won't be able to paint.'

'You are too straightforward, Vasu.'

'My father followed a crooked path. He made money by taking bribes. Which is why I'm trying to be straightforward.'

Sahadevan was keeping up his correspondence with Shreekanta Panicker, giving him all the latest news in Vasu's life. He had informed him of his new accommodation in Tilak Nagar.

Shreekanta Panicker didn't know that Vasu had stayed with Rosily before that. Sahadevan had decided that there was no need for him to know. He believed that not everyone needs to know everything. Likewise, he believed that not everything one knows needs to be revealed to others. Even if it has to be revealed, one ought to wait for the most opportune moment.

Like he had waited for the opportune moment to reveal Vidya's and Rahul's love to her mother and brother.

Vasu didn't accompany Sahadevan and Pinky to watch P.C. Sorcar's magic show that evening. The consignment containing the equipment for the show, weighing one and half tons, had been cleared and delivered to the venue by Sahadevan's company. That was why he had been sent the complimentary passes. When he received them, he had immediately thought of Lalitha.

Lalitha had stopped going with Sahadevan to watch Malayalam movies or to worship at the temple, or anywhere else for that matter. Earlier, she used to take him everywhere. They were good friends. He did not ask her the reason for the change; he didn't find it necessary. Also, he was a busy man now. He struggled to find time to run his business, do his household chores, and write the novel. He felt envious of people who had nothing better to do than lazily wander in Jangpura Market and stroll around near Eros Cinema.

Sahadevan left Vasu at the entrance of the artists' village and walked towards the main road, holding Pinky's hand. They would take a bus or an auto from there.

'Who's that, bhaiya?'

'He's a painter. A good artist.'

'That's why he's so shabby. He smells awful.' She pinched her nostrils together.

'Bhaiya, why are artists so dirty?'

'Baby, art comes out of muck.'

Though he didn't believe it, in that moment the answer felt appropriate.

They came out of the alley into the main road. Different types of water pots were stacked neatly by the side of the road. Among them were pots with their spout shaped like a bird's beak or a lion's face. People only bought these pots after making sure they didn't leak. Anyone looking to buy a pot first poured water into it, then sloshed it around to make sure there were no leaks. Two buckets filled with water were kept nearby for just this purpose.

'Is your didi happy, Pinky?' Sahadevan asked, once they were in the auto. He had not seen Jaswinder for some time now.

Pinky pulled a face and remained silent. He didn't press her further.

They sat in the front row. Pinky watched with trepidation as Sorcar breathed fire and ate broken glass. Sahadevan found his vanishing tricks more interesting. He made humans and birds vanish in an instant.

This was indeed fitting magic for the Emergency.

Dasappan had disappeared from underneath the jamun tree. Back home in Kerala, Kallikkandi Kunhikannan mashu had vanished.

Everywhere, one heard stories of people who had disappeared. Sudhir Bisht, one of Kunhikrishnan's friends and a professor at St. Stephen's College, whom Sahadevan had once met when he dropped in at Lajapat Nagar, was last seen boarding bus No. 502 to the college. He didn't return. The majority of those who disappeared were journalists, teachers and poets.

During the 1971 Indo-Pak war, the police had taken away Rosily, Sathyanathan and Vasu. Though Sathyanathan had escaped, Rosily and Vasu had spent a night in the Defence Colony police station. Four years later, the police rounded up Rosily and Vasu once again. He was taken to the Lajpat Nagar police station. Kallu mochi, who used to repair footwear by the roadside in Guru Nanak Market, was already there. The police picked up people indiscriminately, whoever came into their line of sight. From university professors to cobblers, they all suffered at the hands of the police. Some of them would return; others wouldn't.

'God, why did they pick up that harmless Kallu mochi?'

The straps of Lalitha's sandals snapped often. Even if it was a new pair of sandals, once she started wearing them, the straps would snap. She used to blame the sandals. Kunhikrishnan knew that the problem lay not in the sandals but in her gait. Anyway, this meant that she needed a cobbler close to the house. Kallu was an innocent guy, always smiling and showing his wide teeth. Every day, he cycled over twenty kilometres from Ambedkar Kunj, beyond Palam Village, to reach Guru Nanak Market. He used to wear the same shirt and mundu throughout the year. It had green, red and yellow stains from the previous year's Holi celebrations.

After a few days, Kallu mochi was released from jail. Two of his prominent incisors were missing. Like Dasappan, who had lost his scissors, razor, clippers and soap stick, Kallu lost his chisel, mallet, nails, needles and strop. And his smile. For a few days, he was seen loitering about in the Guru Nanak Market. One day, Lalitha fed him rice and fish curry till he was close to bursting. The next day, he too disappeared.

There was no news of Kunhikannan mashu, either. That he had been arrested from his hiding place three thousand kilometres away from Delhi, locked up and tortured, a coconut leaf spine inserted into his penis, his finger nails pulled out by pliers, did not find any space in the newspapers. However, the news did reach those who needed to know, in Delhi. It reached JNU first. And after that, St. Stephen's College. The college, already simmering after the disappearance of Sudhir Bisht, started to smoke and burn after Kunhikannan mashu's disappearance.

No one in JNU was aware that Janakikutty was the daughter of Kunhikannan mashu. She was proud to be her father's daughter. But she preferred to carry that pride and gratification within her.

The postgraduate students and some teachers on the campus called a meeting at midnight. Janakikutty participated in it. Kunhikrishnan was also present as a special invitee.

The next day, Sathyanathan and Janakikutty went for a stroll together.

'They won't allow achan to remain alive. They will torture him to death.'

'Kunhikannan mashu will escape.'

'You're saying that to console me.'

'Didn't he escape from prison twice earlier? He will, again. If not, the comrades will go and rescue him. Do you think they'll remain quiet while he is in prison? If necessary, they'll set fire to the police station and take him out.'

'It's not as easy as you make it sound. We are living through an Emergency. You are forgetting that, Sathyanatha.'

'It's when they are oppressed that people become stronger. That's when they become more action-oriented.'

'That's all very good to read about in the books. When the policemen smash your testicles with their lathis, what sense of freedom is left in you? How will you become action-oriented? The people who work in the revolution shouldn't adopt the lingo of religious preachers.'

'Whether it's religion or communism, liberationists have a common language, Janakikutty.'

They were walking through Hauz Khas.

'You shouldn't worry.'

'I don't need anyone's sympathy.'

'What should I do then?'

'I need a drink. Will you come with me to a bar?'

As far as he knew, there were no bars in Hauz Khas. At Shagufa Restaurant, where Rosily had once performed cabaret on New Year's Eve, they used to serve beer. But nowadays, restaurants serving alcohol were rare. Only the five-star hotels had twenty-four-hour bars. But neither of them had that kind of money. Moreover, Janakikutty was allergic to five-star hotels.

'It's not good to drink at noon, Janakikutty.'

'Don't advise me, please. Don't I keep telling you that? I don't like anyone telling me what to do.'

If your father has been thrown into jail, what can a daughter, sitting three thousand kilometres away, do other than drink?

'Come, I know where we can go.' Taking her hand, he crossed the road and got into an auto.

'Where are you taking me?'

'To Jangpura. There's a bar there that's open twenty-four hours.'

'Interesting. I didn't know that.'

'Have you had alcohol before?'

'I have. I know what your next question is going to be. I'll answer it even before you ask. When was the first time I drank, correct?'

'Correct.'

'Last week, in my hostel room. My roommate had a bottle of vodka. When I drank some, all my worries vanished.'

They got to Jangpura Market. The mirror on the jamun tree was missing. The space beneath the tree was deserted. The noon show was in progress at Eros Cinema.

Sathyanathan climbed the stairs of Om Prakash Jain's double-storey house and reached the first-floor veranda. There were pots with roses and bird's eye chillies growing in them. Sathyanathan took a key from one of the chilli pots and opened the door.

'Sit down, girl.'

She looked around. Near the closed window stood a writing table, and atop that, an ink pot and pen. There was no writing paper. In the right corner was a bed, neatly covered with a batik bed cover. There was no dust anywhere. From its appearance, one couldn't tell it was a bachelor's pad. Sahadevan liked to live a tidy life.

There was a small wooden wall cabinet next to the door. Sathyanathan opened it; his hunch was right. There was half a bottle of Old Monk rum inside. Thank God!

'How will we drink this without ice or cold water, Janakikutty? Old Monk is best with cold Coca-Cola.'

'Coca-Cola? No!' she said, annoyed. 'Try and get soda. It goes well with rum.'

'Someone here is quite up-to-date about alcohol, heh? You wait here, let me see if I can get one.'

Sathyanathan went down and fetched a bottle of soda. He was actually in a mood to sit quietly and ruminate. But what could he do when Janakikutty, her father under arrest and possibly being tortured brutally, wished to drown her sorrows with him? Other than fulfil her wishes, what was he to do?

He added the cold soda to their rum.

'They must be inserting coconut leaf spines in my father's penis now.' Janakikutty's voice was low, almost a sob.

'We are sitting here and drinking so that we don't worry about anything.'

'How can I not worry about my father, eda?'

'Then why did we come here?'

'To drink and worry.'

She had lost her mother when she was two-and-a-half years old. Kunhikannan mashu had brought her up all by himself, bathing her, feeding her, singing lullabies and putting her to bed. How could she not be worried about him?

'I'm sure I won't see my father alive again. I'm dead sure,' she sobbed.

'My Janakikutty, only now do I see how faint-hearted you are.'

She didn't reply. She poured more rum into her glass.

'Enough, stop!'

They looked up, startled. Kunhikrishnan stood at the door, a smoking pipe between his lips. He had stepped out of the room without being noticed.

They didn't know that he had been living here in secret to escape the attention of the police.

7

THE SPECTRE OF TIHAR

Lalitha arrived in Delhi in 1962. Thirteen years had passed. She had endured the freezing cold winter of 1975. It was after the Emergency was declared that the Delhiites understood that Indiraji and Sanjayji had power over nature too. That year, June was blazing hot. There was acute water shortage. People fell dead on the streets from sunstroke; so did cattle. The winter was equally bad. As Christmas approached, the cold worsened. The homeless poor who used to sleep in front of closed shops and shuttered stores froze to death by morning.

It was a winter of loneliness for Lalitha. Her heart used to tremble when evening fell and the sky became drab and colourless, following a sunless afternoon. The cold air needed but a narrow slit to come through. The doors and windows were kept closed all the time. Inside these rooms that remained closed, there was only silence.

'Why are you sleeping alone? If you ask her, Deviyechi will come over, won't she?'

'No, I don't need anyone. I want to learn to live alone.'

'This is not the time for that. You need someone with you. Sleeping alone every night is not good.'

'It used to be a problem earlier. Sleep wouldn't come. But now ...'

'I know you don't get any sleep. Don't lie to me. Don't I know how brave you are?'

There was silence. She was thinking. Then he could hear her sobbing. Lalitha was forever energetic. He had rarely seen her face fall. He had never seen her cry.

He put down the phone and sat lost in thought for some time. Then he took a woollen jacket from the armchair where he had dropped it earlier. He locked the cupboard and slipped the key into his pocket.

'Divakara, I need to go to Lajpat Nagar urgently. After you reconcile all the bill entries of Motilalji, you can leave too.'

He pushed a pile of papers towards Divakaran. His single-room office was filling up with import-export documents. He had a turnover higher than Gulshan Wadhwa's in the days when he used to work with him. Slowly, he was getting ahead of Wadhwa saab.

He had heard no news of Wadhwa saab; it had been a long time since he last met him. Once, when he was passing through Paharganj, he had thought of stopping by the old office to meet everyone. But he couldn't. Wadhwa & Sons was closed; there wasn't even a signboard.

Of the two assistants in his office, Divakaran Potti was the efficient one. He could handle all kinds of work, including troubleshooting. He knew all the rules and regulations to do with Customs and trade. A young man who was already balding in front, Potti had come to Delhi from his native place somewhere along the banks of the Bharathapuzha. The other assistant, Abdul Ameen, had recently married, and with that, had lost interest in work. He had time only to talk about his bride, Firdous. He had also begun to ask for advances against his salary.

Stepping out of the office, Sahadevan felt as if he was being smacked across the face by the crowd with their many palms.

The cold air added its punch. Despite the number of people, the usual liveliness of Turkman Gate was missing. After the Emergency had been declared, it was as if young people had given up walking aimlessly through the alleys. The usual crowd of burqa-clad women milling around the huge copper vessels of biryani held up by tripods was missing too. Only a few naked urchins, standing on dark verandas and looking hungrily at the biryani pots, could be seen through the wooden windows. The biryani was not selling out either. These days, the lights went out early in the tenement buildings stacked on either side of the narrow streets. The disappointed biryani vendors disappeared into the darkness with the tripods held over their shoulders and the pots on their heads.

The usual jostling and sounds were missing. Through the darkening alleys, still fragrant with the smell of mutton biryani, he walked in search of an auto rickshaw.

Why did all the people around him suffer so much? Sahadevan asked himself as he walked.

He had lived for about twenty years in Kerala. Back then, he was surrounded by poverty. When he came to Delhi, he had encountered war. He saw communalism and bigotry at work. And now, he was witnessing disappearances.

What else could be in store for him?

When he first came to Delhi, he had stayed with Shreedharanunni. Into the lives of that happy if poor family, Zhou Enlai had sent a bolt of lightning. Before the wounds could heal, Vidya had disappeared. With that, Devi's life had burnt down.

Then there was Uttam Singh and his family. Uttam Singh couldn't sleep, haunted by nightmares of Jaswinder coming to harm in her in-laws' house. He looked more like a beggar than a carpenter. His excessive love of chicken and alcohol had emptied his pockets and destroyed his health.

Rosily's condition was also piteous. She was now on the Kalkaji police station's list of women of immoral character. With the money that she earned selling her body, the policemen of Kalkaji bought lipsticks and sandals for their wives, ice cream and toys for their children, and took their families to movies at Plaza Cinema.

Among his circle of friends, there was only one person who seemed peaceful—Vasu. He lived without knowing either happiness or sorrow, devoid of thoughts about his past or future.

After all these years, Sahadevan was still unable to accept Vasu's lifestyle. But he didn't criticise it either.

Only once, in spite of himself, he blurted out, 'Eda, you are leading the life of a vegetable.'

'Do vegetables shit? I shit.'

'Your life has no spice, no excitement. Do you call this living?'

'My life is for me to consume. I'll decide if it has enough spice or salt. It concerns only me.'

Sahadevan wasn't the sort to consume anything ravenously, not even life. He had money in his pocket, but he was a cautious spender. Yet, whenever he went to Hazrat Nizamuddin's dargah, he gave alms liberally to the Bangladeshi child-beggars there. The children recognised him now as the one who gave them fifty paise or even one rupee, while others handed out ten paise. They would get excited at the very sight of him. One of the bigger boys, Jamaluddin, had survived the previous winter because of the ankle-length sweater Sahadevan had given him.

'There's a Muslim in your family now. Is that the reason for this new-found love for Muslims?'

'In my family? Who's that?'

'Abdul Abdunnissar. Isn't he a moplah?'

Though Sathyanathan was joking, it made Sahadevan indignant. Caste and religion were not important to him. When he saw the circumcised children around the Nizamuddin dargah, it never crossed his mind that they were Muslim.

'There's nothing wrong in calling Christians Christians and Muslims Muslims. It doesn't make us any less secular,' Sathyanathan said.

Sahadevan had his own views on caste, creed and politics, and these were not aligned to the views of Kunhikrishnan or Janakikutty, who leaned towards the radical left.

Kunhikrishnan had been unnerved when he came to know that Kunhikannan mashu had been jailed, though he had been expecting it. He feared that mashu would not survive the Emergency. What troubled him the most was the realisation that he could do nothing to help him. The sense of helplessness was suffocating.

'I came to console you. But I don't know what to say,' Sahadevan said.

'There's nothing to be said. I can read what's in your mind.'

'May he come to no harm.'

'The chances are very slim. I won't be able to see him alive again, I'm certain.'

No one knew where Kunhikannan mashu had been taken to. There was no news in the media. There was no phone call or even a one-line letter from anyone.

'You should be careful. If they come to know you are his daughter, they won't think twice. They'll take you away. That's my worry now. It would be better if you stay away from the campus for some time.'

'Come and stay at my place. We have Vidya's bed and razai to spare.'

'If there are any signs of danger, I'll come. I can't always live in fear.'

'Danger doesn't come with any advance warning. We have to take precautions.'

There were many portents of danger in Lalitha's life. They first came in the form of nightmares. The day they came to know of the disappearance of Professor Sudhir Bisht, Lalitha had a disturbed night. She woke up several times, soaked in sweat. Kunhikrishnan was up all night, typing by the light of a table lamp.

He had quit his job at the newspaper due to differences of opinion with the editor. He had turned into a freelance writer.

'I don't have to write about things I don't want to. Finally, I have my freedom.'

'How will we live without a salary?'

'A salary is not the most important thing. It's peace of mind.'

Her anxieties vanished quickly. She was amazed at the fat cheques that landed in the mail. Some days, he would sit with a pipe in his mouth, bent over and typing till the wee hours of the morning. The cheques were the reward for all the hard work.

He had started writing a book. Unlike Sahadevan's, it didn't get stuck in the middle. Kunhikrishnan had a clear vision for it. He worked hard and was knowledgeable too.

'Does a journalist live here?' a policeman in mufti from the Lajpat Nagar police station enquired.

'No.'

'Then who lives here? What does he do?'

'My husband does business.'

'What business?'

'It's a clearing agency. The office is in Turkman Gate.'

'What is its name?'

'V.P. Agencies. Business is poor these days. We are having a difficult time. We are struggling even to pay the rent.'

Lalitha wiped her eyes.

After giving her a long stare, the policeman went away.

'Well done,' Kunhikrishnan congratulated Lalitha, as he might a goalkeeper who had leapt to save a goal.

'I can't keep up this act. I'll blurt out the truth one day.'

'Don't worry. The policemen won't come again. Why should he? I haven't done anything wrong.'

What wrong did Kunhikannan mashu and Sudhir Bisht do? Lalitha asked herself. She had heard from Sahadevan that Dasappan was missing too. What crime did that poor man commit?

'I can't take this stress any longer. Please kill me.'

Leaving the dying pipe on the ashtray, he went to her and hugged her tight. She shivered. Hot tears burst forth.

'I don't have children. I have nothing. If I lose this love too …?'

'Has there ever been a time when I didn't love you?'

'You work all night. You come to bed after I'm asleep. Have you had enough of me?'

That night, his typewriter remained silent. Instead, the sound of her moans could be heard from the bed. Her breasts were tender in his hands.

'Listen! Someone just rang the doorbell.'

'At midnight? You are imagining things.'

He got up and went to the toilet. She heard the sound of his dense urine falling into the closet.

'Kunh'ishnetta, come quickly. There are policemen outside.'

'It's your imagination.'

He switched on the light and opened the front door. There was no one there. The yard was flooded with the light of the moon in the autumn. He was lost in the beauty of the night. For a few moments, he forgot that it was the Emergency and that his friends had been disappearing one by one.

'Kunh'ishnetta, switch off the light and come back in. Don't stand there. The police will see you.'

The next day, when Kunhikrishnan went to the Amar Colony post office, ten minutes away, the police came again. The New Double Storey colony didn't have a post office. They had to go to Amar Colony for everything—buying stamps, registering letters, sending money orders.

The policemen ransacked the house. They flung around the books that Kunhikrishnan treated like his darlings. They smashed the photo of Mao that hung on the wall. Lalitha had told him to remove the photo, but he never listened to her. It was the first thing the policemen noticed when they entered the house.

'Where is he? Where has he gone?'

'He has gone home. Father is very ill. Very serious.'

'You are lying.'

She remained silent. She prayed that Kunhikrishnan wouldn't return from the post office in a hurry. If that happened … She shuddered.

The policemen went away, leaving the mess in their wake. Before they left, one of them asked, 'What's your name?'

'Indira.'

After subjecting her to a close scrutiny, they stomped off noisily.

He returned after some time. How much longer could he avoid them? Tihar was filling up fast. If they delayed any further, there would be no space left in the jail.

8

WINTER OF FEAR

The winter of 1975 was a period of agony not only for the inmates of Tihar Jail, but also for the ordinary folk of Delhi.

The virulent disease of nasbandi spread quickly, all over the city. There was no inoculation against it. Even if there were, who would come forward to be inoculated? Thousands of forced vasectomies were conducted in the premises of government primary schools, municipality compounds, and big hospitals such as Safdarjung, Ram Manohar Lohia and Lady Hardinge. Those who had undergone the surgery had no place to rest afterwards. Their relatives had to carry them away. The petrified men—cobblers, tailors, rickshaw pullers—howled as if they had been castrated. More than the pain in their testicles, it the humiliation and fear that overwhelmed them.

Pinky alighted from a cycle rickshaw and walked towards her school. Suddenly, a van came and stopped near her.

It was the mortuary van of a government hospital, the black van used for taking corpses to the mortuary and to fetch bodies for post-mortem. She was scared.

When the rear doors of the van opened, four or five villagers tumbled out, as if they were cattle being pulled out by the rope attached to their nose. Their shirts and dhotis were bedraggled. There were bits of straw and tiny insects in their hair and clothes. The school employees who emerged after them pounced on them as they tried to escape, subdued them, and forcibly dragged them towards the tent that had been erected on one side of the school grounds.

The hapless men were bleating like lambs being taken for the slaughter. They didn't have the strength to resist, having lived on half-empty stomachs all their lives. The little strength they had, fear had drained them of.

Kuldeep Singh, the headmaster, was despondent. His school had been given a quota of twenty-two vasectomies that month. He had received warnings that if the quota was not fulfilled by 31 December, action would be initiated against him and the school. They were already well into January.

He had requested his relatives and friends; fallen at their feet. Among them were men who had four or five children. No one budged. They didn't even condescend to listen to him.

'Sardarji, first you get it done. Then come to us. What idiocy!'

What they said was true. He should set an example. But the fifty-one-year-old father of three would not do it. Even if his salary was blocked and he was dismissed from service. It would shatter the self-respect of the Sikh who could only walk with his head held high.

When the salaries were stopped, the teachers and other staff started agitating. Especially the lady teachers. They had no other source of income.

'We haven't paid our rent. The landlord is threatening to cut the electricity connection.'

'What can I do? I'm in the same boat as you are.'

Finally, hassled by his staff, the sardar suggested a way out.

'We are about thirty-five men here, aren't we? Let's do it ourselves. Let twelve people volunteer.'

Among those thirty-five were newly married and childless men. They were shocked by his words. They valued their self-respect as much as Kuldeep Singh did. And so, the tactic failed.

Finally, after much discussion, they decided to use force. The police and other government departments were doing the same. It was against their conscience, but they had to do it to survive.

Before the sky had turned light, the headmaster and his gang descended on Mehrauli Village. Hearing the sound of the mortuary van, all the men ran out of their huts. The buffaloes ran out with them. The villagers hid themselves in the wheat fields and sugarcane plantations. Two crawled into a haystack. The buffaloes, which hadn't learnt to hide themselves, stampeded through the sugarcane fields.

Kuldeep Singh and his followers used force to subdue Lambu and Lakhan from the wheat and sugarcane fields respectively. None of the other villagers came to their aid, not having slept a wink the previous night, terrified by the news of nasbandi. The sight of the mortuary van parked on the edge of the village had doubled their fright and they had run for their lives.

Policemen and municipal workers from the neighbourhood were bringing in their victims, forcibly dragging them to the school tent. The name, age and address of the victim were entered in a document that was signed by a doctor. The age was increased or reduced as per their convenience. The age of the eighteen-year-old Motu, who used to sell hot, spicy samosas at the school's entrance, was increased from eighteen to twenty-five after his vasectomy. The sixty-two-year-old Kanwari, full of phlegm and exhausted from coughing, was forced to undergo vasectomy en route to the hospital. He had neither the will nor the strength to protest. They slashed his age to forty-eight. Kanwari fell on the road, drained by the cough in his chest and the pain in his lower abdomen. As he lay coughing, blood leaked out between his legs and seeped into his torn dhoti.

The Emergency had given the consumptive old man the gift of menstruation.

Unable to comprehend anything, Pinky stood agape at the school gate, her school bag hanging from her shoulder. In the past few days, a tent had come up near the tin-roof urinal stalls on the right side of the school. She had seen people go in and come out. But she had never witnessed such a commotion. She felt the winds of danger, but also some curiosity. Who were these men and why were they trying to escape even as they were being taken into the tent? She would ask Sahadevan when she met him next. He was her dictionary, the one who explained everything to her.

As she entered the school compound, loud cries could be heard from the tent. She shivered.

'Go, get inside,' Kapuria master said loudly, when he saw her standing there, trembling, staring at the tent.

'Someone is screaming, masterji. What is happening there?'

'Get inside and keep your mouth shut. Not a word out of you!'

'I'm scared, masterji.'

'You're a girl, why should you be afraid? It's men like me who have reason to fear.'

'I want to go home.'

'You'll get a slap from me! Now go, sit in the class.'

Kapuria pinched her ear and roughly pushed her into the class. The heavy school bag on her shoulder caused her to stagger. She almost fell.

The teachers forced the children standing in the dilapidated veranda of the school to go inside their classrooms. Even the sixteen- and seventeen-year-olds among them hadn't heard the word 'vasectomy'. Pinky filled them in with the new knowledge she had just gained—what was happening in the tent concerned only men. So the girls weren't supposed look in that direction.

'Sir, can I go and have a look?' the blue-turbaned Gurminder from Class 10B asked the mathematics teacher, Balbir Singh. Balbir carried a sharp kirpan in his waistband. He never stepped out without it.

'What do you want to see? I'll slice you up, sit down!'

Once the bell rang, the children assembled in the yard for prayers. Afterwards, they went to their respective classrooms.

Headmaster Kuldeep walked into the tent, licking the hair-fixer on his moustache to moisten it into shape. A bunch of Sikhs were holding down the newly-acquired victims. Of the five, the first man's scrotum had been shaved and cleaned up. He was a farmer, thin and reedy, darkened by the sun. Lambu, whose lower abdomen had become numb from the local anaesthetic, lay still on the bench, as if resigned to his fate. Yet, when he saw the needles, scalpels and scissors being taken out of the boiling water, he bawled loudly. The children in the classrooms were stunned by the sounds that reached them. Could the starving effigy of a man from Mehrauli shriek so piercingly?

'Stuff his mouth with a cloth,' Dr Bihari Lal said. Kuldeep Singh picked up a piece of dirty cloth lying on the floor, balled it up, and shoved it into Lambu's mouth. Suffocated, Lambu writhed on the bench. Bihari Lal made an incision above his shrunken testicles. Though there was no pain, Lambu looked down at it and screamed open-mouthed. The cloth blocked all sound.

'*Patti daal do uski ankhon pe*.'

The headmaster tied a strip of cloth over the man's eyes. But Lambu could see everything. No one can blindfold the mind's eye.

Bihari Lal continued his work. Through the incision, he hooked and pulled out Lambu's vas deferens. He cut it into two. He cauterised the two ends, causing smoke and the acrid smell of burnt tissue to rise up in response. The wound was stitched up. What normally required half an hour, Bihari Lal completed in twenty minutes. After the Emergency had been declared, in the last six months, he had done hundreds of vasectomies. He had never attempted one before that. Back then, Bihari Lal, LMP, was known as a heart and diarrhoea specialist. From now on, he would be known as a heart, diarrhoea and vasectomy specialist.

'Next, please,' Bihari Lal said.

After completing three or four surgeries, he felt like he was in a trance. With the scalpel held high, he kept urging, 'Next … next … next …'

Lakhan was next in line. He had been shaved and cleaned up and now lay on the bench stiffly. He had lost the vision in his left eye on account of high blood pressure, so he couldn't see Bihari Lal. All he could see was the side of the shamiana billowing out into a pot belly each time the cold wind blew. When Bihari Lal's scalpel touched his scrotum, the blood spurted …

'Next, please.'

Lakhan was let off in twenty-two minutes. But he didn't have the strength to sit up, let alone stand. They lifted him like a corpse from the rickety, wobbly 7B bench that doubled as the operating table, and placed him outside the tent, on the ground.

Headmaster Kuldeep Singh flashed a toothy smile. He didn't have to worry anymore this month. They had completed the quota. Everyone would get their salary, as well as incentives and prizes for fulfilling the quota.

Next month, he planned to go to Sultanpur or Arjan Garh, instead of Mehrauli, to trap some more victims.

It became a common sight, post-surgery victims limping along the roads or lying about and moaning in the slums. Cobblers, beggars, rickshaw pullers and vegetable vendors had become easy prey. When the traffic lights turned red, beggars limped towards cars, begging bowls in hand. Many like Sitaram got infected. It was because of Sahadevan that Sitaram's life was saved. He sent him medicines and food. He also gave him money when it was required.

There were thousands of Sitarams in the city. No one knew how many. There was no news about them in the censored newspapers. There was nothing on the radio. Although hundreds of buildings were demolished, and young men and old alike became prey to forced sterilisation, and journalists, writers, university teachers and human rights activists were arrested in droves, the city wasn't any wiser to these happenings.

Sanjayji blindfolded the entire citizenry and robbed them of their sight, just like headmaster Kuldeep Singh had blindfolded Lakhan. And just like Lakhan could see everything with his mind's eye, some people in Delhi grasped what was going on with their ability to look beyond. Sathyanathan and Janakikutty and their friends, Rohan Sen and Irfan, were among them.

They didn't read the newspapers or listen to the news on All India Radio. Sathyanathan had stopped looking at even the newspaper that he worked for. What was the point?

They were in Janakikutty's hostel room, waiting for the BBC's news bulletin to start. They could gather information about their own neighbourhood only from BBC News broadcasts relayed from England.

'Did you hear that? The BBC says the number of vasectomies has crossed ten thousand.'

Janakikutty could not believe it. More than ten thousand men had lost their capacity to reproduce.

'Who knows how many of them have died from infections?'

Sathyanathan knew the story of Sitaram. Sahadevan had told him.

'If only there were sperm ducts that could produce only girl children ...'

'Rohan, that duct is called vas deferens.'

Sathyanathan owned a rich vocabulary.

Rohan Sen continued, 'If there was a specific vas deferens which produced girl children, all the Punjabis would come running for a vasectomy. They could stop the birth of girl children free of cost. Not only that, they would get a transistor radio as reward.'

'This is not the time for jokes, Rohan. We should do something about it.' Janakikutty was not amused.

'We can do whatever we want. There isn't an inch of space left in Tihar Jail. Where are they going to throw us when they arrest us?' asked Irfan.

All the jails in the country were full. From Jayaprakash Narayan to Kunhikannan mashu, thousands were rotting inside them.

People from Mehrauli, Gurgaon, Chhatarpur, Faridabad and other villages on the peripheries of Delhi had stopped coming into the city. Those who were compelled to do so, took adequate precautions. Milkmen jumped out of the early morning milk train coming from Haryana before it reached the station, and ran. It was not easy to run with their heavy milk cans. Some stumbled and fell, hurting themselves. Some even lost their lives.

The bigger commotion was at the Inter-State Bus Terminal at Kashmere Gate. Police and mortuary vans awaited the tens of thousands of villagers who arrived at, or departed from, the terminus. In the nearby tents, doctors like Bihari Lal were waiting with their surgical instruments and boiling water. The rustic passengers who alighted from the buses—visitors on government business, tradesmen, patients, those visiting relatives—fell straight into their net. Before they could react, the mortuary vans had kidnapped them and they found themselves flat on the benches inside the tents. Injection, incision, stitching up, everything was over in a trice.

Kanshi from Bhandi village, who had come to Delhi for Unani treatment for his back pain, was flung into the mortuary van before he realised what was happening. He wailed from the excruciating pain. When he was pushed onto his back, on the bench, the fifty-year-old villager suddenly understood what was going on.

'Doctor saab, nasbandi has already been done on me. Don't do it again …' he appealed, crying.

'Scoundrel, you are lying.'

Without paying heed to his objections, they tore off his shabby dhoti. The two-week-old wounds on his scrotum from the butchery at Bhandi Village's Primary Health Centre were visible. There were signs of infection on one side. As if he didn't notice any of this, the doctor dug out his scalpel and scissors from the boiling water.

'Bajrang Bali, I'm going to die …'

Kanshi's shriek could be heard over the sputtering and growling of the Haryana Roadways bus that had just come into the terminus.

The committee guys took down his name and address. They inked his finger and pressed it down on the document.

When twice-vasectomised Kanshi tried to get up from the bench despite his unbearable back pain and the searing sensation in his genitals, he flopped back and collapsed on the spot. For two days, he lay there, with not a drop of water to wet his lips. Then, he disappeared.

Now, passengers smelt the perils awaiting them and jumped out of the buses before they entered the terminus. Running down roads teeming with tongas, phut-phuts and cycle rickshaws, they escaped. Some skidded on horse dung and fell as they were fleeing. Municipality workers chased them down. They were overpowered and taken to the tents.

'We shouldn't be sitting around twiddling our thumbs. We must do something.'

'What Janakikutty says is true.'

'But Sathyanatha, this is the Emergency. Whatever we do, it will be risky. I'm not saying we shouldn't do anything. Just that we should be fully aware of the risks.'

'We may not be able to do much, Irfan, but we should do something. At least for our peace of mind.'

'Okay, Janakikutty. Let's go.'

That was how they decided to intervene in the vasectomy camps in Old Delhi.

9

RUCKUS IN CHANDNI MAHAL

The next morning, Janakikutty, Irfan, Rohan Sen and a few of their friends bunked classes and headed to Chandni Mahal. Vasectomies were being performed there at a rapid pace. Rukhsana Sultana, a friend of Sanjayji, was leading the charge.

Sathyanathan joined the protestors. Some students from St. Stephen's College were also present. The disappearance of their teacher had kindled a fire in their hearts. Altogether, there were twelve of them. This journey could end for them at Daryaganj police station or Tihar Jail. Everyone had filled their pockets with cigarette packs. You couldn't get cigarettes in prison. And what else could serve as a soulmate in these tense, trying times?

There was no place even to stand in the bus. It was an old piece of junk with broken fenders, tread-worn tyres, and dents and tears all along its body. It plied on one of the busiest routes in Delhi, route No. 501.

There was hardly anyone on the roads. The unease that the Emergency had brought into the JNU campus was manifestly recognisable in the alleys and markets of Old Delhi. The numerous dark alleys and narrow bazaars between Kashmere Gate and Delhi Gate usually celebrated poverty like a festival. It seemed as if the festival had lost its sheen. The greying, hennaed beards, the burqas, the attar-scented kerchiefs around necks seemed to be in an unusual hurry. It was as if they were picking their way through a cemetery at midnight, not strolling through the alleys they'd grown up in.

'Rukhsana Sultana's camp is in Dujana House.' In that group of twelve, Irfan was the only Muslim.

Huge banners had been strung up in front of the camp. They proclaimed that the water shortages in the country were due to a population explosion, and therefore, there should be no more births, and for that, everyone should volunteer to be operated upon. Volunteers pressed notices into the hands of passers-by. There were young women among the volunteers, wearing white salwar-kameez and dupattas. On top of that, exhortations and threats were being shouted through the loudspeakers.

This was the first nasbandi camp set up in Old Delhi. All the arrangements had been made. Doctors, assistants and volunteers stood ready. But no one was coming forward to be operated on. The normally crowded environs of Dujana House were deserted. Even the shadows of men didn't pass by here. Occasionally, a burqa-wearing form or a child wearing a white skull cap might come along. But even they hurried past, not daring to look around, as if someone might be following them.

Occasionally, a police van or a municipality vehicle drove up. The volunteers would rush to it. They would pull out a bedraggled, woolly-haired scarecrow and drag him into the camp.

After an hour or two, they would bring him out, supporting him on either side. Into his trembling hands they would put hundred rupees and a cheap transistor radio before sending him on his way. He might try to walk. But after a few metres, he would fall on the road, exhausted. Urchins would materialise from the dark alleys and pinch the transistor lying by the side of the fallen man and disappear. Someone else would extract the notes from his clenched palm and make off with them.

Janakikutty and her group were witness to one such incident. They wanted to rescue the man, but with no knowledge of his family or relatives, who could they hand him over to? Where would they accommodate him?

'What shall we do?'

'However much we want to, we can't do anything, Rohan. The Emergency has rendered us impotent and incapable. We have been emasculated without realising it.'

Sathyanathan took a deep drag of his Charminar. The smell of toasted tobacco spread in the air. The tips of his right index and middle fingers had started to turn dark brown from his incessant smoking.

The women who lived on the floor above the furniture and sweet shops gathered on the road below and stood looking at them curiously. Of late, they viewed everything and everyone with suspicious, fearful eyes. Far too many people who didn't belong here were coming and going. Foreigners wandered about, toting heavy tape recorders on their shoulders and holding microphones. When they spied a policeman, they quickly disappeared.

'Let's meet Rukhsana Sultana and talk to her.'

'What shall we tell her, Janakikutty? We don't have permission to even open our mouths.'

'Then why did we risk coming here?'

'We have to do something.'

They threw away their cigarettes and walked towards Dujana House.

'Who are you? What do you want?'

A man wearing white pyjamas with knife-edge creases stopped them. His scalp was visible under his neatly combed back, jet-black hair. An indication that he would soon go bald. There were three pens in his kurta pocket. It was clear from his demeanour that he held an important post.

'We are volunteers who have come to help you,' Sathyanathan said.

He looked at each of them, one by one. He had a penetrating stare. He could have been a policeman in mufti or a spy.

'When we need you, we shall contact you. Leave your numbers here.'

'Can we tell you something?'

'What's the matter? Tell me.'

He had started walking away, but turned around now and looked at Sathyanathan's face.

'We are not against the sterilisation movement.'

'No one is. We won't allow anyone to oppose it.'

'We have a difference of opinion. Kindly allow us to convey that.'

'Difference of opinion, opposition … we have removed these words from the dictionary.'

This was not the language of a policeman or a spy.

'We will send those who oppose us to Tihar Jail.'

'But does it have any space?'

He looked daggers at Sathyanathan.

'Family planning is essential to control the population. Our objection is only to the way it's being carried out. It's not right for you to indiscriminately round up young and old by force and vasectomise them. We have come to say this to Rukhsanaji, and if possible, to Sanjayji, directly.'

The man laughed. It was a mocking laugh.

'Neither of them seems to be here. So maybe I could tell you what we have to say. Though we don't know who you are …' Sathyanathan was interrupted by a loud cry.

A group of volunteers, aided by the police, were dragging along four or five men from the neighbourhood. A crowd was following them. They could have been the parents or wives or relatives of the men. One sickly-looking old woman cried, 'Let go of my son. He is a child. He is not married yet.'

His engagement had just taken place. The wedding was scheduled for January.

'Old hag, we don't care if he is married or a bachelor. We only see if he is a man. Get lost!'

The man pushed the old woman back. She followed the group for some more time. Then she collapsed in the middle of the road and lay there.

A stone came flying and hit a policeman.

From the ancient buildings surrounding them, men wearing white taqiyas came out.

Suddenly, it grew into a mob. There was violence in the air. They shouted slogans.

Before they knew what was happening, Sathyanathan and his friends had become part of that crowd.

The policemen from the Chandni Mahal police station rushed in, swinging their lathis. A few from the crowd ran away. In their place, more people came. It became a bigger crowd. They were pushing and shoving, running and then returning and regrouping.

The police contained the crowd outside. With their help, the volunteers pulled their victims into the camp. Those who protested were silenced with the butts of rifles. The police didn't hesitate to ram their lathis into the mouths of those who were crying. Some of them surrendered. Some tried to shake off the volunteers and escape. They were brutalised even more.

Again, stones came flying from the buildings on either side of the alley. The incensed policemen swung their lathis at the faces around them. Blood sprouted, along with two teeth, from the mouth of an old man wearing a taqiyah. His jaw was splintered. Drops of blood stained his beard.

In that mêlée, the twelve friends got separated. A lathi smashed into Revathi Gaur's forehead. Irfan got hit on his knee; he reached the road, limping. With his eyes closed, he tried to bite down on the pain.

After a while, the others arrived one by one. One of them was missing.

'Where is Sathyanathan?'

Janakikutty searched all around. He was not to be seen anywhere. Here and there, people were hanging around. The volunteers and the policemen were inside the camp. Wails and shrieks continued to be heard for a while. After that, silence was the only thing that escaped the victims who had been rendered mute as animals.

Janakikutty stood in front of Dujana House, filled with dread. Where was Sathyanathan?

He had not been able to escape from the octopus-like grip of the volunteers. They had overpowered him and forced him to lie down. On a bench.

10

THE BULLDOZER ARMY

18 April 1976.

A date Sahadevan would not forget.

A date no one could forget.

Since it was a Sunday, he didn't have to go to the office. Although, the truth was, he took no holidays at all. He went to work on all the days of the week. That Sunday, he was in the mood to write, to sit down and nurse his memories. He liked to ride the wave of his darker memories. It was from the past that he gathered energy—even if this habit had turned into a problem when it came to his friends.

Kunhikrishnan, Sathyanathan and Janakikutty worried constantly about the future. They said he had his head buried in antiquity and tradition, burrowing backwards like a great bandicoot rat. Only Kunhikrishnan realised that Sahadevan was a fellow-traveller on the path of progressiveness. He urged him to be more energetic and bring clarity to his observations and insights.

During winter, even a small intake of water causes the bladder to swell. Visitors to Connaught Place often chose the Life Insurance Corporation Building, which housed the airline offices, to relieve themselves. Against its wall, Delhiites could be seen urinating in line; the frothy urine flowed down the pavement and formed puddles in some places. For Malayalis, who hesitated to urinate in the open, all too aware of the women and children passing by, the only refuge was the toilet at the Kerala Club.

Thus, the Kerala Club became a sanctuary for those with a literary impulse and an urge to empty their bladder.

A walk down from Ajmeri Gate brought Sahadevan face to face with the fruit sellers lined up in front of the New Delhi railway station. The stink of horse dung wafted up along with the smell of sweet limes and apples. In front of the station, villagers walked barefoot. God knows how many of them contracted tetanus from the horse dung on the roads.

Since setting up his own business, Sahadevan had done a lot of work with the traders of Old Delhi. He exported attar, carpets, sandalwood oil and spice compounds. He imported olive oil, Arabian dates, pistachios and crystal ware. Many of these traders were illiterate. They only knew the language they had learnt at the madrasa. Hundreds of their invoices used to be typed up by Sahadevan. These days, the task fell to Divakaran Potti or Abdul Ameen.

When Divakaran Potti first came to Delhi, he stayed with a Dalit in Ambedkar Nagar. He couldn't afford a room for himself. Since he was a vegetarian, he prepared his own meals. In an airless, dingy kitchen, in stoves kept side by side, mutton curry and okra curry were cooked at the same time.

Close to Sahadevan's office was a tiny attar shop, squeezed between a staircase and a Unani clinic. The breeze carried the fragrance of attar to him as he went past it every day.

On the walls, from which swathes of plaster had fallen off, one could see the names etched by unknown persons—Zakina, Qultum, Latifa, Naseefa, Anjum, Habiba ...

'As-salāmu 'alaykum.'

Attarwala Fajruddin would wish him as he walked past. Everyone in the alley knew Sahadevan.

'Wa 'alaykumu as-salām.'

Sahadevan would stop in front of Attar Bhandar and chat with Fajruddin. In the beginning, he did not recognise the popularity of the insignificant little shop. Then, one day, he saw an Arab walk inside. He picked up each bottle of attar and smelled it. Those that he liked, he kept to one side. The first one he chose was a green crystal bottle of majmua. Next, he chose rouh-al-oud. The Arab didn't even care to smell the cheaper mukhallat or abdul akhir attar. He bought ten or twelve two-hundred ml bottles of rouh-al-oud, which cost eighteen thousand rupees each. Fajruddin's main customers were Arabs, Palestinians and Iranians; occasionally, a European Jew or two.

Sometimes Fajruddin would put a drop of one of his extra-special attars on his fingertip and affectionately apply it on Sahadevan's temple. The scent would remain on him till night-time, when he went home and had a bath. Sometimes the smell lingered for a couple of days.

Also close to his office was the Rice Hut store, which sold all kinds of grains. On really hot days, its owner, Abdul Bari, would come to his office and say, 'Madrasi bhai, come. Let's go and have a glass of cold lassi. Come.'

In alley No. 29, there was a lassi shop. It was as famous for its lassis as Fajruddin's Attar Bhandar was for its fragrances. Or Abdullah Bawa's teashop in Khan Market. Sahadevan and Bari would walk to the shop, chatting about politics and local affairs. When he drank the iced, rose-milk laced lassi served in a tall copper glass, Sahadevan felt sated; after that, he knew neither hunger nor thirst. Abdul Bari would get himself a strong, tobacco-infused paan after his lassi. Sahadevan would smoke a Charminar.

There was one thing Abdul Bari couldn't comprehend at all.

'Madrasi bhai, don't you want to do a nikah? At your age, I had three wives and seven children.'

Abdul Bari didn't know how many children he had now. Fifteen or sixteen.

Sahadevan smiled disarmingly whenever anyone mentioned marriage.

Fifteen children. If Sanjayji were to hear of it, a nasbandi camp would be set up in front of Abdul Bari's house immediately.

'Become a Muslim. I'll give you my most beautiful daughter in marriage,' Abdul Bari offered.

Sahadevan was not against the idea. If he were to marry at all, he used to tell himself, it would be someone from outside his own religion. But it was not yet time. His responsibilities weren't over.

Whenever he had some free time, Sahadevan would stand in front of Abdul Bari's shop. The street was always full of pigeons and sparrows. Even pigeons from as far away as Jama Masjid came to Abdul Bari's shop. They would peck on wheat, millet and corn, eat their fill, and fly back. One rainy morning, while going that way, Sahadevan saw a flock of red-beaked parakeets. He stood for a long time, watching.

Also within walking distance of V.P. Agencies was the bungalow of Abdul Ameen, past alley No. 29. The bungalows in that area were one hundred and fifty to two hundred years old. Sahadevan had heard that there was a two-hundred-and-fifty-year-old haveli there. He was keen to see the old heritage buildings, but Abdul Ameen never invited him home. It took Sahadevan some time to understand the reason.

'Saab, ours is an old bungalow. Four or five generations were born there and have lived there. There are twenty-eight adults living in our house. And their children.'

A lecturer at the Jamia Millia Islamia, a bird seller who sat in front of Jama Masjid, men who went around repairing carpets and watches, and tailors who made burqas, they all lived under the same roof with their families.

Abdul Ameen was reluctant to take Sahadevan to such a house.

'*Achhi baat hai*. Do one thing. You and Firdous come to my place one day.'

'When will Firdous find the time, saab? Even I get to see her only after midnight.'

'What a shame.'

'One of Firdous's dreams is to have a photo taken at the studio in Chandni Chowk. But she doesn't have time even for that.'

Sahadevan sympathised with Abdul Ameen and Firdous. They had started their married life in a house with fourteen families.

One day, while out on a stroll, Sahadevan happened to walk past Abdul Ameen's house. It had a high wall. Dusty branches grazed its top. From the alley, it appeared as though there were only trees inside the compound. Suddenly, a man with a long beard walked out, opening the wicket gate in the wall, and Sahadevan caught a glimpse of what was inside. It was not a house; it was a world in itself.

One Sunday, when Sahadevan was working in the office, Abdul Ameen came in unexpectedly. Behind him, clad in a burqa, was a short, slim form.

'We're off to Firdous's house.'

They would take an inter-state bus from Kashmere Gate. Her family lived in Aligarh.

'Listen, saab. Firdous has a BA degree. She is much better educated than I am.'

Sahadevan turned to look at her, pleased. But he could not see her; not even her face. All that was visible was the burqa that covered her from head to toe, and white fingers which peeped out from it with much reluctance.

'She wants to know something. She keeps asking me.'

'What is it?'

'You ask, Firdous. Aren't you the degree holder?'

'Saab ...'

The sweetness of the voice from behind the burqa surprised Sahadevan. It reminded him of a thumri singer. *Jao wahin tum shyam …*

'Saab, what do the V and P stand for in V.P. Agencies?' she asked softly, hesitantly. It was a question that no one had asked him so far.

'It stands for Vidya and Pinky Agencies. V for Vidya and P for Pinky.'

He smiled at her invisible face.

'Who are Vidya and Pinky, saab?'

'My little sisters.'

Firdous wanted to know more about Vidya and Pinky. Though she wore a burqa, she spoke freely. He thought perhaps she covered herself for the sake of someone else. Though he told her all about Pinky, he was reticent about Vidya. He didn't answer many of her questions.

Sahadevan had stayed back in his room that day so that he could read, but all he did was reminisce.

He had cooked lunch—rice, dal, sautéed long beans and curd. He washed his hands and was stepping into the kitchen when the phone rang. The telephone was like that—it rang when he entered the bathroom after oiling his head, when he sat at the table with food before him or lay down in bed after switching off the light.

'*Saab, jaldi aayiye.*'

'What happened? What's the matter?'

'Please come quickly.'

Sahadevan could hear Abdul Ameen panting over the phone. The bulldozers had reached Turkman Gate.

11

THE BALLAD OF TURKMAN GATE

It was the month of April, and Delhi was turning warmer after having bathed in the colours of Holi. Compound walls, cement park benches, buses and cars, were all stained with colour. Vegetable vendors, cobblers and sweepers moved around in Eastmancolor clothes. They didn't have anything else to change into.

Abdul Ameen was panting as he conveyed the news of the appearance of bulldozers at Turkman Gate. In his panic, he didn't even complete what he had set out to say.

Sahadevan felt no panic. He had seen rifle-toting soldiers march in front of Jama Masjid. They had not shot anyone. On Guru Gobind Singh's birthday, he saw caparisoned elephants walk grandly along Chandni Chowk. They didn't go in and gore or trample anyone to death. On Republic Day, he saw gun-mounted tanks rolling along Delhi Gate. They didn't shoot anyone. As part of the Republic Day parade, he saw fighter planes fly past Old Delhi. They never dropped bombs on the old buildings. In much the same way, the bulldozers too would pass through Turkman Gate. Let them pass without knocking down anything or leaving a scratch on anyone, he told himself.

He was unsure about why the bulldozers had come to Turkman Gate in the first place. But he decided to first go to Sewa Nagar after eating lunch and reading for a while. Since it was a Sunday, Devi and Sathyanathan would be home. It had been some time since he had met Sathyanathan.

After last winter's episode at Dujana House, Sathyanathan was always in a foul mood. He refused to talk to anyone. Unlike Sahadevan, he bottled everything up and choked on his own silence.

The day when he went to their place after hearing of the incident, only Devi and Sathyanathan were at home. As he stood in the veranda with his heart thudding inside him, his hand on the doorbell, Sathyanathan shouted from inside, 'No! No one should come in. I don't want to see anyone. Please go away!'

The foot he had lifted to enter froze in mid-air.

'My son, it's our Sahadevan.'

'I don't want to see any devan now. Leave me alone!' Sathyanathan screamed.

He was lying in bed, shirtless, wearing loose pyjamas. As if to conceal something, a folded bed cover had been placed across his waist. A pack of cigarettes, a match box and an ashtray lay on the bed. The ashtray was full of cigarette butts. The room was thick with the smell of cigarette smoke and burnt tobacco. He had no qualms about smoking in the house and in front of his mother. His adolescence was well behind him; he was now an adult.

Sahadevan waited at the threshold. Devi was relieved to see him. She opened the door. He was the one person who always comforted her.

'My son's life is over. Why is God so vengeful towards me and my family, Sahadeva?'

'Don't come near me. All of you get out, leave, go!' Sathyanathan shouted again.

Sahadevan stood nonplussed.

Devi dabbed her eyes and tried to recover her equanimity.

'He's very angry. When that girl came, he didn't even allow her to see him. She waited outside for a long time and then left.'

Deferring to Sathyanathan's wish, Sahadevan sat in the veranda and didn't go inside. He could empathise with him. Anyone else in his place would have felt destroyed too.

'When I see his anguish, my heart breaks. His father is no more. Then Vidya disappeared. Now, he is in this state. What ungodly sin did I do to suffer all this?'

'Everything will be all right.'

'When? After I'm gone?'

Sahadevan looked at Sathyanathan from the veranda. The left side of his face was swollen. His left eye had been reduced to a slit. Purple bruises were visible on his forehead and shoulders. He looked like someone who had tried to fight off the devil alone, and failed.

Sahadevan felt a tightness in his chest, like he was being choked. He realised that neither Sathyanathan nor he could win any battles on their own. Only a mob could do it. He wished to be part of such a mob. But where was the mob? The problem with a mob is that it cannot lead itself. It needs a leader to carry it forward.

Just as Shreedharanunni's living room had a photograph of Zhou Enlai and Kunhikrishnan's bedroom had one of Mao, Sahadevan too had a photo in his room.

One day, two policemen came to his place looking for Kunhikrishnan. They stood in front of Jayaprakash Narayan's photo and asked him, '*Yeh kaun hai*?'

'Shekharan Nambiar, my father.'

'*Tumhara baap*?'

'*Haan ji*.'

Shekharan Nambiar and Jayaprakash Narayan bore no resemblance whatsoever to each other. But they believed him.

Those who wield power can't distinguish reality from fantasy, Sahadevan told himself. He felt gratified at having fooled the representatives of a power that flung its citizens into jail, razed their houses and forced vasectomies on them.

He knew that no one could confront authority head on and stop them; especially for someone like him, it was impossible. Bush fighting was the only way out.

One day, a month after the Emergency had been declared, Jangpura suffered loss of power for a full twenty-four hours. In the night, holding a pen knife, he had stumbled down the stairs. The darkness must have read his mind and come to his aid. The big, wood-framed hoarding was placed not far from the jamun tree under which Dasappan used to sit. It was as tall as the tree. He had seen the poor labourers headed for Bhogal, the school children and the beggars looking at it with awe and reverence.

He pulled the nails off the frame, causing the hoarding to tilt to one side. He hacked the canvas, tearing through the khadi kurta and shredding the pyjamas. Then he cut the thick spectacle frame into bits. All that was required was a pen knife to destroy the hoarding, with darkness as his ally.

In the last ten months, he had stealthily vandalised seven such hoardings in Jangpura and Bhogal. It was a secret he kept to himself. He'd had a close shave once, when a police patrol spotted him. He had run through back alleys unfamiliar to the policemen, to get away from them.

Since it was a Sunday, he was wearing a mundu. He hadn't bothered to change into trousers. He took an auto rickshaw to the office. Abdul Ameen must be hopping around on hot coals. Or the bulldozers would have left the place and he might be back in his bungalow in alley No. 29. The latter was more likely.

Sitting in the auto, Sahadevan thought about his youngest sister. He didn't know how she had come into his thoughts. She was in no way connected to what was happening around him.

Shyamala was past what was considered a marriageable age back home. But she hadn't had to find a partner for herself as Vanaja had. There had been a delay, that was all, and it was not due to his inability to pay for the wedding. He had been ready three or four years ago.

'There are proposals. Why wouldn't there be? Who wouldn't like my daughter, once they've seen her?'

'Then, ammae, why is it not happening?'

He had gone to visit them on a one-week break.

'How can it work? Didn't the eldest one go off with a moplah? That too, one with a twelve-year-old child? Which self-respecting family will choose an alliance with us?'

Many things had changed, but not this. Religion and caste were still more important than a girl's character and education. Sahadevan was bitterly disappointed.

'Curse me if you will. Everything is my fault. But let no one think I'm defeated. I'll bring you a better man than I got for myself,' Vanaja said aggressively.

Finally, she did find such a man. Balaraman was a college lecturer—a relative of the headmaster under whom Abdul Abdunnissar worked. More educated than Abdunnissar. More handsome than him. And they were perfectly matched in terms of age too. What more could anyone ask for?

After the monsoon ended and just before Onam, they would be married. Sahadevan would go, not for a week, but for a whole month. Let Divakaran Potti manage the show in his absence. He had been given a visiting card: B. Divakaran Potti, Manager, V.P. Agencies.

By the time his ruminations reached this point, the auto rickshaw had reached Ramlila Maidan. Through the dust raised by the bulldozers that had gone ahead of him, he could see Turkman Gate. His heart skipped a beat. He started to hyperventilate, just like Abdul Ameen had.

Sahadevan stood in front of the bulldozer with his hands raised. It was moving in the direction of V.P. Agencies. Though the attar seller, the Unani doctor and the spice-exporter of Turkman Gate knew him well, he was a stranger to the man who drove the bulldozer. The driver wondered if this man standing in front of him with raised hands was mad. No sane man would stand in front of a bulldozer that could pulverise him in a moment.

'Please don't go any further. There are women and children standing here, blocking your way. You're not just razing their homes and workplaces. It's their whole life.'

Sahadevan spoke in English. That made the driver slow down. If he had used Hindi, the language of liberation used by Mahatma Gandhi and Jayaprakash Narayan, he would have speeded up the bulldozer.

The potbellied, khadi-clad leader of the Nehru Brigade materialised from somewhere.

'Kaun hai tu? Hat jaa.'

'I have to tell you something. I'll go after that.'

'Who are you to talk to us? Shut up. If you say anything, you'll be shot.'

'We are living in the biggest democracy in the world. You have no right to ask me to keep quiet.'

'Democracy? *Woh kya cheez hai*?' The leader of the Nehru Brigade frowned. He had not heard that word before.

'The people who live in Turkman Gate were born and brought up here. They have lived here for generations. If you destroy their homes, where will they go?'

'That will be decided by Sanjayji. *Hat jaa raaste se*.'

He was surrounded by members of the Nehru Brigade.

Poor Nehru.

'*Chhod do bande ko. Madrasi hai.*'

The demolition squad and the Nehru Brigade pushed Sahadevan out of the way. The bulldozer moved forward. He escaped falling prey to it only because he spoke English and was a Madrasi.

People were running out of the alleys which looked like distended veins between the buildings. There were women and children among them. They lay on the road, blocking the path of the bulldozers.

'Why are you destroying the homes and workplaces of these helpless people? To beautify Turkman Gate? To have an uninterrupted view of India Gate from Jama Masjid?'

'Have you started your sermon again, Madrasi?'

'*Goli maaroon bande ko*?' The CRPF soldier had his finger on the trigger of his rifle.

The area around Jama Masjid was full of dilapidated buildings, it was a place of poverty and squalor. It needed cleaning up. If one looked south from Jama Masjid, one should be able to see the majesty of India Gate. The buildings in Turkman Gate blocked this view. All such obstructions had to be removed; the buildings had to be razed. It was the aesthete in Sanjayji that had persuaded him to beautify Turkman Gate.

There was one more reason. Turkman Gate was a mini-Pakistan. Sanjayji used to tell his friends: There's no need for a Pakistan in the capital city. It will not be permitted.

'It's from the fear psychosis in your leader's head that the idea of a Pakistan in Delhi has been born. The indigents of Turkman Gate have neither chapati to feed their hunger nor a place to sleep. All they have is a mosque to pray in. Tell your leader—there's only hunger, and not Pakistan, in the heads of these wretched, famished people.'

Far away, on the top floor of a hotel, dressed in a white khadi kurta-pyjama and sporting thick-framed spectacles, a young man was observing the scene through a pair of binoculars. He watched the bulldozers moving in the midst of the dust and smog as if on a cinema screen.

The Nehru Brigade, the demolition squad and the CRPF soldiers went ahead with their mission, ignoring the dhoti-clad Madrasi blathering at them. The demolition squad, with their crowbars and pickaxes, and the CRPF soldiers, fully armed and trigger-happy, lined up on both sides of the road. In front of them, men and women blocked the path of the bulldozers which were moving to demolish the buildings in which they had been born and where they had frolicked, married, made love and bounced their babies on their knees. The women and children wailed loudly. They could not stop the heartless, steel-limbed bulldozers. One of the bulldozers drove over a burqa. There were shrieks and howls of protests from all sides. Stones started flying in from all directions.

'Teargas!'

The teargas shells exploded, blinding the women and children. Taking them for gun shots, collective wails rose from the buildings and alleys. People came running from Dujana House and Jama Masjid.

Blinded by tears, the lunatic Madrasi couldn't see anything anymore. However, his hearing was unimpaired. He listened to the growl of the bulldozers, the roar of the falling buildings, and dwarfing these, the cries of the people. Having lost his mundu in the mêlée, he sat down by the roadside with his hands covering his eyes.

When the teargas failed to have the desired impact, the guns kicked in. The bulldozers moved steadily onward, in between, and over the fallen, bloodied bodies.

The next day, the newspapers arrived as usual. There was not a word in them about the Turkman Gate incident. But via BBC News, the whole world came to know.

Janakikutty, Sathyanathan and their friends set off for Turkman Gate. Sathyanathan was still not able to walk properly.

He looked like he was dragging something between his thighs. Because of the curfew, they could not get very far.

There was a funereal silence everywhere. Metal and mortar debris, and the detritus from knocked-down buildings, shops and homes lay in heaps on the road and in the alleys. Amidst them, broken chairs, smashed pots, prayer mats, broken spectacles, clothes and footwear lay scattered. Smoke was rising in a few places. Sahadevan's V.P. Agencies had vanished. There was an open-mouthed vacuity in its place. The front wall of Abdul Bari's grain shop had been knocked down. Rice, wheat and pearl millets lay in heaps in the alley. No birds were feeding on them. Fajruddin's Attar Bhandar had been looted. Smashed bottles of rouh-al-oud, majmua and abdul akheer lay on the ground. The intoxicating fragrance of the attar had turned into a piercing, migraine-causing odour. The sherwani-clad corpse of the Unani doctor lay prone in the gutter. One of his legs had been crushed under a bulldozer. The compound wall of Abdul Ameen's bungalow had been levelled. Stray dogs were sniffing at the corpse of a small child. Inside Dargah Faiz-e-Ilahi, the naked body of Firdous, stripped of her burqa, lay frozen in rigor mortis.

The blood between the tread tracks of the bulldozers was still wet, despite the hot sun. There was nothing but deathly silence all around, bearing witness to the ballad of Turkman Gate.

Part Five

Desires and Disappointments

Everything has been figured out, except how to live.
—Jean-Paul Sartre (1905–1980)

1

THE VACANT THRONE

Only a few thin strands of hair stuck to his scalp. Black glasses with thick frames. White pyjamas and knee-length kurta. A quiet, tranquil gaze, even when he was seething inside.

JP.

Jayaprakash Narayan.

A framed portrait of Jayaprakash Narayan hung in Sahadevan's room in Jangpura. When he first hung it there, he had not seen JP in person. Since then, he had been in the presence of JP, he had heard his voice ... When he spoke of it to his friends, he brimmed with enthusiasm. But Janakikutty displayed a pointed indifference each time.

'JP's Sampoorna Kranti doesn't move me.'

'But it's attracting and moving crores of people, Janakikutty.'

'Isn't JP a product of Vinoba Bhave? What happened there, Sahadeva? Vinoba Bhave supported the Emergency. Mother Teresa also supported it. Sarvodaya, the Bhoodan Movement, nothing's right. There's God and religion in all of them. Harijans shouldn't be given land received through begging. It should be done through a revolution ...'

Sahadevan could never win an argument with Janakikutty. She and Sathyanathan were good at polemics. Sahadevan, on the other hand, did not wish to best anyone in an argument.

Kunhikrishnan intervened, 'No need to argue. There's sense in what Janakikutty says. Yet, in the present political scenario, we can't deprecate JP either. If Indira Gandhi is afraid of anyone, it's JP.'

JP and his Total Revolution appealed to Sahadevan. Which was why he grabbed every opportunity to listen to him.

The first time was just before the Emergency had been declared. He had disembarked from the bus at Ajmeri Gate, on his way to the office. He saw a crowd at Ramlila Maidan, at a time of the day when it was usually empty, except for a few grazing buffaloes and the washermen who were putting up bamboo poles on which clotheslines would be strung up later. Thousands of pieces of clothing would fly in the wind like flags on hundreds of these lines. You might also see a few vagrants, drug addicts and hippies wandering aimlessly. But that day, it was very different. There were banners and posters everywhere, declaring that Jayaprakash Narayan would be delivering his message of Total Revolution against the government at Ramlila Maidan.

Sahadevan spent the morning in his office, attending to work, and went back in the afternoon. All along the route, he saw streams of people headed the same way. They arrived at Ramlila Maidan in buses, trucks, tongas, and on foot. He joined the tide. Pushing and shoving, he got to the front, close to the dais. He wanted to see JP from up close.

By 5 p.m., there were more people gathered there than at the annual Dussehra celebrations. He had never seen such a big crowd. When JP arrived, they roared like the sea.

JP spoke against dictatorship, and demanded citizens' rights and the alleviation of poverty for Dalits. Surveying the heaving crowds, he raised his arms towards them and quoted from a poem by the Hindi poet, Ramdhari Singh Dinkar:

'Abhishek aaj raja ka nahi,
Praja ka hai

Samay ke rath ka gharghar naad suno
Sinhaasan khaali karo ki janta aati hai.'

[Today's coronation is not the king's
It's of the people
Listen to the rumble of the chariot of time
Vacate the throne, for the people are coming.]

Two years had passed since then. Indira Gandhi had withdrawn the Emergency and announced general elections. The Janata Party won, racking up 43 per cent of the votes. On the morning of 24 March 1977, Jayaprakash Narayan arrived at Raj Ghat, with the victorious members of Parliament. By that time, a large crowd had gathered there, as big as the one at Ramlila Maidan approximately two years earlier. Standing at Raj Ghat, JP took an oath to continue his activism, following in Gandhiji's path, for the welfare of the people. In that sea of people, Sahadevan was a wavelet. There were journalists there, and writers and artists, with long hair and with cloth bags slung over their shoulders.

JP's speech was suffused with hope for the country and for its individual citizens. These hopes were mirrored in the crowds that thronged Raj Ghat. The hope that there would no longer be midnight knocks on the door; that those who left for work in the morning would return home safely; that nobody's home would be razed to the ground; and everyone would be able to speak fearlessly. The faces in the crowd looked like those of passengers on a train, emerging into the light from an interminably long tunnel. Mature wheat fields, sapota trees bowed down by the weight of their fruits, clear streams breaking against rocks with shiny, white pebbles at the bottom, and village belles dressed in bright, flowery clothes with copper pots on their heads, singing gaily: the faces in the crowd reflected the relief and happiness of winning back these sights that had been lost to the darkness.

Sahadevan stood in the crowd with tired eyes and an unshaven face. Though he was exhausted, there was also the light of hope. A new country, a new world. He didn't think about V.P. Agencies, which had been turned into rubble.

Although mortified at losing his mundu, he had been thankful that he was still alive and somehow managed to reach his house. On reaching home, the first thing he did was to wrap a lungi around his waist and sit down at his writing table. Then he lit a cigarette. That night, he wrote for a long time. Always unsatisfied with his creations, his usual practice was to mercilessly tear up whatever he had written the previous night. He had torn up hundreds of pages in that fashion. However, not one word of what he wrote on Sunday, 18 April 1977 was destroyed. Each and every word was a glowing coal with a long life.

From their experiences of those nineteen months, Delhiites had come to understand that freedom was as essential as food and a roof over their heads. Nobody, and that included journalists, teachers, politicians, writers, and the common person, could sleep in peace without worrying. Others had fallen into a dark abyss where sleep was no longer required. Kunhikannan mashu was one of them. Although he was alive, Kunhikrishnan could be included in the list too. Grabbing the edges of the abyss, he had climbed out and emerged into the light. But his life was like that of the living dead; he would have been better off dead. And no one knew what had happened to Sudhir Bisht.

Janakikutty had given Raj Ghat a miss. But some of her friends were present, including Sathyanathan.

We should be ready to make compromises to avoid the recurrence of those dark abysses: Sahadevan recalled Kunhikrishnan's words.

More than a thousand houses and workplaces had been razed. No one had the statistics on those who had lost their lives, mangled by the caterpillar tracks of the bulldozers and at the receiving end of bullets. More than ten thousand men had lost their reproductive capacity. No one knew how many had died in Tihar Jail or were viciously tortured. Those days of torment must never return. People were ready to stand with JP and do whatever was required, in order to ensure this.

Janakikutty left for Kerala to see her father one last time. She travelled without a reservation. There was no water to drink or food to eat. But her mind was not on these things. It was full of thoughts of her father.

It took her a while to recognise him. His face was disfigured from the torture and the bullets that had gone through it. One of his legs was broken and misshapen.

At the press conference, the minister claimed that he had been killed in an encounter. A journalist stood up. 'Do not lie about the dead,' he said.

They wrapped his body in a red flag and sent him on his way. Now her father would be confined to being the subject of speeches, orations and articles by others.

Janakikutty returned to Delhi. She was no longer drinking vodka—not out of deference to her father or the ideology that he stood for; she just didn't feel the need. But sitting under the trees in the JNU campus and enjoying the salubrious breeze, she smoked a lot of cigarettes. Her political opponents alleged that revolution was just fashion for her now. That her political enlightenment was only imaginary. That she didn't have the high idealism of her father. That she was a CIA informant in the guise of a communist. Her habits of drinking and smoking were cited by them as proof to substantiate their allegations.

'Lenin and Stalin drank vodka to escape from the sub-zero temperatures. Russians drink because of the cold. Why does she drink when the temperature is 44 degrees in Delhi?'

'I don't care. Get lost,' she said.

From the moment she heard that the Emergency had been withdrawn, Lalitha had sat with her eyes trained on the road.

When she heard the sound of auto rickshaws going through Guru Nanak Market, she hoped Kunhikrishnan was on his way and that her long wait was ending. She had lived through two lonely winters without him. As she lay shivering under razais as thick as mattresses, only memories of him had sustained her. She prayed that nothing had happened to him. She was not sure if these prayers were directed at God, because doubts had started rising in her mind about Him. Maxim Gorky had asked the writer whose side he was on; she had started asking God the same. She had matured rather abruptly, to ask such questions in her mind.

Devi invited Lalitha to Sewa Nagar, but she wouldn't go.

'You lock the door and sleep. I'll sleep outside,' Sahadevan told her. She didn't agree.

Janakikutty offered to stay over during the weekends. Lalitha refused.

'You are very stubborn.'

'It's not stubbornness, dear.'

'Then what is it?'

'I'm trying to steel my mind. Otherwise, it's difficult to live in this world. The gods and the politicians will not let us live in peace.'

This was one of the changes that the Emergency had wrought in her. Earlier, her response would have been, 'I've made an offering of vellattu to Parassinikadavu Muthappan. The Emergency will be withdrawn shortly.'

She believed that she had become mentally strong. A police jeep passing by didn't make her heart skip a beat. She had developed enough sense to recognise that when the windows rattled at night, it was the wind and not the police.

Sahadevan and Sathyanathan noticed these changes in her. They called often, to check on her. They offered to fetch things from the store and asked if she needed any money.

One afternoon, there was an unexpected visitor. It was Vasu. He had tied up his long, dandruff-ridden hair at the back, using a rubber band. When he came closer, she smelt varnish.

'Don't worry, everything will be all right.'

Vasu placed a bag of apples in front of Lalitha. As though he were visiting someone in a hospital. He had been walking back from Garhi Artist Village after visiting friends. But, as usual, he had lost his way. Sometimes he had to ask for directions even to get to his barsati in Tilak Nagar.

'Hope Kunhikrishnan sir is keeping well.'

'Vasu, what are you saying? There has been no news of him since he was taken away. I don't even know if he's alive.'

This was news to Vasu.

'I thought Kunhikrishnan sir calls every day.'

He scratched his head with his paint-stained fingers.

Sahadevan had once told Lalitha that Vasu lived elsewhere, not in this world. She could see that for herself now. Which prisoner could call his wife from jail, that too, during the Emergency? What an insensitive man he was.

She went to the kitchen to make tea. Vasu sat outside in the cane chair. When she returned, he was kneading something warm in his left palm. Dust and fragrance rose from it. After filling his cigarette, he put it between his lips.

'Chechi has lost weight. Must be because Kunhikrishnan sir is not here. You should eat well.'

He drank a mouthful of the hot tea. Smoke from the tea and the cigarette hovered around his lips intermittently. The normally taciturn Vasu chatted with Lalitha for a long time. He would have stayed for lunch if she had asked him, but she had not cooked today. Her appetite had left along with Kunhikrishnan; her hunger was locked up in Tihar Jail. Her happiness was also behind bars.

'Kunhikrishnan sir is a follower of Mao, isn't he?'

'I know nothing of politics, Vasu.'

'I like Mao very much. Have you noticed his face? It's like a pumpkin. In America, during Halloween, children draw eyes and noses on pumpkins. I've seen pictures. Just like Mao.'

At 1 p.m., as the students of Frank Anthony School headed for home, Vasu left for his barsati in Tilak Nagar. The smell of his cigarette still lingered in the house.

Acquaintances from back home, as well as friends, visited regularly, to ask about her welfare. That should have pleased her. However, for some strange reason, it only deepened her sorrow and increased her unease. Having studied in a Malayalam-medium school in a village, her knowledge of English was poor. Had it been as good as Sathyanathan's, she might have said, 'Leave me alone, go!'

She didn't know what was happening to her. Sometimes she felt an intense pain. Sometimes it was a nameless, indescribable fear and disquiet. Sometimes, hatred and anger. Sometimes, nothing. Only emptiness.

All the white-uniformed students of Frank Anthony School had gone home. The road in front of Guru Nanak Market was deserted. An auto rickshaw stopped in front of their house. When she opened the door, there stood Kunhikrishnan ...

For a while, they stood looking at each other without saying anything.

'You've lost weight. Just skin and bones.'

'If you'd come any later, there wouldn't have been any skin or bones. My empty form would have opened the door when you rang the bell.'

Kunhikrishnan looked at his wife in amazement. Had the Emergency, which had killed the words on every tongue and pen, sown seeds of dark poetry on her tongue?

'You haven't lost weight. You are the same as when you left.'

He never lost weight, whether he ate or not. That was the way he was built. But other changes were visible. His face looked pasty. His once beautiful, luxuriant, grey-streaked hair had vanished. In its place was the short crop of a prisoner. No one would have recognised him at first glance.

He entered the house. She had kept everything neat and tidy. There were no wrinkles in the starched and ironed curtains at the windows. The cushions on the sofas and chairs were spotless. There was no dust on the ceiling fan. The embroidered cover on the radio was neatly ironed too.

Instead of lying sleepless at night, she would wash and iron clothes.

'How much you must have suffered in my absence! You don't even know how to withdraw ten rupees from the bank. That was my worry.'

'You've come back in one piece, and that's all I asked for.'

'I thought we'd never meet again.'

'We'll talk later. Go and have a bath, and then we'll eat. How long has it been since we ate together?'

They were interrupted by a loud honking. Kunhikrishnan had forgotten to pay the auto-rickshaw driver who had brought him home from Tihar Jail. It was with much reluctance that the driver had agreed to come to New Double Storey. He was sure that Kunhikrishnan was a rapist or a murderer.

'Do you have ten rupees?'

She found the money and offered it to him. He stood still.

'What, Kunh'ishnetta?'

'Nothing. Give him the money, will you?'

When she returned after paying the driver, he was standing exactly as she had left him. His troubled look and unusual stance sent a bolt of fear through her.

He said slowly, 'Lalitha, both my hands have become useless. But you shouldn't feel sad. We can make it all right. At least I've come back alive. That's a great thing in itself.'

She went up to him and looked at his hands. His left arm was broken and hung loose from the shoulder. When she interlocked her fingers with his, he didn't feel them. His fingers had lost their sense of touch.

She stood there for some time, unable to speak.

'Don't cry.'

'How can I not cry?'

'Only my hands have been lost. I'm still alive. Don't you remember Sudhir Bisht? From St. Stephen's College? They chopped off his penis in the jail …'

She shuddered.

She sat him down in the bathroom and applied oil on his body. She couldn't see a single wound or scab. They had focussed on his hands. They only feared his hands which used to fly over the keys of the Remington typewriter.

She bathed him, towelled him down, dressed him in a fresh shirt and mundu, and seated him at the dining table. She sat next to him, rolled the boiled rice into little balls and fed him. There was only rasam to go with the rice. She had no pappadam or lime pickle to offer him. Yet, he ate with relish.

'Tomorrow, I'll make yellow cucumber curry for you.'

Though Kunhikrishnan had come back, she could not go back to being the old Lalitha. The Emergency inside her mind still continued.

Sathyanathan and Sahadevan felt the same way. Sahadevan had lost his company and Sathyanathan his ability to reproduce. Kunhikrishnan had lost both his hands.

The Emergency continued in the lives of thousands of poor people in Turkman Gate, who had lost their partners, children and livelihood.

2

NO LOCKS OR KEYS

Nenmanda Shreekanta Panicker didn't have the confidence to travel alone to the big city. So he came with an attendant, an ex-serviceman who had travelled the length and breadth of the country for sixteen years, in and out of uniform. Shreekanta Panicker was driven by his desire to meet Vasu. The only things he had ever pined for as much were brandy and boiled duck eggs.

'I won't forget you, sir.' Shreekanta Panicker embraced Sahadevan with his large arms. They reminded Sahadevan of ducks.

'I haven't been able to help you enough, sir. I'm sorry for that.'

'No, no, you shouldn't say things like that, sir. I've got my son back only because of you.'

Panicker's breath smelt of brandy. He must have been drinking on the train. He had taken the Jayanti Janata Express, which brought one directly to Delhi from Kerala without having to suffer mosquito bites in some lodge in Madras while waiting to change trains.

Shreekanta Panicker surveyed the scene with his disproportionately small eyes. The Jayanti Janata terminated at

Hazrat Nizamuddin railway station after its long journey. On the crowded platform, a pushcart filled with earthen water pots went past them. Another pushcart, piled with pakodas and samosas and with a swarm of flies on top, stopped in front. Coolies and beggars tailed them hopefully. Though Panicker had a rather large suitcase with him, he didn't need a porter. The ex-serviceman's strong arms carried it as if it were a tiny chick. When the smell of fresh shit assailed his nose, Panicker showed his displeasure. Shit splattered as it fell from the latrines in the bogies and lay wet between the tracks. He wondered if this was really the capital of the nation.

Sahadevan had asked himself the same question when he first came to Delhi in 1959.

Why had Vasu left his verdant land of rivers and gentle breezes for this hell? Shreekanta Panicker asked himself. The possibility that Vasu was as passionate about travelling as Panicker was about brandy and boiled duck eggs didn't occur to him. Did that mean big thoughts occurred only inside small heads?

'I've booked you a room in a hotel.'

'I'll sleep at my son's place.'

'Vasu asked that you don't go there. He requested me to reserve rooms at the South Indian Lodge in Karol Bagh. Since the area is full of South Indians, you won't have any problem, sir.'

'Did my son say that?'

'Yes. But you shouldn't take it to heart. Vasu is a loving guy. He has the mind of a child.'

'Sir, I know that. He is my son. Till he was nineteen, my wife and I looked after him. It's a good thing she is not here to hear this.'

They walked out of the railway station.

'When can I meet Vasu?'

'Go to your room, have a bath, eat and take some rest. Vasu will come by then.'

'Sir, I haven't come to Delhi to eat or rest. I've come to meet my son, you know that.'

'He'll come. If he doesn't, I'll bring him.'

'So, it has got to the point where I need to take an appointment to see my own son.'

After that, Panicker sat in the taxi silently. He seemed to have regained his equanimity.

The area around Nizamuddin was still full of Bangladeshi refugees. Most of them were children. They came running with their begging bowls as soon as any cars stopped at the traffic lights. Sahadevan recognised Jamaluddin among them. He was no longer the kid who used to go about naked. Right in front of his eyes, he had grown up from a hungry, scrounging kid to a big boy. But Sahadevan could still see the ribs sticking out on his shirtless torso. Last year, he had seen the photo of a camel that had starved to death in Rajasthan. Jamaluddin reminded him of that camel, all skin and bones.

After dropping Panicker at the South Indian Lodge, Sahadevan returned to Jangpura. He was full of sympathy for Panicker. His grouse against Vasu had always been that he was not anchored to the ground. Sahadevan believed that even the best of artists shouldn't live the way Vasu did. A real artist walks with both feet on the ground.

He was no longer poor. He didn't wait for hours in queue for Amritsari roti and dal at the gurdwara. Even if he had no money in his pocket, he was well-fed. Yet, he chose not to improve his lifestyle.

One day, when Harilal Shukla had turned up unexpectedly at Garhi Artist Village, he had been greeted by the sight of Vasu fighting for two chapatis. The place was frequented by many artists. There were different studios for painting, pottery and sculpture. What attracted Vasu the most was the old etching press in the graphics studio. But the reason he went there was not only to learn the workings of the press.

The inmates of the village were like Vasu. They dressed as they pleased and wore their hair and beards long. There was a twenty-five-year-old, grey-haired Bengali sculptress among them. Rooposhi sat amidst incomplete terracotta figures. Some were without lower limbs, some headless. Some without eyes and nose. She never completed a sculpture. She was a sculptor of incompleteness.

Vasu was very hungry when he entered. In between the kiln and the wet, kneaded clay lay a chipped plate with three chapatis and vegetable curry. Without much thought, Vasu tore a chapati into four, scooped up some curry with a piece, and put it in his mouth. When he had eaten two chapatis, Rooposhi, who had gone to wash the clay off her hands, returned.

'Those are my chapatis. Paid for by me. How dare you eat them?'

She rushed in and grabbed his hand. Though one roti was left on the plate, Vasu had polished off the curry.

'I was hungry.'

'So you ate someone else's food? If you are hungry, buy your own and eat it. Idiot!'

'I have no money.'

'Then starve, it's rude to eat someone else's food.'

'Propriety is not for the hungry. It's for people whose stomachs are full.'

'First you steal my chapatis, and then you have the audacity to argue with me?'

Rooposhi really lost it then. She transformed into Kali, the goddess. Hearing the uproar, the watchman and other artists came over. By that time, she had grabbed and ripped Vasu's shirt.

That was when Harilạl Shukla walked in, clad in a sparkling white pyjama-kurta and chewing paan. Though his hair was still black, his moustache had turned grey.

'*Kya hua Vasu? Kya baat hai?*'

'He stole my chapatis.'

'*Bas*? That is all?'

'I paid for those chapatis. What will I eat now? He's not an artist, he's a thief.'

'Don't worry, Rooposhi. What would you like to eat?'

Harilal Shukla gave some money to the watchman and told him, 'Buy her three parathas, dal makhani, kadhai paneer.'

'Isn't Rooposhi a Bengali and don't they have a sweet tooth?' he said. 'Get a plate of ras malai too.'

'Get a kulfi instead,' Rooposhi corrected him.

'Vasu, are you still hungry? Do you need something more?'

'I want to eat her, this Kali.'

Harilal Shukla laughed. He walked out leading Vasu by his hand. His shirt, ripped at the shoulder, made him look like a beggar.

'What did you do with all the money I gave you?'

'I sent it to the Railways.'

'What?'

'I owe the Indian Railways a lot of money. I travelled everywhere without tickets.'

Harilal Shukla had paid Vasu after selling one of his smaller paintings. That should have sufficed for two or three months. But Vasu had got a draft made for that amount and sent it to the Divisional Manager of Northern Railways with a note.

'*Respected sir, I owe the Indian Railways a lot of money for travelling ticketless. Please credit the enclosed amount to my account.*'

'You are mad, yaar, stark raving mad.'

Harilal Shukla rubbed his hands in despair. He disliked seeing Vasu starve. He was an artist with a great future. No artist should starve. That was why he kept giving Vasu money. But what was the use? Whatever was given was frittered away within hours.

Vasu's face and the piteous look in his eyes as he stood there with a half-eaten chapati stayed in his mind. That same day, he made arrangements for him to eat at three restaurants in the city. He could go to them anytime and eat as much as he wanted. The bill would be paid by Harilal Shukla. One of the restaurants was on the rooftop terrace of Mohan Singh Place. It was popular with families, children and courting couples. They came for the spicy potato cutlets and steaming-hot tea.

One day, Vasu went to the restaurant in Mohan Singh Place with two beggars in tow.

'Masala dosas and espresso coffees for these guys. Two idlis and black tea for me.'

The restaurant was crowded. They found seats with some difficulty. Vasu sat between the two beggars. He started to smoke the cigarette he had rolled earlier.

The customers sitting close to them protested. Then they got up and left.

The restaurant manager went up to Vasu. He didn't get into an argument.

'Do you have money to pay for the masala dosas and espressos?'

'Harilal Shukla will pay.'

'No. He will pay only for what you eat. That is Shukla saab's instruction.'

Vasu created a scene. The people seated on the terrace, enjoying the evening view with their potato cutlets and coffee, became uneasy. Some of them walked out. More than Vasu's shouting, it was the beggars and their rank smell that bothered them.

Vasu also walked out, holding the hands of the beggars.

He never went back to the restaurant.

The accommodation Harilal Shukla had arranged for Vasu was spacious—more than double the size of Lalaji's place in Govind Puri, which he had shared with Rosily. There was a large room, kitchen and bathroom. And a large terrace. The building belonged to Sunil Chitkara, a relative and friend of Harilal

Shukla. Chitkara, a rich man with furniture shops all around Delhi, had offered Vasu the barsati without rent. Vasu had only to gift him a painting once in a while.

'Now you can paint comfortably.'

'No one paints in comfort,' said Vasu. He sat on the terrace, looking into the distance. He could see the high watchtower of Tihar Jail and the silhouette of the armed policeman on watch. Vasu was not pleased by the sight of the jail.

'All jails should be shut down. Humans don't require jails.'

'Then where will the thieves and murderers be incarcerated?'

'This whole world is one big jail. Thieves, murderers, all of us are inside it. Why do you need any more jails?'

'So, you are saying that Tihar Jail should be closed? All right. I'll have it shut down,' Harilal Shukla said, his smile revealing his red, paan-stained teeth.

Vasu had always hated the idea of jails, like those that Gandhiji had been locked up in during the Independence struggle. Jayaprakash Narayan had been sent to jail too, during the Emergency. After the Emergency, he hated jails even more. It was in Tihar Jail that Kunhikrishnan's arms were crushed, leaving them useless.

One day, he picked up a stone lying on the parapet and flung it angrily, with all his strength, in the direction of Tihar. It travelled less than a hundred metres and landed near a hungry stray dog on the road below. The dog leapt up and howled with its infected, ulcerous throat, its face turned towards the jail. Its voice was as weak as Vasu's throw had been.

Vasu did not align with any particular ideology, Congress or Communist. But if there was anything that required stoning, he was ready to cast the first stone.

Irrespective of the Vasus of the world throwing stones and mangy mongrels howling at it, Tihar Jail was there to stay.

This was a line in Sahadevan's novel.

'Here's the key.'

'Why do I need a key? Is it to lock myself in?'

'You should lock up whenever you go out. All your paintings are in the room.'

'A burglar who steals paintings is yet to be born.'

'They will be.'

Harilal Shukla laughed, looking at Vasu. He put the key away safely. It had rusted due to long years of disuse. He had to use Dalda to remove the rust.

Vasu had never used keys in his life. He didn't even know if a key was to be turned to the right or the left to unlock a door. Or to lock it. He never locked the barsati when he stepped out.

When he stayed with Rosily, he used to watch her latch the door and secure it with a big Godrej lock. Even though it had duplicate keys, she never gave him one. Vasu spent most of his time in the shade of the neem tree and not inside the house. He didn't need a key to enter the yard.

On the second day of his arrival in Delhi, at around 3 p.m., Shreekanta Panicker went to Vasu's barsati, accompanied by Sahadevan.

At the end of the long auto rickshaw ride from Karol Bagh to Tilak Nagar, his eyes were bloodshot and his loose white trousers and shirt were drenched in sweat. The heat drove him crazy. He hadn't been able to sleep at all, the previous night. He couldn't decide if it was the thought of meeting Vasu, the mosquitoes or the heat that kept him awake. All three, probably.

Though Vasu had said he would come to the lodge by the evening, he hadn't turned up. Panicker's eyes hurt from watching for his arrival. Disappointed, he had called Sahadevan at 9 p.m.

'He will come, sir. It's only nine o'clock. Please relax.'

'It's been five or six years since I saw my son. Except for you, who else can I talk to about my sorrow, sir?'

'If he doesn't come, we'll go to his house tomorrow. Don't be upset,' Sahadevan consoled Panicker.

He stood outside the lodge with his eyes peeled. Ajmal Khan Road was still crowded. During the summer, people come out in the late evenings to shop. Garments, shoes and sandals were cheap in this market.

Vasu did not come.

And so, Panicker set out for Tilak Nagar with Sahadevan's assistance. Vasu had told Sahadevan that under no circumstances must his father be brought to his place. But Sahadevan was certain that Vasu would have forgotten his own instruction. He would even have forgotten that Shreekanta Panicker was in Delhi.

Sahadevan rang the doorbell. There was no response. He pushed the door open. Though the fan was on at full speed, there was no one inside the room. Sahadevan guessed that Vasu had gone out without locking the door, as usual.

Shreekanta Panicker looked around. This was the house his son was staying in. There were two faded cane chairs and an old sofa to sit on. Harilal Shukla had bought the scruffy furniture off a scrap trader in Tilak Nagar. The floor was covered with cigarette butts and sheets of paper. Piled in one corner were paintings and un-stretched canvases. On the mattress, which lay on the floor covered by a shabby sheet, underwear, an unwashed lungi, a shirt and a towel were strewn about. Since the windows had no curtains, a hot breeze blew into the room. There was a single painting on the wide walls, of a naked woman bathing. Shreekanta Panicker turned pale looking at it. He didn't know it was a print of Ingres's *Bathing Woman*. Even if he had, it wouldn't have made a difference. It was a good thing his mother wasn't here to see it.

They waited for Vasu. There was no question of Panicker leaving without meeting his son. It had been five or six years since he had seen him. He could wait no longer. Wasn't that why he had suffered the heat in the Jayanti Janata for three full days?

Seated in the cane chair, Sahadevan's eyelids drooped and he started nodding off in the afternoon heat.

He woke up at the sound of a jeep braking to a stop. He heard the loud voice and laughter of Harilal Shukla.

'Vasu has come, sir.'

The father stood and gazed at his son as he climbed up the dark stairs. When Vasu reached the terrace, a blinding light fell on him.

He was no longer the handsome, boyish Vasu his father remembered. He was a man with long, dry hair and a wispy beard. His face was marked with pimples. His bare feet were caked with mud and dust. His ill-fitting shirt had no buttons and there was a tear on one shoulder. Panicker thought he looked like some beggar he had seen in Chinnakada.

He couldn't take his eyes off his son. Suddenly his large, aged body started to shiver as if with malaria. He stuffed a handkerchief in his mouth to stifle the sob that threatened to wrench out of him.

Why had his son chosen such a life?

3

THE TEARS OF SAIFUL ISLAM

A few months after the Emergency was withdrawn, one day in July 1977, at the height of summer, when everyone kept looking up and waiting for the rains, Sahadevan, Divakaran Potti and Abdul Ameen went into a tea shop. It was a makeshift lean-to with a roof made of asbestos sheets, and five plastic chairs, and it stood by the side of a big building. In the turgid oil boiling in a centuries-old, burnt wok, bread pakodas were being deep-fried. Sahadevan ordered three teas. One with less sugar for Divakaran Potti, in whose blood the sugar was rising. Cardamom and ginger-infused masala tea for Abdul Ameen. One normal tea for Sahadevan. He was ever the normal person.

'How's your new job, Divakara?'

'Back-breaking work. The salary is hardly anything. And it's never paid on time. Today is the sixteenth, isn't it? I still haven't got this month's salary.'

Divakaran sighed. There was a seared, sun-burnt look on his face. He used to look so much smarter in his full-sleeve shirt and tie, with three or four ballpoint pens in his pocket, back when he was with V.P. Agencies.

'How are you going to manage after your wedding?'

'I'm not planning to bring my wife here immediately. She can stay with my mother for a while.'

'That isn't right. After marriage, the girl should stay with her husband. That's the proper thing to do.'

'Where will we stay if I bring her here? Can we sleep on the road? My salary being what it is, I can't even afford a barsati.'

He was sharing a room with four other bachelors.

There was despondency and disgust in his voice. Thousands of people lived on the city's streets. A new set of refugees had joined the Bangladeshis: the occupants of the buildings razed by bulldozers during the Emergency. Many of them had lost their livelihood and the roof over their head, and now, begged on the city's streets. They had become refugees in their own country.

'Then why are you getting married in such a hurry? Why don't you hold on till you have some money?'

'Honestly, I'm not marrying for myself. It's for my mother. She doesn't let me be. Her letters are full of this one thing.'

I don't have a mother like that. That's why I'm single and unattached even though I'm close to forty, Sahadevan told himself. What a joke.

'Will you have something to eat?' he asked Abdul Ameen, who was blowing into his steaming-hot masala tea. He shook his head. The usually ebullient Abdul Ameen looked glum. He had suffered the greatest loss amongst them. How could he get over losing Firdous?

'When is your nikah, Abdul Ameen?'

'Soon. As soon as the repairs on the bungalow are complete.'

The bulldozer had brought down the compound wall and one side of the bungalow which had housed twenty-eight adults and their progeny. It had entered the narrow alley, knocking down structures on either side. Afterwards, the joint family had got scattered. They were all living in different places now. It would cost them a lot of money to build the compound wall, but the building itself would have to be repaired.

Abdul Ameen did not have a job anymore. The family of the girl he was going to marry were helping him out. So, he was able to survive. He wore new clothes. His skull cap was also new.

Good, Sahadevan said to himself. If new clothes and a new prayer cap can help him forget Firdous, why not?

He lit a cigarette. Abdul Ameen stepped out to buy paan at the paan bhandar across from the tea shop. Divakaran Potti didn't want anything. He only had two things on his mind. After fantasising about it for so long, he was finally going to marry. But he would have to leave his wife with his mother and return alone. The second was a misgiving: What if the girl rejected him when she saw his bald pate?

If he craned his neck a little, Sahadevan could see the plot of land on which V.P. Agencies had stood. It looked like the mouth of a cave. Everything had been knocked down. There were piles of stones and mortar all around. The front wall looked as if it would collapse any moment.

After the bulldozers had left, he had returned to Turkman Gate. In that eighteen-foot-by-thirteen-foot space was the life he had painstakingly built. That life was no more.

There were policemen and soldiers everywhere. The area was under curfew. Since he knew all the alleyways and by-lanes, he used their labyrinthine network to reach his destination. The signboard of V.P. Agencies, with an aeroplane in mid-flight in the left corner, lay in pieces. Amidst the rubble, the table lay broken in half. The arms and legs of the chairs had been smashed. The telephone, having lost its voice, was swinging by its cable. His new Remington typewriter was missing. Someone must have made off with it.

The files on export and import consignments were scattered everywhere. Most of them were soggy with the water leaking from the broken pipelines. He tried to retrieve as many as possible. The spice sellers and prayer-cap sellers in these alley were going to suffer huge losses. His mind was overwhelmed by the thought of how he would face them, and what answers he could give them. Picking up the documents and files and tying them up in a bundle, he stepped out and took the same route back. He saw soldiers with their guns raised and ready. There was no other sign of human life. Only a deathly silence.

'Sir,' Divakaran Potti put his cup back on the table and asked, 'what are you going to do now?'

At least Potti had a job. Abdul Ameen would be taken care of by his bride's family. They were traditional chicken traders who supplied chicken to Moti Mahal in Daryaganj, Ajmeri Dhaba in Chandni Chowk, and many of the biryani vendors. Although V.P. Agencies was no more, Divakaran and Abdul Ameen would survive. What would Sahadevan do?

He had thought of restarting the agency by renting a smaller place in Turkman Gate. But where would he find such a space? All his office equipment was destroyed, and so were the documents of his clients. He would have to start from scratch. He no longer had the strength for it.

In due course, Divakaran Potti got married; Abdul Ameen's second nikah also took place.

Sahadevan went to Kerala for his sister's wedding, which had been delayed by the Emergency and the miseries it had brought upon everyone.

'Do you have a lot of days off? Will you be here for a long time?'

Sahadevan didn't reply. He was on a permanent vacation. Quite at liberty. He could go anywhere, whenever he wished to.

He didn't tell anyone that he had lost everything in the Turkman Gate disaster. His father was not alive to be informed. If he told his mother or sisters, they would be sad and it would diminish the pleasure of the much-awaited wedding. He acted like nothing had happened. He exuded happiness. After all, it was a big fat wedding, with plenty of gold for the bride and a big feast for the guests. What more could one ask for? He would handle everything else once he was back in Delhi, like he had first done in 1959. He would look for a job. He would find a place to stay … As he thought about it, the image of a play formed in his mind. The actors play the same role in the same story, again and again.

'Come once more. This visit was not really enough,' Sahadevan said.

'We want to come. Vanaja is really keen on visiting you. But with two small children, travelling that far is not easy.'

'Is your boy two already?'

'Saiful? He'll be two next month.'

Sahadevan was upset that he didn't know his own nephew's age.

His full name was Saiful Islam. Sahadevan assumed that it meant the sword of Islam. He could not see why such a ponderous name had to be given to a small child. When he grew up, would he snip off his surname like Sahadevan had done? Except, a stand-alone sword is a dissonant and dangerous thing. A sword that protects Islam was preferable.

He preferred the name they had given to the second child. There was God in it, and religion, and a bit of eroticism too. Not yet six months old, her name was Radha.

Sahadevan paced the yard of the new house Abdunnissar had constructed, carrying Saiful Islam in one arm and Radha in the other. There was a stiffness in his knees as he walked. Ignoring it, he walked up and down the gravel-filled yard.

'Edi, are you happy?'

'Can't you see it in my face? Why do you still ask?'

'To make doubly sure.'

'Do you value my happiness so much?'

'What do you think?'

Sitting in his arms, Saiful Islam, without provocation, suddenly planted a kiss on his unshaven, bristly cheek. What came over you, you little moplah kid? To cause this sudden rush of love for your uncle?

Vanaja fell in step with him.

'You found someone for yourself. You also found a good man for your sister. You did what had to be done. You are a smart one!'

'My responsibilities are not over. They have only increased. Two sisters are now well-settled. One brother is yet to settle down.'

'I'll look after myself.'

'When? You've lost all your hair.'

'When it's time, I'll tell you.'

'Do you have anyone in mind? I've heard Punjabi girls are great beauties.'

Abdul Abdunnissar had told her.

He didn't answer her question. Marriage was something he didn't like to talk about or, for that matter, even think about.

They walked for some more time in silence.

'Did you like Balaraman mashu?'

'Seems to have a taste for literature.'

'He writes poetry. He's a fantastic reader.'

'Both my brothers-in-law are teachers.'

'Isn't that a good thing?'

They could see someone coming towards the house. He seemed to favour one side while walking. Even from that distance, she recognised him.

'Your old friend, Unnikuttan. That's him.'

He was the same age as Sahadevan. If time had manifested itself on Sahadevan's head as thinning hair, on Unnikuttan it was as baldness. He only had some hair above his ears. The rest of his head was bald. His moustache had been dyed extra dark.

'I've come with a request for help, Sahadeva. I'm in dire straits. I've to provide for three children. The oldest is twelve. As for me, I don't have a regular job or occupation. I'm running a chit fund and sell lottery tickets. How can I run a family with that? There's no gold left on my wife's body. I pawned the jewellery first and then sold it all. Two days ago, she lost her temper and told me that since I had sold everything, it would be better if I sold her too. It's not that I don't understand her distress. I'm not made of stone, am I? She was born into a good family and was brought up without any woes. The bad times started for her after she became my wife. You are the only one who can help me. If you put your mind to it, I'll be saved. My children can live without hardship. Will you help me? Don't tell me you can't. It will break my heart.'

'What should I do for you, my friend?'

'Give me money to go to the Gulf.'

'How much?'

'About forty-five or fifty.'

Before the Emergency, he could have tried. He had never possessed such large sums of money even then, not at any point. Yet, he could have tried to help his childhood friend by taking a loan. But who would give him a loan now? What could he show as collateral?

'Why are you not saying anything?'

'How can I arrange such a big sum at such short notice? My sister's wedding is going on.'

'So, that's all there is to our friendship. When I ask for some money, then there's no friend, no friendship. *Phthhoo*!' He pulled up the edge of his mundu, tied it around his waist defiantly, and stomped out. Before leaving, he hawked and spat at the fence and the wall of the neighbouring house. *Phthhoo*! When he saw a sturdy tree, he stopped and urinated against it.

The wedding was a grand affair. All the female guests praised the bride's jewellery and her saree. The feast was sumptuous.

Gratified, Sahadevan prepared for his return journey to Delhi. Saiful Islam bawled loudly as he watched Sahadevan leave with a burning cigarette in his hand, carrying an empty suitcase.

Sahadevan felt like it was he who was crying.

4

THE DISMEMBERED

Two years had passed since the Emergency. It had been twenty years since Sahadevan arrived in Delhi.

He was going to Chandni Restaurant after a long gap. Eros Cinema, the dry cleaners and the sweet shop in Jangpura looked the same. But he couldn't help feeling that something had changed. Gradually, it came to him. He was missing Dasappan. The barber could have come back and started work again under the jamun tree. The street vendors selling golgappa and aloo tikki had already returned. The owner of Chandni Restaurant had encroached on the pavement in front of it and placed tables and chairs there. People sat till late in the night, snacking and drinking lassi.

What did not return to status quo were the shanties on either side of the railway tracks. The bulldozers had levelled the slums during the Emergency. No one knew where the people who used to live there had gone. A new lot of sweepers, sewage workers, bicycle repairers and ice-water sellers had settled there. When he crossed the tracks on his way to Lajpat Nagar, he didn't see any familiar faces.

Abdullah Bawa's shop in Khan Market had also shut down. He had disappeared during the Emergency, and never returned.

One day, Sahadevan asked the kerosene seller in Khan Market if he knew where Abdullah Bawa had gone.

'We don't have a clue,' the man said.

Where did he go? What had happened to him? All Sahadevan knew was that Abdullah Bawa was a resident of Karbala. Without the exact address, it would be difficult to trace him. Yet, one day, he did go to Karbala. He walked along the narrow alleys and near the dargahs, hoping to run into Bawa somewhere.

Whenever he went to Kunhikrishnan's house, he would scan the Guru Nanak Market. Kallu mochi wasn't there. Another cobbler had taken his place.

Where did he go? What had happened to him?

After Dasappan's disappearance, Sahadevan had lost interest in getting his hair cut. Once every month, he had sat on the chair facing the mirror on Dasappan's tree, covering himself with his old mundu, not merely to get a haircut. It was also for the small talk and the moments of friendship. Sahadevan considered himself to be an insignificant man. Dasappan was the one who had made him aware that there was a world of people even more insignificant than he was, and opened the doors to that world for him.

He sat for a long time outside Chandni Restaurant, smoking. It was past 9 p.m.

'Guddu, what's today's special?'

'Baingan bharta. And mango pickle.'

'That's good enough for me.'

Guddu wiped the table with the piece of cloth on his shoulder, and then used the same cloth to wipe his face as he went inside. The warm smell of rotis rose from the tandoor. Guddu reappeared and placed a plate of sliced onions, green chillies, pickle and a glass of water before him. He dipped his finger in the pickle and licked it. Then he took a deep drag of his cigarette.

He had nothing to do now, as he had no job and no office to run. He spent his time doing every possible chore he could think of. He boiled the scruffy curtains, washed and made them sparkling white. He went to a tailor with a pair of trousers that had been kept aside because of a broken zip and had it replaced. Almost every day, he spent two hours at the Max Müller Library or the American Center Library on Curzon Road. He would then go to Nava Kerala Restaurant in Shankar Market and have dosa and beef fry, polishing it off with a cup of strong tea. He would not eat for the rest of the day.

In the evenings, if he didn't go out, he would add Coca-Cola and ice cubes to a glass of Old Monk rum and sit with it on the veranda. After finishing the drink, he would go out and stroll aimlessly, thinking about the novel he was writing. He would end up on Mathura Road. Though he thought about the novel a great deal, he did not write even a single line. With so much time on his hands, he didn't feel like writing.

When he left Chandni Restaurant and headed to his room, it was past 10 p.m. All the shops in the market were closed. The late show had started at Eros Cinema and the street outside it was deserted. The policeman on duty had returned to the station.

He wanted to get to his room and write. He was in the mood for it. He remembered not having switched off the light near the stairs when he left. But when he reached the top, he found that the door to his room was open.

'When did you two come?'

'It's been half an hour.'

'Sorry, eda. I had gone to the restaurant.'

They had let themselves in with the key under the flower pot. They had taken three glasses, washed them, and placed them on the table. The rum bottle had been retrieved from the cupboard. Sahadevan had given them permission to come over at any time, open the house and do whatever they wanted. Another person who had been given this freedom was Vasu. But he never came.

'Today is Monday. Both of us forgot it's a dry day.'

'Eda, are you turning my room into a bar?'

'We have no other place to go to in an emergency.'

There were no dry days in Sahadevan's house. The bar was open twenty-four hours.

'You can come whenever you want. There's always rum in the cupboard.'

Sathyanathan poured rum into two glasses. Sahadevan stopped him before he could pour a third drink. 'I've already had dinner. I don't need a drink.'

There was only enough rum for two. Let the two of them enjoy it, he thought.

After Sathyanathan joined the newspaper, he had started drinking regularly. But never too much. He had total control over himself when it came to smoking and drinking. However many hours he spent in the Press Club, he never drank more than two large pegs. But he couldn't do without cigarettes or alcohol.

He used to smoke at home too, but he never had a drink. His father had not approved of alcohol. Was his mother against it too? He didn't know. She had never told her son not to. She only said, 'Son, you are more educated and knowledgeable than your mother. You decide what is good and what is bad.' And then she would add, 'Take care of your health. I've no one except you.'

'What's happening with your case? I've been meaning to ask you.'

'Why are you asking me now? You don't think I'll win, right?'

'Let victory be yours. But it's like suing God. God is everywhere, but no one knows where he is. The Emergency is like that. Where will you go and find those who brought it on?'

'Wait and see. Sathyanathan doesn't give up so easily.'

He had sued for damages, and was spending a lot of time and money on the case. Janakikutty supported him in this.

If he won a favourable verdict, Sitaram, Lambu, Lakhan, Kanwari and tens of thousands of people would be entitled to damages. It was this possibility that had persuaded Sathyanathan to take legal action. Those who had committed the mass murder of sperms would have to pay for it. They should be punished. He was adamant. He was ready to go to any extent with the litigation.

But who are you grappling with, little one?

'Be careful,' Kunhikrishnan had cautioned. 'Beware of a car or a truck knocking you down.'

The rum was over. Janakikutty poured a little water into the bottle, sloshed it around, poured it into her glass and downed it. Sathyanathan had a fire inside him that couldn't be doused, however much he drank. But what was troubling her?

One of the changes that recent events had wrought in Sathyanathan was that he had stopped thinking of Vidya. All his thoughts now hovered around the Emergency and its victims.

Janakikutty had stopped going home to Kerala. As soon as she stepped off the train, the press would be waiting to interview her. Kunhikannan mashu's daughter was a star in their eyes. Someone or the other always recognised her on trains and buses. There would be photo sessions and autographs. Janakikutty detested it. Who was she to get all this attention? The inconsequential daughter of a colossus of a father.

'It's eleven. Don't you have to go? Isn't your mother alone?'

'It has become routine for amma. Sleeping alone in the house is not a problem for her anymore. Earlier, she wasn't able to sleep when I was away on night duty. She used to say that unwelcome thoughts came into her mind and stayed there. But she's still very lonely. There's no one for us to visit or to be visited by. Lalithechi has no time now for anything. Kunhikrishnettan can't do anything alone. He needs help even to wear a shirt. One day, when I went there, I saw Lalithechi feeding him rice and bitter gourd curry with her own hand.'

Lalitha had always been Devi's sole friend and companion. If Devi confided in, and shared her sorrows with anyone, it was Lalitha. Now, Lalitha had more sorrows to deal with than her.

It was a time for grieving.

Devi had read somewhere that drinking a glass of warm milk helps you fall asleep. But all it did for her was to make her tummy pop out; there was no sleep, early or late. At least she had got used to being alone at night. Who did she have to fear? She was no longer the girl Shreedharanunni had taken on his bicycle to Sarojini Nagar Market. She was an old woman with pendulous breasts and grey hair.

'Sathyanathan's amma is trying to persuade him to get married. She asked me too, to get him to say yes. But who's going to broach the subject of marriage with him? He gets furious when he hears the word.'

'Please shut up, Janakikutty. Don't spoil my mood.'

Sathyanathan picked up the pack of cigarettes and the match box from the table and stood up. Janakikutty followed suit.

'How will you go so late in the night? Will Janakikutty get food at the hostel? There's some bread here. Shall I make an omelette?'

The JNU campus had dhabas where food was available till late into the night. They would be crowded too. For the students, night and day were the same. On the poorly lit paths between the thickly growing trees, they walked about even after midnight.

'What's the news from Kunhikrishnettan?' asked Sathyanathan, poised at the top of the stairs.

Kunhikrishnan had gone to Kottakkal Arya Vaidya Sala for treatment. Two weeks of different types of massages using oil and poultices. He had sent Sahadevan two letters from the hospital. He had even called once. He remained hopeful. Sathyanathan was the one who had forsaken all hope. All the doctors he consulted carried out detailed examinations and then pronounced that the procedure was irreversible.

They went down the stairs. The light was inadequate. Sahadevan wondered if he should change the sixty-watt bulb for a hundred-watt one. He stood by the window and watched them walk away in the light of the street lamp, towards the old sardar's taxi in front of Eros Cinema.

He thought of Kunhikrishnan. Would he be sound asleep after a massage, soothed by the smell of the herb-infused oil used in the ayurvedic poultices?

Perhaps it wasn't proper to think about him that way. He might be lying sleepless, staring at the ceiling.

Eda, your world is full of people who have lost their sleep. Still talking to himself, he switched off the light and lay down on the bed. A faint light from the street lamp seeped in through the windows. He lay sleepless, staring at the ceiling.

5

RAKSHA BANDHAN

Standing on the balcony, Sahadevan took several deep breaths. There were more flowerpots now than before. He had just bought five from the potter who came through the back lane, his donkey loaded with flower pots. Good, loose soil was available beneath Dasappan's jamun tree. He had filled a sack with it, hauled it up to the first floor and filled all the pots. Only then did he wonder what to grow in them.

Already, there were seven pots, and a bird's eye chilli plant flourished in one of them. Because of his love of spicy food, he gave it special attention. Four of the pots had different types of money plant growing in them. He had heard that growing a money plant would bring money into the house. But it wasn't for the money that he grew them. It was because they needed little tending. Even if they were not watered for a long time, they didn't wilt.

Lalitha grew money plants in cracked glasses, chipped cups and bottles, after filling them with water. They were arrayed both inside and outside the house. She had developed a love for money plants after Kunhikrishnan was thrown into jail. There was nothing else for her to do.

In one of the other pots, Sahadevan was growing royal jasmine. He was not enamoured of its fragrance. He was growing it to remind himself of home.

He decided to grow vegetables in all the five pots. Tomatoes in one, bitter gourd in another, and spinach in two. Using a plastic string, he goaded the vine of the bitter gourd to grow onto the chicken wire mesh of the balcony. Okra seeds went into the fifth pot. Watering the plants regularly and removing the pests camouflaged amidst the leaves, he tended to them as he might his children. With his ministrations, they would grow well.

Sucking in his belly, he breathed in as much as he could. As the breath was released, the stomach slowly slackened and returned to its normal state. Belly breathing. He did it to reduce the stress in his mind. He had started this recently. He had seldom done any exercise, except for walking, before that.

'Are you not well?'

'No, I'm fine.'

'You look like you're not well.'

'I'm very tense.'

'What happened, my friend? If you sit at home without a job, you'll get depressed. That's normal.'

'That's not the problem.'

'Then what is?'

'I'm just coming back from Kunhikrishnan's house. He's in bad shape. I feel sad looking at him. He was always so healthy.'

'How is he? What happened to him? He doesn't come here any longer. I haven't seen him for a long time.'

'He hasn't been going out at all since he came back from jail. If he has to go out, he needs someone's help.'

'What's wrong with him?'

'They broke both his arms in jail; they are quite useless now. He's still under treatment.'

'My God!'

There was silence between them. Om Prakash Jain had met Kunhikrishnan often, when he came to visit Sahadevan. He didn't know that Kunhikrishnan had stayed hidden away here for a few days. He normally kept track of everyone's comings and goings. He was very particular about discipline. He was also against the consumption of alcohol.

'We are strict vegetarians. Meat and fish are not allowed here. As far as possible, avoid onions also.' That was all he had said when renting out the house to Sahadevan. It wouldn't have occurred to him that this virtuous-looking man drank Old Monk rum mixed with Coca-Cola.

Jain was the sort of man who was unable to hurt any living creature. Even if he hadn't eaten himself, he would feed the birds and ants nearby. Once a week, he visited the birds' hospital in Chandni Chowk. It housed birds suffering from various ailments and also those wounded by human, kite, canine or feline attacks. He helped look after these birds and feed them. Once, when he found a pigeon on the road, bitten by a dog and bleeding from the neck, he had rushed it in an auto rickshaw to the hospital. His religion was kindness. It stood against all forms of violence.

'I'll tell you a way to reduce tension: belly breathing. I practise it regularly even though I don't need it. Simple deep breathing doesn't help. You must use your abdomen to breathe. Only then will the lower sacs of the lungs get oxygenated.'

Standing in the balcony, Sahadevan took deep breaths using his nose and abdomen. He heard the sound of an auto rickshaw below. It must be Om Prakash Jain returning after dropping his children to school. They both studied in the nearby Delhi Public School on Mathura Road.

Sahadevan had nothing to do today either. He had seen an advertisement for a tutor in English and mathematics for two children studying in class one and class three. He hadn't given tuitions to anyone so far. He hadn't received tuitions either.

During his student days, there was no homework or tuition. His interest had been piqued by the address given in the advertisement: Sunlight Colony, near Ashram Chowk, a place where the not-so-well-to-do lived. He thought about going there in the evening and checking it out. He was wasting time doing nothing. Teaching children could be gratifying.

When Vidya and Pinky were children, he used to teach them.

Hearing footsteps on the stairs, he turned around. It was the sound of high heels.

'Where are you coming from, so early in the morning?'

He was surprised to see her. She never woke up before 10 a.m. How had she got to Jangpura so early today?

'I came early so that I could meet you before you left for the office. I won't detain you long.'

She didn't know that he had no office to go to.

'It's no trouble at all. I'm happy that you've come. Let's sit inside and talk.'

She had come to discuss something important. He knew that she wouldn't have come to his place otherwise. She sat on the chair and put her handbag down—the big, violet-coloured one that she usually carried. She leaned forward, her head bowed. Something was amiss. What could have happened? These were bad times for everyone. Unhappy times. He hoped nothing bad had happened. She was a good-hearted, harmless girl. Circumstances had forced her into becoming the person she was.

'Why are you not saying anything? Will you have something to drink? Shall I make you some tea?'

'Oh, no, sir!'

'Then tell me, what's the matter? Don't keep me on tenterhooks.'

'Will you help me?'

'Who else will I help, if not you?'

'I brought some stuff. Please keep it safe for me.'

She took a polyethylene pouch out of her handbag. Inside it was a packet wrapped in paper and secured with tape. He assumed it contained something valuable. What could it be?

'What is inside this?'

'My entire savings.'

'Which means?'

'I'll open it and show you.'

'No, don't open it. Just tell me.'

'My jewellery, documents pertaining to my bank and post office deposits, and some cash.'

He was taken aback. He didn't know what to say.

'It's not safe here. This is a bachelor pad. No one is here during the day. I won't tell you that I can't keep it. You can do as you please. But it's risky,' he said slowly.

He didn't even have a sturdy almirah in the room. He hadn't bought a Godrej almirah because he had nothing valuable to keep in it. Now, even if he wanted to buy one, he didn't have the money to do so.

'What should I do? Sir, where will I go and keep all this?'

'Where did you keep it till now?'

She remained silent. Suddenly, her eyes became moist.

His anxiety grew. He pulled his chair close to hers. Gently, he put his hand on hers. It was burning, as though she had fever. Maybe she did have fever.

'Don't worry. We can solve it, whatever the problem is. Tell me.'

'I can't stay on in Govind Puri. I'm looking for another place. But no one will give a single woman like me a roof over my head.'

'Why are you leaving? Did Lalaji ask you to leave?'

'He did—he said that I've to vacate my room in two days. If not, he'll throw my things out on the street.'

Sahadevan could not believe it. Would that good man do such a thing? The angular face of the turban-wearing Lalaji came to his mind. But then, he can't be blamed, he corrected himself.

When she had arrived from Kerala, Georgekutty had arranged a place for her to stay. For the first six months, she stayed with many people in many places. One month in Kidwai Nagar, two months in Ber Sarai, sixteen days in Khichripur. Her worst days were in Khichripur. It was a dark alley where prostitutes and chain-snatchers lived. She did not know then that she was going to become one of them. Did Georgekutty put her there on purpose?

After six months she shifted to Govind Puri, all by herself. She had stayed there happily until now. Lalaji owned farmland in Chhatarpur and buffaloes in Govind Puri. He was an elderly man with the uncomplicated mind of a villager. He never asked her any questions. Never demanded anything of her. When she got a telephone connection, he used it to make calls once in a while. That was all. He used to call her beti. He had no problem with anyone visiting her at any time. He had even tolerated Vasu.

But now ...

The policemen from Kalkaji police station had started it all. Govind Puri came under their jurisdiction. Her troubles began when she was included in their list of call girls. Every now and then, they called and asked her to appear at the police station. They harassed her at every turn. They counselled her, threatened her. She understood eventually why they were doing it. She began carrying money with her when she was asked to report at the station. She paid and left quickly. Though they had her address, they never visited her at home.

One day, they turned up.

Raksha Bandhan was approaching. Rakhis were being sold on the pavements. Vasu had narrated the story of Raksha Bandhan to her. Yamuna was the sister of Yama, the god of death. On a full moon day in August, she had tied a rakhi on Yama's wrist and sought his protection. Yama was pleased and gave her the boon of immortality.

Delhiites, being devotees of Rama, had a different story to tell. When Krishna suffered a cut on his arm and began to bleed, Draupadi tore off a piece from her raiment and tied it around the wound. Pleased by the gesture, Lord Krishna accepted Draupadi as his sister and offered her his protection, for all time.

Rakhis in dazzling colours and designs were displayed in the Kalkaji and Govind Puri markets. The sweet shops attracted crowds two days before Raksha Bandhan. After the girl tied a rakhi on her brother's wrist, they would both feed each other sweets. After that, the brother would shower gifts on his sister.

Once, Lalitha had tied a rakhi on Sahadevan's wrist. He had only fifty rupees with him at the time. He gave it all to her and promised to protect her forever.

When he lived in Amritpuri, Jaswinder and Pinky used to tie rakhis on his hand. On his way to the office, he could see rakhis on every man's wrist. Some of them had three or four, and they displayed them proudly. Sahadevan also held up his hand to attract attention to his rakhis.

A policeman from the Kalkaji station had dismounted from his bicycle in front of Lalaji's bungalow and demanded, 'Is there no one here?'

The sight of the policeman made Lalaji nervous. For some reason, he was afraid of policemen. Till now, no policeman had stepped inside his compound.

'Where's the girl?'

Hearing his voice, she felt a flame shoot through her. Cursing herself, she came out of her room. She saw Lalaji standing in the yard. That made her even more nervous.

Why the hell had he come in full regalia? They could have summoned her to the police station as usual. She looked daggers at the policeman. He looked familiar.

'You can go. I'll come to the station.'

She was afraid to talk to the policeman in front of Lalaji. Who knew what he would blurt out? Though she had been staying here for years, Lalaji didn't know anything about her. He had taken months to learn her name. Yet, he used to call her beti.

'The day after tomorrow is Raksha Bandhan. Don't you know that? I have two sisters. I've to give them half a tola of gold each. Bring me whatever you have.'

'I don't have any gold. I'm a poor woman.'

'You're lying. I've seen you with jewellery on your ears and neck. We are policemen. Don't try to hide anything from us. We see everything.'

'I'm penniless. All my jewellery has been pawned.'

'If you have no gold, then bring me money. Or has that too been pawned?'

Stroking his moustache, the policeman stared at her menacingly.

'I don't have anything. I'm telling you the truth.'

'Move aside. I want to search your room.'

'No, don't!'

'Who's inside? Have you started doing your business in the daytime too?'

He tried to push her aside. She resisted.

'Please have mercy on me,' she pleaded.

'It's because I'm showing mercy that you are even living here. Else, you would be living inside a jail or a Nari Niketan. Immoral women belong there. In Nari Niketan.'

Lalaji stood there, taking in everything.

The policeman only left after taking money for one-and-a-half tolas of gold.

Lalaji saw that too.

Sahadevan looked closely at Rosily. She was not the same girl he had seen at the INA Market bus stop in 1971. Her eyes had lost their innocence. Once, her face and laughter gave her the comeliness of a Nazrani lass. That was missing now. There are people who can recognise a call girl in any crowd at one glance. They could pick out Rosily very easily.

'Give it to me.'

He extended his hand. She gave him the packet.

It contained everything she had earned and saved. It contained her hopes and dreams. It was her future, her life.

From now on, the responsibility of guarding it was his.

On the morning of the full moon day in the month of Shravan, after having a bath and wearing a silk saree, she came to visit him and tied on his wrist a beautiful rakhi with silver stars embroidered on it.

6

ADIEU TO SEWA NAGAR

Kunhikrishnan took it slow, undertaking repair and maintenance on his body. His life moved forward, driven carefully like an old, overhauled automobile, brake fluid refilled, filter and oil changed, new condenser fitted.

It was the fifth anniversary of his release from Tihar Jail.

'I thought I'd never be let out of the jail. And even if I did, I thought I would die soon. It's a miracle that I've been alive for five years.'

'It's the result of my prayers.'

There was no god that Lalitha had not prayed to. There was no temple to which she hadn't promised an offering. She had vowed to make offerings to the deities of small, remote shrines Kunhikrishnan hadn't even heard of. He used to wonder who had told her of these. Man creates gods as per his exigencies, he mused.

'I shouldn't thank the gods for being alive. It's my wife I should thank. She has done and suffered so much for my sake, Sathyanatha.'

Kunhikrishnan didn't criticise the gods in front of Lalitha. After his time in jail, he had stopped speaking against the gods. When she held forth on the miracles wrought by gods and godmen, he listened intently. Earlier, he might have said, 'Oh, shut up, you and your God,' and walked off.

Now, when she talked, not only did he listen, he nodded his head occasionally as if validating what she was saying. He did it consciously, to please her. For her sake, he was ready to behave as though he was a believer and make any compromises. He might even have accompanied her to meet Rohtak Baba if asked to do so now. Not because he believed in Baba, but because he believed in Lalitha.

Baba's photo had been on their bedroom wall for longer than the prescribed sixteen months. One day, he had removed it and put another picture in its place—an oil painting of Vatsyayana. He had bought it at the Cottage Emporium for a fairly high price. It was many days later that Lalitha had realised it was Vatsyayana. She didn't know exactly who he was, but he appeared to exude divinity, even more than Rohtak Baba did.

'Who's that?'

'He's a great ascetic.'

'If we pray to him, will we have children?'

'If we do as he says, yes.'

It was a cruel joke. But he was like that. Which was why he avoided cracking jokes as far as possible.

'How can one tell that the painting you bought is of Vatsyayana? No one has seen him. So how did the artist draw him?'

'Do we draw Jesus and Buddha after seeing them, Janakikutty?'

Sathyanathan and Janakikutty were regular visitors at their place. She was now Dr Janakikutty. Like doctors without patients, who spent time in their clinics swatting flies, she was roaming around without a job, even after earning a PhD.

'Do you need us to do anything? Tell us what you need. Janakikutty and I can come and help you.'

'Thank you. I'll tell you when I need help.'

Kunhikrishnan needed a lot of help. He could neither write nor type. How could others help with that? Could someone else's arms replace his? He couldn't change his clothes on his own. He couldn't towel himself after a bath. He couldn't feed himself. Whenever he tried, the rice slipped through his lifeless fingers. Though he craved a smoke even more than before, he could neither fill the pipe nor strike a match. Nor could he lift and put the pipe between his teeth. He needed help for everything. Lalitha's help.

'Lalithae, please come here.'

He called out to her just when she had gone into the bathroom to wash clothes. The newspaper he was reading had fallen down. He could bend down from his armchair, but he couldn't pick up the paper. She had to hand it to him.

'Lalithae ...'

He would call when she was on the way to the terrace to hang up his mundu and singlet, which she would have finished washing after dipping them in indigo for whitening. There was sunshine there, and a constant breeze. The clothes would dry in minutes.

'Please come here,' he would call impatiently. Leaving the wet clothes in the bucket, she would run to him.

'The pipe has gone out. Please light it for me.'

After considerable effort, he had taken the pipe out of his mouth and put it on the ashtray. His hands couldn't strike the match to light it again.

Lalitha took the pipe and placed it in his mouth. For some reason, the picture that came to her mind was of a mother placing a bottle in her baby's mouth. She struck a match and held it over the bowl of the pipe. After he had inhaled strongly three or four times, the tobacco lit up and started to crackle and burn.

'Don't call me again, Kunh'ishnetta. Let me hang the clothes to dry on the terrace. There's good sunshine now. You never know when it will rain. I have to get them to dry before that.'

She went up the stairs carrying the bucket. It was an open terrace and there was no barrier between the rooftop of one building and another. One could do the distance of a whole block and return the same way. The residents used to joke that they had been constructed that way for the convenience of thieves.

In a shaded part of the terrace, two women were sitting and chatting in low tones. When they saw Lalitha, they stopped talking. She understood that their discussion was not for her ears.

They were talking about her. If the conversation could have been rewound, it would have gone something like this:

'Edi, do you know, Kunhikrishnan can't do anything by himself.'

'What can a man do if both his hands are paralysed? How is he bathing? She must be bathing him, no, chechi?'

'Bathing and changing clothes are not a big deal. I'm thinking about something else. How will he wash himself after crapping? She must be doing that too, no?'

'Ugh.'

'What?'

'It's nauseating.'

One day, when she was feeding him, Lalitha saw two kids peeping from behind the compound wall.

She realised that she and Kunhikrishnan had become a topic of conversation, and sometimes the butt of jokes, for their neighbours. Let them talk, she thought. Let them say what they want.

Lalitha behaved as though she didn't hear or see anything. She had no time for that. She only had time to clean the house, wash the clothes, cook food and feed him. Initially, he was completely dependent on her. He could not even hold a glass of tea and drink from it. She took care of him and protected him like she would a baby. She brushed his teeth; shaved him; bathed him; dressed him; combed his hair; fed him; filled his pipe; lit it again when it went out; scratched his back; covered him when he felt the early morning chill. She had forgotten that he was her husband. She treated him like he was her baby, compensating for her unrealised motherhood.

After his return from jail, for one year, it was all hospitals and examinations. Orthopaedicians and neurologists took turns examining him. On all those visits, either Sahadevan or Sathyanathan accompanied them. After the Turkman Gate disaster, Sahadevan didn't have any work. He was willing and happy to go anywhere with them. He had always been like that, even when he had a job.

These days, one didn't need to go to Karol Bagh or INA Market to buy curry leaves and drumsticks. All of these things were available in Ouseph's shop in Guru Nanak Market. They were a little more expensive, of course.

On Friday evenings, the Jayanti Janata Express brought all kinds of goods from Kerala. On Saturdays, there was a big rush in Ouseph's store. Malayalis from Amar Colony, Dayanand Colony, Sadiq Nagar, Amritpuri and other places arrived early in the morning. Ouseph displayed their favourite nenthran bananas, coconuts, shallots, yam, tapioca, pumpkin, etc. in cardboard cartons and gunny bags. Aware of Lalitha's difficulties, he would personally go to her house with a bag containing all that she needed.

'Lalithae, come, I'll teach you how to deposit a cheque.'

Kunhikrishnan used to receive cheques once in a while—royalties from the sales of his book *A Republic of Hunger*, and payments for the columns and articles he wrote in the newspapers. He no longer wrote these columns. How could someone with maimed arms write? The body is run by a coalition. If a coalition partner changes allegiance, governance comes to a standstill.

She sat beside him with the blue pay-in slip.

'On the top, write the branch name first.'

She wrote: Lajpat Nagar, New Delhi 24.

'Now, write the date. Below that, the account holder's name. Meaning, my name. Then, my account number. Below that, the drawee bank's name, which means the name of the bank that has issued the cheque we are depositing. Next, the cheque number and date. The number on the left side is the cheque number. Not the one on the right side. Now write out the amount in figures and words. You can sign, there's no need for me to sign. Have you written everything? Then give it to me.'

He took the pay-in slip and checked it.

'Forty is f-o-r-t-y, not f-o-u-r-t-y. There's no "u". Still, very good. I'm giving you ninety-nine marks out of hundred.'

Gradually, she started to do things on her own. She encashed cheques at the bank. She stood in queue at the electricity office and paid the bill. When the telephone bill arrived, she went to the counter, joined the queue and paid the amount. On the first of every month, she went to the Amar Colony post office, filled the form and sent a money order to Kunhikrishnan's father.

The only thing she could not help him with was his articles and columns. His typewriter sat idle on the table. It hadn't moved since he went to jail. It lay silent, as good as dead.

One day, at 11 a.m., after completing all her chores, bathing Kunhikrishnan, dressing him in a starched mundu and shirt, she changed into a saree to go out.

'I'll be back soon, before twelve. Till then, sit in this room. Don't go out into the yard. You might stumble and fall.'

'Where are you going?'

There was a typing institute in Amar Colony. She had joined a three-month course there.

'Why are you learning typing now?'

'To help my husband.'

'Where do you have the time for it?'

'It's only half an hour daily. After learning the basics, I'll sit at home and practise.'

With the enthusiasm of a school kid, she went to the typewriting institute clutching sheets of paper and her umbrella.

She returned before 12 p.m., bathed in sweat.

'Started? What did you learn today?'

'My fingers are not moving. When I type "*a*" it's "*s*" that shows up on the paper. The instructor scolded me.'

'You only started today. It takes time. If you practise hard, you'll learn faster.'

'I'll have to make time to practise at home.'

'Take it easy, Lalitha. Don't I see your daily drudgery? You shouldn't have joined the course. If you wear yourself out like this, without any rest, you'll soon be laid up.'

That night, Kunhikrishnan had a dream. Both his arms recovered their power. In the dream, he went and sat in front of his Remington typewriter. He started to type an article on it. The movements and sounds of the typewriter gladdened him.

He woke up feeling elated. Lalitha was missing from his side. The wall clock showed ten minutes past one. Light poured in from the next room. He could hear random, disorderly clacking sounds from his typewriter.

When Devi arrived, Lalitha was typing. Kunhikrishnan, seated next to her, was dictating slowly, carefully. Clenched between his teeth was a pipe emitting puffs of smoke. He had learned, long ago, to talk with the pipe in his mouth.

'The point I would like to drive home is that ...'

'How will the *point* drive to the *home*, Kunh'ishnetta?' she asked as she typed. Her question made him smile.

'You have learnt typing. Now learn some English too. You needn't go to any institute for that. I'll teach you. Then I'll appoint you as my secretary, okay?'

They heard the sound of the gate opening. Lalitha assumed it was a beggar. But it was Devi. When she entered the house, the typewriter fell silent.

Devi was visiting Lajpat Nagar after a long time. She had come a few times after Kunhikrishnan had returned home from jail. She was solicitous about their welfare. Then, she stopped coming. She would telephone Lalitha to get all the news. She knew that Lalitha had cleared the Lower Typing Test.

Devi's world was now completely restricted to the Secretariat and Sewa Nagar. She had stopped going anywhere else. Sleep and solitude were her only companions. She had lost interest in everything else.

'Amma, it's not good for you to sit alone all the time. You should go out once in a while. Meet people, talk to them. I have a holiday tomorrow, let's go to Connaught Place. When were you there last? We'll catch a movie at Regal and have dinner at Nirula's. You'll feel happier.'

'I'm happy sitting here alone.'

'When achan died, you were so brave. Everyone was talking about your mental fortitude, your courage. Where has all that gone?'

'I'm not able to forget my daughter, eda.'

'It's been five-six years. If she were alive, she would have come by now. We shouldn't wait for her. She won't come; she's dead.'

'Sathyanatha …'

'We need to face the reality. Let's console ourselves by imagining that she is at our father's side and happy. Otherwise, there'll be no end to our sorrow. Every day, we'll have to live grieving like this.'

'You won't understand the pain of a mother, Sathyanatha.'

'Don't say that, amma. Who can understand your pain more than me?'

Sathyanathan looked at his mother through his glasses.

'Come in, Deviyechi. Do you want to see me typing? Come!'

Devi sat down and surveyed the room. She was visiting after several years, but there were no discernible changes. She thought the number of books on the shelf had increased.

'I was typing Kunh'ishnettan's article.'

'You have passed Lower, haven't you? Good for you, Lalitha. One can't do much these days without knowing typing.'

If you could type forty-five to fifty words per minute, you wouldn't starve. You could get part-time employment at least.

'Didn't Kunhikrishnan go for physiotherapy today?'

'He has to go only twice a week. It looks like he'll have to do it lifelong, Deviyechi.'

'Everything will be okay.'

'You look ill, Deviyechi. Sathyanathan was saying you don't eat anything. Have you had anything since the morning? Shall I make you a couple of chapatis? There's cauliflower curry.'

Devi remained silent.

'I'm fed up with people advising and forcing me to do things.'

'What happened, Deviyechi?'

'Did Sathyanathan say something to you?'

'He did. That he wants to shift to another house. His office would pay the rent. He doesn't understand why you won't agree to it.'

'I came here to talk to you about that. He won't let me be in peace. How can I leave Sewa Nagar?'

Devi wasn't scared of death. But she was afraid of leaving Sewa Nagar. She had lived there from the time she first came to Delhi with Shreedharanunni. So many memories lay buried there.

'You are becoming overly sentimental,' Sathyanathan had told her. The truth was, she had no courage left. The little that remained was fast draining away. It was the opposite with Sathyanathan: he was becoming stronger. He had always been like that. He had stumbled and fallen only once, after the Dujana House incident. But he had regained his courage and rationality quickly and was doggedly pursuing the legal case.

He was also reconciled to the loss of Vidya. She, like her father, would never come back. But Sathyanathan was finding it difficult to get through to his mother. She was unable to think logically. Else, why would she want to continue living in Sewa Nagar?

The government quarters, built in the time of the British, were disintegrating. The sight of the buildings with broken plaster and leaking sewage pipes was repulsive. No one who had lived there in Shreedharanunni's time was still around. Bansilal had quit the place decades earlier.

What Sathyanathan was saying to his mother was this: During straitened times, four people had stayed happily in a cramped house for many years. There was no longer any need for that. With the housing allowance given by his office, they could rent a good apartment in a residential area like Green Park or Hauz Khas and live in comfort. His mother's sentimentalism was obstructing this.

'If he insists, let Sathyanathan go and live where he wants. I won't leave Sewa Nagar for any other place.'

Devi's voice had an uncharacteristic edge to it.

Kunhikrishnan and Lalitha exchanged glances, unsure of what to say. Lalitha thought Sathyanathan's stand was wrong. Kunhikrishnan felt otherwise. It's forgetting that enables one to go on. If you can't forget, you won't be able to go forward.

One more year passed. There was an earthquake in Delhi. After a few days, everyone living in Devi's block received a notice from the government. All the occupants were asked to vacate immediately on account of repairs and maintenance of the dangerously weakened structures.

The coolies loaded the household items onto a tempo standing by the roadside, shaded by moringa and guava trees. There wasn't enough to fill even one tempo. Devi had kept a carton under her bed containing Vidya's salwar-kameez, socks, school bag, the plastic lunch box she took to school and college, and a few other things. Two days earlier, Sathyanathan had taken them out and donated them to an orphanage. Many days earlier, he had removed the faded and moth-eaten photo of Zhou Enlai. Devi hadn't noticed. Even if she had, she would have remained silent.

Sahadevan came with a taxi.

Sathyanathan said, 'Ammae, let's go.'

Devi came out with her son, empty-handed. After standing with her head bowed for some time in the yard, she went and sat in the car.

There was no one to say goodbye to.

As they drove away, Sahadevan told himself, it's not only Devi and Sathyanathan who are moving away from Sewa Nagar. I am leaving too.

This had been his first nest in Delhi.

Part Six

Bloody Yamuna

It was a time when only the dead smiled, happy in their peace.
—Anna Akhmatova (1889–1966)

1

CHAPATIS AND ONIONS

Even after the annihilation of the office at Turkman Gate, somehow, he held on. When poverty pointed a gun at him and asked him to hold up his hands, he didn't surrender.

In the beginning, he was not too worried. Vanaja was in a happy place. Apart from his vocation as a teacher, Abdul Abdunnissar had the additional income from his father's coconut trading business. Besides Saiful Islam and Radha, they now had another daughter called Mariam. Shyamala was also doing well. Balaraman master had already published two books—a collection of his poems and a comparative study of the language of O.V. Vijayan and Kovilan. Sahadevan's mother was not dependent on his monthly money orders. Her daughters would look after her. Still, he had continued to send her money, the amount diminishing steadily, until now.

'What happened, bhaisaab? Aren't you sending your mother any money? Today is already the twentieth.' Sukhdev, the clerk at the sub-post office in Jangpura asked when they met on the road. He was the postmaster, clerk and peon all rolled into one and they knew each other well.

The following month was the same: he had no money to send to his mother.

'Have you forgotten her? Amma doesn't need your paltry money order. I'll look after her. But you shouldn't forget your own mother,' wrote Vanaja. Her pen had a sharp point. He wondered which brand she used. It couldn't be Parker or Hero. The Chinese who killed Shreedharanunni in 1962 were hard-hearted, but their Hero pen wasn't. Letters dropped off its nib onto the paper like flowers gently falling in the breeze. Many were the young men and women who wrote love letters using a Hero pen. And how many dejected young Malayali men had written suicide notes with it!

Thirty days later, he sent the usual money order to his mother. But he didn't pay Om Prakash Jain the monthly rent.

'If you don't have a permanent job, that's your problem.'

'Are you trying to say that it's out of choice that I'm not working?'

'I didn't say that. You are not trying hard enough. Look at me. I've lost the use of both my arms. Nevertheless, I'm living better than when I had them both. If you look around, you'll land something. You know the import-export procedures well. There's an export boom in Delhi right now. You should show more enthusiasm. You should go and meet people,' said Kunhikrishnan.

There could be some truth in what he's saying, Sahadevan mused. He was not motivated enough in his search for a job. In this land where crores of people were job-seekers, it was not easy getting one. Yet, crores of people did find work. So, it must be a lack of diligence on his part.

He thought of Gulshan Wadhwa. It had been years since he had met him. He wasn't sure if Wadhwa & Sons still existed. His girls would be of a marriageable age now. Was he still going around, his head throbbing, thinking about their dowries?

While he was still running V.P. Agencies, Sahadevan had once found himself walking through Chawri Bazaar to meet a recalcitrant client who owed him money. He didn't take auto rickshaws any more. He wouldn't get into a hand-pulled rickshaw either, even if it was blazing hot or freezing cold. He didn't think it was right for any human being to have his weight hauled by another human being. Once, in Ballimaran, when it was 44 degrees in the shade, he had seen a skin-and-bones rickshaw driver stumble and fall while pulling a rickshaw with three corpulent men seated in it. After that, he had stopped using rickshaws.

That day, in one of those alleys of Ballimaran, Sahadevan had found a visiting card lying on the ground. A screen-printed, rich-looking card. Curious, he had bent and picked it up. Gulshan Wadhwa, it said. Managing Director, Wadhwa & Sons International, Clearing Agents & Movers.

Sahadevan had put the card safely in his pocket. The new office was in Gol Market, close to Connaught Place.

The bulldozers had destroyed more than the buildings in Turkman Gate. In his mind's eye, he saw his future, scooped up, bitten, chewed and spat out by the bulldozers. Many victims of the Turkman Gate episode were still vagrants in Delhi and survived by begging. His subconscious mind kept telling him that he too should be in that group. Why must he alone escape? At some level, his reluctance to find a job stemmed from this.

But not all the victims of that time were like Sahadevan. Sathyanathan had dressed the wounds inside him and healed them quickly. He was an energetic daredevil; a hardworking journalist. He had scaled great heights in a short time. He had left the newspaper he had started with and joined a weekly magazine as the coordinating editor for financial news. Sahadevan had heard him on television recently, speaking about the new economic principles of the state.

'One day, Om Prakash Jain will take you by the scruff of your neck and throw you out.'

'He'll never do that. He's not greedy for money.'

'Sahadevetta, who will let anyone stay without rent? You know the landlord of my flat in Hauz Khas? If the rent is delayed by two days, he comes down to meet me. Do you know what I've done? I've given him six months' rent in advance, so I can avoid seeing his inauspicious face every month. But amma didn't like it one bit. In her mind, she's still living in Sewa Nagar.'

'All landlords are not like yours. In that, at least, the good deeds of my past life seem to be helping me. Though he was poor and stretched to the limit, Uttam Singh never increased my rent. Even if I was late in paying him, he didn't mind. You know what he told me when I was moving from Amritpuri to Jangpura? He said, I don't need any rent, you stay here as long as you want, little brother. Om Prakash Jain is the same. He's not interested in money. His greatest happiness is feeding ants in the morning. Delhi has people who drive bulldozers over women and girls, but it also has some who feed ants and birds, Sathyanatha.'

'There are people in Delhi who feed cows when humans are starving. For them, cows are more important. You know that. They don't know the value of human beings. It's such men who turn into fascists. I despise them.'

'I just cannot see Om Prakash Jain as a fascist.'

His landlord didn't say a word about the rent. But he kept reminding Sahadevan that he should find a job soon.

'Do you know how to type?' he asked one day, when Sahadevan was returning after buying cigarettes.

'Yes, I do.'

'How's your speed?'

'Not bad.'

He knew he couldn't match Lalitha's speed. She had passed not only the Lower, but the Higher too.

'Then go and meet this guy I know. I'll give you a letter. He's a good man. He'll help you.'

Om Prakash Jain's friend, a lawyer in Patiala House, needed a typist.

And thus, Sahadevan, who used to go around wearing a tie and carrying a briefcase in his hand as the owner of V.P. Agencies, became a typist who wore a shirt with a worn collar and commuted in overcrowded buses, hanging on to the overhead bar, to reach his office, drenched in sweat.

One of the many miseries wrought by Indiraji and Sanjayji.

What else was there to say?

In the mornings, after making and eating two wheat dosas, chased down by a cup of strong tea, and smoking a cigarette, he left for Patiala House. If he got a seat in the bus, he would light another cigarette. The bus went along Mathura Road, past Sundar Nagar, and reached India Gate. Though there was a stop at Patiala House, he alighted one stop before it. He would walk from there, basking in the early morning light and the mist, and enjoying his cigarette, the third in one hour. In the distance, like an oil painting, he could see India Gate and Parliament House.

Though he didn't have Lalitha's speed, the lawyer, Kashyap Saxena, was happy with his work. Not only did he not make any mistakes, Kashyap noticed that Sahadevan would correct any mistakes that had crept in. When he wrote 'I look forward to see you', Sahadevan would quietly change it to 'I look forward to seeing you'. Impressed by his command over the language and his intelligence, the lawyer began leaving blanks when he couldn't find a suitable word to complete a sentence. Sahadevan would fill each one beautifully. Yet, Saxena only paid him eight rupees per hour, the amount handed over each day for the previous day's work.

It wasn't enough even for Sahadevan's requirements of food, cigarettes, a newspaper and magazines. When he was feeling particularly lonely, he wished he could have a couple of pegs of Old Monk, but immediately, he would chide himself. Are you the kind of person who wants to have rum when you can't settle the arrears due to Om Prakash Jain or send money to amma?

Alcohol was never an indispensable thing. Yet, he seemed to be experiencing the withdrawal symptoms of an alcoholic.

Some days, Sahadevan went to Saxena's house and worked till midnight. He ended up typing for so long that he developed a chronic pain in his shoulder bones.

During this time, he shifted from Jangpura to Malviya Nagar. It was a small room, more like a cowshed. During the summers, it was suffused with heat. In winter, it was wet and chilly. It wasn't large enough to accommodate his bed, table, chair and bookshelf. So, he kept the table and the bookshelf on the bed, pushed the chair against the wall, and put the mattress on the floor. In one corner of the room, he placed the kerosene stove on which he made rice, curry and chapatis. When he didn't have enough money to buy vegetables, he ate chapatis with sliced onions. Countless poor people in Delhi survived this way—eating chapatis and onions. Sahadevan was becoming one of them.

When Sathyanathan came to visit him, he stood as if struck by lightning.

'Are you staying here?' He couldn't believe it.

'Don't people live in worse conditions, edo?'

When he said that, images of the dark, stinking room in which Dasappan and the Bihari workers had stayed flashed through his mind. Surely his room was better than that?

'You mustn't stay here any longer. Come to my flat. We'll manage there for the time being,' Sathyanathan insisted.

Uttam Singh invited him back to his house. The two rooms used by Sahadevan and the two Malayalis had been let out in anticipation of Pinky's marriage. That was his major worry now. He was collecting every paisa for her dowry. He had sworn upon the holy Guru Granth Sahib that he would not give her hand in marriage without a dowry. Pinky herself wanted to study further and become a doctor, but nothing had come of that yet.

When he saw how well she had grown and the way her body had filled out, Uttam Singh's heart would flutter. She looked like Jaswinder just before her marriage. No one could take their eyes off her once they looked at her. Wahe Guru had bathed her in youth and beauty.

From Malviya Nagar, at the edge of the southern border of the city, Patiala House was far away. Buses were infrequent. Some days, Sahadevan walked most of the distance. When his legs began to tire, he would board a bus and get off at India Gate.

The days went by in this fashion. He turned forty-five. A quarter of a century had passed since he had first arrived in Delhi. Yet, his life was stuck exactly in the same place.

Back to square one.

2

VASU THE GREAT

'Vasu, open your eyes.'

Harilal Shukla pulled up a chair next to Vasu. Vasu opened his eyes and looked around him. As usual, there was dirt on his long, unkempt hair. It had been many days since he had had a bath. He had dried paint not only on his arms and legs, but also on his nose and beard. Was he turning into a living, breathing painting himself?

'Vasu, do you know how much that man at the German embassy paid for the painting you made during the last Durga Puja?'

'No.'

'It's your painting. You should know.'

Vasu didn't say anything.

'Don't you remember? After deducting my commission, I had paid the entire amount to you in cash. Don't you remember that either?'

'I don't keep unnecessary things in my mind.'

'You must. The painting was made by you. It's your money.'

'Money is beyond my horizon.'

Harilal usually charged a commission of 50 per cent. But for Vasu, he had reduced it to 40 per cent. He had handed over the total amount, minus his commission, in bundles of currency notes. But Vasu didn't remember anything. How had he spent all that money? Who had he given it to?

'Okay, don't remember then. It's your money and you can do what you want with it. None of my business. But I have to talk to you about some other things. The money that painting fetched has become the talk of Delhi's art circles. It's an all-time record as far as a beginner is concerned. The prices for your paintings will zoom up. You are no longer the sketch artist near Regal who makes portraits for passers-by at ten rupees each. So, you need to be careful about your image. You may grow your hair and beard long like the Sikhs. Ill-fitting clothes are fine too. Have hashish and bhang if you like. Even LSD, if needed. All that will only help your image. But you can't go around looking filthy. When clients come from America or Europe to meet you, you cannot appear before them with lice in your hair or dirt in your beard, trailing a foul odour. When you come close, your body smells like stale semen. I don't know if you indulge in excessive masturbation. That is your personal choice. I don't want to interfere. But I will interfere in the matter of cleanliness and hygiene. I'll send a girl over from a beauty parlour in Sundar Nagar. She'll shampoo your hair and beard and wash them. She'll trim the nails on your fingers and toes ...'

'Will she apply nail polish on my nails?' Vasu asked soporifically without opening his eyes. Harilal continued as if he hadn't heard him. 'I'll also send someone to sweep and clean your house. He'll wash all your dirty linen and dry and iron them. After that, we'll have to spruce up your house. There should be a sofa for visitors. Good-looking curtains. A fridge. For visitors from Europe, we should have chilled beer even if it's winter. That will please them. Also, don't take the bus to Connaught Place, Mandi House or Chanakyapuri; you shouldn't be seen getting off a bus there. Only take a taxi to such places. You have to improve your image.'

'I don't want any image. Should I bear that burden too now?'

'I'll bear the burden,' Harilal said, laughing. He took out a paan from his jacket pocket, put it in his mouth and started to chew. He got up, came around, and peered closely at the painting Vasu was working on. He nodded his head in approval. That nod was like the official seal on a government paper.

He stayed a while longer, then got up to leave.

'Don't forget all that I've told you.'

He shook Vasu's hand and left.

Vasu's first solo exhibition in Delhi opened on 12 November 1983. It was the biggest event in his life as an artist. When he looked up, he could see the shining summer rain clouds of fame gathering above Rashtrapati Bhawan on Raisina Hill.

All the important art exhibitions in Delhi took place in winter. The season started in November and went on till March. After Dussehra and Diwali, when the air became cooler, paintings would bloom in Delhi, turning it into a veritable garden of arts. Dhoomimal Gallery in Connaught Place, Triveni Gallery and Art Heritage Gallery in Mandi House, Wadhera Gallery in Defence Colony, they all got a new life.

The better known galleries were booked out two or three years in advance. Vasu had managed to get the space only because of Harilal Shukla's influence. Five years ago, Harilal had thought that Vasu was unlikely to mature into an artist worthy of a solo exhibition. Though his drawings and palettes had originality, he thought that he had a long way to go when it came to artistic growth. He had predicted that if Vasu was ready to work hard and undergo intense training, he would find a place on Delhi's art map in five or six years. Lack of discipline was the one deficiency Harilal Shukla saw in him. Whether artists needed to be disciplined at all was a subject of debate in the city's discussion forums. Internal anarchy in an artist was acceptable, but in the case of art per se, discipline was essential, he used to argue. Vasu had no opinion on the matter. Anarchy was not an issue for him; neither was painting.

The maturing of Vasu into a fine artist had happened suddenly, Harilal thought. An unmistakable self-confidence became evident in his brush strokes. The missteps in the alignment of space and balance disappeared. The colours became bolder. Each step of Vasu's development as an artist amazed and pleased Harilal Shukla, who followed his evolution closely.

'Well done, young man,' Harilal said, closely inspecting the paintings that were propped up against the wall, one by one.

'I don't want anyone to praise me. I don't like it.'

'I'm not praising you. You've improved so much. I'm just telling you that without holding back.'

'Okay.'

Every day, Harilal went to Tilak Nagar to watch Vasu paint. He was astonished when he saw Vasu on his feet for hours together, painting without sitting down even once. Vasu didn't even notice Harilal coming and going. He was oblivious to hunger and thirst too.

'I'm going to book the Triveni Gallery.'

'What for?'

'To exhibit your paintings, what else? You already have enough paintings for an exhibition. There's no need to wait any longer.'

'I have no interest in exhibitions.'

'Why?'

'I'm not painting for others to see. I don't care about people coming and seeing my paintings.'

'Why are you painting then?'

'Ariyathilla.'

'What? What did you say?'

Communicating with Vasu was not easy. He had his own logic and language. Sometimes he spoke in Malayalam.

Harilal was slowly picking up his lingo, a mixture of English, Malayalam and sign language. What worried him was Vasu's lack of social etiquette. When he was introduced to foreign visitors, he either did not say a single word or responded with 'I don't know' in Malayalam. Ariyathilla.

'He doesn't know English, he's from the South,' Harilal Shukla told them, so as to avoid embarrassment. When the French and the Germans heard this, they beamed. They weren't fond of Englishmen and their language. They encouraged Vasu to speak in his mother tongue.

'Your friend is highly talented. But he doesn't know how to behave with others. He has no manners. The other artists in Delhi behave with respect, maintaining a certain decorum when foreigners come to view their paintings. They call them "sir". And this guy? He won't ask them to sit. He goes so far as to offend them. I have seen him laugh and mock them. In short, I'm fed up with your friend. I don't know how to tame him. The world of art is very competitive. If you are not careful, you can be thrown out very quickly. A return would be well-nigh impossible. Vasu has not entered this dog-eat-dog world yet. The doors should not close for him even before he makes an entry. That's what I'm trying to ensure. But he's not cooperating with me.'

Harilal Shukla wrung his hands in despair.

'No one should try to change him. He cannot be civilised. He is what he is.'

'That's not true, Sathyanatha. An artist cannot but be civilised. He owes some debts to society. To fulfil these, he has to be civilised. Creativity alone cannot make an artist grow or sustain himself. He should be socially conscious. He should be educated and knowledgeable,' said Janakikutty.

'My friends, my worry is only about the clients. When I try to bring them closer to Vasu, all he does is reject them and try to keep them away. I have only one hope—if the foreigners can understand his paintings, they will understand him too.'

'You've got that right,' Sathyanathan said.

Thus ended one of many discussions about Vasu in his absence.

'Shouldn't we name your paintings?'

'No.'

'At least for the catalogue, we need titles.'

'Okay.'

'Let's start then. First this poor man, his wife and three children. What will the title be?'

'Family.'

'That's not market-friendly at all. We need an adjective for the family.'

'A Poor Family.'

'I can suggest a better one. A Dalit Family. It's a politically correct title and very market-friendly.'

It was a reasonably big painting, five feet by four. The emaciated earth-toned man painted against the dark background was the head of the family. He stood on the left end of the painting. His caved-in belly, ribs that stood out, and matchstick-thin limbs spoke of his dire poverty. Next to him was a pair of shrivelled, desiccated breasts, his wife. A small, stunted penis curved like a fishhook—their eight-year-old son—was right next to her. Next to it were two tiny vulvas that looked like half-faded exclamation marks, symbolic of their six- and four-year-old daughters. That summed up the Dalit family.

'Normally, the head of the family is placed in the middle. You have pushed him to the margins by putting him at one end of the canvas. That is the originality of this painting. Another distinctive feature is that the wife is depicted as a mere pair of breasts and the children as genitals. Deepak Ananth, the Europe-based art critic, while analysing the works of Sarkis, the Turkish installation artist, said …'

'I don't want to hear.'

'You must, for you are a painter.'

'No one should call me a painter.'

'Then what should they call you?'

'Varayan.'

'What does that mean?'

'One who draws.'

Harilal continued as if he hadn't heard him, 'The greatest intellectual and financial transactions take place in the world of art. I'm going to price this painting of yours as high as J. Swaminathan's or Krishen Khanna's works. No one will buy a beginner's work at such a high price. Which is exactly what I want. No one should buy the painting. I'll keep raising its price till it's sky-high.'

Harilal Shukla spent the whole day in Vasu's barsati, giving titles to paintings, stretching and stapling the canvases, and selecting frames from a catalogue. Dusk had fallen by the time he left. The next morning, he came with a helper, loaded all the paintings to be framed into his jeep, and drove to Chemould Frames. He summoned the designer and discussed the design of the exhibition catalogue; spoke with the photographer about the colour photographs and transparencies of the works to be exhibited; drafted the invitation and made the list of invitees.

Vasu had never wondered why Harilal Shukla, superior to him in education, knowledge and age, was doing all this hard work to help him. He was attentive to every little thing that concerned Vasu. In the midst of it all, he suddenly remembered something that had slipped his mind earlier.

'Arrey, Vasu. What are you going to wear for the inauguration? Do you have anything?'

'I'll go naked.'

'Stop your silly jokes. Do you know the kind of people who will come to it?'

'Is Rosily coming?'

'All the diplomatic missions in Delhi will be represented. The business community too. I've made all the arrangements.'

Harilal Shukla took him to the Cottage Emporium in his jeep. He bought a silk jacket for Vasu. He bought fabric from Connaught Place and got trousers made for him. Artists could wear trousers and jackets. But they couldn't wear a tie like diplomats and businessmen did. He was au fait with the protocol. He bought a long, black woollen muffler for Vasu to wear in place of a tie. He rounded off his shopping with a pair of branded shoes.

He employed an attendant for Vasu, to take care of him till the exhibition was over. She arrived at Vasu's place on the afternoon of the inauguration. She washed and shampooed his long, feminine tresses. She trimmed the errant hairs of his moustache and beard. By 4 p.m., she had bathed and dressed him.

Harilal Shukla took a long look at Vasu, dressed in black woollen trousers, silk jacket and black muffler, with his shiny black hair combed and tied back. He gave a nod of satisfaction.

'Fine, all right.'

Passing by the mirror, Vasu saw a stranger reflected in it. He looked back at Vasu.

'Who's this?'

'Vasu the Great.'

3

ARTIST'S SLUMBER

Just before the wars of 1965 and 1971, Sahadevan had felt a pall of silence descending on Delhi. All was still. He had heard that such a state precedes death in terminally ill patients. Memories of even insignificant incidents are rekindled in the mind. A few hours before his death, Sahadevan's father Shekharan Nambiar had remembered the time when a cow had tried to gore him, when he was five years old. He spoke of it in great detail, as if it had happened the day before. He even recalled that the cow was lame in its left foreleg.

'I forgive the cow that butted me,' Shekharan Nambiar said. Vanaja had told Sahadevan all this later.

Sahadevan wondered if the city was recalling its past, as if it had heard the footsteps of some imminent calamity. During his last days, Shekharan Nambiar had only memories of a lame cow to recall. The city of Delhi had more than a cow to remember; it had elephants and horses too. In Lodhi Gardens, from where Vidya had disappeared, a stone bridge was still visible. During the reign of Ibrahim Lodhi, war horses used to gallop over it, their manes flying in the wind. The generals leading the troops used to sit on the backs of elephants and ride into Indraprastha amidst clouds of dust, through Delhi

Gate, now gnawed bare by time. Was the city recalling the number of attacks it had outlived?

Sahadevan had no military attacks or lame cows to remember. Though he had walked among cows grazing in meadows and standing on the roads, none of them had tried to butt him. Had he spent all his life avoiding confrontations? Was he unable to raise flags of rebellion? When life rushed at him to bite him, instead of confronting it, did he try to run away? Shrivelled memories and nostalgia appeared before him as question marks, reopening old wounds.

Leaving his faraway memories where they belonged, he embraced more recent ones.

Where was Rosily?

She wasn't centuries old like the stone bridge in Lodhi Gardens. She was from his own time. Yet, he didn't know where she was.

He worried when he didn't see her for any length of time. He had been reading in the newspapers about the police rounding up and putting girls like her in jail. His heart would skip a beat each time, and he would check to see if her name figured in the list of those arrested. Almost immediately, he would realise the futility of checking. Call girls were never known by their real names. He wished she hadn't dropped her real name, Rosakutty, redolent of the smell of fresh sap dripping from a tapped rubber tree. It was such a beautiful name.

For a long time, he had been the custodian of her jewellery, bank deposit certificates and passbooks. It had caused him great worry. What if someone burgled his house and took away all her savings while he was away in Kashyap Saxena's room in Patiala House?

He changed the latch on the outer door. In Chandni Chowk, he purchased a heavy, made-in-Aligarh padlock. He began to lock the house with it whenever he went out. Often, he would double back to check that he had locked up properly. Once, his bus had already reached the third stop when the suspicion began to grow in him; he got down and took another bus back. After tugging at the lock to make sure he had turned the key properly, he walked back to the bus stop.

'Mr Sahadevan, why do you need such a big lock?'

'The menace of thieves has increased all over Delhi. Every day, there's news of some burglary or the other in the newspaper.'

'Jangpura is very safe. As far as I can remember, there has been no burglary here.'

'But we should be careful, take necessary precautions. There's no point in regretting it after something happens. The Delhi Police are useless. Have they ever caught a thief?'

'It's not right to blame the police. They have enough work to do. All their attention is on the Sikh terrorists. Thieves are not on their list of priorities.'

'I'm being cautious, that's all ...'

Om Prakash Jain went back in without saying anything more. Before leaving, Sahadevan eyed the lock again. It was not suitable for a house. He had seen such locks only at warehouses and jewellery stores. Why would someone staying in a barsati, who couldn't even pay the rent, need such an enormous lock? Was that what Jain was thinking?

After she was thrown out by Lalaji, Rosily had found it hard to get a place to stay. Like a rain cloud driven by the wind, she floated around the city. She stayed briefly in many places, alone and otherwise. Sahadevan didn't know where she was these days. He didn't know if she had a telephone connection, and even if she did, he didn't know the number. What if a burglar broke open the door and took away her hard-earned savings? Without a contact number or address, how would he get in touch with her; how would he give her the shocking news?

She had turned a novelist into a genie guarding her treasure.

This was also the reason he could not move to Malviya Nagar immediately, even after deciding to leave Jangpura. He had to first find her and return her things.

Just to try his luck, he called Rosily on the old Govind Puri number. Lalaji's bungalow and the neem tree rose to the top of his mind. Sparrows used to perch on its branches.

'Is Rosily there?'

'What?' A gruff voice replied.

'Isn't this Rosily's number?'

'*Tum kaun ho*?'

'I'm an acquaintance of hers.'

'She isn't here. Do you want someone else? Can send.'

'I want Rosily's phone number.'

'Don't you have a telephone directory? Look in that. Call me if you need a girl. Understand, sister-fucker?'

He pulled on a jacket and locked the door after himself. The jacket smelt of kerosene. The dry-cleaning charges at Band Box and Snow White were very high, so he used to give his woollen clothes to a small dry-cleaning shop in Bhogal. These smaller shops used kerosene for dry cleaning and its smell lingered for weeks together. The man in the seat next to him probably took him for a kerosene trader.

The DTC bus turned the corner and reached Tilak Nagar. Joginder's footwear shop was in the market here. Jaswinder was probably at the cash counter. He had seen her sometimes, sitting there proudly. It had been a long time since he had any news of Uttam Singh and his family. It had been months since he had visited Kunhikrishnan and Lalitha too. The last time he had met Devi and Sathyanathan was during Dussehra. He just didn't go anywhere or meet anyone these days.

In past years, he would go to Ajmeri Gate to watch the Dussehra celebrations at Ramlila Maidan. Once, when Pinky was a little girl, he had taken her along. When they got off the bus in front of the hospital, in the distance, they could see huge effigies of Ravana, Kumbhakarna and Meghnad, standing as tall as multi-storey buildings. Crowds were flowing towards the grounds, just like they did before the Republic Day parade. Tens of thousands walked together in a procession led by a band. Small children bearing bows and arrows walked in the front. Tableaus of Rama, Sita and Hanuman passed by on decorated trucks. As the procession entered the grounds, there was an upheaval in the crowd. He held Pinky's hand tightly so as to not lose her.

Rama took aim at Ravana's effigy and shot an arrow with a burning torch at its head. Children and adults shot arrows at Ravana, his brother and son. The fireworks stored in Ravana's belly caught fire. But the first to burn and collapse was Meghnad. Kumbhakarna followed. Ravana exploded with a big bang. Fire shot out of his eyes and ears.

'I'm scared.' Pinky had tightened her hold on his hand. He held her close to him.

Both young and old cheered loudly. When Ravana fell to one side, enveloped in smoke and fire, chants of 'Ram, Ram' rose from the crowd. Some people shouted, '*Indira Gandhi ki jai*.' If M.F. Husain could draw Indira Gandhi as Goddess Durga, it was hardly surprising that the cobblers, peanut sellers and vegetable vendors of Ajmeri Gate looked up to her.

The devotees of Rama rushed towards the still-burning effigy of Ravana to pull out bamboo splits. It was believed that keeping these at home would bring prosperity till the next Ramlila came around.

Sahadevan picked up a burnt piece of split bamboo for Pinky.

'What do you want to eat, baby? Aren't you hungry?'

'I'll have an ice stick, chhote bhaiya. A red one.'

Before they boarded the bus, he got her an ice stick in a bleeding red colour. By the time they reached home, her face and hands had turned the same shade of red. The front of her dress was stained red too.

When he got to Vasu's barsati, he immediately noticed the changes. There was the smell of fresh paint on the terrace. He saw flowers in full bloom, in pots arranged in a row along the parapet wall.

When he entered through the open door, more surprises lay in store. Expensive-looking sofas and chairs. A fridge in the kitchen. In the bedroom, a new Jaipuri bedcover. Winter sunshine slipped through the thin lace curtains on the window and fell on the bed.

'Vasu,' he called gently.

No one answered. Could Vasu have gone outside, leaving the door open as usual? He looked around.

Then he saw him curled up on the cold floor, snoring in his sleep. Vasu found it difficult to sleep on a clean, soft bed.

He opened the fridge. The light came on, but there wasn't even a bottle of water inside.

Sahadevan tried to wake Vasu, but he wouldn't budge. He slept most of the time now. His sleep was white in colour and empty like his fridge. There were no shapes, colours or movements. Let alone the genie who guarded Rosily's treasure, even if real genies had tried to wake him up, he would have remained oblivious.

Sahadevan squatted near Vasu and touched his shoulder.

'Vasu, open your eyes.'

'What for?'

'You've got to help me. Where is Rosily staying? Do you know her phone number?'

'Six-two-nine-four-one-four.'

There was a phone in Vasu's room. He dialled the number. It rang for a long time. Eventually, he heard a tired voice at the other end.

'Edi, how long I've been searching for you … Don't you want your jewellery and papers and all?'

'Yes, but where am I going to keep them? They are safe with you.'

'I'm moving house. I'm shifting to a small room. It won't be safe there. So please come immediately and take it away.'

'Why are you moving house now? It's such a good place. And very safe.'

'Rosily, you don't know the state I am in. I don't have money even for the rent. I owe Om Prakash Jain one year's rent already.'

'Don't leave Jangpura. There's a brown purse in the packet I gave you. There's money inside. Take as much as you want and pay the arrears.'

'No. I'm moving to Malviya Nagar. You give your jewellery and stuff to Sathyanathan. Deviyechi is there. There's nothing to worry about.'

Silence.

'Why aren't you saying anything?'

'They are all big people. If someone like me visits, it's a matter of shame for them.'

'Did Sathyanathan say something to you?'

Again, silence.

Their conversation ended there.

He hung up the phone and picked up his jacket to leave. There was a cold breeze outside. He loved winters. Wearing a woollen jacket, with his hands stuffed into his trouser pockets, he could walk for hours on end, talking to himself. These conversations contained whole novels, philosophies and ideologies; crisp-fried bread pakodas at Chandni Restaurant and Old Monk rum also featured in them.

'We can keep Rosily's money and jewellery here. It's safe,' Vasu said, his eyes still closed.

Sahadevan had been mistaken in assuming that his silence and stillness meant he was lost to the world. He had the power to see, hear and understand.

The next day, Rosily came to Jangpura and took away her valuables. Sahadevan could finally breathe easy. I'll sleep well tonight, he told himself.

'Rosily has trouble keeping her gold and money safe. She has no place of her own. Shouldn't we have helped her?' he asked Sathyanathan one day.

'Amma doesn't like it when she comes home. One day, when she rang the bell, amma asked me not to open the door. She asks if it's right for someone to marry their sweetheart after earning money working as a whore. In a way, it is. But amma can't think like we do.'

'It's a shame. You shouldn't have hurt her like that and turned her away. Who does she have here but us?'

'She's not one of us. Her life is not easy, but that's a decision she made. She has to take the responsibility for it. But what's her problem now?'

'She has no place to keep her money and gold.'

'People find it difficult to make money. *That* is a problem. Her problem is keeping money safe, is it?' After a pause, Sathyanathan said, 'She can get a locker in a bank and keep everything there.'

Eventually, that was what Rosily did. She leased a locker in the Karol Bagh branch of Syndicate Bank. Her savings were safe there. Once every month, she would open it and place a bundle of currency inside.

'Edi, haven't you saved enough? Why don't you go back home and marry Jomon?'

'I'm going, chetta,' she said with a sigh. 'It's time to go.'

Sahadevan felt a wave of affection for Jomon. He had been waiting for her for years. Finally, they would become one.

Yet, even in the middle of this happy thought, his heart beat erratically, with misgivings. A nameless unease grew within him.

4

GUNSHOTS IN SEWA NAGAR

'I need to go, son.'

'The place is crawling with police and army men. You won't even be able to enter. Why are we going there?'

'He was your father's friend. They led strikes together. After your father died, he used to walk from Andrews Ganj to Sewa Nagar to check on us every day. The least we can do is to go and see what is happening. Otherwise, your father will never forgive me.'

With the passage of time, Shreedharanunni's old colleagues had drifted away, one by one. Even Bansilal seemed to have forgotten them. Only Sukhram continued to visit until they moved out of Sewa Nagar. He used to sit and talk of old times while drinking the cardamom-laced tea she made for him. He spoke of the strikes he had been part of while at the Secretariat. He had retired as a gazetted officer but was never able to reconcile to the higher grade. With his grey stubble and his grimy shirt collar, he looked the part of a busy trade union worker. And he never stopped riding his bicycle to work.

The day after his superannuation, Sukhram had come to Sewa Nagar. 'I feel like I've taken a heavy load off my head. I'm so relieved.'

He looked about sixty-eight or seventy years old. The stubble on his face was fully white. The skin and muscles of his neck hung loose.

'If Shreedharanunni was alive, we would have retired together. We are of the same age.'

Devi sighed.

'I have to vacate the R.K. Puram quarters within six months. I must get a small house constructed before that.'

Till his promotion to the officer cadre, he had stayed in Andrews Ganj. He had bought a small three-cent plot of land not far from there and given it on rent to a man who owned buffaloes. In a shed with a tarpaulin roof, seven or eight buffaloes could be seen lying on the floor and chewing the cud. The place stank of buffalo dung. People came with aluminium vessels every day to buy the fresh, warm milk.

'I have to evict the buffalo man. I don't know if he'll agree.'

Sukhram had sat with them for a while, discussing this and other matters.

A few months later, he had moved into his newly built house in Sant Nagar.

For Delhiites, a house is a huge luxury. Their dreams don't usually extend beyond an apartment. Most Malayalis, after coming to Delhi, gave up on their dream of owning an independent house. A DDA flat was all they could hope for. Matchbox-like flats built one on top of the other. Within months of moving in, there would be seepages and leaks. The corroded water pipes would break in one's hands.

'One day, you must come with your son to Sant Nagar,' Sukhram had told them.

After moving to Hauz Khas, Devi had stopped going anywhere other than her office. As a trade unionist's wife, she couldn't adjust to her new surroundings. She was familiar with buildings with broken-off plaster and leaking pipes, roads that were crowded with bicycles, vegetable vendors and pushcarts, and people who lined up early in the morning at the DMS milk booths with empty bottles.

On the Hauz Khas roads, there were no bicycles. The bungalows had marble staircases, covered garages, and front yards where colourful dahlias bloomed in the winters. The grey, scraggly-haired woman in her worn chappals, standing at the bus stop at 8.30 a.m. with a plastic lunch box in her hand, did not fit with the affluence all around her. Those who alighted at Devi's bus stop in Hauz Khas were ayahs or helpers who did the gardening or took care of the pets in the bungalows.

'Son, how much rent are we paying for this flat?'

'Not much.'

Sathyanathan grinned, flashing his white teeth, and looked at her through his glasses.

'Tell me, eda, I want to know.'

Devi was astonished when she heard the figure. It was more than her monthly salary.

'Son, isn't it a waste? It's just the two of us. Can't we do with a smaller flat?'

'Amma, if we have the money, we should live comfortably. We had a hard time in Sewa Nagar. I used to sleep and study in that narrow veranda, even in the winter. Did you and achan have any privacy at night? There's no need to live like that any longer. I won't allow you to suffer any more.'

'Will my sorrows disappear because you want them to? No one can get rid of them. It's only when I breathe my last that they'll leave me alone.'

He guessed that Vidya was on her mind. Had she been alive, she would be about thirty now, maybe a wife and a mother.

Neither Devi nor Sathyanathan spoke about Vidya. Lalitha, Kunhikrishnan, Sahadevan, they had all forgotten her.

Sathyanathan had set apart a room for Devi in the flat. He had bought a bed from a shop in Panchkuian Road for his amma to rest and sleep on. He had bought a Dunlop mattress and

Bombay Dyeing sheets. He had bought a transistor radio so she could listen to music. In one corner of the room, he had arranged a few photographs of Parassini Madappura Muththappan and Guruvayurappan for her to pray to. From the Kerala Emporium, he had managed to get a small brass lamp for her to light after her morning bath. As the winter set in, he got her a soft blanket to cover herself with. He bought two expensive woollen sweaters from Connaught Place for her to wear to work. They were white and blue because he was not fond of bright colours. He didn't share Shreedharanunni's fondness for red.

On a wall in Devi's room hung a photo of Shreedharanunni. His portrait had been extracted from a group photo of union workers and enlarged. A zero-watt bulb burned above it all the time. At night, when all the other lights were off, the light from this bulb would flow down the walls and onto Devi's bed. Once, Devi had thought of hanging Vidya's photograph next to Shreedharanunni's, but the very next moment, she stopped herself. Where was the proof that Vidya was no longer in this world? What would they do if, one fine day, she walked into the house?

Devi struggled to cope with the luxuries in the flat. She would lie sleepless on the Dunlop bed and stare at the ceiling helplessly, with nothing else to do. One night, when Sathyanathan peeped in, she was sleeping curled up on a single sheet on the cold floor.

When she was fifty years old, Devi developed a pain in her knees. When she touched fifty-three, her knees started to swell and the pain increased. With her lunch box and painkiller tablets in her bag, she would bravely walk to the bus stop. Usually, there wasn't even standing room in the buses going towards Central Secretariat. But she would manage to squeeze in somehow. The pain was excruciating when her swollen knees got kicked and knocked about by others. Nevertheless, she went to work every day, suffering.

'I have something to tell you, amma. Will you listen to me?'

'When have I not done what you asked me to?'

'Amma, stop going to the Secretariat.'

'Where else can I go? My office is there.'

'You should leave this job. You don't need it.'

Devi had guessed he was going to broach the subject. She could read his mind. Hadn't she given birth to him and suckled him?

'Say something, amma.'

'I had Sewa Nagar and then the Secretariat. Sewa Nagar is gone. Only the Secretariat is left. If that too is gone, where will I go? How will I live?'

'From now on, Sewa Nagar and Central Secretariat are all in this flat. What do you lack here? I'll get you anything you want. On the first day of every month, I'll give you the salary you receive at the Secretariat. What more do you want?'

She sat with her head bowed, silent.

'If I stay at home without doing anything, I'll go mad.'

'I'll buy you books to read. I'll get the *Deshabhimani* delivered from Kozhikode. We'll buy a record player and LP records. On Saturdays and Sundays, I'll take you out. We can go to the movies. Have dinner at Nirula's ...'

'Eda, stop it!' She covered both her ears with her hands.

'What do you want me to do then? Do you want me to die? I can do that too.'

He went to her and hugged her tight. Her body smelt of eucalyptus. Or was it the smell of old age? During his childhood, her face always smelt of talcum powder.

'Son, I'll do whatever you want, obey you in all other matters, but don't ask me to leave my job at the Secretariat. That's where your father used to work. I want to work there till I die.'

Sathyanathan understood. His father's smell lingered in the dark corridors stacked with musty files. In the mornings, her hair still wet from her bath, she went to his father's side under the pretext of going to the Secretariat. His father must be riding the bicycle along Rashtrapati Bhawan, with her seated in the front. Like he had taken her on his bicycle to Sarojini Nagar, he must be going with her to Rajpath.

Sathyanathan never spoke to her about quitting after that.

Devi didn't like going out. On weekends, she stayed at home. She cleaned the house and washed Sathyanathan's clothes. She kneaded the dough. When he saw her working, he would scold her.

'Why are you doing all that? We have a maid now.'

His anger would drive her back to her room. A room stifled by the enduring loneliness of a widow who had lost her husband at a young age and a mother whose daughter was missing.

Sathyanathan found a solution for his mother's isolation during the weekends. On Saturday mornings, Janakikutty would come to Hauz Khas with a bag on her shoulder and round-rimmed spectacles perched on her face. The shoulder bag contained books, a pack of Gold Flake, and plastic packets of achappam and murukku. The last two were for Devi.

'Ammae, I hope the pain in your knees is gone?'

'It won't go anywhere. It'll stay with me till the end.'

'Ayurveda is better for arthritis. Shall we go and consult the Arya Vaidya Sala on Pusa Road?'

'No, dear. Just let it be, as long as I'm able to walk. When that too is no longer possible, I'll lie down. What else can I do?'

Devi was mentally prepared to accept old age and its infirmities.

Janakikutty applied balm on Devi's swollen knees and a herbal liniment on her whole body before she bathed. Then they took an auto to Chittaranjan Park to buy fish.

Some nights, Janakikutty would stay over. If Vidya was alive, she would have been approximately Janakikutty's age. Devi had started seeing Vidya in her. In their childhood, Sathyanathan and Vidya were close to the point of being inseparable. They used to have tiffs, sulk, stop talking to each other, and then fall asleep side by side. Now, Sathyanathan and Janakikutty behaved the same way. They quarrelled, got annoyed at each other, stopped talking, and then lay in bed together, reading.

But then, one day, everything turned topsy-turvy.

'Eda, where are you?'

The sound of water running in the shower stopped and Janakikutty peeked around a half-open door. She was usually careful not to call him by the familiar eda, poda, in front of Devi. The eda in that sentence astonished Devi.

'Get me a towel. I forgot.'

Sathyanathan, who was talking to Devi in the drawing room, got up and went towards the bathroom after picking up the towel. Instead of extending her hand through the gap in the door and grabbing it, Janakikutty took it with the door held half open. Her naked, wet body could be seen through the gap. What did this prove? That they were not merely friends. They had gone beyond friendship. Devi sat there, thinking.

That evening, Janakikutty returned to the hostel. Devi could not sleep the whole night. Suddenly, Vidya had gone out of Janakikutty. After that, however much she tried, she couldn't see even a shadow of Vidya in her.

'Sathyanatha, I want to know something.'

He had changed into his work clothes before seating himself at the breakfast table. Devi usually left half an hour after he did. Breakfast was idli and coconut chutney today. The chutney had been ground in the mixie, which Devi didn't like. The flat-topped wet grinding stone and its companion pestle had been left behind in Sewa Nagar when they moved. Sathyanathan had insisted, although they had brought along the earthenware pot, the puttu maker and the coconut scraper. There is a mixie for grinding, he had said.

'What do you want to know?'

'There's no need to prolong this anymore. If you both like each other, why are you waiting? Why don't we formalise it?'

A bulb lit up in Sathyanathan's head.

'We haven't thought about marriage, ammae. What's the hurry?'

'You and Janakikutty have been going around together all this time. I've seen both of you lying on the same bed. You shouldn't do all this without getting married. It's not right.'

'It's not a done deal, amma. I'm not even sure she'll agree, if I ask her. There's still time. We can think about it at leisure and decide. You shouldn't worry your head about it.'

He could not give his mother a grandchild. Sanjayji had robbed him of that forever.

The cases he had filed had been dismissed for lack of evidence. In the meantime, Sanjayji's life had been robbed by a rogue plane.

Sathyanathan rose from the table in a hurry. Through the leafy branches, he could see the office car waiting for him outside the gate.

Unexpectedly, there was no crowd in front of Sukhram's house in Sant Nagar. The work on the tiny house had not yet been completed. The granite blocks meant for the compound wall were still lying on the road, where they had been unloaded. A parked police jeep blocked the narrow lane. Their taxi stopped in front of the wheat mill. Devi and Sathyanathan got off and walked towards Sukhram's house, until they were stopped by the police.

'We are family friends of Sukhramji.'

'Sorry. No one has the permission to go inside.'

'When is the cremation?'

'We don't know.'

Three or four men were talking, standing in front of the wheat mill. Sathyanathan tried to listen to what they were saying.

'Sukhramji had come out for his morning walk. Usually both of us go together. But today, I felt lazy and didn't go. That's why I'm alive and standing in front of you.'

Khalistani terrorists had come in a car and shot at the morning walkers. Three fell dead on the road. Sukhram breathed his last on the way to Safdarjung Hospital. He had been shot in the abdomen.

There was no wailing or breast-beating, nothing one would associate with a sudden death. People seemed too scared to cry. Even those waiting outside were mute; afraid to talk.

'Let's go.'

'Shouldn't we see him once, for the last time? He was your father's friend. How many years they worked and sat on satyagraha together ...'

'We won't be allowed to see the body, ammae. We'll come again, another day.'

Sathyanathan took his mother's hand and turned back. The road was empty. All the windows and doors on either side were shut. There was no one outside. Sant Nagar, usually crowded and bustling, looked like a haunted place.

Devi returned home, sad that she could not see Sukhram one last time.

There was a second attack by the Khalistani terrorists, this time during Durga Puja. They shot and killed devotees congregated in a Puja pandal in Chittaranjan Park.

No one knew when bullets would fly from passing cars. People waiting at bus stops tried to stand behind trees and lamp posts to avoid getting hit.

The buses ran empty once dusk fell. Even cinema halls showing Amitabh Bachchan movies were empty. The lights went off early in all the markets.

Fear was everywhere, and everyone carried it in their hearts.

It was the kind of fear that Sahadevan had experienced a long time ago.

5

THIRTY-THREE BULLETS

Clouds driven by the winds from Punjab gathered over the gurdwara. The edges of the dark clouds that grazed the golden domes of the Bangla Sahib were tinged with the scarlet of the rising sun and reflected in the pond within its precincts. Disturbed, the pigeons roosting in the domes flew away in search of distant lands of peace.

31 October 1984 was a Wednesday.

Sahadevan was on his way to Patiala House when a black Ambassador and a jeep went past his bus. Inside the car was Peter Ustinov, who was in India to make a short film on Indira Gandhi. The jeep carried the recording and lighting equipment he would use. They were on their way to Indiraji's house on Safdarjung Road.

Sahadevan had been in no mood to go anywhere. After Durga Puja, the early mornings had turned chilly. Through the open window, a slightly nippy breeze entered the room. He pulled the sheet up till his neck, turned on his side, and dozed. He felt cold without his shirt on.

Usually, he always wore a shirt, even when he was indoors and alone. His landlord, Ashok Chibber, on the other hand, walked around in his underwear. He even stood at the gate in his underwear and chatted with passing acquaintances. And his wife? Sahadevan had seen her dressed only in a petticoat and blouse when she was at home. Delhiites were generally allergic to clothes, Sahadevan thought. Was it because of their influence that he was shirtless today? His unventilated, airless room always pulsated with heat. He felt a little better when his chest was bare. If he spotted anyone coming, he would hurriedly put on a shirt. He was sensitive about his chest, and mortified each time it occurred to him that no woman would want to see it.

He wished he could sleep in for a longer time. But Kashyap Saxena reached Patiala House at 9 a.m. He was supposed to be there by then. Saxena didn't give him anything in writing now; he dictated. Sahadevan had not learnt shorthand, so he would take it all down in long hand and type it up later.

When the bus went past Indiraji's house, Sahadevan saw Ustinov's car and the jeep parked there. He saw the gun barrels peeking out from behind piled-up sandbags. Security guards were hidden behind these, holding guns at the ready. Soldiers stood vigilant, holding rifles and Sten guns behind the walls, in the tall watch towers built atop them, and on the roof of the house. These security details had come into place after Operation Blue Star, which had been launched to flush out the terrorists holed up in Amritsar's Golden Temple. Before that, Indira Gandhi used to stroll in the garden at 1, Safdarjung Road, tending to flowers, without even a personal bodyguard. Those passing by could look in and see her; Sahadevan had done so too, a few times.

Saxena's chamber was closed. That was when Sahadevan remembered—Saxena had told him that he was not appearing in any cases that day. He had gone to Punjab to attend a wedding in the family.

Though he was stingy with money, Saxena was a progressive lawyer. He mostly took up cases that could benefit society. He believed that lawyers and judges should be socially conscious and committed. The case he was dealing with now concerned the rights of workers. But for that, Sahadevan would not have stuck around for more than six months. Also, as things stood, if he stayed with Kashyap for six months more, he would be able to repay all his debts—the biggest one was to Chandni Restaurant—and have some savings too.

He had stopped sending money to his mother. She alternated between staying with Vanaja and Shyamala. Her letters had become irregular. Maybe she didn't need him any longer. She didn't talk about his marriage either. Maybe she was fed up.

'Good-for-nothing,' she was probably telling everyone about him.

He went to Guru Nanak Market. Ouseph's Malayali Store was prospering. Another cobbler occupied Kallu mochi's space. Beneath the jamun tree where Dasappan used to cut his customers' hair and shave their beards, another barber had established himself. He was from Uttar Pradesh or Haryana. With that, the Malayali suzerainty over the space below the jamun tree ended.

Seen from the outside, there were no visible changes to Kunhikrishnan's old house in New Double Storey. A small, two-room abode within a yellow-painted barrack-like building. Nothing remarkable about it.

Inside, though, there were many changes. Near the bedroom door, a Kelvinator fridge had appeared. A Japanese-made National rice cooker sat inside the kitchen. Wash the rice, fill the required amount of water, put it in the cooker, switch it on and go. The cooker switched off by itself once the rice was cooked. All the ladies in the neighbourhood had come to see this miracle. A woollen carpet decorated the living room. Not just the bedroom and the living room, even the toilet was full of books, most of them hardcover editions. Kunhikrishnan spent hundreds of thousands of rupees on books.

'Did you forget the way here? It's been such a long time since we've seen you. You don't want to hang out with Lalitha and me anymore, eh?'

'I don't get the time. I'm always so busy.'

'I thought bachelors are never busy. They are not tied down. They can cook and eat what they want, go where they please and when they please. No one is waiting for them at home. You're enjoying your freedom, aren't you?'

'Married men have more time for leisure than bachelors. They don't have to cook, clean the house, wash their clothes or anything. She'll do it, won't she? If there's a wife at home, the man can sit in an armchair, smoke cigarettes and read books.'

'How old are you now, Sahadeva?'

'I was born in '39.'

'Muthappa, so you are on the very wrong side of forty. An old man. When are you going to find yourself a wife? After you've lost your teeth?'

It was not only Sahadevan who had aged. Lalitha was no longer the woman he had first seen in her wedding album. Nor the one he saw on the bus near INA Market, the day war broke out. She had put on weight. Her face was fleshy. There were copper coloured strands here and there in her hair, darkened by the use of Black Rose henna.

'One must marry when it's the right time to do so. That there's no money, or that your sisters have to be married off first, these are all excuses. Kunhikrishnan understood the value of a wife when he lost the use of both his hands.'

'What she's saying is true, Sahadeva.'

His left arm hung loose from his shoulder. Treatment and physiotherapy had returned partial movement to the fingers of his right hand. He could smoke his pipe without help from others. He was able to clean the pipe, fill it with tobacco and light it, all with one hand. But he couldn't do much more than that.

Two of his books had been published in England. Both manuscripts had been typed up by Lalitha. Not merely her typing, her English had also improved substantially. Her vocabulary often surprised him.

'My third book, I'm not going to dictate. You write it yourself. Can you?'

'Are you teasing me? I don't have the nous for it.'

What would he do if he were Kunhikrishnan? If he were to lose the use of his hands, he would have to take help from others for everything, wouldn't he? But whose help could he take? Who could he depend on? There had to be someone.

Once, when Sahadevan was discussing this with Rosily, Vasu had asked, 'How does Kunhikrishnan sir wash himself after he shits?'

It was true. You can depend on others for almost everything. But not this.

Sahadevan sat flipping through Kunhikrishnan's new books. Most of them dealt with abstruse subjects. Sahadevan preferred novels. His reading was confined mostly to fiction and studies of novels.

Kunhikrishnan was speaking about Sikh terrorism.

'The Green Revolution alienated the Sikh community. Their traditional farming methods were disrupted. They lost the right to decide what to sow and when to sow. These decisions were taken for them by IAS officers sitting in Delhi. Sahadeva, when modernity is imposed in the place of tradition, its natural outcome is terrorism.'

He was interrupted by the sound of the telephone ringing. He picked up the receiver with his right hand and put it close to his ear. His normally grave face turned more severe.

'Sahadeva, Indira Gandhi has been shot dead.'

There was a huge crowd in front of the All India Institute of Medical Sciences. Most of them were Congress Party workers.

Journalists walked around with writing pads and ballpoint pens in their hands. Press photographers milled about, carrying heavy cameras with big lenses. There was a ring of policemen outside the Institute. Police jeeps kept coming and going. Some of the women in the crowd were wailing and beating their breasts. Others shouted the name of Indiraji. All eyes were on the main, multi-storey building. Inside the operation theatre, surgeons were trying to remove the seven bullets lodged in Indira Gandhi's body. Several more bullets had passed through her.

A Buddhist monk appeared suddenly from nowhere, praying in silence for Indiraji, who was fighting for her life.

Sahadevan stood outside, amidst the massive crowd.

The concerted wail of police sirens sounded. The President's convoy was speeding through INA Market. The crowd, wailing and praying for Indiraji, wouldn't make way for him. The policemen tried to create a path by swinging their lathis. The crowd responded by pelting stones at the car. Dressed in white and wearing a turban, the Sikh President of India sat inside the car, trying to look tranquil.

The crowd outside AIIMS didn't know when Indiraji's soul flew to where her father Jawaharlal Nehru and ex-husband Feroze Gandhi waited. They continued to pray for her life. But no one's prayers could have saved her that day. Beant Singh and Satwant Singh had fired thirty-three rounds into her. Perhaps every single Sikh among the millions in Punjab, Delhi, America and Canada wished to shoot Indira Gandhi for having desecrated the holiness of Harmandir Sahib. The day the army went in, they had raised their eyes to the heavens and said, '*Hukum karo, sachche padshaon* ...' They had waited for the command of Wahe Guru.

The city's residents gathered before their radios. But All India Radio was silent. Indiraji's death wasn't confirmed until ten hours after it happened. However, people like Kunhikrishnan, who listened to foreign radio stations, got detailed reports from the BBC. The news started to travel through the city.

The cobblers and vendors of ice-water, peanuts and bananas abandoned their carts and stood in front of AIIMS, mourning. One-legged and blind beggars dropped their bowls and prayed for Indiraji. Many of them were victims of nasbandi. But they had forgotten that.

Within minutes, the streets emptied. People withdrew into their homes. DTC buses let off their passengers midway and returned to Shadipur Depot. Cars and private vehicles disappeared; shops were shuttered. Just as Rajesh Khanna was trying to embrace Mumtaz, singing and circumambulating a tree, at Regal Cinema in Connaught Place, the screen trembled and went blank, as if the film reel had snapped. Thousands of typewriters in the Secretariat fell silent. The thousands who had arrived at the Old Delhi railway station from Punjab, Uttar Pradesh and Bihar couldn't find buses to continue their journey to their final destinations. On the operation tables at Safdarjung Hospital and Ram Manohar Lohia Hospital, pregnant women with distended bellies lay waiting for C-sections to be performed by surgeons who had disappeared. The long bell rang in schools and children ran out of their classrooms. Worried mothers rushed to kindergartens and nurseries to bring their little ones home.

Joginder Singh dug out the crackers left over from the previous Guru Purnima.

'No ...'

Jaswinder tried to stop him. She caught hold of his hand. Joginder slapped it away. She, and her pregnant belly, fell back against the wall.

Crackers continued to be burst in Jaswinder's yard. Tilak Nagar, Hari Nagar and Trilok Puri, where Sikhs lived in large numbers, drowned in the flashes and sounds of firecrackers bursting in abandon.

By sundown, the city's residents could see the lifeless body of Indira Gandhi, wrapped in the tricolour, on their black and white screens, the images telecast by Doordarshan. In the background, Kishori Amonkar sang bhajans.

Sahadevan gazed at the road, which was bereft of vehicles. He was not worried about how he would reach home. Twenty minutes of walking would get him to Hauz Khas. He could seek refuge with Devi and Sathyanathan. He wanted to walk alone, talking to himself.

Indira Priyadarshini, where did you go wrong? he asked aloud. There was no one to hear him on that lifeless, deserted road, which seemed frozen with fear. And yet, he continued.

You slid out of Chacha Nehru's lap, straight onto the throne, without pausing to read and understand history. You failed to see even your own shadow lying fragmented on the pages of history. You forgot the abject defeat you suffered in the 1977 elections. You may not recall the photo that appeared in all the prominent newspapers the day after the rout, but I, as a failed novelist, remember. It was one of those big wall posters with a large photo of you and 'Vote for Congress' printed on it. The whole world saw that picture, torn in two, lying on top of the rubbish heap on Kasturba Gandhi Marg. The prime minister, the daughter of Pandit Jawaharlal Nehru, on top of the rubbish heap on a city road.

You were responsible for demolishing my workplace and destroying my life. Yet, when I saw your photo lying on that mound of rubbish, I felt pity for you. Even if they are penniless, our countrymen are citizens with the right to vote. And when they unite, they can make any throne tremble. Priyadarshini, you alone didn't realise that. Seven years later, you failed again to read the minds of the public—the believers. You sent the army into the Golden Temple, one of the holiest shrines in the world. Today, you have been erased from the face of this earth, without even being able to say goodbye. Though you were the empress of errant ways, you were a woman and a mother too. They should not have emptied their guns into your chest.

It was past midnight when Sahadevan finally reached Malviya Nagar. As he lay sleepless on his shabby bed, violence emerged, cutting open the night's womb and displaying its bloodied head. Like a new-born animal that starts to walk as soon as it is born, it started to move through the night towards the parts of the city where Sikhs lived in large numbers.

6

THE HUNTERS OF AMRITPURI

In Shreedharanunni's time, a radio was a rare thing. On the day China attacked India, Sahadevan had to cycle all the way to Kunhikrishnan's home to listen to the news. That was twenty-two years ago.

Today, Sahadevan wanted to watch Indira Gandhi's funeral procession on television. He liked to be an active participant at events, whatever they may be.

There was no television in Kunhikrishnan's home. Would Sathyanathan's place have one?

It had been a long time since he went to Hauz Khas.

'Why aren't you coming over anymore? Amma keeps asking about you. We have a Bengali lady as our cook. She cooks hilsa very well. Call before you come. I'll go to Chittaranjan Park and get fresh hilsa to eat with rice. We can have some vodka or rum before that. Amma doesn't complain about those things now. She is no longer the old amma.'

Sahadevan had no desire to have rice with hilsa curry. What he wanted was two pegs of rum. In the old days, there was always a stock of Old Monk in the cupboard at home. Now, even a pint of rum had become a luxury. Some days, he would walk around thirsting for a drink. He would dream of drinking rum with chilled Coca-Cola and smile in his sleep. It was one of the few luxuries he permitted himself—rum and Coca-Cola.

He put on his shirt and trousers. Recently, he had bought a funky blue cotswool shirt with large black checks. He had discovered a small store that sold export reject garments and trendy shirts that didn't burn a hole in one's pocket. And, even if he wore the shirt for a week, it didn't become shabby. Since October had ended, it wasn't humid and sweaty anymore.

Just when he was ready to leave for Hauz Khas, his landlord Ashok Chibber appeared in his underwear.

'Where are you off to, bhaiya?'

'Hauz Khas.'

'Don't go anywhere. Riots have started in Tilak Nagar. It's risky to go out.'

When Sahadevan had first moved here, his landlord rarely spoke to him. He preferred to remain aloof from his tenants. Collect the rent on the first of the month; don't say anything; don't ask anything. After eleven months are over, ask for a hike in rent. If they don't agree, ask them to vacate. If they don't vacate, throw out their things, lock the room and leave. That was his philosophy.

But, gradually, Chibber had come to like Sahadevan. He never gave him any trouble. He didn't play Peeping Tom with his wife or daughters. He paid the rent on time. Once he got back from work, he stayed in his room. He often came home with his hands full of books from various libraries.

One night, at around 3 a.m., Chibber had woken up to answer the call of nature. He saw that there was a light on in Sahadevan's room, and unable to contain his curiosity, he had tiptoed to the window and peeped in. He saw Sahadevan bent over, writing on a sheet of paper. There was a halo of smoke above his head. Chibber knew then that he was no ordinary tenant and many grave matters must weigh on his mind.

'Why are you going to Hauz Khas now?'

'To watch TV.'

'What?!'

'To see Indiraji,' he clarified.

'Don't go so far for that, my friend. My nephew has a TV. We can go to his place and watch Indiraji together.'

Sahadevan nodded his head in agreement. Under normal circumstances, he wouldn't have gone to a stranger's house to watch TV. But this was no ordinary day. Everything was extraordinary today. It was a day that established that a gun can kill its owner. A historic day.

Chibber's nephew lived one street away. He was in the business of buying pieces of old furniture, repairing, polishing and reselling them. In a shed next to his house were broken chairs, writing and dining tables, beds, dressing tables with cracked mirrors, and sofas with missing cushions. Chisels, glue, varnishes, polish and other things were scattered around. The carpenters hadn't turned up today. They too must be watching Indiraji on TV.

When he saw the chisel lying in the shed, Sahadevan thought of Uttam Singh.

Though the nephew's room was small and narrow, it had a comfortable sofa. Sahadevan sat down and lit a cigarette. Whatever happened around him, he needed a burning cigarette between his lips. It was a quarter-century-old habit. The nicotine stains were well entrenched on the edges of his teeth. No amount of brushing could get rid of them.

'Mummy ...'

Roby, Chibber's nephew's son, who had been playing cricket outside, on his own, rushed into the room. His little face was pale with fright. What had he seen to frighten him so much?

Their eyes followed his pointing finger.

An old sardar was lurching like a drunk down the deserted street. He was wearing a white shirt and trousers. On his feet were canvas shoes. He could have been out for a morning walk.

Except, the front of his shirt, from the collar down, was soaked in blood. One side of his face was smashed in as if it had been hit with a stone. Blood was oozing from his forehead and the side of his head. He looked like he would collapse any moment now.

'Who's that, Chibberji?'

'Dilbagh Singh. He lives down there, on that street. Both his children live in England.'

'He's going to fall.'

The old man needed help. He looked like he would fall face down on the road, any moment now.

'No!' Chibber restrained Sahadevan.

He went out and put a lock on the gate.

Dilbagh Singh didn't fall as Sahadevan had imagined he would. He walked on and out of sight, rounding the corner.

There were sounds of a crowd from somewhere close by. Could it be the mob that had attacked Dilbagh Singh?

'Get in.'

The nephew shut and locked the door behind them. He drew the curtains and lowered the volume of the television.

Sahadevan was reminded of the 1975 war. He was staying in Uttam Singh's house in Amritpuri then.

There were loud voices and the sound of footsteps outside. Someone was shaking the gate vigorously.

'Who lives here? Are you sardars? Come out.'

'This is not a sardar's house. Go and mind your business, people.'

'You're lying. Open the door.'

Someone struck the gate. They were pushing against it now. It was coming loose with each push. It could fall any time now.

Chibber opened the door.

'Am I a sardar? Do I look like a sardar to you?' he asked angrily.

He had no beard or moustache and he wasn't wearing a turban. How could he be one?

'Have you hidden any sardars inside?'

'Come in and take a look.'

The banging on the gates stopped.

How did Chibber find the courage to step out?

The mob went from house to house, asking if any sardars lived there.

No sooner had their footsteps faded away than another mob appeared at the end of the alley. They were carrying iron rods and swords. One man was carrying a trident. Blood dripped from it.

Would such mobs be roaming around in Amritpuri too, carrying rods and swords?

When he thought about Uttam Singh and his family, he felt a sudden dread. If a Sikh girl got caught by a bloodthirsty mob like this ...

He had to save her at any cost.

'I'm leaving.'

'Don't you want to watch TV?'

'No, Chibberji.'

The entire city was turning into a large TV screen. What was there to see on this small one?

How could he reach Amritpuri? There were no cars or buses on the roads. How could he get to Uttam Singh and Pinky?

Sahadevan walked to Amritpuri. He had walked long distances many times before. But it had never been like this. He had never felt so frightened. His mind was in turmoil.

Why are you going to Amritpuri now? Will you be able to save them? No. Go back. Go to your lair in Malviya Nagar, take off your shirt and try to write, Sahadevan told himself.

Without heeding his own voice, Sahadevan walked on. He still had a long distance to go. As he walked along the Hauz Khas forest, an armed gang of young men went past him in an open jeep. He wanted to run into the green darkness of the wooded forest where the deer were grazing and wait it out till the riots ended. But even as he thought that, his legs kept moving, not straying from their path.

Fire and smoke welcomed Sahadevan into Amritpuri.

Balbir Singh's small store, which used to sell bread, jam and eggs, was burning. Sahadevan had bought bread and butter there innumerable times. Balbir Singh and his family lived in the same building. Its front veranda had been converted into the shop front.

What had happened to them? Could one of the Hindu families have given them refuge? Had they escaped?

Sahadevan walked to the end of the lane, towards Uttam Singh's house. He rang the doorbell, then noticed that the wire was hanging loose. He knocked on the door. No response. Could Uttam Singh and his family have left? Could they have gone to a safe place?

There was no lock on the door. He knocked sharply, once more.

'Who?'

It was the tremulous voice of Gunjan bhabhi.

'Open the door. It's me.'

Uttam Singh didn't recognise the familiar voice of Sahadevan. Fear had numbed his senses.

'We have not killed anyone,' he wailed.

'Sardarji, it's me, Sahadevan.'

The door creaked open, as if it had opened by itself. Sahadevan slipped inside. Though it was close to noon, there was barely any light. He realised that it was Pinky who had opened the door for him.

Uttam Singh sat at the dining table with a glass in hand. In front of him was a half-empty bottle of santra. For years, he has been drinking the cheap lime-coloured alcohol, which was available in abundance in Palam Village. It was known to turn people blind and give them intestinal ulcers.

'They will come now. Save us, bhaiya,' the sardarni pleaded. Pinky started to weep. She stood close to him.

What could he do? How could he save this family?

Gunjan bhabhi was holding a thin, soiled book. It contained the Mool Mantar from the Guru Granth Sahib, written in the Gurmukhi script. She had brought it when she first came to Delhi from Gurdaspur as Uttam Singh's bride. She clutched it tightly. '*Ek onkar sat naam … Aad sach, Jugaad sach, Haibee sach, Nanak hose bhee sach …*'

The night before, as they lay sleepless, she had heard her daughter say, 'I'm hungry, mummy.'

They had not eaten anything after hearing of Beant Singh and Satwant Singh emptying their guns into Indira Gandhi. Pinky had gone foraging inside the kitchen and found a single mathi. She ate that, drank some water to wash it down, and went and lay down near her mother again.

Armed mobs were moving about on Amritpuri's main streets, looking for Sikh houses. They knocked on all the locked gates and doors and checked if there were any Sikhs inside. When they were told that there were none, they were disbelieving and went inside to check. Then, following the scent of Sikh blood, they went into other lanes and alleys.

Another mob reached Balbir Singh's store. They entered the hut of Billa, who ironed clothes. It was a small lean-to by the side of the road, with only a tarpaulin for a roof. The men in that mob were not from Amritpuri; they had come from elsewhere. The presswallah knew better than anyone else where the Sikhs lived, as he went from house to house, collecting clothes for ironing.

'Tell us, are there any sardar houses here? Show us.'

Billa shivered in terror, looking at the rods and swords in their hands.

When the point of a sword touched his neck, Billa pointed towards Uttam Singh's house.

'Who stays there?'

'Carpenter Uttam Singh.'

'Who else?'

'His wife and daughter.'

Sahadevan listened to the sounds of the approaching mob. Pinky stood at the door, shaking with fear.

'Will they kill us, bhaiya?'

'No, baby. Come, shall we go?'

He took her hand.

He offered his other hand to Gunjan bhabhi.

'No, bhaiya, no!'

She could only think of Pinky. He should take her and leave right away. Young and beautiful, she should not fall into the hands of the mob.

'If you stay here, they'll set you on fire.'

'Let them. One has to suffer for one's sins.'

Uttam Singh didn't move from where he was sitting. The source of the uproar outside had reached their gate. He poured what was left in the bottle into his mouth.

'Bhaiya, go! Run!'

Shouts of '*maar do*' rose from outside.

'Go away!'

Gunjan bhabhi opened the backdoor and pushed Pinky and Sahadevan out. The door opened onto a pitted lane filled with debris. Clutching Pinky's hand, Sahadevan ran. The legs of the forty-five-year-old gained the strength of a fifteen-year-old's. He knew each lane and alley of Amritpuri. As they ran, they could hear cries from houses on all sides. Smoke was rising from some of the buildings.

The flimsy doors of Uttam Singh's house went down with a great noise.

Indira Gandhi ki jai.

Indiraji amar rahe.

The rods and swords rushed inside. In his alcohol-fuelled fugue, Uttam Singh collapsed on the table. Sardarni clutched her prayer book tightly.

Wahe guruji ki fateh.

7

STREETS ON FIRE

Vasu slept on his side, curled like a millipede. That way, he couldn't see the stars shining above his head. He was allergic to stars, moonlight and flowers.

Harilal Shukla had arranged for him to stay here, knowing that a barsati was a good place for artists to be in, to think and paint. No one came up here and disturbed him. It helped that the landlord lived elsewhere.

Vasu had never lived in a more calm and serene environment. Harilal Shukla looked after all his needs. He would bring apples, grapes, bananas, eggs, butter and bread each time he visited. The fridge was always full. Just like he was averse to moonlight and stars, Vasu was not fond of fruits either. And like Om Prakash Jain fed ants, Vasu used to feed sparrows and squirrels. He came to be popular among these creatures and soon became their star. His popularity spread to mice and chameleons. They marked their presence every morning on the terrace, waiting for him to wake up. The mice gnawed at the mangoes and quince he offered them. Then they climbed down the drainage pipes and vanished.

Vasu never cleared out the fridge; he got Harilal Shukla to do that too. One day, when he opened the fridge to keep the container of ras malai that he had brought, a foul smell hit him along with the cold draught. He saw Vasu's shoes lying on top of the mangoes and bananas. The shoes were frozen and in the eyelets for the laces, there was frost. When he had enough space in the barsati to keep a hundred thousand shoes, why had Vasu chosen the fridge to stow them in? Harilal Shukla was very annoyed.

'Vasu, this is too much. You are crossing the limit.'

'What did I do?'

'You took off your shoes and kept them in the fridge. That's all.'

'Did I do that?' Vasu had no recollection of it.

Harilal brought out the shoes and put them in the sunshine. The frost melted almost instantly and water drops formed around the shoes.

He switched off the fridge, took out all the foodstuff and dumped them outside. No one could eat them now. He used a damp cloth to wipe the inside of the fridge clean.

When he was leaving, he told Vasu, 'You should make a painting. An open fridge. Bright light coming out of it. In that bright light, fruits, and in the midst of the fruits, Bata shoes.'

'I don't paint to others' instructions.'

Though Vasu had spoken in Malayalam, Harilal understood.

Vasu had done the same thing at his maiden exhibition as well. It was in unadulterated Malayalam that he answered the questions of the journalists. They had stood with their mouths agape, unable to understand a word.

Vasu was woken up by a burning smell and fumes. Streaming in through the open window, the winter sunlight lay on his bed, the colour of mustard flowers. He got up and went in search of the source of the smell. The Contessa car which was parked on the street below was burning. It belonged to Gurminder Singh, who owned a furniture shop on Jail Road. When Gurminder

Singh came to meet Vasu for the first time, he had greeted him by saying 'Sat Sri Akal'. The elderly sardar had assumed that Vasu was a young Sikh, looking at his long hair. He talked to Vasu in Punjabi. Though he didn't know the language, Vasu had understood what he said.

From the terrace, Vasu could see a scooter burning farther away, in front of an automobile workshop.

Near the radio repair shop stood the skeleton of a burnt auto rickshaw.

There was not a single human being around. Were all these vehicles burning spontaneously? Vasu racked his brains till his head started to emit smoke. He didn't know that riots had already broken out in Sultanpuri and Mangolpuri, across the Yamuna. He also didn't know that they had spread to Tilak Nagar.

He knew of Indira Gandhi's death, but not about its repercussions.

In the morning, an armed mob had arrived from Hari Nagar via a shortcut. They had canisters in their hands. The roads were deserted. Occasionally, a car or scooter passed by.

The mob appeared to know the area well. They zeroed in on the shops owned by Sikhs, sparing those owned by Hindus. Using crowbars, they broke the locks and forced open the shutters. Their first target was Mukat Singh's churidar-kurta shop. They pulled out the brightly-coloured churidars and colourfully embroidered and sequined kurtas, which used to catch the covetous eyes of all the women who passed by. They made a bonfire of them on the road. They prised open Mukat Singh's steel locker and pocketed all the money inside.

That was when they noticed the scooter, being ridden by a man in a blue turban. They jumped out of the shop and blocked its way. The young man braked, and the scooter skidded and threw him off. The blue turban flew off his head. His hair and face resembled that of Vasu. At one glance, he could be mistaken for Vasu. He was a lecturer named Sumeet Singh, from Khalsa College. He had got married only eleven days ago.

The mob poured the petrol from the canister on Sumeet Singh's head, lit a match and set him on fire.

He was Sikh after all. Eleven days of honeymooning was all that he was entitled to.

A mob was moving through Tilak Nagar Market. Joginder's footwear store was set on fire early in the morning. There was nothing in it that the rioters could take away. Gone were the days when Joginder measured Jaswinder's feet and presented her with the latest fashion in footwear. His business had declined day by day. There was competition all around. He had failed to source trendy footwear and understand changing tastes. His stocks remained unsold.

'Accursed woman! It's after you set your inauspicious foot in this house that my son's business began to go down. Your arrival without dowry was the beginning of the end. The blasted luck of my son.'

Joginder's mother cursed her every day.

From the moment Jaswinder came to her in-laws' house, she heard only imprecations. The realisation that one should not agree to get married without a proper dowry came to her too late. Joginder's love and affection had given her strength. But these days, even his love seemed to be on the wane.

'She didn't give you any dowry. She hasn't given you a son. Who cursed you with such a fate, my child?'

The mother-in-law continued to lament.

Jaswinder had become pregnant after a long wait. While she retched and vomited with such ferocity that she feared she would expel her own pharynx, her mother-in-law told her, 'If you give birth to a girl, I won't leave you alive.'

Jaswinder lost weight steadily. The fullness of her breasts, the rhythm of her hips and the swing of her buttocks left her. She was not even a shadow of her old self. Her mother-in-law did not allow her to visit her own home. She wouldn't allow her parents to come and meet her either. A house next to Joginder's had a phone connection. Uttam Singh called there and requested them to call Jaswinder to the phone. He waited till the line got cut. She didn't come. The truth was, she couldn't come.

One day, when he happened to go to Jail Road to buy a yardstick—he had been using his old one for as long as he could remember and it had finally broken—Uttam Singh went to Joginder's house to meet his daughter. It had been years since he had seen her. He badly wanted to look at her and hear her voice.

When she saw Uttam Singh approaching, the sardarni came out and stood in his way.

'Why have you hauled yourself here?'

'To see my daughter.'

'If you come as you should come, you can see her. If you've come empty-handed, you may return just as you have come.'

'It has been two years since I saw my daughter. Where is she? Call her. I'll see her and then leave.'

Standing on the road, he looked at the house. It had all the shortcomings of a DDA flat. Electric wires and cables were hanging loose everywhere. The cement steps of the staircases were cracked. Sewage and drain water had stained the walls black.

'Joginder has had only hard days after your daughter set foot in this house. His shop was doing so well. She has destroyed everything.'

Uttam Singh swallowed hard.

'Come back with money. At least fifty thousand. Joginder needs at least that much to renovate the store. Go, get the money and come.'

Forget fifty thousand, he didn't have even five thousand rupees with him.

That day, Uttam Singh returned without seeing his daughter. It was a good thing that he didn't get to see her scarecrow look. He couldn't have endured it.

He didn't go directly home. He got off at Okhla and bought a bottle of santra from the bootlegger behind the vegetable market. Since he didn't want to spend the little money he had on bus tickets, he used to walk as much as possible. Impatient now, he used his teeth to open the bottle cap and poured the yellow liquid directly into his mouth. That gave him some self-confidence. '*Phtoo!*' he snapped at the sardarni. 'Sister-fucker!' he threw at his spineless son-in-law. Then, licking and savouring the remnants of the alcohol on his lips and beard, he walked in silence towards Amritpuri.

Moments before Uttam Singh reached the Garhi Artist Village, Sahadevan had passed that way. If he had seen Sahadevan, Uttam Singh would have felt pity for him. Like Jaswinder, he too had become very thin. She had lost weight because of the mental torture she was subjected to, and her pregnancy. But Sahadevan? He was neither tortured nor pregnant. Why had he become so thin?

Sahadevan had spent some time in the morning in the artists' village. Sculptors, painters, graphic and terracotta artists from various parts of the country stayed there and created art. He was attracted to the graphic press in particular. The pottery section was also interesting. He gazed fondly at the artists making pots with wet clay, their hands covered with sludge. They were in touch with the earth every day. Even after they washed their hands, the marks would remain on their faces, knees, elbows and legs. In his view, the real artists were those who kneaded clay, cast it in moulds and fired it in the kiln to create art.

Harilal Shukla had toyed with the idea of arranging a studio for Vasu here. But he had changed his mind, knowing that it would be difficult for Vasu to stay with the other artists. How would they tolerate the man who had stolen and eaten Rooposhi's lunch? With that one incident, he had become notorious.

Vasu watched the burning vehicles from his terrace, becoming increasingly agitated. He saw Sumeet Singh being beaten like a mad dog in the middle of the road, his beard and hair coming loose, and his body set on fire after being doused with petrol. From this distance, it looked like a shadow play. Not everything was clear.

Why was this happening? Why were the mobs setting fire to cars, auto rickshaws and scooters?

His phone rang.

'Chhotae bhaiya, I've called to tell you something. Riots are taking place in Trilokpuri and other areas. Tilak Nagar has a large population of Sikhs, so be careful, don't step out of your place. Stay inside the house. If you need anything, give me a call. Under no circumstances must you go out. Got it?'

Harilal Shukla could bring him everything—canvases, colour tubes, linseed oil, paneer tikka, rumali roti—but he didn't know where to get what Vasu needed just now. Even if he knew, he would not be able to buy it.

The hashish that Vasu craved was available in Old Delhi, near Jama Masjid. And the men who sold it? Rickshaw pullers. They wrapped it in the foil paper found inside cigarette packs and hid it under the seats to evade the eyes of the policemen. They made it available only to people they knew and trusted. Vasu was among their older clients.

Vasu's unease over all that he had seen gradually turned to a deep melancholy. He felt a tightness in his chest, as if he were having a heart attack. What he really needed was a few long, deep drags. But his stock was over.

He pulled on a shirt and set out for Jama Masjid. Still feeling the tightness around his chest, he started to walk along the deserted road filled with the smell of fire, burning tyres and smoke.

Joginder's mother howled on hearing the news of her brother Jagmohan Singh's death. His neck had been slashed by the mobs. He had lived in Mangolpuri. She wept like a mass of women crying together. The sound pierced through their block and carried all the way to the road.

Jagmohan had gone to Ludhiana to pick up stocks of readymade garments, which he used to sell in the street markets. When he was getting off the train at Old Delhi railway station, a mob of ten or twelve men holding iron rods pulled him down to the platform and slashed his throat. They set fire to his turban and threw it between the tracks. Burning turbans lay scattered across the platform.

A group of sardars had gathered in the C Block park amidst its dried up trees and ripened red grass. Some of them had kirpans in their hands—they were prepared to defend themselves. One group said that the attackers should be met with whatever weapons they were able to muster. Joginder argued that it wouldn't help. There were not enough Sikhs to match the Hindus, who were an overwhelming majority. They knew that the gangs which were killing and looting on Jail Road and in Tilak Nagar Market would soon reach their colony. Someone suggested that they seek refuge in the gurdwara. But how did they know the mobs wouldn't attack the gurdwara, Joginder countered.

Get hold of any vehicle that you can and flee across the Delhi border. Now. Don't think about your property or money. Leave all that to Wahe Guru. That was what they finally decided.

'Mother, take only jewellery and cash. Leave everything else behind.'

'What about my blanket?'

'No. There won't be space in the jeep.'

The sardarni needed a blanket to wrap around herself from November onwards. When December arrived, she would need a razai. Those who have layers of fat under their skin do not feel the cold, or so people said. But the sardarni was always cold.

'What should I take?'

Jaswinder came in silently, supporting her swollen belly. She didn't have the strength to walk around much.

People believed that if a woman's belly was big, she would have a boy. When Jaswinder became pregnant after a long wait, the sardarni had gone to meet an ascetic who used to recite shabad kirtan at the gurdwara. He had predicted that it would be a baby girl. His predictions were never wrong.

'You have destroyed this family. Do you want to give birth to a girl and bring her curses down on our heads? I'll finish you off!'

Sardarni had picked up a bottle of kerosene and attempted to pour it over her head. Jaswinder was saved by Joginder arriving at that moment. She had never cried as much as she did that day.

'Shall I take my yellow suit?' she asked Joginder now. The bright yellow salwar-kameez with mirrors sewn around the neck was a gift he had given her before their marriage. He had bought it in Chandni Chowk. It was something she treasured. A memento of their happy days.

'You don't need to take anything,' her mother-in-law said. 'You aren't going anywhere.'

'Ma, please take me with you and leave me at my home,' Jaswinder said.

'Son, you can still get a beautiful girl. Also, a Contessa car and a DDA flat. That Bunty was telling me again yesterday.'

She had heard the mother tell her son about Bunty Singh, the marriage broker, earlier too.

Everyone was ready within the hour, waiting for the jeep to turn up. The sardarni didn't allow Jaswinder to either pack or change her clothes. She cried, with her hand over her swollen belly. Everyone pretended not to notice.

The jeep arrived before it was noon. There was another Sikh family in it.

'Hurry up,' Makhan Singh, the driver, said urgently. The attackers could appear at any time and from any direction. If the mobs saw them, there would be no escape. They would lose their lives.

The sardarni pushed Jaswinder back into the house. She had followed Joginder, holding up her belly. No one heeded her wails. They pushed her into the house and locked it.

'Come, boy.'

She took her son by the hand and walked to the jeep. Joginder followed his mother without even a glance back at his wife. The jeep took off, spreading the smell of burning diesel. The thin cries of Jaswinder from behind the locked door followed the jeep momentarily.

Their aim was to cross the border as soon as possible.

Sikh families were travelling towards the Delhi border in jeeps, cars and tempo vans. Packing whatever came to hand and fleeing for their lives, leaving behind their homes and more.

Before the sun set, thousands of men, women and children had crossed the border into the neighbouring states.

8

BLOOD RUN

Sometimes good news comes at the most inopportune times. Sahadevan had had such an experience once, when he was eleven years old. He had found a four-anna coin on the road. In those days, one anna could fetch a glass of tea and a parippuvada, a pazhampuri, a bonda or a sukhiyan. Four annas could get you mutton chops, bread and tea. Drinking a mouthful of hot tea after eating a piece of bread dipped in gravy spiced with black pepper—the very thought of it was heavenly.

But when he reached home—with the coin in his pocket, fantasising and talking to himself about the things he was going to do with it—the yard was full of people. His grandmother's motionless body lay on the floor of the inner room, with a lamp at her feet. Sahadevan wanted to cry. When no one was watching, he took the coin out of his pocket and threw it away.

On 1 November 1984, sometime in the afternoon, a telex message arrived from the Italian embassy. When the whole country was mourning the death of its prime minister, were the white men sitting and working in their embassies? Harilal Shukla hadn't known that the Pope's countrymen were so hardworking. Perhaps the message had been drafted overnight and left on the telex machine.

Harilal Shukla knew that it was due to his efforts that this had come about. But not merely because of him. Genius and originality were the main criteria, and his young friend had both in ample measure. That was the reason he was going out of his way to help him. But was that the only reason? He couldn't say.

In normal circumstances, he would have immediately written out a press release and sent it off to the news agencies, along with photographs. The news was bound to appear in the next day's newspapers. Today, however, there was no one at the newspaper offices, even though they were open. Most of the staff hadn't reported for duty. Non-Sikhs had no reason to be afraid. No one was going to harm them. No one would snatch the turban off their heads, set it on fire, and throw it on the railway tracks. Yet, fear congealed in everyone's heart. Many of them felt the tightness that Vasu felt in his chest.

Harilal Shukla decided not to inform the press till the city returned to normalcy. The body count was rising every minute. Delhi was a city of tombs. Thousands of damaged and broken sepulchres were scattered all around, their stones rendered cancerous. But now, it was a city not only of lifeless tombs but also of corpses on which the blood was still wet.

He dialled Vasu's number. The call didn't go through. When he tried again, it rang at the other end.

'Vasu, Harilal here. Good news for you.'

Silence from the other end.

He kept the earpiece close to his ear and waited. Hadn't Vasu woken up yet? But he had called him only a while back and cautioned him against going out. Harilal Shukla recalled that Vasu always did the opposite of what he was told. He may have gone out. Possibly to buy hashish. Or he may have gone for a stroll. He was unpredictable.

He rang the number over and over again. There was no response. The phone, ringing far away in the barsati, keened like a wartime siren in Harilal Shukla's ears. He felt fear swell within him.

He started his jeep. On the way, he saw mobs moving about on the streets. They didn't spare even the smallest of shops owned by Sikhs. At one point, he saw them looting a sweetshop where the alley met the main road.

They stuffed themselves with laddoos, jalebis, barfis and kala jamuns. Then they filled as many bags as they could find with sweets. They threw the rest out on the road. Stepping on the sweets scattered around, twirling their iron rods and swords and screaming for blood, they walked onward.

One of the men threw a laddoo towards Harilal as he drove past. '*Lo, muh meetha karo.*'

What were they celebrating by distributing sweets? For the first time after the riots had broken out, Harilal Shukla also felt a tightness around his chest.

The telex from the Italian embassy about the Venice Biennale slipped out of his mind. He stepped on the clutch and the brake at the same time, and changed the gears unthinkingly, so that the jeep wheezed and lurched. A tempo van filled with swords, iron rods and granite pieces sped past him. The weapons were to be distributed among the rioters in Tilak Nagar. They waved their tricolour flags furiously at Harilal Shukla.

'Maar do saare sardar logon ko … maar do …'

He jumped out of the jeep without switching off the engine, and ran up to the barsati. He usually took the stairs one step at a time; he was a watchful man who took all the necessary precautions. But he had always kept an eye out for Vasu, with the passionate fondness of an art trader towards an artist. As the prices of Vasu's paintings rose, so did the intensity of his relationship with him.

Harilal Shukla had made his entry into the world of art as a promoter of a new generation of artists that emerged in the '80s. He had remarkable insight into the world of contemporary art and the vision to predict its future. And he had very little interest in artists from Kerala. He did not care for the over-sentimentalism and lack of sophistication in their paintings. He thought they were very loud.

Vasu was different. You couldn't tell his country of origin from his work, or the cultural tradition he came from. The people in his pictures pulsated with life. He didn't pin the labels of nation or religion to the travails and miseries of human beings. And Harilal Shukla was an art critic and trader who wished to see the borderlines of culture and nation being erased out of art. In his opinion, identity politics and regionalism were just bullshit.

The extraordinary market prices for Vasu's paintings had brought other gallery owners and agents to his barsati. They came with shampooed and well-tended beards, in unwrinkled woollen trousers and jackets, smoking cigarettes. Sometimes they were accompanied by ladies wearing sleeveless blouses and sarees slung low at the waist, revealing their navels. They examined his paintings, standing up, squatting down, head tilted to one side, leaning and listing; they took photos. Oblivious to all that was happening around him, Vasu would sit there, staring at the sky.

He didn't know that he was a painter whose works fetched a million rupees or more in the market. Nor did he realise that in the sophisticated art world of Delhi, he had pushed out many and raced ahead of many others. He was not even aware that he was Nenmanda Vasudeva Panicker. He was Vasu, as introduced to himself and to the world at large by Delhi's number one art dealer, Harilal Shukla.

'Vasu, you must understand some things. You are now one of the most successful painters in Delhi. This must reflect in your speech and behaviour.'

Vasu looked at Harilal Shukla, uncomprehending.

'You are a very valuable asset. Measured by weight, you would fetch at least one crore rupees. Do you know that?'

'I don't.'

'Don't you understand all that I'm saying?'

'No.'

'All right. You don't have to understand anything. Just do as I tell you to. Agreed?'

But Vasu wouldn't obey him. Even if he was told repeatedly to lock the door when he went out, he didn't. He always left it wide open.

One day, when Harilal Shukla came to visit, he saw a familiar car parked on the road. He felt a twinge of anxiety. As usual, the door was open. A conversation was going on inside. He saw the owner of one of the famous galleries in Saket and an industrialist—a buyer of art—examining Vasu's paintings. She was explaining his techniques and the philosophy behind his art to the industrialist, who kept nodding his head.

'What the hell are you doing here?'

The normally placid Harilal Shukla exploded. There was an argument. He demanded to know how they had come uninvited and without Vasu's permission. She countered by asking him who had given him the right to speak on Vasu's behalf. He said he paid the rent for the barsati. She said the sale of Vasu's paintings more than compensated for the rent. He claimed that he had taken the starving artist who sketched passers-by near Regal Cinema and made him a famous painter. She said Vasu was a gifted artist and didn't need anyone's help to grow. He said that genius alone didn't make a painter famous. She said public relations alone couldn't create an artist. He asked why she was interested in Vasu's affairs. She asked why *he* was so interested. He said that he owned all of Vasu's paintings. She said that was a lie. He said he knew more about Vasu's art than anyone else did. She said that, too, was a lie. He said that Vasu's art could be understood and appreciated only after reading Suzi Gablik's essay on minimal art in *Concepts of Modern Art: From Fauvism to Postmodernism*, edited by Nikos Stangos, and that she should only talk to him after she had read it ...

He entered Vasu's barsati, panting. The door was open as usual. Vasu was not there. An hour ago, he had left for Jama Masjid. But Harilal Shukla did not know that.

He went downstairs and got into the jeep. He had no idea where to go next or where to look for Vasu. He drove around slowly, scanning both sides of the road.

Many of the roadside shops were on fire. In the middle of the road were scooters and cars gutted by fire. Near an overturned bike lay the corpse of a sardar who had bled to death.

What could happen to Vasu after all? He was not a Sikh; he didn't wear a turban. Maybe he was being anxious over nothing.

He drove through Hari Nagar and reached Mayapuri. It was the industrial belt of West Delhi. From cast-iron gates and railings to spare parts of auto rickshaws and motorbikes, everything was manufactured here, in hundreds of sheds. The residents were mostly street vendors, carpenters and labourers. A large number of Sikhs also lived here.

Harilal Shukla could see the flames and smoke rising from the sheds which had been set on fire. In the far distance, he saw a man, his long hair loose and flying in the wind, running down the Mayapuri road. The road was deserted. Not just Sikhs, everyone was afraid to be seen outside. Buses had stopped plying. A screaming mob was chasing the running man. They held rods, sword canes and kerosene canisters. There were smaller groups of people lurking in the alleys. They emerged, holding sharp stones in their hands, and joined the larger mob.

'Kill him. Kill that dog ...'

'I'm not a Sikh ...' the man screamed as he kept running. Until, out of breath, he could run no more. One stone hit him on the back of the head. Soon, the mob had surrounded him. Unable to speak, he pleaded silently for mercy. Blinded by their thirst for revenge, they caught hold of him by his long hair. There was dried paint on his face and hair. They overpowered him as he tried to break loose. One man poured kerosene from the canister in his hand over his head. He was blinded by the pungent, volatile kerosene falling into his eyes. He felt the heat on his head. The next moment, his whole body was on fire.

Harilal Shukla went back to the barsati in Tilak Nagar. He sat on the chair for a very long time, his head in his hands. Suddenly, his eyes sparkled. He stood up and looked around. He smiled, looking at the collection of finished and unfinished paintings leaning against the paint-stained walls of the large room. In his mind, this room in which Vasu ate, painted and smoked hashish was turning into an art gallery.

At his first exhibition, each of Vasu's paintings had been priced at over one lakh rupees. Yet, as soon as the ribbon-cutting and inauguration were over, red, dot-shaped stickers had started appearing under them. On the very first day, all the paintings were spoken for. 'Exhibition Sold Out', he had written on a piece of paper, and stuck it on the wall.

Now, Vasu's paintings were valued at several lakhs each. In fifteen or twenty years, they would be worth crores.

Vasu had been invited to the Venice Biennale, to attend as a special invitee. He wouldn't be able to go now. But Harilal would go. He would go with Vasu's paintings. His eyes lit up with a blinding glitter.

He closed the windows, switched off the fan, and went out of the room. He locked the door, dropped the key safely into his pocket, and climbed down the stairs. The receding sounds of his jeep sounded like loud laughter.

He, Harilal Shukla, was the owner of an invaluable collection of paintings.

After hiding in Garhi for three days, Sahadevan and Pinky emerged into the open. They saw the city once again. He had thought they would never see it again, and had silently bid adieu to it.

They were hungry, thirsty, exhausted from lack of sleep because of the mosquitoes. And weakened by the tension and fear that was uppermost in their minds.

After leaving Uttam Singh's house, hand in hand, they had run through back lanes and shortcuts. If they ran into the mob, perhaps nothing would have happened to Sahadevan. He had no facial hair pasted down with hair-fixer, or even a turban. But Pinky looked like a sardarni. Her fair complexion and tall, voluptuous body would have given her away.

On the first day, the mob had sought out the homes of Sikhs and attacked them. Then they found out that Hindus were hiding Sikhs in their homes. So, they searched the homes of Hindus they suspected of harbouring Sikhs. One glance would have been enough for them to know that Sahadevan was helping Pinky to get away.

Just as he knew the by-lanes and shortcuts of Chandni Chowk, Jama Masjid, Turkman Gate, Jangpura and Sewa Nagar, Sahadevan knew the topography of Amritpuri and its environs like the back of his hand. He had quickly fixed on Garhi Artist Village as a potential sanctuary. It was a place where artists lived. They would give them refuge. He was also acquainted with the studio in-charge.

Running and walking along the narrow passages between the buildings and through open buffalo sheds, they reached Garhi. Pinky trembled with fright each time they heard footsteps behind them.

Garhi was a centuries-old village with high walls and tall Mughal-style gates. It must have been the fiefdom of some nawab. Inside, the granite walls of many of the rooms had crumbled and fallen down. Most of the studios were housed in rooms which had been rebuilt or renovated. Several artists lived there.

The watchman who usually stood twirling his moustache in front of the village was missing. Perhaps he had run away when the rioting started. There was a lock on the heavy door, but it wasn't in place. When Sahadevan pushed the door with one hand, it made a sound like the low bellow of a rhinoceros. When he gave it one more hard push, enough of a gap was created for them to squeeze through. Then he turned and pushed it back into its original position. No one should suspect that there were people inside.

'Pinky, we'll stay here till the rioting ends. It's safe here.'

'Who lives here, chhote bhaiya?

'This is an artists' village.'

'Then where are the artists?'

Sahadevan went looking for them everywhere. There wasn't a soul inside. All the workshops were deserted. The rooms the artists lived in were locked. Everyone had apparently upped and left. The press was silent in the graphic studio. There were no sounds of chisel and mallet from the sculptors' space. The village lay abandoned, like a burial ground. Even the birds that built their nests on the trees that grew between the studios seemed to be maintaining a studied silence.

'Till the rioting is over, this shall be our home.'

'Mummy?'

'They must have escaped.'

He could not look her in the eye. There was little chance that they would have been spared. How could the old sardar and his wife have escaped? Who would have rescued them?

They sat silently, close to each other. He could feel her breath on his neck.

Occasionally, they heard shouts and screams from outside. Pinky trembled at the sound of a gun being fired. There was no assurance that the mob wouldn't enter Garhi. They were forcing their way into any place they had doubts about. By evening, the gang leaders had distributed copies of census reports to their men. Weapons were also provided. They marked the residence of every Sikh family in every ward according to the last census. Their prey could neither flee nor hide.

Once, they heard loud conversations and footsteps right outside the door. The mob was resting on the steps of the village.

When darkness fell, a cold breeze sprung up. Pinky's teeth were chattering. She had not eaten anything in a long while, but her mind didn't register the need for food. Suddenly, it became dark in the sculpture workshop where they had taken refuge. In the trees above, birds began to flap their wings and screech. He looked up at the sky, waiting for some stars to appear. But the autumnal clouds lay spread above them. Not a star was to be seen.

'I'm scared, chhote bhaiya.'

'Why, isn't chhote bhaiya sitting next to you?' he comforted her.

He realised that he had taken on a very big responsibility. The riots had just begun. How many more days would they go on? What was going to happen? He felt dizzy thinking about it.

He had to save Pinky at any cost. He would ensure that there was not a scratch on her body. That felt like the sole purpose of his life, in that moment.

V.P. Agencies had ceased to exist. The first to drop off from its name was the V of Vidya. But the P was still there, and still alive in his mind. It should always be there.

After a while, the clouds moved away and the stars began to shine. In the hazy light, they sat wordlessly amidst the half-finished sculptures. Some of them were headless, others limbless. Female torsos with no hair and only breasts. Unnaturally elongated, thin and distorted male forms in the Giacometti style. Heads of indistinguishable gender lay on the floor. Arms that had fallen off. Contorted legs with broken knees. Faces with no lips, nose or eyes and only large, displaced teeth. In the starlit night, the forms terrified Pinky.

'Let's go.'

'Where to, baby?'

'I'm scared.'

He realised that the sculptures were the cause of her fear.

He helped her up and led her towards the painting section. There was very little light there. But even in the darkness, the smell of paint was discernible. He found a stool and made her sit on it. As their eyes adjusted to the low light, brush strokes on canvas became visible. In their colours she found solace. And he did too.

They tried to sleep on the rough floor, amidst the smell of paint. Then the mosquitoes started to attack them. Something crawled over their bodies. After midnight, the cold intensified. They wished they had something to cover themselves with. That was when he remembered seeing the banner announcing the Artist Camp of Lalit Kala Akademi outside the main entrance of the Garhi Artist Village. He got up slowly, pulled open the door and went outside. There was silence everywhere. All the Sikh houses in the locality must have been attacked. Those who had been spared would have fled.

He untied and removed the banner. He covered Pinky with the Artist Camp.

The next morning, she opened her eyes with a demand for water. Sunlight fell obliquely on her through the window. The shadow of one of the window bars rested vertically on her face. Mosquito bites and rashes could be seen on her face, arms and legs. He remembered seeing a pot of water in the sculpture workshop. Luckily, there was some water left in it. He poured the water directly from the pot into her mouth. Some spilled down the front of her pale yellow kameez. She took her dupatta from the floor and wrapped it around her neck, then stepped out of the room. She was searching for something.

'Over there.'

He pointed towards the rear. It was an isolated area. Grass as tall as a human being grew close to the high compound wall. She was afraid to go alone, so he accompanied her. When she entered the toilet which had no latch, he stood guard. An owl perched on the jamun tree looked askance at him with its round eyes. A smile came to his lips. Did this owl know him?

Once the water in the pot was over, there was nothing left to drink. In the last twenty-four hours, they hadn't eaten anything. He knew that she was terribly hungry. But when they heard the sounds of people moving around outside, she would forget her hunger. When everything quietened down, she would tell him, 'Bhaiya, I'm hungry.'

'Will you be afraid if I leave you alone? I'll come back soon.'

'No, bhaiya, I'm not hungry. Please don't go anywhere.' She squeezed his hand hard.

By the evening, she was completely exhausted. He decided to go out in search of food.

He managed to force open the lock on the studio supervisor's room. He made Pinky sit inside and locked the room from the outside.

He got out of the village and started to walk. It was like walking in a ghost-town. Empty roads. Closed doors. In the distance, he saw a military vehicle with soldiers holding their rifles pointed and ready. Shoot-at-sight orders had been issued. He froze, thinking of what would happen to Pinky if he fell to their bullets. He could not take a step forward.

He returned to Pinky.

They spent three days and nights in Garhi without even a drop of water to drink. By the fourth day, she didn't have the strength to stand up. He carried her to the toilet guarded by the owls. He had to help her undo the strings of her salwar and fasten them again.

They stepped out into the light, pushing open the heavy door reinforced with wrought iron strips. The light and warmth of the sun gave her legs the strength to walk again. Her hand gripped his tightly.

The smoke from Balbir Singh's grocery shop had snuffed itself out. The glass window panes of the majority of the Sikh homes were shattered. Stray dogs were licking the congealed blood on the ground.

Only the walls and terrace of Uttam Singh's house remained. Everything else had burnt down. Smoke was still rising from the smouldering windows.

All the other Sikh houses were shut. Though they could see Pinky, none of the neighbours came out of their homes. They would have recognised Sahadevan too, he had stayed there long enough. Asking Pinky to wait by the roadside, Sahadevan went into one of the houses.

'Pinky is hungry. She hasn't eaten for three days. Please give us something. Please give us water.'

The door was slammed shut in his face.

They continued to walk aimlessly.

While they sat amidst the sculptures and paintings in Garhi, murder and arson had gone on, unhindered. Many vehicles had been reduced to ashes on Ring Road and Mahatma Gandhi Marg. Sikhs were lying dead in trains shunted into Old Delhi railway station and in buses at Shahdara DTC bus depot. Stacks of corpses, burnt and bloated, were blocking the drains. Dead bodies were heaped by the side of the railway tracks in Tughlakabad. When gurdwaras went down in the conflagration, the women and children who had taken refuge there were burnt to death. In deserted houses, sardarnis lay frigid in the cold, stripped of all their clothes, unmoving.

'Come, baby.'

'Where to, chhote bhaiya?'

'I don't know.'

Sahadevan didn't have a clue where to take Pinky. The world had shrunk so much that there was no place even for two people to sit close together.

As the tired light of the November sun gathered over the blood-tinged Yamuna, Sahadevan and Pinky, near-dead from thirst and hunger, and with the stench of the dead in their nostrils, walked hand in hand, drawing strength from each other's proximity. Delhi appeared to them like a huge painting made with blood.

9

KEEPER OF DREAMS

Uttam Singh, Gunjan bhabhi, Jaswinder and Vasu were erased from the face of Delhi in a matter of hours. A wet January sun opened its eyes above a city that missed them as well as several others.

As the light became brighter, Sahadevan stood with his gaze fixed on the Yamuna. The river looked bloody, as if one was looking at it through eyes suffering from conjunctivitis.

Preparations were on at Rajpath for yet another Republic Day. Workers standing on tall ladders were using a frothy soap solution to clean the names of the martyred soldiers carved on India Gate. The VVIP and VIP galleries were being erected.

'Come, Pinky, let's go.'

She lifted the bag she had prepared, a cheap one bought in Palika Bazaar. It was half empty, even after she had put in everything she owned: two salwar-kameez and a pair of sandals that Sahadevan had bought her. That was the entirety of her worldly possessions. Everything else was lost. She must study and play hockey well; she must win a medical seat on the sports quota; she must earn enough as a doctor for her dowry, and marry into a good family. Even she had forgotten these dreams. But Sahadevan remembered them.

He was the keeper of other people's dreams.

Much later, in her last year at college, she amended her dreams a little. 'Don't let anyone think they can marry me after taking a dowry. I won't give a single paisa as dowry,' she told Sahadevan. He smiled at her, happy and proud.

Pinky's sandals were made of cheap rexine. When Jaswinder was alive, she used to wear fashionable sandals which were the envy of her classmates.

Not only her parents and sister, she had lost everything. The uniform she wore to Khalsa School, her schoolbooks, the autograph book in which her classmates and friends had written messages and signed their names—she had stored them all in a metal box. That too had been destroyed in the fire.

Chibber, the landlord, came in.

'Bless you.' He placed his hand on her head and said a benediction. He pressed a small brown paper envelope into her hands.

He and his family had helped them.

'It was a good thing that you did. Very good deed. You saved a girl's life,' he had told Sahadevan.

But he could not save Uttam Singh and Gunjan bhabhi.

'Why are you quiet, my friend? What's the matter?'

'I'm feeling dizzy, Chibber saab.'

'Why do you feel dizzy now? Isn't the looting and arson and killing over? Hasn't the curfew been lifted?'

'My troubles are not over yet. What will I do with this girl? I feel dizzy when I think of it.'

Chibber hadn't accounted for such a problem either. After the riots were over, when Sahadevan and Pinky landed up in an auto rickshaw, he hadn't even wondered who she was. He was filled with relief that Sahadevan had returned. He had disappeared the day the trouble started. On the first night, Chibber had waited up for him till past midnight, without switching off the lights, eyes straining for his return. When Sahadevan didn't turn up the next day, he decided he had come to harm.

'Doesn't she have anyone else?'

Chibber found it incredible that Uttam Singh, after living for so many years in Delhi, didn't have any friends or relatives.

Uttam Singh did have relatives and acquaintances, and in the old days, they used to visit Amritpuri. They had last come for Jaswinder's wedding. But they had found it unacceptable that she was being sent off without a dowry. They considered it an insult to the entire community. Many had stayed away from the wedding itself. When the rumour spread that she had seduced Joginder, all the others had distanced themselves too.

Gradually, the relatives living in Punjab also stopped coming with their gifts of desi ghee, sugarcane and jaggery. Uttam Singh, lit up on moonshine, would tell Gunjan bhabhi that money made the mare go, and that when there was no money, everyone stayed away.

The only one who continued to visit them was Pinky's uncle, Gurcharan Singh, carrying Bhaiya di barfi, the famous sweetmeat of Faridkot. He used to come without fail for the Gurupurab celebrations in November. As the procession of warriors, elephants and horses led by the Panj Pyare wound down the road, Gurcharan Singh would be in the vanguard, carrying the Sikh standard. On Basant Panchami day, Sahadevan had seen him dance the bhangra vigorously. Eventually, the infirmities of old age had put a stop to his visits too.

Relief camps had been opened in many areas, mainly inside gurdwaras, for those who had been orphaned by the riots. There was a camp close to Malviya Nagar. Sahadevan had gone with Pinky one day to see it. There were children there, who had lost their parents; women who had become widows; parents who had lost their children. There were people with broken arms, facial burns and deep skull wounds. Lying on iron cots under shamianas, the injured and the sick moaned aloud. Though they had woollen clothes to wear and blankets to cover themselves with, they were shivering from the cold.

Sahadevan could not have abandoned Pinky to that world.

'I'm not going anywhere. I'll stay with you, bhaiya.'

'Pinky, I don't have a family or children or anyone. How can you stay with me?'

'Didn't we stay together for three days in Garhi, bhaiya? We can live here like that. I'll make chapatis for you. I'll make you poori and chole, to take to office for lunch. I'll wash your clothes and iron them. And I'll keep the room tidy and clean. See, bhaiya, the table and the chair and even the books are covered with dust.'

'No, Pinky. The world is not as simple as you think it is. Somewhere, there are people who have a right over you. I'll find them for you.'

She sniffled and wiped her eyes.

'Let her spend a few days here. But that won't be a solution to her problem. We have to find a permanent solution, eda.'

'To be honest, I have sympathy for her. She has no one, and she is an innocent girl. But I cannot allow her to live here. It's a big responsibility. I've suffered a lot after Kunh'ishnettan lost the use of his arms. No more. The rest of my life, I want to live in peace. Sahadeva, don't think that I have no affection for you or Pinky. I just can't suffer any more. I can't.'

Sahadevan understood. He had no grouse against anyone.

'I've spoken to amma. She has agreed. It will be a help for her too. She won't have a great many things to do. We have a washing machine for the clothes. Sometimes she may have to go to Hauz Khas Market and fetch fish, meat or vegetables. Money is not an issue. Sahadevetta, you can name the amount. I'll pay you every month.'

'Let me think about it.'

Sahadevan had to bite down on the fury that was rising in him.

'What is there to think about? I'm only doing this to help you.'

'Let me think it over.'

Sahadevan had spent the last two months in Malviya Nagar suffering such suggestions and conversations.

He took the bag from Pinky now, and they walked down the road. They stopped the first auto rickshaw that came their way and got in.

The city had not returned to its old ways. The roads had been cleared of the gutted buses and cars. But there were overturned auto rickshaws and half-burnt motorbikes in the gutters still. A turban lay in the stagnant drain water in a gutter. Members of the Sikh community were nowhere to be seen. Many had forsaken their turbans and shaved off their beards and moustaches. The city of Delhi, in which they were born and grew up, had suddenly stopped being their city. They had become outsiders.

My own Delhi shorn of me.

The sentence formed part of the novel which Sahadevan had started twenty-five years ago and still lay incomplete.

The Punjab Mail steamed into Faridkot after its twenty-hour journey, filling the station with smoke. It was a tiny station. A red-painted overhead sign pointed the way to the exit. Cycles, rickshaws and tongas awaited passengers.

Sahadevan and Pinky took a bus going to Line Bazaar. From there, they took an auto. The roads were dusty and gravelly. They saw a bullock cart filled with sugarcane going along the Sirhind Canal. After about an hour's travel, they saw greenery all around them. The sight of wheat and mustard fields softened their hearts. Only turbaned Sikhs were to be seen everywhere. There were all kinds of beards, from grey, wispy ones to lush, bushy ones. The residents of Faridkot seemed to love bright colours. The sardar driving their auto rickshaw was wearing a green lungi, a yellow shirt and a red turban. Along the way, they saw colourfully painted trucks, tractors and bullock carts. Though it was a small place, Faridkot was full of life.

'Gudiya, have you been to Faridkot before?'

'No, I've been to Gurdaspur and Amritsar.'

Which follower of the Sikh religion would not have visited Amritsar? Even Sahadevan, who was not a Sikh, had been there. He had bathed in the Amrit Saras Kund. It was not only the holy gurus who had brought him close to the Sikh community. Uttam Singh's family had a big part in it too.

Punjab was the land of Pinky's forebears. The memories of that land were in her genes. He had noticed the sparkle in her eyes as she gazed at the wheat fields. Most people in Delhi, who survived on chapatis, had never seen a wheat field in their life.

For the first time in two months, Pinky's face was bright and cheerful. She had been silent for a long while after that night. But she had a strong, brave heart. Anyone else in her place would have crumbled. It was her courage that had helped Sahadevan too. Else, he would have had a breakdown.

'It's taking very long. Where do you want to go?'

The auto-rickshaw driver was getting impatient. He had been driving for one and a half hours through wheat and sugarcane fields.

Sahadevan took out a chit of paper from his pocket and ran his eyes over it. Written in the Gurmukhi script, it was the description of the route to their destination. But he didn't understand head or tail of it. He looked at both sides of the paper and gave it to the driver, who looked like he understood it. After vigorously shaking his head once, he returned the paper to Sahadevan and revved up the engine.

The auto entered a large yard in front of a house. Heaps of hay lay on the ground. Brightly attired farm workers were loading bundles into a bullock cart. An old man was lying on a charpoy under a peepal tree, swathed in a blanket. His eyes fell on Pinky ...

Women came running out from the mud house. Collective wails rose from the yard. They cried loudly, beating their breasts. Hearing them, the neighbours came running. They too joined in the mourning. In between the wailing, they sang paeans of praise for Uttam Singh and Gunjan bhabhi. They extolled the beauty of Jaswinder. The communal weeping went on for about five minutes. Then it stopped, like a sudden rain does.

Gurcharan Singh got up from the charpoy with great effort. The legs which had borne him from Chandni Chowk to Lajpat Nagar, and danced the bhangra in Uttam Singh's yard, were now swollen and immobile. He embraced Pinky, then allowed the women to take her into the house.

They would apply mustard oil on her body and bathe her in water drawn from the well. They would comb her hair, seated in the gentle sunshine in the yard. She would be fed parathas made with desi ghee and sarson da saag. At night, in the large mud-brick-walled hall, she would sleep cosily under a razai in the company of the other girls.

She would learn to draw water from the well and irrigate the fields with the water from the canal. She would learn to make Bhaiya di barfi by boiling and reducing milk. She would learn to hem a dupatta on the sewing machine placed in a corner of the hall. She would learn to bathe, feed and milk the buffaloes. She would learn to balance a heavy basket filled with wheat grains on her head and walk along the ridge of the field without missing a step. After the winter, when the mustard fields flowered, she would learn to dream again.

Now I can return to Delhi in peace and continue my life, Sahadevan told himself.

Part Seven

Return Journeys

Home is the place where, when you have to go there,
they have to take you in.

—Robert Frost (1874–1963)

1

JAYANTI JANATA EXPRESS

All journeys end at home, where they begin, Sahadevan told himself. If not to one's own house, a return to God's house was inevitable. Robert Frost was mistaken. The doors of a house may not always be open to the returnee. But the doors to the mansion of God are never shut. Everyone is welcome there.

The return journeys started in the winter of 1984. People went back in different ways. Vasu, Kunhikrishnan, Rosily, Devi ... some of them reached their own homes; some God's house; some reached nowhere.

The first traveller was Vasu.

Sahadevan wasn't aware of Vasu's death. Nor were Rosily, Sathyanathan or Kunhikrishnan. They were stunned when they heard that Uttam Singh and Gunjan bhabhi had been roasted alive. The shock remained with them for a long time, but they were not surprised. Nearly six thousand Sikhs had been butchered in a matter of three days. Uttam Singh and his sardarni were merely two of them.

Jaswinder's death was really one and a half deaths. Along with her, her much-wished-for and long-awaited baby also perished. But none of them had known Jaswinder in person. None of them had even seen her. So her death didn't affect them.

The hunted were all Sikhs. So why was Vasu, born into the religion of the hunters, killed?

No one could believe it.

After coming back from Faridkot, Sahadevan bought a bottle of Old Monk and drank as much as he wanted, sitting in his room in Malviya Nagar. He took a long drag of his cigarette after every sip of rum. Others might lick a finger dipped in pickle; he filled his mouth with smoke. Cigarette butts filled the ashtray and spilled over to the floor. The level of rum in the bottle reduced steadily.

That was when he recalled that it had been months since he had seen Vasu. He had last met him before the start of the riots. He was late in sending his monthly report to Nenmanda Shreekanta Panicker.

In the place of the small, burnt-down grocery store in Malviya Nagar, another one had come up quickly. A brick-walled and asbestos-roofed store. It opened only in the mornings and the evenings. The owner, Uddham Singh, was employed as a clerk in a government office. After selling bread, butter and eggs till 10 a.m., he left for his office in Nirman Bhawan. He worked there between 11 a.m. and 4 p.m. Once he was back from the office, he opened the store again. In the evenings, buns, rusk, mathi and other fried and salted snacks were sold. No one could say Uddham Singh was a Sikh by looking at him. He was clean shaven and had a short crop of hair. Many Sikh youngsters had given up their turbans too. They didn't wish to be identified as Sikhs. Who knew when the next riot would break out?

Though the store had reasonably good sales, Uddham Singh's main income was from the telephone. At 6 a.m., when he arrived to open the store, people would already be queuing up. There was no other public phone in the area. Till 10 p.m., when he closed the store, people kept coming to make telephone calls.

'*Kya haal hai, Madrasi bhai*?'

'I'm fine, thank you.'

'Didn't you go to the office? Are you on leave?'

'I didn't go today.'

Saxena didn't need Sahadevan as much as he used to. He had a secretary now. Her skin was ash-coloured. Sahadevan had assumed she was from Kerala or Karnataka or Andhra. But she turned out to be a Bengali.

'What's the number?'

Uddham Singh never allowed anyone else to dial the number. He asked them for it, then dialled it himself and handed over the receiver once the connection came through.

Sahadevan gave him Vasu's telephone number. Vasu, who was no longer on this earth. The phone rang in the barsati in Tilak Nagar but no one answered. How could Vasu have taken the call?

'There's no reply.'

As the afternoon sun dimmed, a cold breeze sprang up. He put on a crumpled jacket over his shabby shirt. It had been days since he had swept his room or cleaned the toilet. Unknown to him, a sense of apathy and detachment was growing inside him. A kind of disinterest. A form of complacence.

He would go to the barsati in Tilak Nagar in search of Vasu for the sake of Nenmanda Shreekanta Panicker. Personally, he was indifferent. He had no other interest in Vasu.

He took a bus from Malviya Nagar depot to the Safdarjung Hospital stop. After taking two buses and walking a longish distance, he finally reached Vasu's barsati.

One of the buses that had been set on fire on 1 November was lying by the roadside, its charred ribs exposed. The remnants of similarly charred and partially burnt vehicles of all sizes could still be seen on the city's roads. For several months after the riots, sandals, shoes, dupattas and turbans floated in the drains.

Sahadevan lit a cigarette and climbed the stairs. His legs were unsteady; he had drunk a lot of rum. And he was famished. He thought he would go out with Vasu and get a plate of aloo tikki or samosa. Vasu was always ready to go out and get something to eat; he was hungry all the time. The fridge contained fruits, eggs, yoghurt and other stuff, bought and kept there by Harilal Shukla. But Vasu was too lazy to help himself. He would rather remain hungry.

There was a big lock on the door. That was unusual. The key must be under a flower pot. Sahadevan lifted up every pot and searched under it. But the key was not to be found.

He decided to wait.

There used to be rattan chairs on the terrace, but it was empty now. He wanted to sit down. He felt dizzy from the rum, from hunger and tiredness. He started to hallucinate. Visions such as he had never seen before appeared in front of his eyes. They created disquiet and fear in him. As he stood leaning against the parapet, his eyelids started to droop, and he fell asleep, standing up. He experienced sleep as if he were sinking into fetid drain water. He started to choke from the muck that entered his nose and mouth. Then he slipped down and sat against the parapet. Again, he had strange visions. The kind of visions Vasu used to have while smoking hashish. Could Vasu's soul have transmigrated to Sahadevan?

'*Kaun ho tum? Kya kaam hai idhar?*'

'I'm waiting for Vasu.'

'*Kaun Vasu? Woh kaun hai?*'

'The artist who lives here.'

'*Yahan koi artist nahi hai.*'

'The artist with long hair and beard. Where has he gone?'

'The tall artist? Oh, he is dead.'

'Vasu is dead?'

'The artist is dead.'

'How?'

'Ask Harilal Shukla.'

Harilal Shukla said, 'Yes, my friend, Vasu is no more. No more.'

Sahadevan returned to Malviya Nagar at dusk, just as the mist was descending. He vomited copiously into the stained and chipped washbasin. Along with the rum, his intestines were also expelled. Then came his liver and kidneys. They lay writhing in the vomit in the basin.

Sahadevan lost consciousness. If he had remained conscious, he might have asked himself, what do you need consciousness for?

Sahadevan got ready to leave for Saxena's chamber. He had brushed his teeth with Colgate toothpaste, shaved with a 7 O'Clock blade, bathed with Rexona soap, and put on a starched and ironed shirt and trousers, and shoes. He had already made breakfast—bread from Uddham Singh's store and a single fried egg. He sprinkled black pepper powder on the egg. He put the water to boil on the stove and lowered the flame. By the time he was through with breakfast, the water would be boiling. He had to drink his tea hot. After straining the tea into a glass, he went and sat on the bed. At such times, memories of the narrow veranda of the Jangpura house brought with them a sense of loss. He used to love sitting on that veranda with a teacup in his hand.

He combed his hair, looking into the mirror. Not many years left before he turned fifty. He smiled, looking at his own reflection.

Hearing the sound of laughter behind him, he turned around to look. Rosily stood there, laughing. It was rare for her to be in such a jovial mood.

The best medicine for healing wounds was indeed laughter. He had never seen Vasu laugh. Kunhikrishnan and Sathyanathan were solemn most of the time. When Sahadevan had first come to Delhi, Devi used to laugh a lot. After Shreedharanunni's demise, she forgot how to. With the disappearance of Vidya, the forgetting became complete. The only one who still laughed was Lalitha.

'Edi, how come you're in such a happy mood?'

'You're also in a happy mood, chetta.'

'Have you ever seen me sad?'

'I've only seen you that way. Your face is never radiant.'

'You liar. Lying to my face!'

'I never lie. You know, chetta, as a child, my appachan taught me this—one should never lie. Jesus doesn't like liars.'

She sat down by his side.

'Would you like some tea?'

There was some tea left. And bread and eggs, if she wanted. But she was not hungry. She was full of happiness.

'So, what's the news? Tell me.'

'I'm leaving.'

'Where to?'

'Back home. I won't be coming back here.'

A piece of news he had been waiting to hear for a long time.

'Why aren't you saying anything, chetta? Don't you like knowing that I'm going back?'

'I don't know what to say, I'm so happy.'

'I never wanted to be here this long. I had planned to go back after five or six years. That's what I told ammachi, appachan and Jomon when I left. Yet, I have spent so many years here. My sweet Jesus, I'm not able to believe it, chetta.'

'You are going back. That's what matters.'

'You thought I'll never go back, didn't you, chetta?'

'I never thought that, not even once, Rosakutty.'

'Whaaa … what did you call me?'

'Rosakutty. You are returning to your old life as Rosakutty. Jomon will be waiting for you in his boat, with the oar in his hand. If you are leaving this week, you'll be in time to catch the moonlight over the lake in the backwaters.'

'Sometimes you talk like writers do.'

He laughed.

About fifteen years ago, Vinod Duggal, the manager of the Shagufa Restaurant in South Extension, had transformed Rosakutty into Rosily.

But she was no longer that old Rosily whom he had first seen during the war of 1971. She was past thirty-three years of age. Long use of make-up had desiccated her face. She had black circles under her eyes. She had become plump. He was sure that she was dyeing her hair, at least partially.

He could not believe that Jomon was waiting for her. Did he love her still? If so, the lovers to celebrate in verse and legend were not Laila-Majnu or Ramanan and Chandrika, but Jomon and Rosakutty.

'When are you leaving?'

'Monday. On the Jayanti Janata.'

'I'll come and help you with the packing.'

She had no one to help her. There was a time when Sathyanathan and Vasu were her friends. Vasu was no more. Sathyanathan had gradually drifted away from her. Devi's aversion for her was not the only reason. People had started recognising Rosily, and not in a nice way. There was something in her face and comportment that declared she was a woman of easy virtue. He noticed the dirty looks thrown at him once, by two young men, as he walked past the Kerala Club with Rosily.

She had no one but Sahadevan to help her or sympathise with her in a crisis. Georgekutty had stopped calling her a long time ago. She had called two days ago to inform him that she was leaving. He showed no interest at all. She could go or come or do what she liked, it was no skin off his nose, he seemed to suggest.

Georgekutty was no longer the Georgekutty of yore. The store he owned in INA Market, which sold ladies' undergarments, was still open, but he didn't go there. His primary business was of exporting nurses' uniforms to Saudi Arabia, Libya, Iraq,

USA and many other countries. He owned a large, modern factory in Kirti Nagar and employed five hundred workers. He lived in a massive bungalow in Maharani Bagh, where his next-door neighbour was an ex-chief minister of Delhi; scientists from CSIR and foreigners lived in this part of the city. In the '60s, when nurses thronged to far-flung countries in search of a livelihood, Georgekutty had chosen to remain behind. He had become a multimillionaire by supplying uniforms to these Florence Nightingales.

Sahadevan made an omelette and served it to Rosily with four slices of bread. She ate with relish.

When Vasu left Govind Puri, she had cooked a feast for him. She decided that before leaving Delhi for good, she would give Sahadevan a feast too. She would cook and serve him with her own hands.

On Sunday, Sahadevan arrived at Rosily's house. It was his first time there. It was an old house in a narrow lane between Sunlight Colony and Bhagwan Nagar. Bala Sahib Gurdwara and Guru Harkrishan Hospital were close by. Rosily lived in one room. In the other rooms, a printing press was running. Rough-looking people were standing at the gate and in the corridor leading to her room; other people arrived and left continuously. It was not a pleasant atmosphere.

'Why are you living in a place like this?'

'Should I live in a mansion like Georgekutty, then? Who will give their house on rent to a woman like me?'

At least for now, her troubles were ending. She was leaving the next day. The return journey of Rosily. The homecoming of Rosakutty.

But would her difficulties end for real?

Sahadevan felt nervous and fearful. Would her dreams turn to nought? When she returned after a decade and a half, would Jomon welcome her home? What would happen if he learnt of the kind of life she had led in Delhi? Hadn't Rosily been unfair to Jomon for the past fifteen years? Jomon, who was waiting for her with his boat and oar? Sahadevan's heart murmured to him that Rosakutty's future life would contain more ordeals than her past.

Sahadevan helped Rosily pack. Sarees and salwar-kameez lay in heaps on the clothesline and inside the wardrobe. The sarees weren't as flashy as the ones she used to wear in the early days. The kameez were stitched in the latest fashion. When he started to fold the sarees, she stopped him.

'No, chetta, not those. I'm not taking any of them.'

'What will you wear back home?'

'I've bought new ones.'

A suitcase placed in a corner of the room contained the sarees and salwars that she was going to wear at home. She was leaving behind all her old clothes. Her old life too.

He wrapped up the sandals in various designs that she had got from Karol Bagh and Palika Bazaar. She had also bought a bolt of cloth for Jomon from Bombay Dyeing; he could get a suit stitched in time for their wedding. One small bag contained talcum powder, all sorts of moisturising face creams, shampoos, hair oils and scented soaps. She had bought Jaipuri bedspreads and cushion covers from Ajmal Khan Road, and two ladies' shoulder bags from Lajpat Nagar Central Market. From the Tibetan Market on Janpath, she had picked up a copper vase and from Panchkuian Road, paper flowers to keep in it.

Everything fit into two suitcases and one airbag.

Sahadevan was there to load everything into the taxi summoned from Ashram Chowk. She kept chattering and laughing all the way to Nizamuddin railway station. He had never seen her so chirpy or overflowing with happiness. It spilled out, not only from her eyes, but also her mouth and the pores of her skin.

They drank cardamom-laced tea from earthenware cups. Soon afterwards, the Jayanti Janata Express pulled into the station. She had come to Delhi in a steam-engine-drawn train from Madras. Her return was going to be in a long-distance diesel-engine train, and faster too.

'What are you thinking, chetta?'

'Whether I should thank Georgekutty.'

'Thank him, what do we lose?'

She laughed again. She had turned into a compulsive laugher at the age of thirty-three.

When the Jayanti Janata Express left the station, he retraced his steps along the route on which her laughter and happiness lay scattered. To his home.

Whose would be the next return journey?

And when?

2

THE CHANGING MANUSCRIPT

It was his birthday. Sahadevan was turning fifty.

It was not a very warm day. He had woken up in the morning with the caress of the moisture-laden breeze carrying the smell of the Yamuna. Proximity to the river made it humid and sweaty in the summers. But inside the room, it was always cool.

It's the duty of your mother or your wife or your children to remind you that it's your birthday. He had no one. The few people he knew and cared about were immersed in their own lives. Five years ago, when the mass murder of Sikhs had taken place in Delhi, no one from home had even sent him a postcard asking about it. Everyone was concerned only about themselves, Sahadevan mused. It was his turn now. He was going to live a self-centred life, concerned only about himself.

He had remembered that it was his birthday quite by accident. Kuber Lal, his new landlord, had been talking about ration cards. One's date of birth and father's name were needed for filling in the form.

'Hey Ram! You don't have a ration card? I can't believe it.'

He had lived for nearly three decades in Delhi without a ration card. Sahadevan himself could scarcely believe it.

A ration card was not merely for buying wheat, rice and sugar at subsidised prices, and candles and firecrackers during

Diwali. It was also an identity card. An authoritative and credible testimony that he was alive on the face of this earth. Without a ration card, it would be impossible to prove that he was a resident of the city.

There was no real requirement for him to produce such proof. To show whom? Yet, he decided to apply for one. Let not the lack of a ration card be held against him. His life had been full of lacunae so far. There had to be some achievements too. When he took his last breath, he could at least be satisfied that he too had a ration card.

He didn't know how long he would continue to stay in Delhi. Others had already started their return journeys. Sahadevan, Kunhikrishnan, Lalitha, Rosily, Vasu …

Kuber Lal gave him an application form. He had a collection of forms, of every kind. If you had to send a telegram, he had the form for that; if you wanted to open a savings bank account, he had that too; if a train ticket needed to be booked or a gas connection was required or a Public Provident Fund account had to be opened in a post office, he had the appropriate forms for each of these. Sahadevan was surprised to see one for the use of the municipality electric crematorium too. Kuber Lal had stacked all the forms neatly in the drawer of an old table stained with the remnants of food, tea and mustard oil.

Each of Sahadevan's landlords had made his presence known in a unique way: Uttam Singh of Amritpuri by lamenting incessantly about his failure to give his daughter a dowry; Om Prakash Jain of Jangpura by feeding wheat flour to ants that lived under the roots of trees; Ashok Chibber of Malviya Nagar by chatting up passers-by in front of his house, clad only in his underwear; and now, Kuber Lal, by distributing forms to those in need.

Sahadevan expected Lalitha or Devi or Sathyanathan or someone else to call, to wish him a happy birthday. His own expectation surprised him. Even when thinking of bigger things, in his heart of hearts, he was a person of small needs. An ordinary man. A very ordinary man, waiting for birthday greetings …

If Rosily were in Delhi, she might have called and wished him. She was very mindful about such things. But she had boarded the Jayanti Janata Express and left, accompanied by two suitcases and one airbag.

An ordinary man, right? He decided then that he might as well celebrate his birthday. It was not an ordinary birthday; it was his fiftieth. A half century. Cricketers hit a lot of half centuries. But he would have to be satisfied with a single one. This auspicious day that would not come again needed to be celebrated.

He went out and dialled the number of his office in Shaheed Bhagat Singh Marg. He asked for a day's leave, which was promptly granted.

'Go and enjoy,' Gulshan Wadhwa told him.

His new workplace was very unlike Kashyap Saxena's office. Most of the rooms were air-conditioned, and many people worked in them. If one or two didn't turn up on a particular day, it didn't affect work too much.

Sahadevan shaved. He had a bath. He ran his eyes over the shirts in the wardrobe. There was no time to buy a new shirt. He picked one that looked relatively new. He wore a white mundu with a black border. A mundu was definitely more appropriate on one's birthday. He dusted talcum powder on his face and combed his hair. There wasn't much left. It had started falling soon after he turned thirty-five. The few remaining strands now stuck to his scalp. Luckily, the hair on his head wasn't as grey as his beard or moustache. How was he to marry if he looked so old, with his hair gone all grey? Sahadevan laughed at himself.

Laughing at oneself is akin to talking to oneself, he thought. If anything is impossible, it is impossibility alone. Everything else is possible.

Touché!

Sahadevan stepped out and took an auto rickshaw to a bakery nearby. He seldom felt like eating the cakes or pastries displayed in its window. But the aroma was intoxicating. It reminded him of the smell of borma-biscuits emanating from the bakery back home. It brought back memories of eating the rustic biscuits stacked like planks, dipped in tea. He used to stand in front of bakeries to take in that aroma, even though he knew that anyone passing by would take him for a glutton.

As usual, the warm aroma of cakes and bread spilled onto the road.

What kind of birthday cake do you want? Sahadevan asked himself.

He glanced at the cakes displayed in the glass case. Vanilla and pineapple flavoured cakes. Cakes with thick icing. Chocolate cakes. Sponge cakes.

'Tell me, which one do you want?' Sahadevan asked Sahadevan.

'Plain vanilla cake,' he answered himself, after a moment of reflection.

He ordered a plain, one kg vanilla cake.

He didn't bother to think about what he was going to do with such a large cake.

'Is it for a birthday?'

'Yes.'

'Do you want something written on it?'

'Happy Birthday to Sahadevan.'

'Tell me the spelling.'

'S-A-H-A-D-E-V-A-N.'

The man wrote the letters on the cake in the blink of an eye. Instead of 'n', he wrote 'm'.

There's a lot of difference between Sahadevan and Sahadevam. But I don't care, he told himself.

'Do you need candles?'

'Yes.'

'How many?'

'Five.'

He returned to his lair with the cake and the candles.

He didn't want to eat out on his birthday, so he decided to make himself a simple lunch. He measured out one-and-a-half cups of rice, good enough for two meals. While the rice was cooking, he diced onions and crushed ginger and garlic. When the rice was cooked, he placed a fresh vessel on the stove. The vessel had been with him since his Jangpura days. When he was living in Amritpuri, Gunjan bhabhi didn't allow him to cook. Whenever she saw him kneading dough, she would come running, catch hold of his hand, and persuade him to eat with them.

He poured oil into the aluminium vessel. When it was hot, he dropped in some mustard seeds and waited for them to crackle. Then he dropped in the sliced shallots he had kept ready, and sautéed them. Dal, cleaned and washed, followed with diced onions, tomatoes, salt, turmeric powder and the right amount of water. When the dal had cooked, he threw in some curry leaves. After that, he diced some beans and sautéed it to make a side dish. It was a simple preparation using only fried mustard seeds and no coconut at all.

When lunch was ready, he placed the cake on the table. He planted the five candles on it and lit them one by one. Then he blew out the candles in the same order as he had placed them, one after the other.

Happy Birthday to you, Sahadevan ...

He cut a small piece of cake with a knife and placed it fondly in his mouth. He arranged the plates and quarter plates on the table. He poured water boiled with cumin seeds into a glass. And then he sat down to a hearty meal of rice, dal, beans, pappadam, tender mango pickle and curd.

By then, it was past 3 p.m. Time for a nap.

Sometimes Sahadevan thought he was in love with poverty. Though there were many attractive, sophisticated places in

Connaught Place, he saw himself fitting in better in the environs of Jama Masjid. He had watched himself walk around there, where life was lived amidst poverty and hardship. Somewhere within him was the desire to avoid luxuries and lead a simple life. Wasn't it his inclination towards poverty that had made him stay in that shed-like room in Malviya Nagar for so many years? On top of that, he had been entirely negligent when it came to moulding his own life. One day, while he was out walking and conversing with himself, he decided to put an end to this negligence. Life was like writing a novel. Corrections and revisions had to be made every now and then. A complete rewrite might be required too.

The next Sunday he bought *The Hindustan Times*, a newspaper he didn't normally read. On Sundays, it had four or five pages of Situations Vacant and Employment advertisements. Even after going through it with a fine-tooth comb, he could find none that suited him. The next week, he continued his search. He felt a surge of excitement when he saw an insertion in the name of Wadhwa International. The name and address were different from those he had seen on the visiting card he had picked up in Old Delhi. Instead of Wadhwa & Sons, it was Wadhwa International, and the name of the street was Shaheed Bhagat Singh Marg.

I've had enough of poverty, he told himself. I must move to a place that is cleaner, sunnier and airier. And I must have a couple of pegs of Old Monk every day. He needed a job that would fetch him that much money, nothing more.

In the three decades he had lived in Delhi, he had watched as many of the Malayalis who came during the '60s reached high stations in life. In the initial days, the writers and intellectuals who came to the literary meets organised by the Kerala Club travelled by bus and arrived hot and sweaty. They smoked cheap cigarettes or beedis. Their shirt collars were grimy. The majority of these men were clerks. Gradually, they changed. They started wearing suits and jackets; many of them drove cars. The Delhi Malayali had acquired a new stature.

Once, Sahadevan had happened to see Georgekutty's bungalow in Maharani Bagh. He was astounded by it. It was a mansion in marble. Security guards manned the tall black gates. Right in front of him, a Mercedes Benz drove into the compound. On the shiny brass plate fixed on the wall, he could see Geogekutty's name.

When he leafed through the Mahanagar Telephone Nigam Limited directory, he saw Malayali names among the company MDs, government secretaries and industrialists. On the gate of a huge mansion in East of Kailash, he saw the name of a man who hailed from Kannur. He was an exporter of crêpe fabric.

Only you have remained a nobody, Sahadevan told himself crossly. You wasted two or three decades living the life of a dreamer. And now, you are a pauper who can't even buy a bottle of rum. For fifteen years after V.P. Agencies was razed by the bulldozers, you did nothing. You could have borrowed money and resurrected the agency. But you did nothing.

I had no desires, no ambition, Sahadevan defended himself against his own accusations. I didn't need anything. But there was loathing in his voice.

After much thought, he decided to meet Wadhwa saab. A long, long time had passed. Would he recognise this aged and changed man? Would he remember him?

'Do you have an appointment?'

'No.'

'Sorry, he doesn't meet anyone without an appointment.'

'I …'

'Please take an appointment and come.'

'It's urgent. I've sent a letter. Wadhwa saab knows me well.'

The receptionist, her navel showing through the low-waist saree, sized him up. He didn't look like someone who would know the MD of Wadhwa International in person. The patina of sweat on his face, the dangling top button of his shirt and the general look of desperation couldn't possibly belong to someone Wadhwa saab knew. Those who came to meet him wore a suit and tie and carried leather briefcases. From Sahadevan's shoulder hung a bulging handloom cloth bag bought at Khadi Gramodyog in Connaught Place. Even Sahadevan didn't know exactly what it contained.

'How do you know Wadhwa saab?'

'That's none of your business.'

His voice was hard.

'Your good name please?' she asked, hiding her discomfort.

She rose from her seat, pulled her saree down to cover her navel, and opening the batwing doors, went inside.

The reception area exuded a fragrance and was cool. Five minutes of waiting in the room and the sweat on his body evaporated. He didn't know if the smell of stale sweat lingered. No one could smell their own sweat. Before starting, he had put on a clean shirt and trousers, and spilled Cuticura talcum powder under his singlet and over his shoulders.

'He's calling you.'

Through the half door she held open for him, he entered the MD's room.

It was even cooler here than in the reception. The glass-topped table had three phones on it. One of them was red. Wadhwa saab was holding a receiver against each ear and talking to two people at the same time. On the table lay a crystal ashtray, a pack of State Express 555 cigarettes, and a gold lighter.

Shifting in his revolving chair, Wadhwa saab pointed to the chair opposite him and gestured to Sahadevan to sit. He had never sat on a softer chair. It was like sitting on a cloud.

'Arrey yaar. Where have you been all this while? What's up with you?'

Sahadevan narrated his story. Wadhwa saab listened, occasionally talking into the black and red phones, sometimes into both of them. He had the ability to talk into two phones and listen to someone sitting across from him at the same time. Sahadevan could only do one thing at a time. Also, he was taciturn. Maybe his business had failed because of that. Maybe that was why he had reached a stage where he could not afford a bottle of Old Monk. He remembered Sathyanathan repeatedly using the term 'multitasking' in a discussion on TV. He didn't have that skill. How could someone who didn't know how to do a single task multitask?

A man brought espresso coffee and cookies in gold-rimmed crockery. While Wadhwa saab was busy on the phone, Sahadevan drank his coffee.

'What kind of a man are you? Why did you struggle so much? You could have come and met me.'

'I didn't want to bother you.'

'Stupid idiot!' Gulshan Wadhwa lost his cool.

As Wadhwa saab talked on the phone, alternating between English and Hindi, Sahadevan noticed that he still spoke ungrammatically and mispronounced his words.

Pushing open the half door, Wadhwa saab came out to see him off, his hand on Sahadevan's shoulder. The receptionist jumped to her feet.

The next day, as fifty-year-old Sahadevan walked into Wadhwa International in a clean shirt and trousers, a fountain pen in his pocket, holding a cheap briefcase he had bought in Palika Bazaar, the receptionist stood up for him.

Are you turning into Ramu, the protagonist of Aravindan's *Small Men and the Big World*? Sahadevan asked himself. Then, he thought, no, I've just made a small amendment in the manuscript of my novel. That's all.

The following month, he shifted to Kuber Lal's Low-Income Group flat in Mayur Vihar. With two rooms, a kitchen and a bathroom, it was more than sufficient for a bachelor. The first room was where he would sit and read the newspaper, watch the news in English on the black and white TV, listen to classical music on the radio, and drink Old Monk after returning from office. The second room was for him to write and sleep in.

A twenty-minute stroll took him to the river front. The banks of the Yamuna.

After a very long time, this man on the verge of stepping into old age felt happy.

How long would his happiness last?

3

THE SCENT OF MANGO BLOSSOMS

One more return journey.

He was abandoning the house. Abandoning a place with which he had grown deeply familiar over twenty-five years and visited almost daily. It was as painful as any return journey.

Sathyanathan had been awakened at 4 a.m. by the need to relieve himself, and found the light on in his mother's room.

Outside, Hauz Khas lay frozen. The light that hung over the houses and on the branches of trees reminded him of buttermilk. In that murky light, Firoz Shah Tughlaq's tomb looked like a watercolour. In the pond built by Alauddin Khalji in the thirteenth century, swans were sleeping even as they swam.

Sathyanathan stood at the door. 'Amma, why do you get up so early? It's only four o'clock. You don't have to go to the Secretariat these days. You don't have to go anywhere. Why don't you sleep a little more?'

Devi never shut the door to her room. She felt suffocated if it was closed. Sathyanathan, on the other hand, could only sleep with the curtains fully drawn and the windows and doors closed. He wore striped pyjamas to bed. He brushed his teeth before turning in. In the morning, he had tea in bed, served by the maid. He seemed to be giving up his Malayali habits, bit by bit.

He conversed with Janakikutty mostly in English, even at home. Sometimes he spoke to Devi in English. 'Ma, I'm off. See you in the evening.' He would leave, taking the car keys.

'Amma, sleep a little more.'

'Eda, I can't get any sleep.'

'That's because you keep thinking about unnecessary things. Take it easy, amma.'

'My life is over. I've gone through it all. Nothing is left. I can die in peace now.'

'Bullshit! Why are you getting so sentimental, amma? When you reach a certain age, you have to retire. It's time to enjoy yourself. Your responsibilities are over. Now live in peace. That's how you should think, amma.'

Would it be so easy to forget twenty-seven years of life at the Secretariat?

The previous day had been her last day there. Devi had spent a good part of her life in North Block, with its hundreds of rooms and long corridors designed by Herbert Baker and built with Dholpur red sandstone. The flag fluttering atop Rashtrapati Bhawan on Raisina Hill and the chhatris or canopies of North Block were sights she saw every day. She had started her life there by dusting tables and chairs, wiping typewriters clean, and fetching tea for the babus. Right opposite, in South Block, was the prime minister's office. Before being assassinated by her Sikh bodyguards, Indira Gandhi had walked into South Block so many times, right in front of her.

Thousands of people from all parts of the country worked in North and South Blocks. The first few days, Devi used to stand and stare, astonished at the sight of the employees streaming in on bicycles, scooters, and from buses. *She* was a part of this massive crowd. During winters, as the gentle sunlight settled on the lawns in front, thousands basked in it as they ate lunch out of their boxes. There was a sincere friendship among them although they hailed from different states and spoke different languages.

There were exchanges of joys and sorrows. They discussed their children's education. Gradually, Devi also became a part of this world of babus.

Twenty-seven years went by.

Yesterday, she had said her final goodbye to the Secretariat. It had given her the strength to cope with the city without Shreedharanunni and Vidya—its countless employees, from the Cabinet Secretary to the peon; the dusty files lying in heaps; the tea-stained and chipped glass tumblers. Devi had been ejected from that expansive complex consisting of India Gate, Rajpath, Parliament House, Rashtrapati Bhawan and the Central Secretariat. Now, she would live out her old age in the shadow of her son, in his Hauz Khas flat.

She hadn't slept a wink the previous night. She kept rewinding and watching her life all over again. So many experiences. An unending chain of memories. The indelible face of Shreedharanunni. Vidya's face, which seared her insides.

She bathed early, as usual. The saree and blouse that she had ironed the previous day were in the almirah. She washed and ironed her clothes herself. Though there was a maid, she didn't allow her to do any of her work.

The shoulder bag and lunch box she used to take to the office were in the cupboard.

She found herself falling into a terrible, insufferable void.

Sathyanathan, meanwhile, had shaved, bathed and dressed in a hurry, as usual. He drank coffee in between. He left in a hurry, grabbing his car keys, books and files. She heard the car start.

There was nothing for her to do the whole day. She was alone in that big apartment. With no one to talk to.

At night, the inevitable call. 'I'll be late, Amma. Don't wait up for me. Have your dinner.'

Devi would go to the kitchen and serve herself some rice or a couple of chapatis. The Oriya maid used mustard oil for cooking. Even when she was asked to use coconut oil, she didn't.

She only knew how to cook with mustard oil, she said. Devi couldn't stand its smell or taste.

It didn't matter to Sathyanathan because he rarely ate at home. His dinner was mostly at the Press Club or the Gymkhana Club. Or in the company of Janakikutty. Once he left in the morning, he returned home only late in the night. Some days, he didn't even come back.

In Sewa Nagar, in that small house, she had lived amidst three people. Though two of them had departed early, Sathyanathan had given her company. He filled that little room so that Devi never knew solitude. He was always with her, like a shadow. She had spent more time with him than with Shreedharanunni. But now, he had become a rare bird. Only occasionally was he even sighted.

Janakikutty had left again for Calcutta. She travelled to Calcutta and Bombay as if she was going to Connaught Place. She was preoccupied with lecture tours and conferences.

Dressed in inexpensive handloom sarees, sporting round-rimmed glasses and a shoulder bag, she came often to visit Devi. She travelled by bus. Only when buses and auto rickshaws stopped plying, late at night, did she use taxis. If the distance could be covered on foot, she walked. Sometimes she came barefoot.

When she came, she cooked rice, vegetables and fish curry. She didn't take much time to do it either. Devi liked having her around.

This time too, before leaving for Calcutta, she had visited Devi. The three of them had sat down for dinner. Devi had cooked this time. The maid had been asked to stay out of the kitchen. Devi did everything—scraping the coconut, grinding it, and cutting the rohu fish. She was not satisfied with the maid's way of preparing it—the scales and entrails were not completely removed, and she detested that.

Sathyanathan opened a wine bottle before they started to eat.

'Amma, isn't Janakikutty leaving tomorrow? This is to say goodbye to her.'

This too had become routine. He would find some excuse to serve alcohol. Last Sunday it was: 'Genuine Jamaican rum. A friend who came from the Caribbean islands gave it to me, amma.' Or 'Let me drink some vodka today, amma. It's a very happy day for me. Our pre-budget economic forecast has turned out to be accurate.' Another day: 'I'm feeling very low, amma. Today is achan's death anniversary. I'm going to have some rum.'

Sathyanathan poured the wine into long-stemmed glasses and offered one to Janakikutty.

The conversation and wine-drinking continued. The rice and fish curry Devi had cooked went cold. She began to doze, sitting in the drawing room.

The maid was asleep inside the kitchen. The watchman's whistle reached them once in a while. Gradually, the sound of cars being parked outside their neighbours' homes also stopped. The late autumn moonlight had an unusually expansive aura. It lit up the white curtain on the window near the dining table.

'Amma, please have dinner and go to bed. We'll talk for some more time. We'll also be hungrier by then.'

'Eda, how will Janakikutty go if it gets late?'

Janakikutty was brave enough to take a taxi even past midnight. She was afraid of no one.

'Amma, Janakikutty is sleeping here tonight.'

They had a three-bedroom flat. One room was full of his bookshelves, table, chair, etc. When she came on Sundays, after lunch, she climbed into Devi's bed and read. Her shoulder bag was always full of books and papers. Like Sathyanathan, she slept very little.

'Let her sleep in my room. I'll get an extra pillow and a blanket.'

'No, amma. Pease go to bed. We're not going to sleep now.'

Devi ate some rice and fish curry. After all, she had cooked the meal herself. She then withdrew into her bedroom.

When she woke up at 4 a.m. and checked, she found Sathyanathan's bedroom locked from the inside.

When they emerged in the morning, it was past 10 a.m.

'Eda, do you need to do all this right in front of your mother's eyes?'

'What do you mean, amma? I don't understand.'

'Eda, which mother can live like this? I've told you no less than a hundred times to get married. Do you ever listen to me? Tie a mangalasutra around her neck. Then do whatever you want to do. This is not your France or America. As long as you are living in this country, you should follow its customs and morals.'

He recognised an uncharacteristic edge to her voice and a hardness in her eyes. It felt like a warning to him.

Without replying, he went into his room and shut the door. Devi felt as if it had been shut in her face.

Two days later, Devi went and sat beside Sathyanathan as he drank his bed tea, leaning back against the headboard. His spectacles lay by his side. Devi put them on, just like that. Immediately, the world around her dimmed. She couldn't see anything. The spectacles that gave Sathyanathan vision had robbed Devi of hers.

'Sathyanatha.'

'Yes, ammae.'

'I'm leaving.'

'Where to?'

'I don't know. I can't live in Delhi any longer, eda. It's weighing me down. It's a burden I can no longer bear. If I stay here, I'll die. Or go mad.'

'Amma, will you leave me here alone and go? No way. Impossible.'

'You're not alone. I'm alone now.'

'What do you lack here? Am I not providing you with everything you need?'

'I don't need anything. And if I ever do, I don't need anyone's help for that. I have my pension.'

'I don't understand anything that you are saying, amma.'

'Precisely why I'm leaving.'

Devi went to her room and shut the door behind her. She too had learned to shut doors.

Sathyanathan, Janakikutty, Kunhikrishnan, Lalitha and Sahadevan accompanied Devi to Nizamuddin railway station. Sahadevan walked with difficulty because of a sudden pain in his knees. Though he was dressed neatly, he had not shaved. His jaw was covered with grey stubble.

There were more people around Nizamuddin station these days. Entire families lived under the trees and behind the bus stops, with gunny bags and torn clothes as sad excuses for screens. They were homeless migrants from Uttar Pradesh and other states, who had come in search of work. The excreta of their children spread a nauseating stench all along the way. Beggars and hawkers had taken up every inch of the available space. Now buses ran from Nizamuddin to all parts of the city. Several were parked haphazardly in front of the railway station.

The poverty that greeted Devi when she first came to Delhi after her wedding to Shreedharanunni had not changed very much, though she had grown into an old woman. If anything, it had worsened. The crowds, the hunger and the squalor of Jama Masjid and Paharganj seemed to have spread like cholera to the residential areas of painters and dhrupad singers. The abject destitution was like a communicable disease that no inoculation could prevent. Delhi placed its handsome men and beautiful women in front, as a screen, to hide its destitution from the rest of the world.

'So, you're leaving, are you?'

Sahadevan had come to know of her departure only the previous day. She had called to inform him. Many months had passed since they had last seen each other. After Devi moved out of Sewa Nagar, they had met only a few times. Sathyanathan and Janakikutty used to come to his Jangpura house in search of Old Monk rum, on dry days. In his barn-like room in Malviya Nagar, there was no stock of rum; even if there was, they wouldn't have come. Also, there was more rum and vodka in Sathyanathan's flat than could be consumed in a hundred dry days.

'It's over the top and ruthless, this thing you are doing.'

'Edo, I need peace of mind.'

'What's ruining your peace of mind here?'

'Have I spent even one day in Delhi peacefully? You know the answer to that.'

'Who do you have back home? Aren't we all here for you? Me, Sathyanathan, Lalitha, everyone?'

'Who said I don't have anyone to go back to? Edo, I'll have the breeze of Vrischikam and the mango blossom. That's all I need.'

4

DIAMOND ON HER FOREHEAD

Sahadevan had once tried to sketch the picture of a big house in Panchsheel Park. He was not much of an artist, and he soon realised that his scrawl didn't do justice to the magnificence of the building. So he gave up sketching and, instead, started to detail the building in words and letters. Oh, man, you are great! He complimented himself. How well you have described Gulshan Wadhwa's bungalow! The readers will see it appearing in front of their eyes.

The huge circular dish antenna on top of the building attracted the attention of passers-by. Perhaps they had seen one like it in Palam airport, but they didn't understand what it was doing on top of a house. People in the know claimed it was a radar. Wadhwa had paid 300 per cent Customs duty to import a colour TV from Germany. The dish antenna that looked like a radar kept sending colour pictures into it. It was a wonder for visitors to his house. For many, Gulshan Wadhwa himself was a wonder.

Behind the bungalow was a heated swimming pool. His three daughters used to swim in it. To keep the neighbours from peeping in, the compound wall was raised very high.

Sahadevan had seen the girls while working at Wadhwa & Sons. The eldest was old enough to be married and Wadhwa saab, like Uttam Singh, was anxious about it. He wished to give away a Maruti 800 car as his eldest daughter's dowry. He was not able to do that. But unlike Uttam Singh, he didn't lament. He used his intelligence; he worked hard and made money. At his second daughter's wedding, he gave away a Mercedes Benz as dowry. After the wedding of his third daughter Shailee, whom Sahadevan knew and remembered by name, Wadhwa saab sent the newly-weds to Europe for their honeymoon.

Then he celebrated his sixtieth birthday with his wife, aboard a cruise liner to Greece. Sahadevan's respect for him grew. Not because he had chosen to travel on a luxury liner. But because, instead of Singapore or Bangkok, he had chosen to go to ancient and eternal Greece ...

'Wadhwa saab ...'

'Tell me, yaar.'

'Why didn't you go to Bangkok or Singapore? Don't most Indian tourists go there?'

'What does Bangkok have that Delhi doesn't? Girls giving oil massages? For that you needn't go so far.'

There was nothing you couldn't find in Delhi.

'Arrey yaar, we are old. It's Greece and Italy that we should visit now. We must see the artistic creations that are the world's heritage.'

He isn't the man I thought he was, Sahadevan told himself. He's not hollow. There's goodness inside him. There's understanding. Sahadevan had left his employment once. Yet, he had taken him back in his old age. And he treated him like a friend, sharing things with him in a way he didn't with his other employees. As he pondered this, his respect for Wadhwa saab grew manifold.

Now, the wedding preparations of his granddaughter, Guneet, were on. He had given out responsibilities to each of his staff members. Sahadevan was charged with the arrangements at the venue, a five-star hotel. It would not have been possible for him to run around on his swollen knees. But he only had to take the staff car to the hotel and oversee the arrangements. Wadhwa saab knew the strengths and weaknesses of each of his employees. Three decades earlier, even before Kashyap Saxena of Patiala House, Gulshan Wadhwa had recognised Sahadevan's competence when it came to the English language. Now, he must have recognised his ability to supervise and manage events.

Sahadevan was allergic to five-star hotels, a fact Wadhwa saab was not aware of. Else, he would have given Sahadevan some other responsibility, such as overseeing the printing and distribution of invitation cards. That was an onerous task and had to be done with great care.

Sahadevan and Janakikutty had something in common. Both of them abhorred luxury. Sahadevan couldn't stand vanity and narcissism. Janakikutty was allergic to rich people, especially the nouveau riche.

'In earlier times, people used to become rich through hard work.'

'And now?'

'Stealing and robbing.'

What about Georgekutty and Gulshan Wadhwa then?

Sahadevan got out of the car and walked to the reception. He was dressed in a suit and shiny shoes. He had got used to shaving every day, and even used a spray to stave off body odour. He had bought it at Palika Bazaar, knowing that though it said 'Made in England', it was made in Chandni Chowk. He also knew that sustained use of the spray would cause his skin allergy to flare up. But he remembered something Gulshan Wadhwa had said at a staff meeting: Avoid bad breath and body odour. Otherwise, however competent you are, you will not make any headway in your career.

A shamiana was being set up near the swimming pool. The poles for it had been erected. He walked around the area; he didn't have anything specific to do. In the forenoon, there were mostly women in the pool. The hotel staff made small talk with him. Even the junior-most employee wore a suit and tie.

He had heard that Wadhwa saab had told someone, 'Let Guneet's wedding get fixed. I'll spend five lakhs just on the shamiana.'

It sounded like he was getting even with someone. Perhaps with himself. He didn't have the money to buy a Maruti 800 for Guneet's mother's wedding. But now, he could afford to spend the equivalent of the price of five such Marutis on the shamiana alone.

'I'll shower my granddaughter with diamonds and gold,' Wadhwa saab said at a staff meeting. Of late, he only spoke of his granddaughter's wedding arrangements. Sahadevan had heard that all the jewellery had been bought from Dubai's Gold Souk.

'How does Wadhwa saab have so much money?' Sahadevan asked himself. Wadhwa International was doing the same work that V.P. Agencies used to do. And yet, Sahadevan had seldom been free from the grip of poverty.

'Your clients were the kite manufacturers and spice sellers of Old Delhi. Wadhwa saab's clients? Most of them are from the African nations.'

Sahadevan remembered the shooting incident at the embassy in Golf Links, many years ago.

'It's all black money, sir. All black money,' Bodhi Narayanan, a clerk in the import department, told Sahadevan one day. He was more or less the same age as Sahadevan, the oldest among all the employees of Wadhwa International.

'Don't spread such rumours about your own master, Bodhisattva.'

'It's not a rumour, sir.'

'What else is it then? Do you have proof?'

'I see it with my own eyes. What further proof do you need?'

With that, he walked away as if he hadn't said anything significant.

From his observation of the swimming pool, Sahadevan realised one thing. Earlier, local residents never stepped into five-star swimming pools; they were meant for foreigners. If an Indian was sighted in the vicinity of a pool, the hotel's security staff would tail him. They would question him and get him to move away. But now, there were as many locals as there were foreigners. One day, he saw Georgekutty sitting under the shade of a palm tree by the side of the pool in his swimming trunks, with a glass of beer in his hand. He noticed many Georgekuttys with their wives and children.

'On her wedding day, the bindi on Guneet's forehead will be a diamond.'

'Won't it fall off?'

'No, yaar, not even if you pour water over her head.'

There was no change in Gulshan Wadhwa's behaviour with Sahadevan, despite the passage of time. He had told him that after Guneet's wedding, he planned to go to Singapore. Sahadevan didn't have to ask him why. He himself explained, 'Look at my head, yaar. I've lost all my hair. I hate this bald look. I'm going for a hair transplant.'

A hair transplant was the new treatment for baldness. Wadhwa saab had wanted to get it done before the wedding. But there wasn't enough time.

One day, Wadhwa saab took Sahadevan with him to the Gymkhana Club. That surprised him. Why was this multimillionaire businessman taking his subordinate to the club with him?

Sahadevan tried to excuse himself. Wadhwa saab wouldn't budge.

'Membership has been closed for the last twenty years. Now, no one can become a member.'

'Aren't you a member?'

Gulshan Wadhwa laughed loudly.

'Yaar, which club in Delhi does not have me as a member?'

'How much did you pay, Wadhwa saab?'

'Only five lakhs.'

'The cost of the shamiana.'

Wadhwa saab laughed.

It was a club that had been famous from the British days. 'No Dogs or Indians' said a signboard displayed at its portals. Sahadevan had no desire to be a guest at such places. But he wanted to see what it looked like inside. He wanted to see all the places that were possible for him to access, and learn from the experience.

There was only one place he had never visited—G.B. Road, the red-light district of Delhi.

When he was running his business in Turkman Gate, he had walked along that road many times. But he had never climbed the dark stairs to visit the women who beckoned to him through the grilled veranda, leaning on windowsills that looked like they were on the verge of dropping off. As they stood there enticing customers, dressed only in petticoats and blouses, their lips brightly painted and their necks adorned with artificial jewellery, the only emotion they evoked in him was sympathy.

Once, when he went to Kerala, his old friend Unnikuttan—who still nursed a grudge against him for not financing his trip to the Gulf—had asked him with great curiosity, 'Eda, why haven't you married till now, though your hair is all grey?'

'Don't other people live in this world without being married?'

'There has to be some reason, and that's what I want to know. We've been friends and playmates since childhood. If you don't tell me, who else will you tell?'

'My dear Unnikrishna, the circumstances were such that it never happened. That's all there is to it.'

'No, there is some reason. You're hiding it from me.'

'What am I hiding?'

'There's some problem with you.'

'Nothing is wrong. Bring a woman and I'll show you right now, right here, that there's nothing wrong with me.'

'Then what do you do? Do you keep someone on the side?'

'Eda Unnikrishna, I don't know what to do with you. Here's some money. Go and get drunk.'

Sahadevan took out fifty rupees and handed the notes to Unnikrishnan. Tucking them securely at the waist, between his body and the mundu, he said, 'How can there be a problem in places like Delhi and Bombay? Aren't there red-light areas? What's the name of that red-light street in Delhi—G.B. Road? I've read about it in short stories and novels.'

'Eda, Unnikrishna, you shouldn't ask anyone such things. Every human being needs some privacy. Don't enter that space.'

In the repository of experiences he had accumulated, this was one compartment that lay barren. Besides that, where had he not wandered in search of knowledge …

The road leading to Lodhi Estate from the Nizamuddin dargah, teeming with famished urchins stretching out their begging bowls. (Jamaluddin must have grown into a young man. Wearing tattered rags and with a sunken belly, he must be extending his begging bowl towards devotees alighting from their cars at Hanuman Mandir and Sai Temple.)

Rohtak Baba's ashram, where he went with Lalitha. (He had read in the newspapers about Baba attaining samadhi. He felt sorry. Not about Baba's death, but his inability to retrieve the jewellery Lalitha had given away.)

The Old Delhi alley where the shrieks of animals being slaughtered resounded, and where the chopped heads of lambs and chicken's legs lay in heaps. (When the craving for chicken became irrepressible, this was where Uttam Singh had come to buy chicken feet, which he would then take home and cook with spices.)

The fetid, miserable room where the naliwalas and Dasappan spent their nights, in a place where shit-eating pigs and excreta ruled the roost. (He still didn't know where Dasappan had ended up. He was certain about the final destination of Shreedharanunni, Vasu, Uttam Singh, Gunjan bhabhi and Jaswinder. What he did not know were the shadowy lairs of Dasappan and Vidya.)

The hut where Sitaram lay howling from a putrefying scrotum and snipped vas deferens. (He felt gratified at having saved the life of that hapless man. And dismayed at not having been able to save the lives of many others who suffered similarly.)

Turkman Gate, where the bulldozers had driven over and pulverised burqas, hennaed beards and circumcised penises under their wheels. (What happened to the wretched people who had lost their homes, parents and children? How long could they have survived, begging on the streets, suffering the biting cold?)

Garhi, cowering among sculptures and paintings while, outside, meek human beings surrendered to death and were immolated alive, their guts spilling out, their skulls broken open. (Poor Pinky was terror-stricken by the rictus of the eyeless and nose-less heads.)

Gurcharan Singh's house in Faridkot, accessed by an auto rickshaw over a dusty road on which sugarcane-laden bullock-carts trundled along.

And now, Gymkhana Club, in the company of Gulshan Wadhwa.

He has visited so many places. Except the body of a woman.

Gulshan Wadhwa seated himself in the midst of a group that consisted of a former Central minister, a nonagenarian diwan of a princely state, an ambassador who had recently resigned his position in Europe, two aged, retired secretaries of the Government of India, and the owner of a pharmaceutical company.

'Have you had Scotch whisky before?'

'No, Wadhwa saab.'

'Then we'll have Chivas Regal, yes?'

'No, Wadhwa saab, I don't want any.'

'You don't drink?'

'No.'

Gulshan Wadhwa looked sympathetically at Sahadevan, who sat before him with his thinning hair and grey moustache.

'You don't have a flat of your own to live in, you have no money, you are unmarried. And you don't drink either. Arrey yaar, what were you doing all this while in Delhi? *Tum bekaar aadmi ho. Bilkul* useless.'

With a full glass in hand, Gulshan Wadhwa circulated between the former minister, the diwan, the former government secretaries and the industrialist. He had ordered litchi juice and seekh kabab for Sahadevan, who sat alone, eating and drinking what was ordered for him.

That was also an experience.

On their way back, Wadhwa saab drove fast, with one hand on the steering wheel and the other on Sahadevan's knee. 'Yaar, you've screwed up your life completely. Don't waste any more time. Stay with me. Don't run away like you did last time. If you had stayed with Wadhwa & Sons, your life wouldn't have been like this. Don't repeat the mistake. How old are you now? You must be past fifty-five? A man can get a girl, however old he is. I'll find you a girl who'll come with a fat dowry.'

'Not a girl. An old woman, Wadhwa saab. An old dame.'

'You're totally mad, yaar.'

5

GOODBYE, MR KUNHIKRISHNAN

Sahadevan was waiting at the Regal bus stop in Connaught Place.

He had spent a good part of his life waiting at bus stops.

Sometimes he had to wait for hours. But he preferred travelling by bus. He couldn't afford to take a taxi or even an auto rickshaw any more. As a young man, he didn't mind waiting for the bus. He used to enjoy it. The waiting and the travelling gave him opportunities to learn about Delhi, to touch, smell and know its residents.

He used to wait at the INA bus stop, along with the Malayali housewives and the nurses from AIIMS, for bus No. 541 to Connaught Place. It used to be full of the fashionable residents of Greater Kailash. As soon as the bus started, the girls would take out books from their bags and start reading. It might be a textbook or an English novel. They never talked to anyone.

Greater Kailash Market was a shopping haven for the nouveau riche. In and around the market, cars would be parked chock-a-block. Sahadevan used to think that the place had more cars than people. It was here that he had sighted a Lexus for the first time.

When he took the No. 440 from Lajpat Nagar's New Double Storey to Central Secretariat, his fellow passengers were not as fashionable. They were mostly government employees and wore shirts with missing buttons or worn out collars, though they were washed and ironed. They carried lunch boxes. Discussions usually revolved around their personal deficit budgets and the next Pay Commission.

There was no direct bus to his place from Mandi House in those early days, so he would take a bus to Connaught Place or Pragati Maidan and change there. At the Mandi House stop, you mostly saw people from the various academies, the National School of Drama, and the art galleries. Both men and women carried cloth bags. Many of the men sported long hair and beards. The women wore no make-up, not even lipstick. Dressed in crushed sarees or churidar-kurtas, they discussed books, movies and art. As they waited for their bus, both men and women smoked, often the same cigarette changing hands. There were also some who used bhang or hashish and sat at the bus stop, bereft of all sense of time and place.

Although Sahadevan spent a lot of time waiting for buses at various bus stops, he did not talk to anyone. The intellectuals or artists sitting next to him did not initiate any conversations with him either. His clothes and manners marked him out to them as an accountant in a grain mill. When they discussed a Latin American novel he had already read, he sat silently, listening to them.

Two buses went by. He could not board them. The age for leaping into buses was over. These days, he could only take the less-crowded buses, and that too slowly. Sometimes he had to wait for more than an hour at one bus stop.

'He's an old man. Let him come in.'

Sometimes, a sympathetic conductor, himself squeezed tight inside the bus, would extend his hand and pull Sahadevan into the bus.

The buses that passed through Connaught Place were full of handsome men and beautiful women. The girls talked in a mixture of English and Hindi. The boys would caress them with their eyes. Fashionable, buxom ladies wearing sheer sarees would have young men, middle-aged men, and sometimes even men of Sahadevan's age, stuck to them from behind. As people pushed and shoved their way into the crowded bus, causing a ripple of movement, their hands would press against the full breasts and buttocks of these women. Delhi's DTC buses were a magical world of erotic fantasies. In that world, hanging onto the overhead bar, Sahadevan would think about his novel.

You couldn't find people like Dasappan, Kallu mochi or Sitaram in Connaught Place. Sathyanathan went there to shop. And Georgekutty and Gulshan Wadhwa. Once upon a time, Connaught Place had small shops selling aloo tikki, samosa and lassi. There was an Indian Coffee House—Shreedharanunni had attended its inauguration by AKG—which sold masala dosa and coffee at very affordable prices. All of these had disappeared, one after another, to be replaced by modern, branded stores from Paris and New York. Lacoste had already set up. McDonald's was on its way. Come evening, Connaught Place turned into New York's Times Square or Paris's Champs-Élysées. A world of illusions created by fashion, beauty and the power of money.

Sahadevan went to Connaught Place only to get hold of the latest books. After spending some time in the bookshop, he would go to the terrace café on top of Mohan Singh Place, have a coffee, smoke a cigarette, and sit for a while. The café wasn't as crowded any more. It was rare to see families at the tables. Children these days didn't ask for samosa and aloo tikki, they demanded hot dogs and burgers. The women wanted Pepsi and vanilla milkshakes. The men preferred pistachio shakes.

He sat alone in the café bereft of families and children, leafing through the book he had bought and smoking a cigarette. In front of him lay the lights and colours of Connaught Place. Was Delhi always so colourful? Not that he could remember. He didn't like glitter and garishness. He wondered if he should buy a pair of dark glasses to wear when he came to Connaught Place. But he didn't like wearing them.

The changes he saw in Delhi were not to his liking. He couldn't tolerate them. Is that my fault, Sahadevan asked himself.

The doubt gained strength when he saw men of his age walking around with their friends or families, joking and laughing. Perhaps his problems stemmed from his failure to live like others. Instead of talking to people, he went around talking to himself. Language is for communicating with one's fellow human beings. To talk to oneself, one needs only thoughts.

Sir, don't you need a language to think in too?

Stop it!

Another day. After smoking two cigarettes, Sahadevan closed his book, put it under his arm and walked towards Barakhamba Road. The trans-Yamuna buses left from there. He now lived in a rented flat in Mayur Vihar, close to Samachar Apartments, the colony of journalists, and within walking distance of the Guruvayurappan Temple.

Come evening, the number of people waiting at the Barakhamba Road bus stop would shoot up. Gradually, it would swell into a crowd and remain that way even after 9 p.m. Buses would chase one another to, and past, the stop.

It was one of his favourite routes home. From the bus, he would look out at the many famous institutions they went past.

The first was Modern School, one of the best-known schools of Delhi. Children from the cream of Delhi society studied there in their blue uniforms: short skirts and shirts for the girls, and trousers and shirts for the boys.

A short walk away from Modern School was Bengali Market. When school was let off, blue-uniformed girls would crowd around the golgappa vendors there. It was a well-kept secret that eating golgappas would help them grow full breasts quicker; the girls believed this.

'We must send our children to Modern School,' Lalitha used to tell Kunhikrishnan, when she first came to Delhi.

'If we put them through Modern School, both of us will have to starve. I'm not sure my salary will be enough for the fees.'

'Our children are our wealth. They should be educated in the best school.'

'The kind of dreams my girl has!'

'No, this is the dream of every mother.'

'But you aren't a mother yet.'

'I will be. So what's the hitch?'

'Everyone can dream, Lalithae. To make dreams into reality, we need money.'

'You have a good education, don't you? Then why did you join a newspaper? Why don't you work in one of the Tata or Birla companies? We could live a comfortable life then.'

A banana seller came and sat near Sahadevan. He was carrying bunches of bananas in the wide, flat basket on his head. He split the bananas along their length, put salt and masala in the cleft, and sold them to the people waiting at the bus stop.

After summer, when the roads were wet from the rains, bhutta appeared on the streets. Charcoal was burnt on chicken-wire grills and corn cobs were roasted on them. The vendors sold the hot corn sprinkled with lemon juice and salt. Children on their way from school and their office-going parents often chomped on these on their way home.

As winter approached, vendors of boiled eggs would start showing up at the bus stops and on the roadsides, with stoves fixed on tripods, aluminium containers, plates and eggs. They attracted a lot of customers. They would remove the shells of the hard-boiled eggs, cut them in four, and sprinkle salt and chilli powder on the pieces. As the winter intensified and the cold became bone-chilling, people would eat two, or even three, eggs.

Once the bus went past Modern School, you could see Rabindra Bhawan. The Sahitya Akademi was located inside it.

There was a life-size bronze statue of Pushkin in the front. Like other statues installed in public spaces in Delhi, this one too had bird droppings all over it. The birds in Delhi must have done something good in their previous lives, Sahadevan told himself. They had the heads of Rabindranath Tagore, Mahatma Gandhi, Alexander Pushkin and Bhim Rao Ambedkar to shit on.

Sahadevan had spent many evenings at the Sahitya Akademi. He had met Latin, Russian and European authors there, though he never interacted with any of them. Not because of any antipathy. There was a writer inside him; he kept a distance even from that writer.

He also usually attended the anniversary celebrations at the Akademi. He would listen to the speeches made by writers from different states. All the invitees would be served a grand lunch of pulao and chicken curry. Every year, Sahadevan received an invitation, though he was not a writer; the patronage mystified him. But he never stayed for lunch. If he was hungry, he would go to Bengali Market and eat makki ki roti and sarson ka saag. Or chole bhature. Afterwards, he would stroll under the shade-giving trees of Todarmal Lane.

When you came down Barakhamba Road and around the traffic circle, onto Bhagwan Das Road, you could see Kathak Kendra, the national school for Kathak dance, on your right. Enjoying the amiable sunlight of wintry afternoons, Sahadevan would sometimes walk to Bahawalpur House, after getting off at the Bhagwan Das Road bus stop. He would watch the dance students practising, dressed in white salwar-kameez with their dupattas tied tightly around their waists. The place resounded with the sound of their ankle bells. When Pandit Birju Maharaj was teaching, Sahadevan would sit in silent meditation at one end of the classroom. The bewitching strains of thumri and bhajans pervaded the atmosphere.

Every year, without fail, he attended the annual Sarat Chandrika Kathak Utsav conducted by the Kathak Kendra. Till late into the night, he would sit on the lawns of Bahawalpur House, entranced, lost to the world. He sat spellbound by Birju's performance of *Kumārasambhava*, for which Aminuddin Daguar had composed the music. As Sitara Devi, dressed in a Mughal-style angarkha, set the stage on fire with her sublime dancing, he sat stunned, watching the spectacle unfold.

One wintry evening, as the moonlight streamed down, Saswati Sen, wearing a lehenga-choli the colour of sandalwood paste, sent Sahadevan into raptures with her performance at the Hamsadhwani Theatre. She was his favourite Kathak danseuse.

As the bus headed to Mayur Vihar, what came next into view was the National School of Drama—NSD to everyone. Sahadevan was a regular at the Bharat Rang Mahotsav, the NSD's annual drama festival. He had seen Ratan Thiyam's *Chakravyuh* there.

Ten minutes later, the bus would be on the Yamuna bridge.

Sahadevan now lived on the banks of the Yamuna.

One day, while waiting at the Nehru Place bus stop, Sahadevan met Lalitha. He had never thought that she might come that way.

His mind travelled back in time with some bemusement. When he had first arrived in Delhi, this part of the city was barren land. A stretch of wheat fields and cauliflower patches lay between Moolchand Hospital and Nehru Place. No one passed that way once darkness fell. The road to Kalkaji was also avoided by most people after sundown. Robbers and thugs lorded over the area.

The wheat fields and cauliflower patches had disappeared since. Wide roads, schools and colleges had sprung up in their place. The barren land had become Nehru Place, with multi-storey buildings, office complexes and markets. Multinational companies opened their offices there. Fashionable men and women got out of buses and cars and sashayed into the office complexes.

It was close to 5 p.m. and the traffic was dense. Lalitha poked her head out of the window of her car, which had come to a halt beside the bus stop.

'Get in.'

'Where are you headed?'

'Get in, Sahadeva. I'll drop you wherever you want to go. Isn't that enough?'

The Redline bus headed to Kalkaji Extension bellowed beside them. The Redlines were infamous for ruthlessly mowing down men and cattle as they sped through the city. When he saw one approaching, he would move to the farthest edge of the pavement. If there were bus stops or shops close by, he stepped into one. Dying held no terrors for him. But he refused to die ignominiously, mowed down by a rogue bus. His fantasy was death by cardiac arrest. Like Shreedharanunni.

Once Sahadevan was seated, Lalitha manoeuvred the car alongside the Redline bus and got onto the Outer Ring Road, heading to Neeti Bagh. He noticed how expertly she shifted the gears. The car didn't jerk and the gears didn't clash when she changed them.

'It's been such a long time since we met. Can't you at least call sometimes, Sahadeva?'

He nodded, non-committal.

There was a time when he used to make regular visits to Lalitha's house. She used to call and invite him over whenever she made something special: tapioca and sardines, muthari with nenthran banana and jaggery, elanchi. There was a time when he used to go with her to Sangam Cinema. And during the period when kerosene had become scarce, she used to give her ration to him. Several years later, he had accompanied her to Kunhikrishnan's physiotherapy sessions.

'What are you thinking about, Sahadeva?'

'About the old days. The good old days.'

'I don't think about the old days now, so I don't suffer from stress. I'm happy.'

Could happiness be achieved so easily?

The car entered Neeti Bagh.

'My office is here. Why don't you come inside with me, and then we'll go to my place.'

'It's past five. Won't the office be closed?'

Lalitha pointed towards her office building. In the front was the signage of a well-known publisher of English books.

Sahadevan couldn't believe it. Lalitha was working in a responsible position in an English publishing house. He had never realised that she was so smart.

'I didn't know any of this, Lalithae.'

'How would you know? You've forgotten me.'

Who forgot whom? Sahadevan asked himself. As time passes, people become forgetful. Perhaps he was among those people.

Lalitha took Sahadevan to her office. Though it was past 5 p.m., everyone looked busy; the phones were ringing; visitors were coming and going. Had the normal working hours of ten to five become obsolete?

It was the same with Wadhwa International. The lights would be on even at 9 p.m and the telex and typewriters would be clacking away.

Kunhikrishnan had had a few books published, both in India and abroad, after the Emergency. At first, Lalitha had helped him with the transcription. Then, she began helping with research and gathering information. Later, having secured the appropriate permissions, she began visiting the Lok Sabha library to collect copies of documents he needed. She learnt to speak and write English well. When she started correcting Kunhikrishnan's manuscripts like Sahadevan used to do with Kashyap Saxena's legal briefs, he was astonished. He said then, what Sahadevan said now: 'You are so smart!'

Kunhikrishnan departed suddenly. He didn't get time to say goodbye. Some people go that way. Some keep saying goodbye but don't get to go.

If he wished, he could have returned to the Vrischikam breeze and the smell of mango blossom. Or to a moonlit lake and the boat waiting in it. He could have gone anywhere. Instead, he went to the electric crematorium.

They say that not everyone has a place to go to. But that's a lie. If nothing else, one can leave oneself, like Sathyanathan did. Or you can leave without knowing the destination. Like Vidya did. Or go to Wahe Guru, like Vasu.

Sahadevan wondered for a moment about where he would go.

'Kunh'ishnetta, what is that burning smell?'

Lalitha had peered out of the bathroom, smelling smoke.

Kunhikrishnan had woken up before she went for a bath and started reading a book. The previous night, he had fallen asleep with it in his hand.

She could see smoke coming out of the bedroom. She was familiar with the crackle and smouldering of his pipe, but this was a different smell.

'Kunh'ishnettaaa ...'

No response.

He was like that. When he was engrossed in something, he wouldn't know even if a gun went off near him. Once, when there was an earthquake and the whole house was swaying, he sat reading. She used to tell everyone, 'As it is, Kunh'ishnettan doesn't fear God. Now, look, he's not afraid of earthquakes either.'

She finished her bath quickly and came out without bothering to wipe herself down.

He was lying with the pipe on his bare chest. The hair and flesh on it had started to burn. When she removed the pipe, she saw a circle, as big as a pappadam, of red, seared flesh.

He lay there as if he didn't know what was happening. There was a suggestion of a smile on his lips.

He had stopped going out of the house after he lost his arms. He hated walking. No walking, no exercise. Only reading and thinking. His body had started bloating because of that. His belly had started to protrude.

'You'll fall sick if your body doesn't get enough exercise. At least go out in the morning and walk. Even old men walk these days. Why don't you go?'

'With both my arms lifeless, how can I walk on the road?'

'Do we walk on our hands? Don't we use our legs? Your legs are quite okay, Kunh'ishnetta.'

One day, after five minutes of walking, he returned home and complained, 'I can't do it. I'm panting.'

He refused to go after that, in spite of her persuasions.

'If I hadn't arrived there then, the whole house would have caught fire, Sahadeva.'

Lalitha was far more courageous than Devi. Devi was only pretending to be brave, Sahadevan told himself.

'Come home, have a cup of tea, and then you can go. I'll drop you to Mayur Vihar.'

'Ayyo, no. I'll take a bus.'

'Then have a cup of tea with me. You've come to my office for the first time.'

He sat in the chair across from her. The table was piled high with manuscripts. Books waiting to be born. Lalitha was an obstetrician, he thought. Her job was to facilitate the birth of books. She was a midwife of books.

For so many decades, his own novel had been carried around in his womb. It might require a C-section to give it birth. How long could he go on carrying it?

He was fed up.

He observed Lalitha as she sat reading from a file, occasionally sipping tea. Her hair was dyed black. Not a strand of grey was visible. Her lips had a thin reddish patina of lipstick. She didn't look like someone who was past her prime. There was dignity and energy in her expression, in her bearing and attitude.

'Lalithae …'

'Huh?'

'It's a good thing you didn't go back to Kerala.'

'How could I have gone? Delhi is my home.'

'But you are alone here.'

'Don't you live alone too? If you can, so can I.'

'I'm a man.'

'It's when I hear this kind of stuff that I lose it. What's the difference between men and women? What a man can do, a woman can do too.'

'I don't believe that. That what a woman can do, a man can do too. Can a man give birth?'

They left the office together. She invited him to have dinner with her at Golden Dragon restaurant. Though it served only Chinese dishes, he went with her and had a bowl of soup.

Before parting ways, she said, 'Sahadeva, I have to tell you something. I'm adopting a child. She'll come home next month. My darling baby. She's two years old. Her name is Indira. We can change it if required.'

'No. Don't.'

6

HER FATHER'S DAUGHTER

The return journeys continued. Some left Delhi. Others left life itself.

Janakikutty's path was different from the others'. She remained in Delhi, alive to the world. And yet, it was a return. Away from Sathyanathan and back to herself.

Sahadevan hadn't thought they would part ways so soon. They shared many things, they were similar in many ways. And there were differences too. Learned people say that this is necessary. Some space should be left vacant between husband and wife, between parents and children, and between friends. When a partner tries to encroach on your space, you need a room of your own to retreat to.

Sahadevan had learnt all this from his reading. He had always been concerned about the happiness and welfare of others, though he didn't dare to declare that he lived for them. He was a solitary social animal. And he had no desire to be part of anyone else's memory either. He only wished to tiptoe through life without making any noise or attracting attention.

'Truth be told, eda, I used to be afraid you might follow in the footsteps of Kallikkandi Kunhikannan mashu.'

That made Sathyanathan laugh out loud.

'Let's assume I did follow in his footsteps. What is there to be afraid of?'

'Who would have been there for your mother, who had already lost her husband and daughter? I was afraid because of that.'

'When one becomes like Kunhikannan mashu, then wife, kids, family, nothing matters. There's only the objective in front of us.'

'Can everyone be like that, Sathyanatha?'

'Yes, it's possible. If the objective has taken root deep inside, it will happen.'

'I can't do it, Sathyanatha. When, long ago, I saw the Bangladeshi refugees begging and dying of hunger, I felt sad that as a man I couldn't do what K. Ajitha,* as a woman, could. But what could I do, Sathyanatha? I can't kill anyone.'

'This arm of mine can kill any number of people, if I so desire. But that is not my path.'

'I would like to kill at least a few. I don't have the power. You have the strength, but you don't want to kill anyone. Sometimes I think life is a farce.'

'I don't think so. Life is for enjoyment and for living well. Work hard for it, fight for it.'

'Is it really Shreedharanunni's son who is saying this?'

'You don't know what a struggle it was. Everyone's eyes were on amma and Vidya. No one was even aware that a person called Sathyanathan was alive in that house.'

Sathyanathan turned his head away, his face full of wrath, and stared into the distance.

'Sathyanatha, there are only two options for people who have a hard life. One, to work hard and get out of their difficulties. Two, to try and make sure that others don't have to struggle like them; to fight for their cause and be prepared for anything, even

---

*Kunnikkal Ajitha, a social reformer and human rights activist, took part in the naxalite movement in the 1960s in Kerala.

death. You chose the first way, didn't you? Isn't that why your mother left Delhi?'

'If that's how it is, so be it. I'm going, I have to get to work.'

Sathyanathan grabbed his leather briefcase, got into his car and drove away. Sahadevan watched till it disappeared from sight.

You are one hell of a guy, Sathyanatha! Is this what you read and assimilated, as you lay shivering in the dead of winter under a forty-watt bulb in the narrow veranda of your Sewa Nagar quarters?

Sathyanathan didn't lose his way. He chose his path. His grave face and the determined look in his eyes were clear proof that he was not one to go astray.

What did Janakikutty think about all this? Did she feel like she had committed a blunder? Could Kunhikannan mashu's daughter, an alumna of JNU and a PhD from London, commit such a blunder?

Long ago, during the Emergency, as she watched Sathyanathan and Janakikutty approaching them, Lalitha had said, 'They're a good match. I hope they get married. They make a wonderful couple.'

Like Lalitha, Sahadevan had also assumed that they would get married. They could tie the mangalasutra at the Guruvayurappan Temple in Mayur Vihar or the Ayyappa Temple in R.K. Puram. Astrologers from every caste, nampoothiri to thiyya, were available to check the compatibility of their horoscopes. But did they have their horoscopes? Where did the children of communists get horoscopes from? Their actions and their sacrifices were their horoscopes. Or at least, that's how it was made out to be.

He did not know Janakikutty as well as he knew Sathyanathan, which was only natural. From the day he had arrived in Delhi, Sathyanathan had been with him. And the place he knew the best in Delhi was still Sewa Nagar.

The first time Sahadevan saw Janakikutty was just before the Emergency. After that, he had met and talked to her many times. But they rarely spent any time in each other's company without the presence of others. It was only fourteen years later that an occasion arose for them to walk together, chatting.

By then, her appearance had changed. Though her face was still youthful, occasional grey hairs had appeared on her head. But she still wore her Gandhi-style spectacles and she was as carelessly dressed as before. Even at the height of winter in January, she did not wear shoes or socks when she was indoors.

Sathyanathan was the other extreme. He had put on weight and become fairer. Now, he had the girth to go with his height. When he went past, the fragrance of Old Spice followed in his wake.

'Did you hear the news?'

'What news?'

'Safdar Hashmi is dead.'

Only the previous week, Sahadevan had seen Safdar Hashmi emerging from Vithalbhai Patel House. He had gone to the FICCI office on some work and was on his way to the UNI canteen to have dosa and coffee. That was when he saw Safdar Hashmi. He didn't know Sahadevan. Nonetheless, they smiled broadly at each other.

Many years had passed since Sahadevan had seen the street play *Kursi, Kursi, Kursi,* performed by Hashmi and his Jana Natya Manch at the India Gate lawns. The spectators had clapped and cheered as the king rose from the throne to cede it to the elected people's representative. Sahadevan, not one to clap easily, had joined in. The play had been performed every day, for eight days running. From the lawn, they could see Parliament House and the national flag fluttering over it. What could be a more appropriate venue for this play, he had thought, pleased that he had caught the performance. He was filled with that familiar sense of satisfaction that came from watching a good play or reading a good book.

'Janakikutty, what happened to Hashmi?'

'Murdered.'

'Who?'

'The people's enemies, who else?'

Janakikutty told him that the attack on Hashmi had taken place when he was performing the play *Halla Bol* on the streets of Sahibabad, across the Yamuna.

'I'm going to see him. Are you coming?'

'Is Sathyanathan coming?'

'He can't get out of the office.'

Safdar Hashmi was an alumnus of St. Stephen's, like Sathyanathan. Perhaps they had known each other.

Hashmi's face was covered. Eyewitnesses said that he had been dragged away from the venue and that his head had been smashed in with stones. His face was mutilated. He had become a martyr at the age of thirty-four.

A small crowd accompanied the body. Sahadevan and Janakikutty walked behind Habib Tanvir and Shabana Azmi. Along the way, workers and students kept joining the funeral procession until it turned into a veritable sea of people. Flags and wreaths were visible everywhere. Tens of thousands of people flowed through Delhi's roads.

Safdar Hashmi ko lal salaam!

Safdar Hashmi amar rahe!

Sahadevan did not shout the slogans with them. In his booklover's heart, some lines from a poem written by the young martyr rose up:

Kitaaben karti hain baatein
Beete zamane ki
Duniya ki, insaano ki
Aaj ki, kal ki,
Ek-ek pal ki

That day, Sahadevan and Janakikutty walked together for a long time and talked. They asked each other why people who fought for humanism and justice were brutally murdered. Janakikutty had her father in mind. Sahadevan's mind was filled with images of people from Cuba, Vietnam, Bolivia and Bangladesh.

As night fell, they turned to their private sorrows and personal problems.

'I don't know what you think about me, as someone who smokes and drinks. You might be thinking I do all kinds of immoral things.'

'I'm not too far behind. I also do whatever you do.'

'Some people think about me that way. In the eyes of Sathyanathan's mother, I'm a dissolute girl. I have slept in Sathyanathan's room. But then, he was going to be my husband. I used to talk to him about getting married. He didn't agree. If we had married then, amma wouldn't have left Delhi. That's one of my greatest sorrows.'

'It's not too late. You can marry even now.'

She took a cigarette from her bag and placed it to her lips. Sahadevan struck a match. They were seated on the terrace of the cafe, on top of Mohan Singh Place. On the table in front of them were steaming cups of coffee. Connaught Place lay spread out, darkness and light intermingling in the fog. No one else had chosen to sit out on the terrace in January's cold.

'No, it's not that easy now.'

'Lalitha used to say that you both are a good match.'

'Just in looks, no?' She laughed. 'But now, not even that.'

Who considers physical compatibility? Isn't mental compatibility the most important thing?

Sathyanathan could never have a child; she knew that. It wasn't important to her. It was the changes which had come about in him during the last few years that disturbed her. He was no longer the man she had known during the Emergency.

Not only his thoughts, even the clothes he wore and the food he ate were different.

'Sometimes I'm not able to recognise him.' She continued after a short pause, 'We fight every day.'

'Why? What do you fight about? You should always remain in love. '

She remained silent, thinking. The rims of her spectacles shone in the thickening fog above the deserted terrace. He could not see her clearly. He could see only her forehead or nose or cheeks, depending on her posture.

They fought over many things. The maid from Orissa had left a long time back. Janakikutty cooked. She was working for an NGO for a meagre salary. It was an organisation that protected stray dogs and cats.

'Did you go to London and get a PhD for this?' Sathyanathan had raged, the day Janakikutty started work.

'This job gives me satisfaction. That's enough for me, eda.'

'What satisfaction do you get? Your body stinks of dogs and cats. When you sit near me, I get nauseous.'

The NGO's office was in Rajokri. At any given time, there were about a hundred injured and mangy dogs and cats in its premises. In the beginning, she was nauseous too. But within a few days, she was over it. She learnt to handle even near-dead dogs with putrefying wounds, trimming their hair, bathing them and applying medicines on their wounds with her hands protected by gloves.

If someone reported seeing a dog lying on the road, bleeding after being hit by a vehicle, her phone would shriek.

'Run, one more dog is going to die. Run, girl,' Sathyanathan would mock her.

She would disentangle herself from his arms and pick up the bedside phone. A dog had been knocked down by a truck near Ashram Chowk. She covered herself with a woollen shawl and stepped into the cold outside. She found an auto rickshaw and went to Ashram Chowk.

'Janakikutty, I thought you would take after Kunhikannan mashu.'

'Why did you think so?'

'Your travels,' said Sahadevan.

Till some time ago, she used to visit the north-eastern states regularly. He used to wonder why she was making those trips.

'In his time, the path my father chose was the right one. But if one wants to do something for the welfare of society, there are many paths to choose from. And society is not just about human beings. Animals are also part of it.'

Sathyanathan did not agree with any of that.

'How can the animals we eat be a part of our society? Edi, animals are either for display inside the zoo, or to kill and eat.'

Differences in opinion cropped up over everything. They argued over the smallest of things.

Janakikutty had turned vegetarian a year back. When they came out of Rivoli after watching a movie, he said, 'Let's eat dinner here. Do you know that McDonald's has opened in CP?'

They could see the yellow glow of the double arch in the distance.

'I'm not going in there. Let's go somewhere else.'

'Where? To have rice and sambar at Madras Hotel? I can't. I want to eat some meat or fish.'

'We can go somewhere else.'

'I like McDonald's. If you eat their chicken burger, you'll never forget its taste in your life. You'll go there again and again.'

'I'm not going there,' she repeated, 'I can't eat meat.'

'Then let's go home. My appetite's gone.'

He went into the Palika Bazaar parking, found his car among the countless cars parked on the three floors, and brought it out. He didn't utter a word during the drive home.

'My boy is very stubborn.'

She placed her hand on his thigh.

'Don't rile me unnecessarily.'

'I care two hoots if you get riled. It doesn't matter if you won't talk to me for the rest of your life. Even Lord Almighty can't make me change my decision. Assuming there is a Lord Almighty.'

They quarrelled every day. One day, he said, 'It's a good thing that I didn't give in to the pressure from amma and marry you.'

Taking off her round-rimmed glasses, she wiped them with the pallu of her saree, gave him a withering look and asked, 'What did you say?'

'At least I've been spared the litigation and the courts. Who has the time for all that?'

'So, that's what's bothering you?'

She replaced her glasses, but she didn't look at him.

After that cold night, when they sat talking on the terrace café in Mohan Singh Place, Sahadevan didn't meet Janakikutty for a long time. He was preoccupied with his ailments. The creatinine level in his blood had gone up. Was it because of the rum he had consumed over three decades? The pain in his knees, his companion for years, didn't abate. Climbing into buses became an impossibility. Auto rickshaws carried him everywhere, to Connaught Place, Chandni Chowk, Rajokri.

He had gone to Rajokri to see for himself how Janakikutty's organisation worked. The place smelt of dog soap. Dogs with their heads and legs bandaged lay whimpering and whining. An infected dog, its raw flesh exposed, looked at him pathetically. A cat with one side of its face crushed in a car accident gazed at him with its only good eye.

'What do you want?'

'I've come to see Janakikutty.'

'She's gone.'

'Where?'

'We don't know.'

Sahadevan never saw her after that.

A few years later, in a photo published in the *Times of India*, Sahadevan recognised a bespectacled woman standing next to Irom Sharmila. Kallikkandi Kunhikannan mashu had followed only one path. Janakikutty was taking many paths. When he thought about it, he realised that she was right in her choice of all of these paths.

7

THE BEGGAR ARMY

When Sahadevan moved to Mayur Vihar after starting work with Wadhwa International, he was very happy. He had never lived in a place so agreeable. A lot of Malayalis lived around him; ordinary people, at that. They were not like the Malayalis of Hauz Khas, who didn't walk despite having legs. They only used their legs to control the clutch, brake and accelerator.

The Guruvayurappan Temple was within walking distance of his house. The vegetable and fish markets were also close by. By late afternoon, villagers from the banks of the Yamuna would arrive, carrying baskets of vegetables. They would lay out bottle gourds, cauliflower, radish and tomato, freshly picked and still damp from the water, by the roadside. Then came the fisherfolk from the banks of the Yamuna, with freshly caught fish, which too would be displayed by the roadside for their Malayali and Bengali customers. The fish would be still gasping for breath, their gills moving.

What made Sahadevan happiest was the view. From the top of his two-storey building, he could see the Yamuna. Whenever he could find the time, he walked up to the riverbank. He looked forward to getting back home in the evenings, so he could see the river. On Saturdays, Sundays and other holidays, he would take the unpaved path to the riverbank, wearing a woollen pullover and a black muffler around his neck. From there, he could see the pontoon bridge built over one of the tributaries of the river, bobbing up and down on the water.

The riverbank was usually deserted. In the distance, people could be seen fishing from small boats. Cranes and other birds wheeled around. He had never seen so many kinds of birds. Sometimes wild hares came running out of the foliage. He had even seen monitor lizards and porcupines. He soon became a familiar sight for the fisherfolk and the farmers who grew vegetables there. They began to smile at him as he sat on a damp stone for hours, smoking. He was a curiosity to them.

Gradually, walking became too painful for him. The pain in his knees became chronic. When the swelling became insufferable, he took steroids. There were days when he couldn't even leave his room; he would be bedridden. He needed to support himself by holding on to the walls to go to the toilet. Cooking became impossible. When there was some relief from the pain, he used to sit at the table, light a cigarette, and pick up his pen …

His Malayali neighbours often came to his aid. They used to bring him tea and biscuits. If the restaurant did not deliver food, and that happened often, they would bring him chapatis.

Till now, he had done all the chores, of sweeping the room, washing clothes, cooking food. Now, he had to depend on others for everything. What made him even more despondent was the thought that though the Yamuna flowed so close to his place, he couldn't go and sit on its banks.

On a good day, when the pain decreased, he would walk to the grocery store with the help of a walking stick.

'Don't go alone, you'll fall,' his neighbour, a Malayali woman, would say.

'Eda Kutta, please go with grandpa.'

Eight-year-old Kuttan would walk with him. He would take the bag from Sahadevan and hold it as they walked slowly to the store. The owner was also Malayali.

'Is the pain better, sir?' he would enquire. 'Why do you take the trouble of coming here? Why don't you send a list? I'll make sure that everything reaches you.'

'I feel like walking a little, son.'

He bought coconut oil for cooking and bathing, Sunlight soap for washing, tea, sugar and dal. Then, suddenly remembering, he asked for a packet of 7 O'Clock blades. He took out money from his pocket after handing the walking stick to Kuttan, then asked, 'Baby, do you like Cadbury chocolate?'

'No, appuppa. Amma will beat me.'

Kuttan looked longingly at the chocolate in the glass case. Sahadevan bought a hundred-gram slab for him, and his face brightened. Then, slowly, they walked back home.

Sometimes Kuttan would come over to his house. He helped him fill ink in the pen and water the plants in the veranda. Though he was only eight, he could fill the pen without spilling a single drop of ink.

On holidays, Kuttan's father would turn up to check on him.

'Don't think you are alone. You should tell us whenever you need something.'

The people who once used to be with him were no longer around. Many had gone away after saying their final goodbyes. The rest had withdrawn into themselves. Sathyanathan didn't even call him anymore. He had heard that he had found employment in Wall Street and had left Delhi for New York. Lalitha still called, though only occasionally. And she was always in a hurry. She spoke as if someone was standing close by, trying to snatch away the receiver.

'The day after tomorrow is Indira's birthday. You must come.'

'I don't go anywhere, Lalithae. My knees ...'

'Don't take a bus. I'll send my car. I have a driver now.'

'No, Lalitha. She has my blessings. Let her study well and become smart. Only good will come to her.'

'Baby, say thanks to grandpa.'

'Thanks a lot.'

There was impatience in Indira's voice too.

One day, after 10 p.m., he received a call that made him happy. It was an STD call from Kerala.

'Who is this?'

'Chetta, have you forgotten me so soon?'

A tinkling female voice.

'This is Rosakutty.'

'Ayyo!'

'Are you okay? It's been such a long time since I heard your voice. Say something, don't be so quiet.'

'First tell me all your news.'

'Jomon is still in Dubai. One summer vacation, Elsy and I went there. Chetta, it's a place worth seeing. Our Delhi is nothing when compared to Dubai.'

'Which class is Elsy in?'

'Class 3B. She is a very good student. Jomon says she looks exactly like me.'

'How do you look now, Rosakutty? Is your hair grey?'

'What a question! When I left Delhi, I was already dyeing my hair. Don't you remember, chetta?'

His memory had become poor.

'Tell me your news. Where do you live? Have you bought a flat of your own?'

'In Mayur Vihar. On rent.'

'Chetta, you're a useless fellow.'

She forgot that it was an STD call and chatted with him for a long time. She asked about everything and everyone and found out all the news. Just as she was disconnecting the call, a long sigh escaped her. It didn't reach him where he sat, three thousand kilometres away.

The following winter, he came down with jaundice. Usually, hepatitis gripped Delhiites during the summers. There was a severe shortage of water. The water coming out of the municipal taps smelt like sewage. However long you boiled it for, the smell remained.

Sahadevan had had problems with his liver earlier too. Now, after Dussehra and Diwali, as the cold rolled in, his eyes turned yellow. His face and hands turned pale, like those of a corpse. When Kuttan came into the house and called out to him, Sahadevan saw a sunflower in bloom instead of his face.

Kuttan's parents took Sahadevan to the hospital in a taxi. For the first time in his life, he lay in a hospital bed. Till now, he had only suffered minor ailments. But he was old now, and staying in various parts of Delhi was no longer sufficient. In between, he would have to stay in the hospital too.

He was shifted from Mayur Vihar Hospital to Ram Manohar Lohia Hospital the same day. The emergency ward doctors said that his condition was serious. They were speaking to Kuttan's father, but Sahadevan overheard them and was saddened. His novel was not complete yet. What would happen to it, if something were to happen to him?

As Sahadevan lay there, troubled, he was put on a stretcher and taken to the Intensive Care Unit. He felt as though it was his corpse that was being pushed along by the attendants. Then he realised it wasn't his imagination, it was actually happening.

With an oxygen tube in his nose and an IV needle in his vein, Sahadevan oscillated between consciousness and unconsciousness. He felt as if he was walking on the pontoon bridge on the river. It swayed in keeping with the swell and ebb of the water. As Sahadevan got on to the bridge, looking down at the little wavelets, it started to sway to his gait.

He felt no pain in any part of his body. Though his knees had folded when he was put on the stretcher, they didn't ache. But he felt nauseous. He wanted to put his fingers down his throat and vomit. Several times, his eyes closed on their own. He should have been thinking about God. Instead, the beggars of Nizamuddin and old acquaintances like Dasappan and Jamaluddin floated into his mind.

Then, suddenly, like at the start of a movie inside a theatre, the light went out of his eyes. Moments later, a weak, shaky picture appeared, as though on a screen. He saw Jamaluddin and Dasappan walking away in the diffused light. Jamaluddin appeared to him as the little naked baby he had seen in Nizamuddin, after the1971 war. He had not grown up despite the passage of so many decades.

Where were they headed? They were walking along the Boat Club lawns, the site of strikes and protests. His eyes closed. Darkness fell. He opened his eyes again. He saw an army of beggars walking with Dasappan and Jamaluddin. Among them were cripples, blind men and women, and the lepers who sat in front of the Hanuman Temple on Baba Kharak Singh Marg every Tuesday. Also with them were the lepers who lined the roads in front of the Sai Baba temple on Thursdays. The beggars who went about begging in the Sunday market at Red Fort, at every traffic light in the city, at Jama Masjid in Old Delhi, were part of the crowd. Walking between the lines of luxury cars parked on either side of Rajpath, the unlikely army marched towards Parliament House.

Don't go, Sahadevan begged of them, they'll shoot you all.

The beggar army was thousands-strong by now. Led by Jamaluddin and Dasappan, they rushed towards Parliament House. They tried to enter it; the policemen on duty stopped them.

We are hungry, the army said. We have no place to sleep.

Fire!

The guns spat bullets. One of the bullets went through Sahadevan's head. Jamaluddin was shot in the belly. His penis was blasted from his body and fell far away ...

The light went out again in the cinema hall. Those sitting in the front row put their fingers in their mouths and produced shrill whistles.

There was darkness everywhere.

AFTERWORD

After a prolonged period of fog, rains and wintry weather, the sun finally showed its face today in Delhi.

The mild sunlight spread over the balcony of my second-floor flat. I wanted to cup it in my palms and drink from it. I brought out my easy chair and lay in it, enjoying the sun-kissed vista. In front of me was the wide bluish road and the shady, light-caressed trees that lined it. Occasionally, buses, cars and auto rickshaws passed by.

I saw an auto rickshaw stop in front of the gate to our apartment complex.

Someone descended from it and, leaning on a walking stick, walked towards the security guard's cabin.

The apartment complex has high walls, and security guards at every gate.

The intercom rang. It was the security guard.

'Saab, you have a visitor.'

'Who is it?'

'He won't tell me his name. He is an old man. Very old. Shall I send him up?'

'Umm, yes.'

I had no desire to meet anyone as I sat basking in the mild sunshine. But he was an old man. I decided that I would meet him. Also, he had refused to reveal his name. That piqued my curiosity.

There was a knock on the door.

I went and opened the door. The old man stood there, leaning on his walking stick. His scalp could be seen through an almost non-existent layer of hair. He had a thick, cotton-wool-like moustache. A fat paper package was in his hand.

'Come in.'

I took him to the balcony and made him sit on a chair. He was walking with great difficulty.

'Where are you from? I don't recognise you.'

'I'm coming from Mayur Vihar.'

'I thought you were coming from Kerala.'

'I've lived here since 1959.'

Many migrant Malayalis have come to meet me over the years. They get their copies of my books autographed, drink some tea, and go away. My wife insists that whoever comes should be served tea at least. If this man had been living here for so long, why was he coming to meet me only now?

'I know how busy you are. I'll tell you quickly what I've come for. And then, I'll leave.'

His eyes had a yellowish tinge. His body was emaciated. Age and disease appeared to have weakened him. I felt a surge of sympathy.

'Here ...'

He offered me the paper package he was holding.

'What's this?'

'A manuscript.'

Oh no. Was it a novel? Many people approach me with their stories and novels. They want me to read them. Find them publishers. Write prefaces. Where do I have the time? It's been years since I slept to my heart's content.

My first instinct was to give the manuscript back to him. But the look on his face stopped me. I opened the packet and had a look. More than five hundred pages of foolscap paper filled with tiny handwriting. The handwriting wasn't beautiful, but it was neat, with adequate spaces between words and lines. Reading it was not difficult.

Delhi: A Soliloquy.

'What is this?'

'A novel.'

I ran my eyes over the first chapter. I liked the quote on the first page, from the work of Black Kettle, the American Indian chief.

'Who is this Sahadevan?'

'That's me.'

'Who has written this novel?'

'I have.'

I understood then. He was asking me to read his novel, help get it published. Maybe write a preface.

I wrapped the manuscript back in the paper carefully and returned it to him. He refused to take it back.

'It's yours.'

'Mine?'

'Consider it a novel written by you. Get it published. Under your name.'

Madness.

Who sent this lunatic to me, early in the morning? I was angry now.

'I'm leaving. The auto rickshaw is waiting for me.'

He stood up and reached for his walking stick.

'Mister, please take this package and go.'

I controlled the anger rising in me. He started walking towards the door, without hearing my words.

'What do you think of me? I'm the author of the novel *On the Banks of the Mayyazhi*. Do you think I need to publish someone else's work in my name?'

'Every novelist writes about other people's lives. But no one needs to steal from my life. I've written and packaged it, and I'm giving it to you.'

'Why me?'

'I like your writing, that's why.'

'Are you in your right senses when you say all this?'

'Listen, I was on the verge of dying from liver cirrhosis. But I have not stopped drinking. I need two large pegs of Old Monk every day. But today, I haven't had a drop.'

'Mr Sahadevan, I don't understand what you are saying.'

'I'll be brief. I know your time is valuable. I started writing this novel when I arrived in Delhi. I completed it two days ago. Writing a novel about Delhi was my dream. That has been accomplished. All I desired was to write the novel. I have no desire to be a novelist. If it gets published, it should only be in your name. Please read it. If you are okay with it, publish it under your name. If you don't want it, throw it off the Yamuna bridge. Let no one read it.'

'Sahadevan, you are giving me a punishment that I cannot bear.'

'I'm sorry.'

Before I could say anything more, he walked out through the door, leaning on his walking stick. After sometime, I heard the sound of an autorickshaw starting up. I saw it moving through the greenery.

Delhi: A Soliloquy was published on 1 November at Thiruvananthapuram. The publishers had made arrangements for a book signing by the author. I reached Thiruvananthapuram early on that day. Two tables stacked with copies of the book with various cover designs were on sale at the entrance to the auditorium. Many people bought copies. They stood in a queue, and one by one, came up to say hello and get the books autographed. The queue became longer; my fingers hurt from signing. I stretched and flexed my arm for some relief.

That was when I saw Sahadevan standing at the head of the queue, leaning on a walking stick.

He extended the copy of the book he had bought towards me.

'What should I write?'

'To Sahadevan, with affection, M. Mukundan.'

I wrote as he requested, signed, and handed the book back to him. He accepted it with both hands, then joined his palms and looked at me.

'I can die a happy man now.'

A HUG OF GRATITUDE

To all those who helped me make this dream book a magnificent reality.

First and foremost, Fathima and Nandakumar, who have rendered this in English so marvellously, capturing the soul of the novel with all its trepidations.

Most importantly, Karthika V.K., editor extraordinaire, who kept me afloat all through the making of this book.

Priya Kuriyan, for the mesmerising cover.

My friends Ravi D.C., Paul Zacharia and A.J. Thomas, who stayed with me when I thought I was sinking.

And for all those at large, for their contributions—in their own way.